A Taste of Darkness

Carly Claire

Content Advisory

This is a slow burn dark romance... the first in a series which gets progressively darker and spicier. This will not be the darkest or spiciest book you ever read. But it *is* dark, so this is the part where I caution you to proceed carefully. Mental health is a real thing, and it is so important. If you read to forget that the world is a place of pain and misery, you probably just want to skip this series altogether. But if you want to lean into that pain and the beauty that goes along with it, then this one just may be your cup of tea.

Themes which may not be suitable for all readers include, but are not limited to:

drug abuse, sexual violence/abuse, human trafficking/slavery, sex trafficking/slavery, human auctions, sexual assault (groping, licking), Murder, torture, kidnapping, suicidal ideation and referenced suicide attempt, references to sexual abuse of under-age persons (not on page), references to rape of aforementioned persons (not on page)

DEDICATION

For the ones who speak up, and the ones who don't.

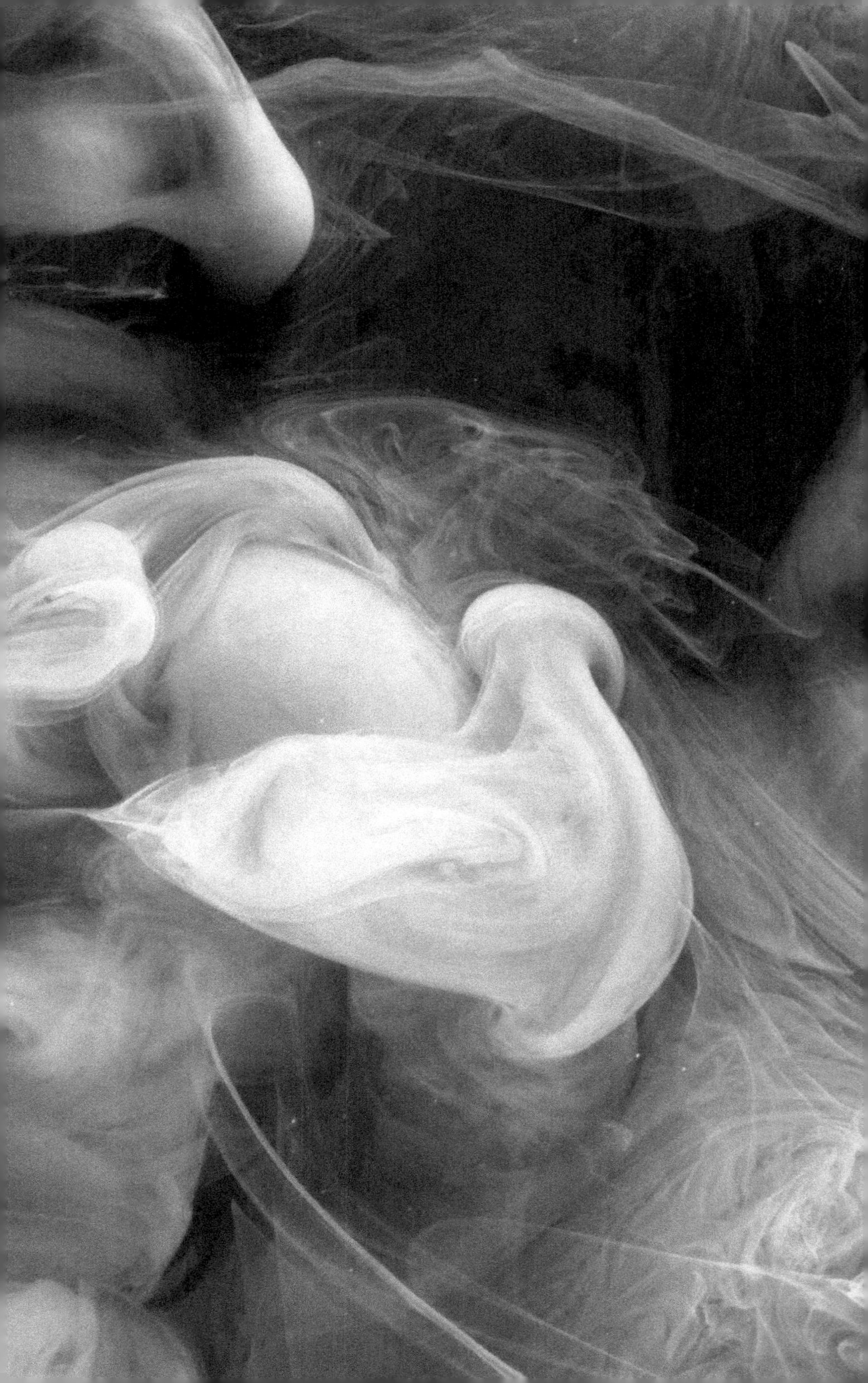

CHAPTER ONE

REMY

I walk through the quiet house, each footstep chasing away the demons lingering from my childhood. It's been years since I walked away from this bit of my life, but the place is like a time capsule, everything still as it was, just the way my mother had liked it. Not so much as a speck of dust gathers on the gilded frames of gauche paintings or obscure photos lining the wall. The massive dining table— where we sat only when we wanted to portray a well-to-do, happy family—is set as if we're prepared to host a small army.

I make my way into the foyer, where a fire crackles in the grate below an oil painting of my great-great-grandfather. Other than the obvious, we share many things: a powerful jaw and chiseled cheekbones, dark eyes, and even darker hair that betrays a hint of curl despite all the effort and gel in the world. The similarities don't end there. We even share the same name. Remington St. Jean had been respected, loved, hated, and feared— just how all great and powerful people are meant to be.

The bar in the corner of the room has also been well-attended in my absence, though I'm not sure all the liquor behind it is enough to get me through this without trying to crawl out of my own skin. Unfortunately, I have to try, so I pour myself a drink that by most standards is too strong, watching the fire reflect off the crystal a moment. Then I raise it up in a toast to my long-deceased grandfather, the family patriarch whom I never met and will probably never live up to.

My parents had made no qualms about the fact that I was the fuck-up, the troubled one, the failure. They didn't have to tell me I'd never achieve the things I aspired to. I know all that, but it's not going to stop me from doing the best I can to right my family's wrongs and carve out my own place in the world, even if I die trying. I've already lost myself to this world they brought me into, but I can still spare my sister.

That's the whole reason I'm here.

The bourbon goes down smoothly, so I fill my glass again and drain it just as quickly before placing it upside down on the bar with every intention of walking away. I don't make it far, because footfalls sound down the hall, heading toward me in a hurry.

I turn just as Monica reaches the doorway, where she stops moving. She was saying something when she walked in here, but whatever it is, it's lost when her mouth falls open in shock. Those painted pink lips spent plenty of time on me when we were younger, on my neck, my lips, wrapped around my cock. They'd trembled when I broke up with her, sliding the metaphorical knife between her ribs just hard enough that I thought she'd leave this whole place behind and never look back.

I'm just as surprised to see her as she is to see me. The only difference is, I don't show it.

"Remy!" She gasps, placing a hand on her heart as if seeing me after all this time is a shock capable of stopping her heart. And then her hand moves to cover her mouth like she can stop herself from being sick, though I'm certain her stomach is churning at the sight of me, the memory of what I did.

I allow her the moment of obvious surprise, and she recovers quickly, smoothing her skirt. "I mean Mr. Boudreaux." She clears her throat, and when she speaks again, her voice is even and composed. "We weren't expecting you."

"You were expecting someone..." I muse, gesturing at the fire. It doesn't even make sense to have a fire in the dead of summer, but I suppose my sister isn't worried about the cost of the electric bill rising to combat the heat. She doesn't worry much about anything, a fact that I simultaneously hate and appreciate. "I expected the house to be closed up. Instead, it's like a shrine."

"Your father has requested everything be kept just as it was." Monica swallows, trying hard to look at me without meeting my eyes. She looks good in her conservative black dress, the fabric clinging to her in all the right places, her skin kissed by the sun and her chestnut hair swept back to showcase her pretty face. It has lost some of the roundness of our youth, and her eyes no longer glimmer with hopes and dreams yet to be chased, but that's an unfortunate side-effect of growing up. Other than her shattered dreams, whatever she's been doing since I left, it agrees with her.

I was prepared for the possibility of running into her now that I'm back in the States. I just never expected it to be in my own family home, within twenty minutes of walking into it. Somehow, the distance between us has done what I had once thought to be impossible. The feelings I had for her were real, and they meant everything to me once. But they aren't as strong as I'd thought they would be. I've worked hard to kill them with every measure of certainty, just as I worked hard to kill her feelings for me. I did a damn good job of it for my part. She looks like she'd rather light herself on fire than be in the same room as me.

"Can I get you something?" She ventures, clearly happy for the excuse to disappear. "Coffee or tea?"

If I was nice, I'd send her on a fruitless mission just to let her get away from me, but I'm not ready to let her walk away just yet. "Bourbon suits me just fine."

I flip my glass again and pour myself another measure of dark liquid into the heavy crystal, deliberately taking my time. I hadn't planned to have another drink so soon, but being in this house has me on edge as it is. Now my ex-girlfriend is staring at me like I'm a stranger who terrifies her. It's fair... I *am* a stranger. This is the first time I've seen her in four years. I effectively erased her from my life, along with my old self. I burnt my former life to the ground, and then I burnt the ashes, too.

She's right to be terrified of me.

This time, I drink more slowly, savoring the smooth and oaky taste of my father's most expensive liquor. Upon turning, I see Monica is still standing there, visibly shaken. Of all the traits that I've learned to embrace, it's the fear that I usually enjoy the most. Of course, it's only fun when it's being enacted on the right people.

"Where's Rhiannon?"

"She was working." Monica purses her lips and glances at her watch—a thin gold band that she definitely couldn't afford on the menial salary my father offers. Perhaps she's moved on then, found a man to care for her, to buy her expensive gifts and give her heart to. But then why would she be working here? "I'm not sure when she'll be home."

"Take a guess." I encourage, eyeing her calmly. "It's Friday night."

"I'm sure it will be a few hours, *sir*." Her chest moves up and down faster than it should. Is it only fear, or does that old desire linger? Is she scared of what I could do to her right now, how I could ruin her all over again? Just a kiss would be enough to do it, I'm sure. Or is she eager to find out whether our spark still remains, naïve enough to hope that I've come back to whisk her away to the life we used to dream of?

She says nothing as I drink her in. She's as smooth as the top-shelf bottle I'm working my way through, but the sight of her doesn't feel like the punch to the gut I expected. There was a time when this girl was the reason I breathed, and now she's just another relic of a past life, like the grand piano in the foyer or the vintage wines in the cellar.

"Are you hungry? I can fix you something."

I *am* hungry, of course. I always am.

By this point, the hunger is as much a part of me as the lie. Nothing ever satisfies it. I sometimes muse that there's a demon in me, and nothing will ever fulfill either of us. But I can at least sate it with whiskey, steak, and the company of beautiful women who don't expect a night of fun to turn into anything more.

"Is Natasha still living in town?"

Monica's eyes glimmer a moment before she blinks the tears away as if they'd never been there. Natasha... her old best friend who she caught me fucking on the couch in the sitting room.

It's wrong of me to ask her about Natasha. I don't particularly care what happened to the bitch, but asking about her serves to deepen the chasm between me and the beautiful woman opposite me. It serves as a reminder of who I am.

Monica doesn't know that I intended to get caught, that I wanted her to see me burning our bridges. She doesn't know that I *meant* to hurt her so badly that she'd be scarred from the wounds I inflicted. But she does know exactly why I'm asking about Natasha now, and it isn't because I care to know how she's doing. "I ran into her at the farmer's market a few weeks ago." She nods, her slender throat bobbing as she works to keep anything more from slipping off her tongue. "Would you like me to call her?"

I arch an eyebrow as I contemplate the offer. I'm pent up and in need of release, and it would be nice to not have to work for it. Natasha most certainly won't make me work for it.

And if Monica is testing me, just trying to see if I still feel anything for her, she's not about to see me fail. There's nothing left of the love that once existed between us, and more than that, there's nothing left of my need for her. My cock isn't even hard at the sight of her despite how beautiful she really is and how much fun we used to have.

"Please do." I nod.

Monica nods too and turns to go but stops when I speak again. "And Monica?"

She meets my eyes slowly, blinking away more tears like that will prevent me from seeing them. "Sir?"

It's not even weird to hear her call me by the formality. The divide between who we were and who we are now—who I was then versus who I am now—is brutally evident.

"You know why I'm here, don't you?"

Her attention turns to her feet, trying to escape my probing gaze. The red tinting her cheeks is enough of a tell even without seeing her eyes. "I'm in no position to guess about your business."

"Maybe you shouldn't." I concede. "But I think you know what I'm here for. And I'd appreciate your discretion until I've had the chance to speak to Rhiannon myself."

"Of course." She grimaces just the slightest bit before she can hide it, but I excuse it as a smile and watch her go, the hem of her dress riding her curves.

Monica's family has been employed by mine for years. It is *their* family business to serve my family in every manner. Her mother was a fantastic cook, her father a sort of advisor to mine, and her uncle was one of several drivers we'd had on hand growing up. Their apparent loyalty was curious, to the extent that rumors had once circulated that they were indentured to my family... that we *owned* them. Knowing what I know now, it's not entirely out of the question. Did her parents know what mine did? Were they involved in the family business, or were they just product bought and sold at auction?

Monica grew up in the servant's house out back, and she always liked me. Even before I cared for her, we were friendly enough. Somehow we became lovers, and we thought we were meant to be together right up until the day I tore her heart out and left it on the kitchen floor.

I was admittedly awful to her in the end, sure to sever the ties between us so crudely that there was no hope of repair. I'd never planned to come back to the States when I left them, and I wanted Monica to break free of her family business the way she'd always talked about. It seems that only half of my plan worked; She wants nothing to do with me, clearly.

But she's still here.

It takes a lot to surprise me, but that fact does it. We always talked about getting out of here, leaving it all behind. The fact that she's still in this prison is disappointing. After the whole show I put on for her, after thinking I'd drive her away from any reminder of me, she decided to stay. I'd worry that I failed at what I set out to do, but it's clear that the spark between us is gone. That spark was the only thing that put her in danger, and now that it's been extinguished, I guess it doesn't really matter where she works.

Of course, I'd like it if she moved far away and never spoke the Boudreaux name again, but I know it's a wasted effort. She's on their radar and will never be off of it. If someone decides they want her at any point, they will do whatever they want to get her. If she is going to stay here, though, I'll have to be sure she gets a pay increase at the very least. I'm sure my father never considered offering more money to the help.

Monica reappears after a few moments, still refusing to hold my gaze when she speaks. "Natasha will be here within the hour."

My throat is dry as I contemplate what to say to her by way of response, so I say nothing, nodding brusquely.

"I'll be in my room if you need anything." She finally looks up at me, blushing furiously as she realizes the way I could take her words. In another life, I would have teased her and made an innuendo about her word choice. But I say nothing, letting her trip over her own tongue instead. "That is to say, I will make myself scarce while Natasha is here. If you need anything, just call me."

"Goodnight, Monica." I turn away from her, finishing the last of my bourbon in front of the crackling fire.

I hear her scurry away and laugh to myself, but it's a sound devoid of humor. Monica has changed. It isn't entirely unexpected... to live is to change. Houses may stay the same, but people don't. They rot as they die, each day stripping them a little more of the innocence of youth, each day leading them further from the light.

I changed first. But was it my own metamorphosis that changed her, too? I really was pretty awful to her.

"Change happens where pain happens." I remind myself, flexing my fingers into a fist. Money, power, women... none of those have ever been in short supply around me. But the most plentiful thing in these halls is *pain*. It exists in every photo, every memory, every cell of my body, every molecule of air in this place.

The ghosts of my past whisper their grievances with me as I watch the slow burn, my grip tightening on the glass. If pain gives life to change, then I'm a different person entirely from who I once was.

That is both a blessing and a curse.

The crystal shatters as it meets the jagged stone at the back of the fireplace, and the flames roar as they devour the rest of the drink I left behind. Orange and red blazes threaten to spill out the sides of the grate, but I don't move. It's an empty threat; The inferno mellows a moment later. I watch it glinting over the shards of broken glass and heave a sigh.

No matter how I try to cast it off or how deep down I shove it, I can never escape the guilt.

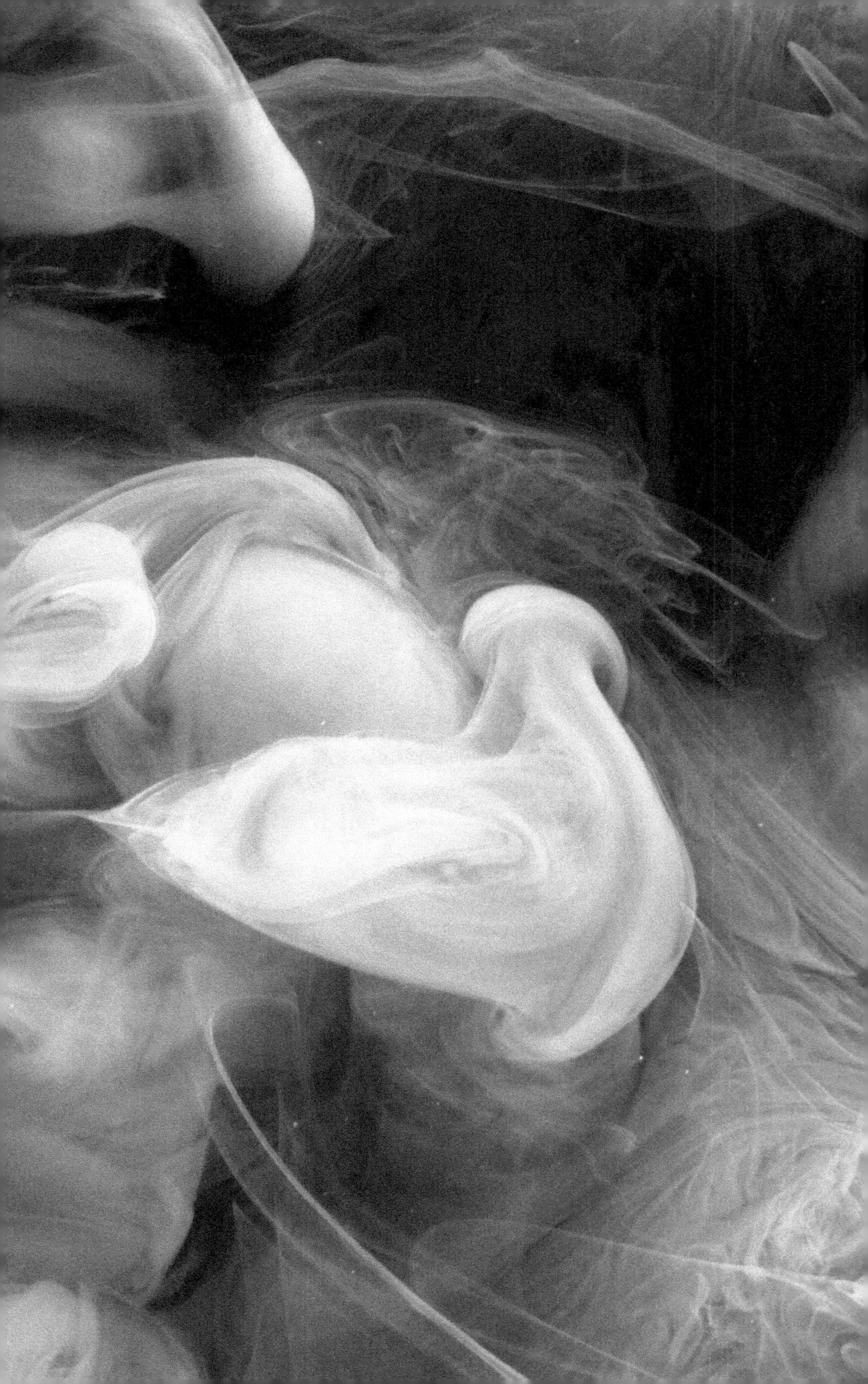

CHAPTER TWO

CLAIRE

Breathe, Claire.

I grip the edge of the countertop until my knuckles turn white, focusing on the cold marble under my touch. It's solid, holding me up in the face of all the relentless anxiety threatening to pull the rug out from under my feet.

Five things.

I groan. It's been years since I've had to resort to coping techniques to keep from falling apart... years since I've felt this gnawing inside me like a rodent trying to chew its way out from under my ribcage. I did so good for so long—right up until this moment, holding back tears in the work bathroom because I'm too proud to let my best friend see them.

Five things.

I let a slow breath free from my chest and keep my eyes down as I turn, trying not to catch a glimpse of myself. I don't want to describe what I see when I look in the mirror; It definitely won't help lessen my situation.

The small bathroom is surprisingly posh: a gold-framed oil painting a la Renaissance, flameless candles adorning the countertop, red painted walls done in broad strokes, a collection of soaps and perfumes cluttering the shelf in the corner, and a crystal chandelier glinting with its own light.

Good. Now what can you touch?

I brush my hair off my face, letting silky strands fall through my fingers before twirling the ring on my right hand in a circle with my thumb. Wiggling my toes in my shoes, I stretch, casting off the jittery feeling in each of my limbs.

Already starting to feel calmer, having taken a step away from the proverbial ledge, I close my eyes and focus on what I can hear. The slow cadence of the broken faucet *drip-drip-drips* water in the porcelain sink behind me. Laughter carries through the heavy wood door as footfalls sound on the other side, retreating just as quickly as they approached.

I take a deep breath, inhaling the scent of berries from my lotion. *Taste. What do you taste?*

The taste of wine lingers on my tongue, but it's burdened by the taste of something else—something that's creeping in around me. Darkness.

I'm only supposed to describe physical sensations, but it's the only word that comes to mind. Sometimes darkness tastes like blood from biting your own lip trying not to cry, or like a sore throat from screaming for the pain to stop. Sometimes it tastes like anticipation, like knowing that the ground is going to fall out from beneath your feet, but not knowing *when*. It's a bitter taste on the back of my tongue that I've been swallowing down for the last month, and it's starting to choke me, which is exactly why I'm presently struggling to center myself in a freaking bathroom.

The first few weeks of summer went too fast, and now I'm spiraling as I try to hold tight to what's left.

As it always does, summer fell away like petals in the breeze. That's the thing I love most about my time at the shore—or the thing I *used to* love. The days come on fast, and they go by even faster, each sunset melting into a bonfire under the stars. The waves that crash on the sand fear no man, and no man has any fear of something more than an empty beer bottle. This town is insulated from the rest of the world, a little piece of heaven... my paradise. Bad things don't happen here, and I can generally forget that they happen at all.

This is my third summer at the shore, and though I am by many accounts different from the majority of tanned, toned, trust-fund kids who call Cove Harbor home, I am an honorary member of their club.

My best friend is their queen.

On the surface, the locals appear to have it all. I know they aren't perfect, but that has never mattered. I don't need perfect. I don't need to feel important or desired, or beloved by all. I don't need extra money in the bank or to be the talk of the town. Rhea thrives on the adoration of our peers, on making friends, and on living her life on her own terms. I don't need all that. All I've wanted for as long as I can remember is simply to be *loved*.

And I have been since I met my best friend. She's the closest thing I've ever had to family, the only person who has ever made me feel that I matter to them no matter what. I let her carry me until I learned to float. But now I can't float anymore. Senior year is looming, and all the old insecurities are knocking on my door. Soon it will be time to sink or swim. Cvc

But not tonight. Not this last, perfect summer. I've had so many things taken from me in life, but this, I won't give up.

Taste, I remind myself. The fruity flavor of Mama's homemade wine still lingers on my tongue. It's light and bubbly, the antithesis of how I feel, but it's the perfect embodiment of these enchanting stays at the shore, and I need more.

Taking one last slow breath, I let go of the insecurity that's plagued me my whole life, locking it away to be dealt with another day. Once I've assured myself that I don't look like I just had a mental breakdown, I rake a hand through my hair and flip the light off before heading back to my table.

Not known for her subtlety, I hear Rhea from across the room before she even comes into view. "Brava, Mama," She plants a loud kiss on Mama's cheek. "That piccata is a work of art."

Mama beams as she clears the counter of our plates and swats my hand away when I reach out to help her, tsking her tongue disapprovingly. "If you won't eat anything else, have some more wine." She demands, pushing the glass pitcher across the table. I'm pretty sure she topped it off since I went to the bathroom; A bit of it nearly sloshes over the side. "It's made special."

I roll my eyes at Rhea, but neither of us can help the conspiratorial grin we share. She knows exactly what I'm thinking without speaking a single word.

Mama is always shoving food at us. I gained a few pounds my freshman year, but by the time Rhea introduced me to Mama, she'd claimed I was still too skinny. She makes it her mission to fluff us up every summer, right in the middle of swimsuit season. I gladly trade her gourmet meals for a few pounds on the scale without hesitation. When we go back to university (and eating like college students) I always lose it so that when we return the next summer, Mama shakes her head while she mutters to herself in Italian and restarts her mission of trying to fatten us up all over again.

But when it comes to her wine, I need no further invitation. Neither does Rhea, who pours us both another glass and then tips hers toward me in a salute. There's a lot to enjoy about summers at the shore, but this is my absolute favorite part. When the shop closes for the night, Gus locks the doors and starts cleaning up while Mama doles out all the new dishes she's been experimenting with. She's a creative chef, and despite the classic Italian comfort food she serves daily, she experiments with all sorts of interesting and delicious recipes, throwing ingredients together and producing magic every time without fail. After every shift, we eat dinner under the twinkling lights on the deck, enjoying the breeze coming off the water and listening to the partygoers yelling and laughing down the beach.

"I think you're supposed to leave room in the glass," I chuckle, eyeing the brimming goblets she filled.

"And waste my time when I finish the first glass and have to refill it that much sooner?" She scoffs. "Never."

That I can't argue with—not with Rhea. Carefree as she is, she's deliberate about not wasting time on anything she doesn't want to do, which reminds me...

"Aren't we supposed to be meeting Ryan at the Piazza?" I don't know what time it is, but I know we've been savoring every moment of our dinner, neither of us in a rush to leave. I also know that Ryan has a way of getting even whinier than usual when we're late.

"I suppose." Rhea sighs, rolling her eyes for dramatic effect.

I laugh, allowing myself another sip of wine and letting it chase away the tension brought upon by Mama's earlier prodding about my plans for the future. I'd barely gotten halfway through my first glass when she brought it up in innocent conversation, and then I'd spiraled until I excused myself to fall apart in private. But now that I've effectively chased away my worries for now, I can really indulge. Her wine is surely the nectar of the gods, and it is *strong*. I can feel my cheeks warming already, the bubbles in my veins.

"If you aren't interested, why don't you just cut it off?"

"Because, *mon petit Cherie*, what's the point?" The fact that she's fluent in English, Spanish, French, and Italian, is just one thing I admire about Rhea, though she sometimes speaks in another language like she expects me to keep up. With her beautiful skin and ample curves, Rhea doesn't just look different compared to the rest of the people I know; She is simply cut from a different cloth. And she's never been ashamed of that. "Summer's over in three weeks, anyway."

"Ugh. Don't remind me." I lift the wine glass and tilt it toward my friend in an honorary toast before draining the rest of it and letting it chase away the complicated emotions threatening to take control again.

It's far too likely that this will be our last summer like this... dining under the stars, breathing in the salt air, raking in enough cash to last the school year without having to do food delivery to drunk frat boys for menial tips, having meaningless flings, and being generally care-free. When we graduate, we'll both be thrown into the world and expected to act like proper adults. I haven't been a kid in a long time—that innocence died with my parents, and whatever was left was ripped away afterward— but the thought of being a proper adult is nearly as terrifying as the past I've run from.

I've been more of an adult throughout my childhood than most people in Cove Harbor have to be in their entire life. The world is cruel, wicked, and unyielding, and I'd all but given up on it before meeting Rhea. She forced me to relax and cut loose for the first time, and though I have no qualms about our enduring friendship, I can't help but stress that real-world pressures after graduation will change our dynamic. And frankly, I'm not ready for it. I was in a dark place—literally and figuratively—before she became my roommate. Once we separate, I'm afraid I'll revert back to the girl I was before... a girl I want to bury more than anything.

I just want to live in our bubble until the day that I die, too full and happy and a little tipsy.

"That's a problem for another time," Rhea says it casually, but the look in her eye tells me she knows where my head is. She stands, taking a deep breath of the salty air. "Come on, let's go see what sort of treat Ryan has for you today. Maybe a candy-coated hunk of man meat?"

I laugh, enjoying the slightest, sweetest wine buzz. The night is young. As much as I don't mind the idea of changing into sweats and binge-watching crappy reality television (as we do most nights), I'm also desperate to cling to everything about our summers for as long as possible, and that includes entertaining the men trying to woo my best friend. Sometimes, it's better than reality TV.

Rhea kisses Mama's hand on the way out, and I wrap her in my arms, thanking her for everything as she presses a kiss to the top of my head. Mama is another thing I'm terrified to lose about this place. She's the closest I've got to a grandmother. She doesn't call me out for holding onto her a beat longer than usual, sensing that I need her warmth more tonight than usual.

The door lock clicks in place behind us. From the corner of my eye, I see Gus blow a kiss at Rhea through the glass. She flips him the bird and then turns around, chuckling to herself.

"Where are we going to change?" I ask, my eyes falling on the glowing neon sign for The Piazza. It's just down the boardwalk, the light cutting through the cloudless night. The bass from the club's speakers rattles the wood under our feet.

"Change?" Rhea scoffs, unfastening the buttons on her dress uniform to reveal that she's been wearing a short, spandex dress under her uniform. I haven't seen that one yet, but it's the kind of dress that looks perfect on her frame. It also looks like the kind of dress that had to have been shifting around under her uniform all day.

"I'm sure that was really comfortable to work in."

"Actually, the elastic on these sides kept riding up every time I'd serve a customer, and this lace bra itches like a bitch. But," she accents, "Beauty is pain, daaahling."

"I guess I'll change in the bathroom." I fail to suppress a shudder.

The bathroom of any bar is a place to be avoided, if possible, but in particular, the restrooms at the Piazza are like something from a horror story. The whole building seems close to crumbling into the sea, really, but there are a few reasons we go back almost every weekend, every summer, and it isn't for their watery cocktails.

"They may not let you in looking like you're fresh off the farm." Rhea teases, dodging the arm that I swing at her before we both dissolve into laughter.

"Vin knows me by now. Besides, I know you well enough. If he tried to turn me away, I could see one of three things happening. One—you'd buy the whole damn place." Rhea tilts her head to the side, considering it, and then nods summarily. "Two—you'd flash him. Not full frontal, but just enough to make him turn to putty in your hands."

"Accurate." Rhea concedes, albeit with a little reluctance.

"And option three—you'd run into the middle of the dance-floor, convince DJ Dave to cut the music, and then tell everybody the party had been moved to your house."

Rhea smirks. "I'm a little concerned with your intimate knowledge of how my brain works, Claire. But you did forget one option. Number four—Report them to Sheriff Jack for serving minors, wait 'til he shuts them down, and then break in through the loft that I still have the key for, and party 'til the crack of dawn."

"You still have the key?" I laugh and then immediately shake my head. "Why am I even asking? Of course, you do."

"You never know when it will come in handy." She shrugs. "Oh shit, there he is."

I look up to see Ryan walking eagerly toward us, his hands stuffed in the pockets of his blazer. Though I went to high school in a relatively impoverished community, we still had the stereotypical teenage cliques: the loners, like me, the jocks, the nerds, and the preps.

Ryan is a prep student if ever I've seen one, always dressed like he's just come from the courtroom where he had to litigate a case for Giorgio Armani. He isn't a lawyer—he graduated a few years ago, but when I asked Rhea what he does, she told me it was too boring to remember. Apparently, he's known Rhea for years because his father had done business with hers, though before this summer, they hadn't seen each other since they were children. Rhea made it clear that her memories of him weren't as fond as his are, but she doesn't seem to entirely hate seeing him, even in spite of the fact that she groans every time he spots her, which is often. Rhea jokes that he must have a tracker on her because he seems to be magnetized to her. I told her he's more of a heat-seeking missile.

He reaches out with open arms, moonlight glinting off his gold watch. Rhea sidles under his shoulder, which is a funny feat considering he's a full foot shorter than her, and that isn't accounting for the strappy heels on her feet. Working in a second-skin dress under your uniform is one thing but serving up drinks in four-inch stilettos is another type of pain altogether. I'd opted for flats with thick cushions hidden inside and my feet *still* ache after a day of waitressing. "You're late, babe." His lower lip juts out in a pout that probably got him anything and everything he ever wanted as a child. As a grown man, it's hardly endearing. "Mama wouldn't let you out to play?"

I bite my lip before I can say anything rude, but Rhea backs down from no one. And bringing Mama up in anything less than worship is a black mark in her mind. "I wasn't sure I was going to show, actually. I've been a little bored lately." She shrugs, stepping away from him with either a practiced apathy or genuine disinterest.

Ryan swallows, trying hard not to look bothered despite being clearly offended. "Ah, Claire!" He says as though he's just realized I'm here too. In his defense, he probably did. "I brought a friend." He turns around, looking for whoever it is that he's brought along to distract me.

I stifle my laughter and give Rhea the side-eye, while she chuckles openly. It's no secret that Ryan sees me as nothing more than the cock-blocking best friend keeping him from getting with his summer conquest. If only he could get me to take one of the bones he's been throwing at me, he's sure he can whisk Rhea away and get the thing he's been seeking from her all summer. We'd actually been talking about it in the kitchen during a rare lull in customers earlier today.

"Maybe on the last day of summer before we go back to Darrington." Rhea had mused. "I don't want to give him any more reason to be obsessed with me in the meantime. What about you? Are you ever going to sleep with someone who you don't plan to marry?"

I'm not waiting until marriage. And I'm not a virgin. But I'm also not anywhere near as casual about sex as she is. That is probably the starkest difference between the two of us.

Each of the three friends Ryan introduced me to this summer has been charming, funny, and would have been more than happy to take me home for the night. But none of them have made me *want* to go home with them. Worse, none of them made me feel safe enough to go home with them if I had wanted to.

When you only get a couple hours with someone, I guess that's a big ask. I'm not opposed to going home with a friend of a friend or having a meaningless but cathartic one-night stand; I just need assurance that I will not end up mounted above their mantle or something. I need to know that I'll be respected and that things only go as far as I want them to go. Unfortunately, all of Ryan's friends are objectively creepy.

"Ah, Wes!" Ryan calls, waving over the crowd gathered at the door to a man with jet-black hair that falls in waves and green eyes that pierce through the night, landing right on me.

Shit, he's gorgeous.

As he breaks into a magnanimous smile, Rhea leans into my shoulder. "I'll switch you." She quips, fanning herself gently.

Wes doesn't take his eyes off me as he joins us, and I can't take mine off of him either. He's pretty in a way that men usually aren't... definitely prettier than me. He's a tall drink of water, and I'm suddenly parched.

And then he smiles at me like I'm suddenly the only person in the world. "Claire, I presume?"

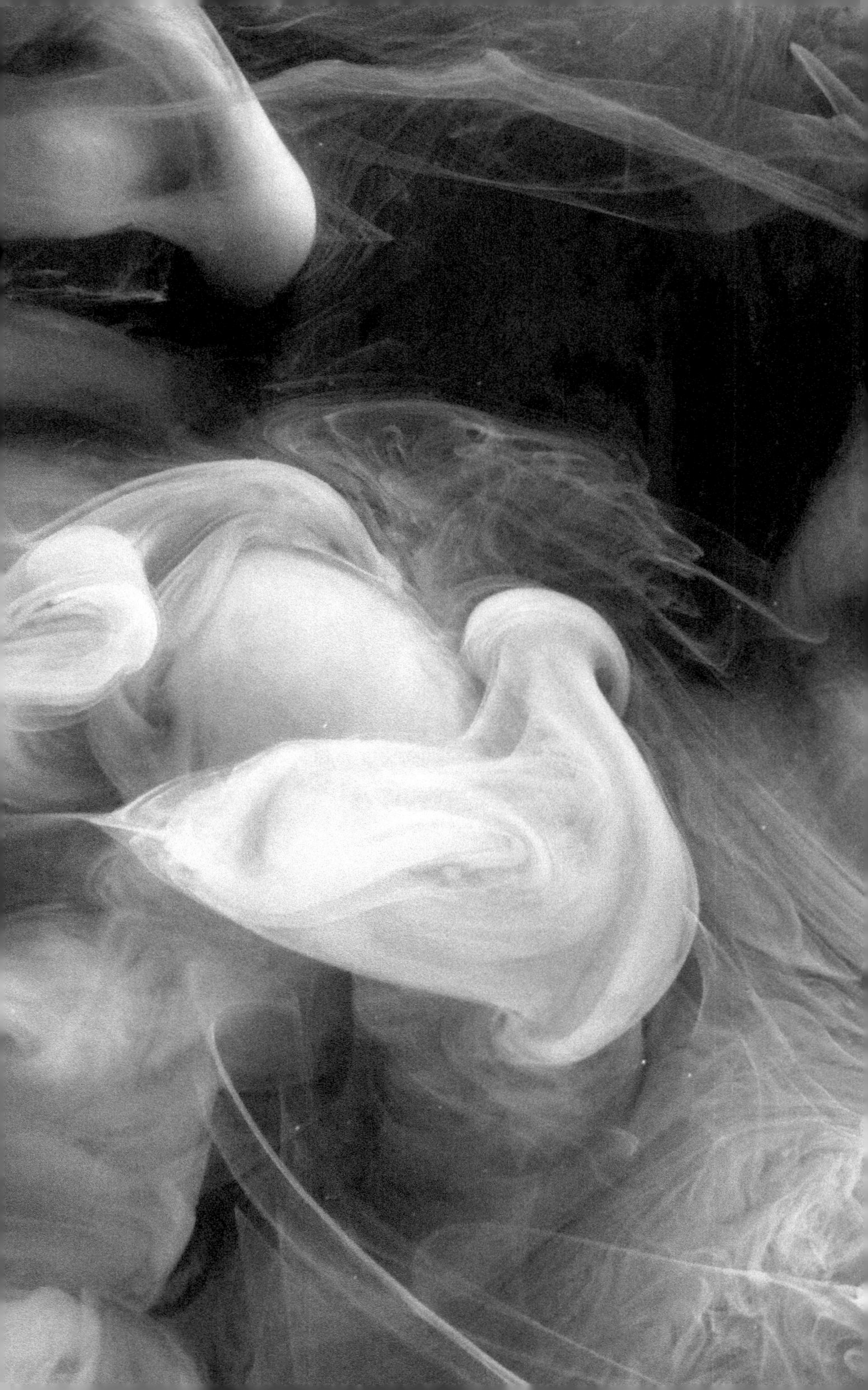

CHAPTER THREE

CLAIRE

"I like the dress." Wes grins, leaning into me so that the dim lighting overhead illuminates the playful look in his emerald eyes.

"Yeah..." I laugh, brushing a loose thread off the yellow dress uniform I'd forgotten I was still wearing. "I need to change." Cheeks heating with the faintest embarrassment, I stand and turn to my friend, who's sitting next to Ryan on the white leather couch he led us to when we got here. Rhea looks bored as he leans into her, whispering something in her ear that he undoubtedly hopes will capture her attention.

"Do you want me to come?" She offers, looking hopeful.

I know it's for her benefit and not mine that she asked. Despite all my insecurities, I am perfectly capable of going to the bathroom alone. I also know that I'm not going to be her scapegoat at the moment. She's been pulling Ryan's strings all summer. For all her talk earlier of potentially sleeping with him, it's never going to happen if she runs from him all night. Besides, if I want to explore anything with Wes—and I do—she will need to be occupied anyway.

"I'll be fine on my own, *mom*." I tease.

Leaning back with her arms crossed under her chest, Rhea pouts. I guess she's still annoyed with Ryan for his comment about Mama.

"What's your drink?" Wes asks, smoothing the buttons on his shirt as he stands up to head to the bar.

"Um..." My little buzz from dinner is fading exponentially. Still, if I mix wine with liquor, it means I'm sure to get drunk fast. Whether or not that is the goal depends on whether Rhea wants to bail early. For my part, I'm certainly more inclined to stay a while than I would be if Wes weren't here.

"Tequila." Rhea bats her eyes, letting me know that the goal is to let go tonight. "Tequila sunrise."

Wes watches me a minute, waiting for my confirmation nod, before turning to retrieve the drinks. I turn away too, laughing.

Apparently, it's going to be a long night.

Despite having the alcohol tolerance of a collegiate linebacker, tequila is Rhea's kryptonite, and she knows it. When she wants to have a little extra fun, she orders me all sorts of tequila concoctions and steals a few sips here and there so that she can take herself higher without getting as obliterated as she would if she ordered it herself.

I don't mind. Though not as impressive as Rhea, I can handle my liquor. I built a tolerance because it numbed the pain well. I don't use alcohol for that anymore—I don't need to. It's fun to see people's shock when they realize my tolerance is pretty impressive for a girl my size.

I've built up an impressive tolerance for a lot of things, honestly. Dealing with drunk people is no exception.

The line for the women's restroom is long, and full of tipsy tourists and a few locals I exchange pleasantries with. The company makes the line go faster, but I seem to be the end of it. In fact, after waiting in line for nearly ten minutes, surrounded by the chatter of care-free women enjoying their summer night and the thrumming music, I end up in the bathroom alone.

As I pull the dress uniform over my head in the cramped stall, awareness pricks at the nape of my neck, making me uncomfortably conscious of how empty it is. The only sound to be heard is the steady drip of a busted pipe and the swish as I drape my uniform over the stall door. I've just put the tight-fitting lace dress over my shoulders and stuck my head inside when there's a little *click* from outside the stall.

The lights go out, casting me into a deeper darkness.

My breath catches in my chest, freezing me in place for a moment, half-dressed in the bathroom stall. Fear seizes me by the throat, and my stomach drops before I remember where I am.

I'm not helpless, I'm not a child, and I'm not alone. Sure, a bathroom stall isn't exactly the pinnacle of security, but it's a hell of a lot better than some of the other places I've been.

You're okay, Claire. You're safe.

"Rhea?" I call once I find my voice again, listening for any sound that might indicate my friend is trying to get payback for ditching her with Ryan.

I tug the dress in place over the few curves I have and then push the stall door open. The creaking sound it makes sends chills down my arms. It's too dark to see anyone or anything, but it doesn't *feel* like I'm the only person in the bathroom now, which is somehow more terrifying.

Eyes adjusting, I squint through the darkness and pick out a cluster of shadows, lighter than the rest of the darkness. It stands, motionless, by where I know the door is.

Chills lace my spine and then crash violently over the rest of my body, sending a full shudder over me. I dig my nails into my palms, assuring myself I'm really here, not just stuck in an old nightmare.

"Rhea," my voice wobbles. "Is that you?"

Only silence answers. Nobody moves... the shadows don't so much as ripple.

You're being silly, Claire. It's probably nothing. Your eyes are playing tricks on you.

The Piazza is a glorified wreck, but maybe they've sprung for motion-activated lights, and they're just glitching. It's the only thought that can explain why I'm standing in sudden darkness. I wave my arms, trying to get the lights to engage, all while not moving my eyes off the shape by the door, just in case the shadows come to life and lunge at me.

In spite of the nervous pounding of my heart, a metallic sound takes me by surprise, as if something is being scraped along the exposed plumbing beneath the sinks. It's not a grating sound, but it *is* haunting. I shiver, suddenly so cold that I'm shaking.

"Who's there?" I demand, my heart slamming against my ribs.

The noise stops as suddenly as it began, and then there's a distinct shuffle of movement as the door opens. I can't make anything of the shadow that slips out, but the music from the bar grows louder before being muffled again as the door closes once more.

With my heart in my chest and the shadow gone, I lunge for the light switch.

The fluorescent box over my head flickers to life, casting the restroom in a yellow glow that reveals I'm completely alone. Shuddering in a small bit of relief, I find the courage to throw the door open, but there's no one on the other side of it either.

It's just a malfunction, I tell myself, looking at my reflection in the full-length mirror bolted to the back of the door. Through the smudges, graffiti, and fingerprints, I see my reflection, visibly shaken.

I'm not imagining things. Someone was in there with me. Did they sneak in and turn the light off as a stupid joke or did they know it would get to me?

Get a grip, Claire.

I square my shoulders and fix my hair, glancing at the bottoms of the stalls as they're reflected in the mirror, just to be sure that no one else is in there. That's when I realize my dress uniform is no longer slung over the stall door.

I glance around once more to be sure I'm alone, and then check it didn't fall on the floor. I am definitely alone, and my work dress is totally gone.

Rhea knows I'm terrified of the dark. She realized as much the first night we shared our dorm room in freshman year. She didn't question me then over the little lamp I left on at my bedside, and she still doesn't. Rhea wouldn't turn the light off on me for a cheap laugh, so who would?

Drunk college kids, of course. That's the average clientele of The Piazza, after all. Some of them are still obscenely immature high schoolers, sneaking in with fake IDs that show them to be five or six years older than they truly are. Someone probably watched me walk into the bathroom alone and dared a friend to do it. Taking my work clothes was probably just some weird sort of trophy.

I muster a smile in the mirror, force myself to exhale the fear, and roll my neck to ease the tension that's building up in my shoulders. I'm on edge tonight because of my earlier anxiety attack, that's all.

When I return to our table, Rhea is exactly where I left her. Still tucked under Ryan's arm, she looks considerably more relaxed. She leans forward when she sees me approaching, gesturing to the table excitedly. "Ryan bought shots!"

"Your favorite." I muse, accepting the cocktail that Wes holds out for me as I take the seat next to him and smooth my skirt under my palm. My hand shakes a little, so I grip the edge of the couch and tap my nails against it.

"I feel warmer already." Rhea grins, jiggling her shoulders so that her tits bounce freely in the low-cut dress. Ryan stares at her like he's just found water in the desert, pressing the heel of his hand over his pants indiscreetly.

"I'm sure you do." I laugh and take a long sip of my own cocktail, hoping it will calm my still-jilted nerves. The taste of the tequila tries to pull at old memories, but I drink it fast enough that my brain doesn't get too long to wander.

"I thought the other dress was nice, but this..." Wes leans into me so I can hear his words as his eyes give me an appreciative once-over. I feel the heat spread across my cheeks as I blush.

"Have a shot!" Rhea reaches down and grabs two of the little glasses, holding them both up. I hesitate for a moment.

"What's in them?"

"Shot roulette!" Rhea cries, pumping her fist in the air like some sort of cheerleader.

"How much did you drink while I was gone?" I chuckle, taking the first shot and peering tentatively inside. The glass is too dark to tell what kind of liquor it is, and the smell is just an alcohol burn. But I don't really care what it is as much as I care how well it will ease the cocktail of anxiety and adrenaline in my stomach. Though nothing actually happened, my nerves are frayed from the bathroom incident.

I toss my head back and drink it down, coughing at the afterburn as I set it down on the table.

"You were gone foreverrrrr." Rhea draws out the last syllable, punctuating it with a roll of her eyes.

"Yeah." I agree. "Long line."

"Of course." She rolls her eyes so dramatically it makes my head ache. "I'm going to start using the men's restroom. In fact, I have to go right now."

"No!" I all but yell, stopping her before her ass fully leaves the couch. A few people turn to shoot nosy glances at me, and Rhea raises an eyebrow in an unspoken question. "If you pee now, you'll be going every twenty minutes the rest of the night."

That placates her, and Rhea taps me on the nose. "Clever, clever, Claire." She giggles and stands, pulling Ryan to his feet. "Come on, I want to dance."

Ryan, always eager to please Rhea, jumps to his feet like a golden retriever and allows himself to be pulled to the dance floor, where they disappear in a crowd of moving bodies. Wes turns to me. "Do you want to dance too?"

"I'm not there yet." I laugh, eyeing the other shot on the table in front of me.

"Thank God." Wes laughs too, grabbing the little glass off the table and handing it to me. "I'm a terrible dancer."

I take it with a smile and choke it down before looking back at Wes with tear-filled eyes. "That burns." I say, fanning my face like that will help chase away the afterburn. "I'm pretty sure that was straight isopropyl."

"Isopropyl." He grins, flashing brilliant, straight teeth. While Ryan looks to be a businessman of sorts, Wes looks like a fringe doctor... a veterinarian or dentist, maybe. He's polished, wearing an expensive-looking watch and shiny shoes, but he also has a much more relaxed vibe than his friend. "I like the way you say that. Are you a nurse?"

"No." I laugh. "That little dress you were so fond of is my work uniform. I'm just a waitress."

"Yikes." He shakes his head like I've just disappointed him. "Just a waitress, huh?"

"Is that not enough for you?" I narrow my eyes on him. I know nothing about this guy and am beginning to feel emboldened by the alcohol to say so.

"I've never dated anything less than a flight attendant." He strokes his chin, thoughtful, and then dissolves into another one of those big smiles. "I'm teasing, Claire. I don't care what you do for work. Does it make you happy?"

"I like it, actually." I admit. "It's low-key, keeps me busy, and the tips are mind-blowing."

"That's cause you're easy on the eyes." As if to prove the point, his own eyes slip over me to assess the statement. "I mean, I'm sure you're good at your job, too, but that's only half of it."

"Um... thanks." I tuck a piece of hair behind my ear, not entirely sure whether that was meant to be a quirky compliment or not. "So, where do you work?"

"No work." He leans back with his hands behind his head, the epitome of casual, and appraises me.

"No work?"

Wes shakes his head as I repeat his answer.

"You're one of *those*... like Ryan?" I don't mean for the contempt to ooze out of my voice, but that doesn't stop it. "A trust-fund kid just seeing where life takes you?" I'm used to being around people who are financially sound, but the thought of dating someone with a sense of entitlement bigger than their personality is a hard pass.

"Not exactly." He lifts his rocks glass to his lips, barely concealing the grin there. "I just graduated med school. I start my residency in a few weeks, actually."

"Wow. That's impressive." I blink. "So that's why you asked if I was a nurse."

"Not many people outside of the medical community refer to it as *isopropyl*. But I must admit, it did turn me on a little."'

I blush but am thankfully spared from having to say anything when a cocktail waitress appears, handing me a drink I don't recognize.

"Oh, I didn't order this." I glance at Wes, wondering if he did, but his face is blank while he waits for an explanation.

"No, that guy at the bar did." She gestures to the crowd of people at the bar behind her, none of which are looking our way except for the guy standing at the edge of the crowd. Sorely out of place wearing severe leather with his stringy hair hanging in a marled face, he isn't easy to miss. His dark eyes collide with mine and he lifts up his flask in a toast just before turning into the crowd. I keep my eyes trained on him as long as I can, but he disappears somewhere in the throngs of teenagers. The waitress sets the drink on the table and teeters away, unbothered by my hesitation.

"What kind of guy sends a woman a drink when she's with someone else?" Wes muses. The touch of irritation in his words sends a slight thrill through me, but I'm not sure yet if it's because I *like* the possessiveness that crept into his tone or if it's because I *don't*. "Did you know him?"

"No." I shudder. "That was weird."

"Well, since it came from the bar, it's safe to drink. Looks like a Blue Russian."

"A what?" I turn, my eyes falling on the drink.

"A Blue Russian. Vodka, blue curacao, whipped cream. It's a pretty sexy drink."

I laugh. "How is a drink sexy? And how do you know what it is? Did you study the anatomy of a cocktail in med school?"

"You don't make it through med school without copious amounts of alcohol, sleep, and caffeine." He shrugs. "It's a cycle."

"So, is this your drink then?" I tease, my lips quirking into a smile as I lift it up, letting it gleam under the light. "You like the girly stuff?"

"I'm an equal opportunity drunk." He shrugs, unbothered, but his lips quirk at the corners a bit. "I like all kinds."

I sip the cocktail, surprised to find it's actually a sweet, creamy orange flavor, almost like a daiquiri. "That's really good, actually."

"Much better than a tequila sunrise, I'd say."

I eye him, the dazzling smile and his eyes like sea glass. With his charm and ambition, I suspect he's firmly out of my league, so why is he bothering? Does he think I'll be an easy opportunity for casual fun, or is he just that dedicated of a friend that he's willing to occupy me as long as it takes?

"And when it comes to women, are you an equal opportunity lover? Do you... *enjoy* all types of ladies?"

He tilts his head to the side, briefly considering his answer. "Only the ones who make the first move."

I raise an eyebrow and finish the rest of my first cocktail before placing it down on the table. I move closer to Wes, and he slips his arm around my shoulder, taking our stance from casual to intimate. "Come here." I motion him even closer.

Wes moves into me, anticipating the kiss that's about to unfold between us. But instead, I press my lips to his ear so that they brush against his lobe as I speak. "I'm old-fashioned. So, I'm afraid you'll have to woo me first. A lady never makes the first move."

Wes pulls back to see my eyes, his mouth inches from mine. "You just did."

I'm leaning into him, our lips just barely touching, when a scream tears through the room, overpowering the tenor of the music, which cuts out a second later. There's a loud scuffling of shoes, a panicked symphony of screeches, and a consuming chaos as everybody scatters. Wes pulls me to my feet just as Rhea appears.

"Time to go!" She yells, grabbing my hand and dragging me toward the back of the room... in the opposite direction of the exit.

CHAPTER FOUR

CLAIRE

I don't fail to recognize the irony, remembering my earlier conversation with Rhea regarding the key to the loft. I've never been so grateful to have a resourceful best friend as I am in this moment, with her pulling me toward the staircase in the corner of the room. I can feel the panic clouding the room and smell the body odor wafting toward us as everyone else stampedes in the opposite direction, every man for themselves as they try to squeeze out the too-small exit.

We run up the steps with Ryan and Wes in tow, followed by the screams of panicked partiers trampling one another in their rush to get out of the building.

Rhea fumbles around in her purse a minute before coming up with a little ring of keys. "Fuck!" She mutters, spinning them desperately to find the right one. When she does, she jams it into the lock and throws the door open with enough force that she and I both tumble in.

Wes is the last one to cross into the apartment, and he locks the door immediately behind him, turning to Ryan to demand an explanation. "What happened?"

"Some freak just full-on assaulted a girl down there!" Rhea yells. "He was talking to her, and then she must have said something he didn't like because he grabbed her hair and started yelling in her face. Another guy went over to break it up, and the first guy pulled a knife on him." She swallows, turning to me, her eyes wide in distress. "A fucking *knife*, Claire!"

I understand her shock. It rattles in my ribcage, making it hard to breathe.

Cove Harbor is a one-sheriff kind of town where nothing bad ever happens. There are the occasional fistfights between drunk frat boys on the beach, but beyond that, it's overwhelmingly safe. We walk home alone at all hours of the night and never have to concern ourselves over whether there is someone lurking in the shadows waiting to attack. I'm not sure anyone here even locks their door at night; I know Rhea didn't until we started rooming together. The thought of someone bringing a knife anywhere in Cove Harbor is wild enough, let alone someone actually pulling it.

My mind flashes back to the bathroom and the person I was sure was standing there watching me. It was easy to dismiss the incident as my mind and eyes teaming up to play tricks on me when everything had been normal, but now that I know someone was down there pulling knives on people, I can't shake the feeling that maybe they were in the bathroom with me. But to what end? Nothing happened, so if someone had been in there, what did they hope to achieve by it?

"Was anyone hurt?" Wes demands, looking between Rhea and Ryan. The way he just assumes control of the situation is both comforting and oddly attractive. I assume it's the med student in him, prepared to take control in an emergency.

"I don't know." Rhea shakes her head helplessly, turning to Ryan, who throws his hands up in frustration.

"I didn't see anything."

"Stay here." Wes warns, unlocking the door again.

"Wait!" I hiss. "You're going down there?"

"If someone is hurt, I have a responsibility to help. Stay here." He repeats.

Wes disappears down the stairwell and into the suddenly unsettling quiet of the club below. I turn my ear toward the hall, listening out for anything that could indicate he may need help.

"How do you have a key to this place?" Ryan asks, looking Rhea up and down with unveiled suspicion.

"I was dating the guy who lived here last summer. He gave me a key so that I didn't have to wait up for him all the time."

"And where is he now?" Unimpressed, Ryan looks around like he expects someone is going to pop out of the pantry. Though it's empty, the apartment clearly isn't *entirely* abandoned. All of Nick's stuff is still as he left it, including the framed photo of him and Rhea sitting atop the TV stand.

"Jail." Rhea snaps, waving a hand at him. "Who cares?"

"I do." Ryan bites back, matching her irritation word for word. "That's why I'm asking."

I wait with bated breath for anything to come out of the silence, but there are no sounds to be heard other than Ryan's mumbling about how he should know these sorts of things about the woman he's seeing.

Sirens wail to life in the distance and Rhea jumps a little at the sudden noise, grabbing my arm.

I turn to find her frozen in place, waiting for a sign that everything is all clear. My best friend is great at taking charge in most situations, but her upbringing has sheltered her to the wicked reality of the world. We balance each other, in that way.

"Wes?" I call, cracking the door just enough to let my voice carry downstairs. Only silence greets me a few beats, and then I hear my own name called back to me from the foot of the stairs.

"Claire? You may want to see this."

Rhea shakes her head back and forth adamantly, not ready to abandon our hiding space.

"Is everything okay?" I ask. Please God, don't make us exit through a crime scene. Blood has always made me a little faint, and even more so when it belongs to someone else. And with the adrenaline and alcohol cocktail roiling in me, I'm not sure I can handle seeing anything too violent.

"Everything's fine." Wes calls back. "I promise."

I let go of a little breath and pull the door open enough to see that the staircase is empty. I descend it cautiously, my eyes sweeping over every inch in front of me just in case someone drops from the ceiling and tackles me. For all I know, we're living the start of the zombie apocalypse right now.

Despite Ryan's objections, Rhea follows right behind me, so I reach a hand behind me and grab her wrist, not sure whose benefit it's for.

Wes is crouched down looking at something on the ground, but he straightens when he sees us turn the corner, holding something in the air for us to see. I'm vaguely aware of Ryan, a very safe distance behind us as we study the scene.

The four of us are alone in the bar. Though you can tell it was evacuated in a hurry thanks to the spilled drinks, shattered glass, and even a pair of stilettos abandoned at the bar, there are no signs of blood on the ground, no body. "Looks like your new friend may have been the one wielding the knife."

My eyes fall on the flask in Wes' hand. It could belong to any number of people; There's nothing remarkable about it. But it could also be the same one that belonged to the man who sent me a drink. The Blue Russian.

"Your *friend*?" Rhea demands, arms crossed under her chest nervously. All traces of her buzz are gone.

"Some guy sent me a drink." I shrug. It isn't exactly unusual to have a drink sent to me, particularly when Rhea is nearby. But it is weird that he'd deliberately made sure both Wes and I had seen him. And that's to say nothing of the bathroom incident, which feels both too random to be connected and too unusual not to be.

"Well, I'm officially sober." Rhea groans. "Let's go home."

"We'll walk you." Wes insists before the objection has even made it off of Ryan's lips.

"That really isn't necessary." I shake my head. Just because we've had a strange night doesn't mean that the town is suddenly a den of evil too sinister for us to make it home. But there's a shudder sitting between my shoulders, a cold, heavy lump of awareness telling me to swallow my pride before I choke on it.

"Um, there is a strange man out there, assaulting girls and pulling knives on people. I'm not too proud to accept an escort. Thank you." She tells Wes, tapping his hand in gratitude as she stations herself next to him. I catch a glimpse of Ryan's obvious sulking as he sidles next to me, and we fall into place behind them.

Most of the crowd has disbanded by the time we leave the Piazza. Those who haven't quickly scatter when the sheriff pulls up. I scan the faces of the crowd, looking for any trace of the man with the flask or the shadow from the bathroom, but neither is anywhere to be seen.

Thankfully, the walk back to the Boudreaux Estate is short because Ryan's negative energy and Rhea's nervous energy are rolling around us in waves, making for a really uncomfortable journey home. No one speaks the whole way there, though Rhea slows enough to fall in step with me and grant me a curious glance.

Rhea's house is an unnecessarily large mansion made of brick and glass that sits just off the boardwalk. It overlooks the sea while still managing to be surrounded by woods and also decidedly isolated from the rest of the town... or at least, it feels that way.

Ryan makes it clear that he doesn't want to walk any further out of the way than he has to. He knows his plan backfired and that he isn't going to get to go home with Rhea. Of the four of us, he seems the most concerned about the possibility of someone coming after us, glancing over his shoulder every few steps. Despite his fear, he decides to wait alone, sulking in the ring of light under the streetlamp as Wes walks us up the long, paved path to the front doors.

The porch light, the lanterns scattered down the steps, and the lampposts on either side of the entrance make me feel immediately safer. Whatever may be lurking in the shadows isn't here, which is an immediate comfort. Despite whatever is going on in the rest of the world, the Boudreaux Estate is a shelter from the storm.

I nod at Rhea, whose fear also seems to have evaporated as she smirks at me, to let her know she can go in and then turn to thank Wes for accompanying us home.

"That was sweet of you to walk us back," I tell him honestly, not bothering to point out that Ryan would have left us to our own devices.

"I wouldn't dream of letting you guys walk alone." He shakes his head, a little laugh escaping him. "Thank you for… an interesting night."

I laugh, too.

'Interesting'. I guess that's one way of putting it.

"So, can I call you?" Wes' eyes are playful now, glinting in the glow of the porchlight. "Maybe we can try for a re-do?"

"Are you asking for my number?" I tease.

"I am." He nods with zero hesitation. "I'm in town for a week, and I'd actually really love to see you again."

"Okay." I nod, not the least bit ashamed of the goofy little smile tugging on my lips at that admission. "Do you want to put my number in your phone?"

"No, no." He shakes his head as if the idea is ridiculous and brandishes a pen from the pocket of his dress shirt. "You're old-fashioned, right?" Grinning, he pushes his sleeve up, presenting his forearm along with the pen.

I eye him a moment, letting myself appreciate the view of a very toned forearm, the thick vein that has no business being so attractive while trying to gauge whether he is serious. I decide he is, and laughing, I take the pen and uncap it with my teeth. Holding his arm steady in my hand, I write my number, then sign it with a heart and my name. "Don't wash that off," I warn, a little bit of lust slipping into my words at the thought of him in the shower.

God, Rhea was right. I need to get laid. And I probably would have if the night hadn't gone off the rails.

"Wouldn't dream of it," Wes says with surprising sincerity, though his voice is also husky.

I return the pen to him and catch a glimpse of some sort of tattoo right above his elbow, obscured by his rolled-up sleeve. He doesn't look like the sort for tattoos, but I want to see it. I want to see a *lot* more of him.

I wait a moment to see if he will make a move, but he only smiles, so I turn and let myself in.

As soon as I step inside the entry, Rhea lunges at me. I haven't even finished spinning the lock in place before she demands me to, "Spill it!"

"He's a nice guy." I shrug, smiling a little. It's been a while since I've met one of those—I was starting to think they didn't exist any-more—and it feels like things between us are to be continued. He asked for my number, so he's clearly interested, but he didn't move in for a kiss. He either wanted me to be the one to do that, or he was trying to be respectful. Either way, the slightest disappointment swirls in me, mixing with hope for our next encounter.

"*A nice guy*?" Rhea parrots. "Did you kiss? Was there tongue? Are you going to see him again?"

"He has my number." I shrug.

"Okay, *details*! You got to spend an hour with tall, dark, and steamy, and I had to get drunk to tolerate the presence of Tristan never-worked-a-day-in-his-life Ryan."

I laugh. "Nothing happened, but I'll tell you everything. Let me get out of this stupid dress, and then I'll meet you in the theater room. It's my turn to pick the movie, and you know what that means..."

Rhea rolls her eyes and hefts a dramatic sigh. "Fine, but I'm still drinking! I need my buzz back if you seriously expect me to sit through a Christmas movie in July."

I laugh as I hurry up the stairs to the room I've called my own the past few summers since Rhea first brought me here. It has the advantage of being just across the hall from her room, which is a time capsule of her teenage years. It's perfect since I often get the creeps being alone in such a massive house with floor-to-ceiling windows looking out into the thick woods. I sometimes get the feeling that I'm being watched, but it usually passes when an owl flutters by or when I draw the heavy curtains that allow me to sleep into the late morning.

I kick my shoes off as soon as I'm inside the room, set my purse on the bed, and shimmy out of the too-tight dress, breathing a sigh of relief when I'm free. I let that fall in a pile with my shoes and cross to the dresser, producing an old tee shirt and shorts, deciding I'll pick that up later. It's as I'm reaching around to unclasp my bra when I realize I'm not alone.

"I could help with that." A husky voice, deep and dangerous, breaks through the quiet, stealing the air from my lungs and causing me to freeze for a split second before I jump, throwing my arms in front of me to cover as much of my skin as possible and scanning the room for the source of the offer.

I find it when my eyes fall on a figure in the corner of the room, mostly cloaked in shadow. I wouldn't even know he was there if he hadn't spoken. But now that I do, I can see the glint of his eyes, sharp and predatory.

He takes a step closer, allowing the moonlight to pass over his face just enough for me to confirm that I do not know him. He doesn't have the same build as the shadow figure from the bathroom, and it's not the man who sent me a drink. That knowledge gives me simultaneous relief and deepening terror. What the hell is going on?

The door to the balcony is open, letting the sultry night air in, and it seems that's where he came from. Did he scale the balcony to get up here? Did I forget to lock the door?

"Go on," He teases, gesturing for me to continue where I left off, his eyes gleaming. "You don't have to stop on my account." His words are hungry, but his voice? It's low and deep, sensuous like a blade wrapped in satin.

"Who are you?" I demand, unable to move. The shock has numbed my body, and though I think of running, my limbs can't even entertain that idea, so I stand there and stare at him.

"You're not Natasha." He says with a small frown. "I don't remember ordering you." He allows himself a long, languid look up the length of my body and then back down. His gaze sends chills shooting over my skin— both the parts that are exposed and the ones that aren't. "Were you sent as a gift?"

"A gift?" I swallow, taking a small step back as he takes a smooth one forward, eliminating most of the space between us. "Who are you, and what are you doing here?"

"You may have technically asked that first, but I was thinking it first." He is close enough now that I can see the danger in his dark eyes, and yet, for some reason, I still can't command my body to move.

He's a large man, tall with a slender frame that's wrapped in muscle... *so* much muscle. The ripple of his stomach makes my own clench, and the dip of his hips where the elastic of his boxers hangs on his hips is damn-near erotic.

His height eclipsed me even from across the room, but now that he's drawing nearer, I feel small by comparison. There's a hint of honey in the color of his skin, and his smoldering gaze threatens to light me on fire, though I'm not sure if that's with the threat, my embarrassment, or the power that seems to radiate off of him.

"Don't come any closer!" I warn, putting an arm out to enforce a distance and leaving myself slightly more exposed.

It does nothing to stop him. He steps closer still, a smirk playing in the corner of his mouth. It reveals a dimple that looks deceptively soft, given how hard the rest of him is. He knows I am no match for him, and I know it too. I also know I could scream for help, but Rhea would be the first to get here, and what if he attacks the both of us? I don't have a single doubt that he could do it easily. No, I don't want to drag my best friend into this sort of situation.

I take another step back, my heart aching with the force of its churning. "I'm not going to hurt you." He says, showing his hands as if to prove that they're empty. But he is an admittedly sexy, shirtless man in nothing but silk boxers who broke into my room through the balcony. The fact that he is empty-handed really is no consolation.

I open my mouth and take a breath, my lungs filling with air as I prepare to run screaming. At least half a dozen staff sleep in a house behind the manor. If I yell loud enough to draw them, maybe it will scare him off before he can hurt me.

But he's fast, closing the distance between us in a matter of seconds so that he's able to wrap one arm behind my back, trapping it between the both of us, and covering my mouth with his other hand. The intoxicating scent of bourbon and cinnamon fills my nose as I try to focus on taking in air, not him. Despite his aggressive move, he's not covering my nose, so he's not trying to kill me... at least, not yet.

His breath is hot on my neck, his lips brushing my ear as he speaks. "You should know that I don't make it a point of hurting innocents. So, you answer my questions and answer them honestly, and we'll go from there." I struggle in vain against him, which only results in him tightening his grip, drawing me further into him. His chest is a solid wall of muscle pressing into my back, and I have no doubt he could hurt me in a dozen different ways in this very moment. But that doesn't scare me nearly as much as the other thing I feel pressing into my back, growing harder as I jostle against him.

He *likes* my fear.

The shape of his erection, large and unyielding, causes me to still entirely, going slack against him as his hot breath whispers in my ear. "Understood?"

I nod, unable to speak with his large hand over my face and the cloying scent that seems to cling to him. The man lets his hand fall away from my mouth, landing instead on my hip. I shiver under his touch, my breath going ragged as I'm aware of how intimate this position is. And what's worse is that I don't hate it. In fact, I feel everything in me clench in desire as he uses his grip to spin me around and pull me into him so that our bodies press together again, skin on skin. He's warm and gorgeous and terrifying, and he makes it clear that there is no way I am getting away from him.

Whoever this man is, he's a lot more prepared to handle me than I am to handle him. "Who are you?"

I swallow, my tongue thick in my mouth. "Claire... Claire Monroe."

He releases my arm finally, at least a little satisfied with that answer. The tension in my shoulder eases, but the fear in me doesn't because he still manages to hold me pinned against him. I'm all too aware of the way my chest rises and falls against his, deepened by the fear crashing through me.

His hand moves instead up my arm, sending static running throughout my body. His touch is delicate but firm as he finds the hollow spot between my collarbones and runs a thumb over it, his eyes never leaving mine. He could easily collapse my throat if I try anything, and he's at least letting me know it as his eyes coax mine into holding his gaze.

"I didn't ask your name," he tells me, his words so delicate as they whisper over my mouth that I almost think he's going to kiss me. "I asked who you are. Try again." His voice is stern even as he whispers the last two words.

It doesn't escape me that although I'm barely clothed, I feel more naked under his touch than I did when he'd been able to see everything from a distance. Something about his eyes, as he looks down at me from this proximity, seems to be exploring my soul. It's almost more intrusive than his touch, prompting chills to race down my spine and erupt again along my exposed arms.

The man doesn't seem to enjoy waiting for an answer. "I've got all night, *Claire*." Something about the way he says my name sends another chill through me, this one spiking in my core until I can't decide if it's fear or arousal that he sparked. "Do you?"

"I... I'm a college student. Twenty-one. I work at a restaurant down on the boardwalk."

Who am I? It's a good question, but I don't have an answer. The cruel irony is that this is the question that plagues me all the time, the reason for my breakdown at work earlier. I'm just one year away from graduating college, and I still don't know who I really am, let alone what I'm going to do with my life.

"Claire Monroe, the college student?" he asks, watching my face for any betrayal of a lie. It's curious; The expression in his dark eyes is stormy and foretells of obvious danger if he doesn't like my answers, and yet as tightly as he is holding me in place, he isn't *hurting* me.

His dark features are beautiful and faintly familiar. As imposing as he is, something about his presence is also calming... authoritative. I'm scared, but there's something foreign mixing in there with that fear. Whatever it is, I can't put a name to it.

"Yes." I breathe, tilting my chin up so he can see I have nothing to hide. I don't know who he is or what he wants, but something in his demeanor is intimidating enough that the idea of lying to him is unappealing.

"Okay, Claire." He nods slowly. "What are you doing in my bedroom?"

CHAPTER FIVE

REMY

That seems to catch her by surprise. The sinful curves of her lips look like velvet when they fall open, and I want, in the worst way, to feel them on me. I've been hard since I turned around to see her breasts begging to be released from that bra that barely even manages to contain them. The sensation only intensified when I pressed her against me and felt her captive under my touch, completely at my whim. Some men wouldn't hold back, and I have to admit, I'm fighting the urge to do wicked things to her. The women who walk willingly into my room know what they're signing up for. They're not there to talk about politics and childhood memories—they're there to be fucked so hard the rest of their pain disappears and they forget they're hollow inside. They're there for me to fuck them so hard that I forget I'm hollow, too.

"*Your* bedroom?" She asks, looking around at the lavish room I grew up in. I haven't been back in years, but much like the rest of the house, it's exactly how I left it... clean, simple, without any trace of the person who lived there. I didn't even notice that it smells like her until she was under my touch, but now her delicate scent surrounds me. It's not floral, but a delicate vanilla, like she's spent the night baking cupcakes or something.

"Wait... you're—"

The door bursts open, cutting off the rest of her revelation. The shock on my sister's face is immediate, swallowing the rest of her words about 'spilling it' as she takes in the scene before her.

"Remy?" Rhea looks from me to the woman in my grasp, and then she charges at us with a hand in the air like she's heading into battle. "Fuck, Remy!" She yells, swatting my hand until it stings. "Let go of her!"

"You know this woman?" I straighten and remove my hand from her delicate neck, unable to stop my eyes from swooping down to admire the peaks of her breasts again, being held up by the cups of a lacy black bra I'd love to peel away from her skin.

"Remy, I've told you about Claire." Rhea snaps. She can't seem to decide between shock and anger as she stares at me like she's seeing a ghost.

"You told me that she exists. How am I supposed to know she is who she says she is?"

"Because I'm telling you she is, you jackass." Rhea swats at me again, but I step to the side, avoiding her hand. "Let go of my friend!"

I release my grip on the girl completely and raise my hands as some sort of bargaining chip, a sign of surrender. Claire steps away from me quickly but doesn't dare take her eyes off mine. Accusation colors her stare, but there's a hint of something else underneath all that indignation. "You can't be too careful," I say coolly.

"No, but you can be too *stupid,* apparently."

"I was just making sure she wasn't a threat."

"A threat?" Rhea's laugh is cold and unamused. I expected this from her; I just didn't expect it to be because I'd accosted her best friend. "What did you think? That she was hiding a revolver in her bra?"

At Rhea's words, I glance over at her friend again, standing still in a bit of shock, her arms crossed over her chest like that's really doing anything to conceal her body from me. My eyes graze what's visible—her pink lips parted slightly with the remnants of shock, the swell of her breasts, and then trail down a flat, smooth stomach. My cock tightens painfully as I imagine what *is* hidden under that fabric. But, no, there isn't quite enough of it for her to be hiding any sort of weapon there, really. My eyes trail down around her hips, where my hand had been moments before, and land on a shapely ass. "Maybe a shiv in the waistband of those panties." I muse, not bothering to keep the smirk off my face.

Claire seems to realize I've let my eyes linger and turns to Rhea. "I'm going to finish what I came up here to do, which is to get dressed."

"Of course," Rhea says, her words weighed down with an apology that isn't hers to give. "You!" She hisses at me, her tone going from apologetic to enraged in a split second. She got that fun trick from our mother. "You get your ass downstairs and start working on your apology. Not only did you show up here unannounced, but you attacked my best friend. My best friend, who, for the record, is more family to me than you've been the last three years."

I almost grin despite the cutting edge of her words. True or not, I know she chose them carefully to wound me. It's not that she doesn't love me. I hurt her first. That guilt often threatens to wash over me like waves in the ocean if I think about it long enough, so I really don't give it the time of day. I push all thoughts of Rhea out of my mind until our monthly call, and even then, I give her only what she needs—essentially just an audience. I listen to her tell me about her life, but never divulge anything of my own life. Every so often she calls me out on it, but then I switch subjects and Rhea recognizes that I'm not going to bend, so we let it die.

"I apologize," I say, brushing gently against Claire as I make my way out of the room. When I catch her eyes on me, they're wild. Fear mingles with something that looks suspiciously like desire. I turn away before I can contemplate that, but not before she sees me smirk.

"I'm so sorry." Rhea groans from behind me. "He is... insane. Are you okay?"

"I'm fine," Claire says, her voice breathy. She's rattled, and something about that is oddly satisfying to me. She seems like the kind of woman who prides herself on keeping it together. "Just give me a minute?"

"Of course. Meet us in the kitchen when you're ready." Rhea closes the door softly behind her.

I'm halfway down the hall by the time she catches up to me. "What are you doing here?"

Suddenly it's like no time has passed at all since I left. Her demanding tone, the accusation, and her irritation are all still there. So is the playful lilt to her tone that she tries so hard to cover up.

"Can't I check on my only sister? Here I was thinking you'd be excited to see me after all these years."

"I *am*." She says it confidently. "But I'm surprised and confused and to be honest, a little frightened by what I just witnessed. I mean..." Blowing out a breath, she shakes her head, trying to reconcile what she just walked in on with the brother who all but died years ago. "What the hell, Rem?"

"I really didn't know she was your friend." I promise, though I'm not sure it would have made much of a difference if I'd known. If Claire is going to be around my sister—one of only two people left in the world that I give a damn about— I'm going to have her vetted. "I always react first and ask questions later. I guess it's lucky you didn't bring a man home instead, or we'd be cleaning his blood off the floor."

"As if." Rhea snickers, nudging me in the ribs as best as she can given our height difference. It appears she hasn't grown at all since I've been gone—at least one thing about her has stayed the same. "You know you'd be calling Monica to come clean up the mess." She turns to look at me then, realization dawning on her face. "Does she know you're here?"

"I saw her." I nod, making it clear that I have nothing more to say about the matter. But I don't have to say anything else because Monica appears in the next instant as though our conversation summoned her. She waits for us to give her our full attention, opening and closing her mouth like she isn't sure how to form words anymore.

"Natasha's here?" She says it like a question, wringing her hands together nervously and avoiding catching my sister's eye.

"*Fuck.*"

In all the intensity of the last ten minutes, I forgot that I'd been out on the balcony, having a drink while I waited for my former lover to come try and ease some of the tension I'm drowning in. And then a half-dressed blonde sauntered into my room and all thoughts of Natasha went out the window.

"Natasha?" Rhea spits the word like it's poison. Her hazel eyes are so wide and full of rage that they look like they're about to pop out of her head. "Are you fucking serious, Remington?"

"Get rid of her," I demand, looking at Monica. She does a good job of maintaining a stoic face, but I know her tells. She bites her lip, pulling it between her teeth and worrying it back and forth. Is she more scared of Natasha than she is of me? She surely doesn't relish the idea of telling Natasha that she's been summoned in the dead of night to see me after all these years, only to be turned away when she actually gets here.

"Sir?"

The word sounds strange on her tongue, but I know what it means.

Monica waits for me to say that I didn't mean it, that I'll go talk to Natasha myself. But Rhea is home, and there's an alluring, barely dressed woman in my bedroom. I'm not taking Natasha up there now, and my need for her is gone just as if it never existed. I simply watch Monica, unwavering, as she turns to Rhea.

"Don't look at me," Rhea says sharply, folding her arms in a show of obstinance. "I haven't seen her in years. She should have known better than to come around here regardless of who called for her."

"Send her home." I say calmly. My tone is even, but it leaves no room for argument. There's a fine line between invoking a little healthy fear and causing sheer terror, and right now, I want to stay in the narrow margin as best I can. It isn't the time for games, and

Monica isn't the type that I want to intimidate any more than I have to. I already have her allegiance just by virtue of my family name.

Monica nods, swallowing her fear, and turns to do as she's told.

"Really?" Rhea stares daggers at me, her jaw set in anger. "You called *Natasha* to come over?"

"No." I lean on the counter, the ghost of a grin flickering on my lips. "I had *Monica* call Natasha to come over."

"You're disgusting, Remington Boudreaux." She says, shaking her head. But her anger is stretched thin over her amusement.

I shrug. "I was trying to kill some time. I expected you to be out a bit longer."

"Yeah, well, our night got cut short. And thank God it did, because if it hadn't, you'd be screwing Natasha in the bed where my best friend is sleeping! I can't believe you had the audacity to—" She stops talking and I look up to see Claire in the doorway, her hair in a messy pile on top of her head. A few pieces frame her face, and now that I can see her in the golden light from the kitchen chandelier, she's even more beautiful than I realized. It's an unassuming beauty, effortless. Unfortunately, she is also considerably more clothed, wearing cotton shorts and a shapeless top that conceals the delicate curves of her body. I want to know what she's hiding under all that fabric, to see her without her desperately trying to cover herself.

I don't even realize the quiet is awkward until she tentatively pierces it. "So... you're Remy?" Claire concludes, taking a barstool at the counter next to where Rhea is leaning back, her arms crossed.

"Yes," I smirk. "I suppose we weren't properly introduced."

A pink tint rises up on her skin, spreading like a wine stain over her fair cheeks. "I suppose not."

I'm not sure what Claire knows of me or my strained relationship with the rest of the family. I only know that she's been sleeping in my bed for the last three years, and a strange sort of homesickness washes over me as I realize the missed opportunity.

"So, you never answered my question. What are you doing here?" Rhea demands with her head tilted a little as if she's trying to read my thoughts. "Besides harassing Claire, I mean."

I feel the air rush out of the room all at once. I knew she would ask. This conversation is inevitable. But that doesn't make breaking my little sister's heart any easier.

My head fills with euphemisms, a dozen little cloaks I could throw over my words to try and soften their impact. But I'm not a man of words—not anymore. Once upon a time, I would have all the right things to say and would have prepared myself for this moment. Now, I'm a man of action, which is why I chartered the jet and made the journey here, despite how much I loathe everything about this place. Phone calls have kept her at bay for the last few years, but they won't cut it now. I have to tell her this in person.

Claire watches me like she knows what I'm about to say, but I can't handle the distraction of her right now. I train my eyes on my sister, bracing myself against her impending reaction. It's best to just rip off the band-aid.

"Father's dead."

My words fall around the room like shattered glass, but nobody moves.

The silence stretches itself out into an uncomfortably long interval as Claire looks at me and then back to Rhea. "Rhea?" She whispers tentatively, placing a gentle hand on my sister's back. "Are you okay?"

It takes a moment before Rhea blinks slowly like she's waking up from a dream and trying to remember what's real. She stares at the cold granite before her, working through what she's just been told. Claire looks at me again, nervous, helpless. I want to be able to offer them comfort, but that isn't something I've ever been good at, so I simply watch her try to console my sister.

"I..." Rhea opens her mouth and then closes it again. She takes a deep breath, swallows, and then looks up at me. "I'm not sure I heard you right?"

"I hate having to tell you," I say as softly as I can, like the delivery will really make any difference here. "He's gone, Rhea."

Rhea stares at the granite again, her eyes filling with tears. I can feel a pit begin to open in my stomach, a hollow darkness stretching wide. It's not a new sensation; the void is my oldest companion.

A woman crying isn't typically something I could brush off, but it also isn't something I've ever learned how to handle. Thankfully, Rhea doesn't let them fall. Instead, she blinks her tears away, and when she looks back up, it's with a quiet acceptance.

"How?"

Claire wraps an arm around her, trying to offer some small comfort.

I guess she really is more family than I. She, at least, is willing to offer my sister something I can't.

I heave a sigh. It's a question I knew was coming and a question I haven't yet figured out how to answer. I spent hours trying to come up with some sort of explanation on the flight, but I still have nothing. Turning to the fridge, I grab a couple of beers and place one in front of Rhea and another before Claire.

Claire doesn't look like the type of girl who drinks lager, but she thanks me as I pop the top off for her.

No easy way to say it. I may as well just treat this like a band-aid, too.

"He was murdered."

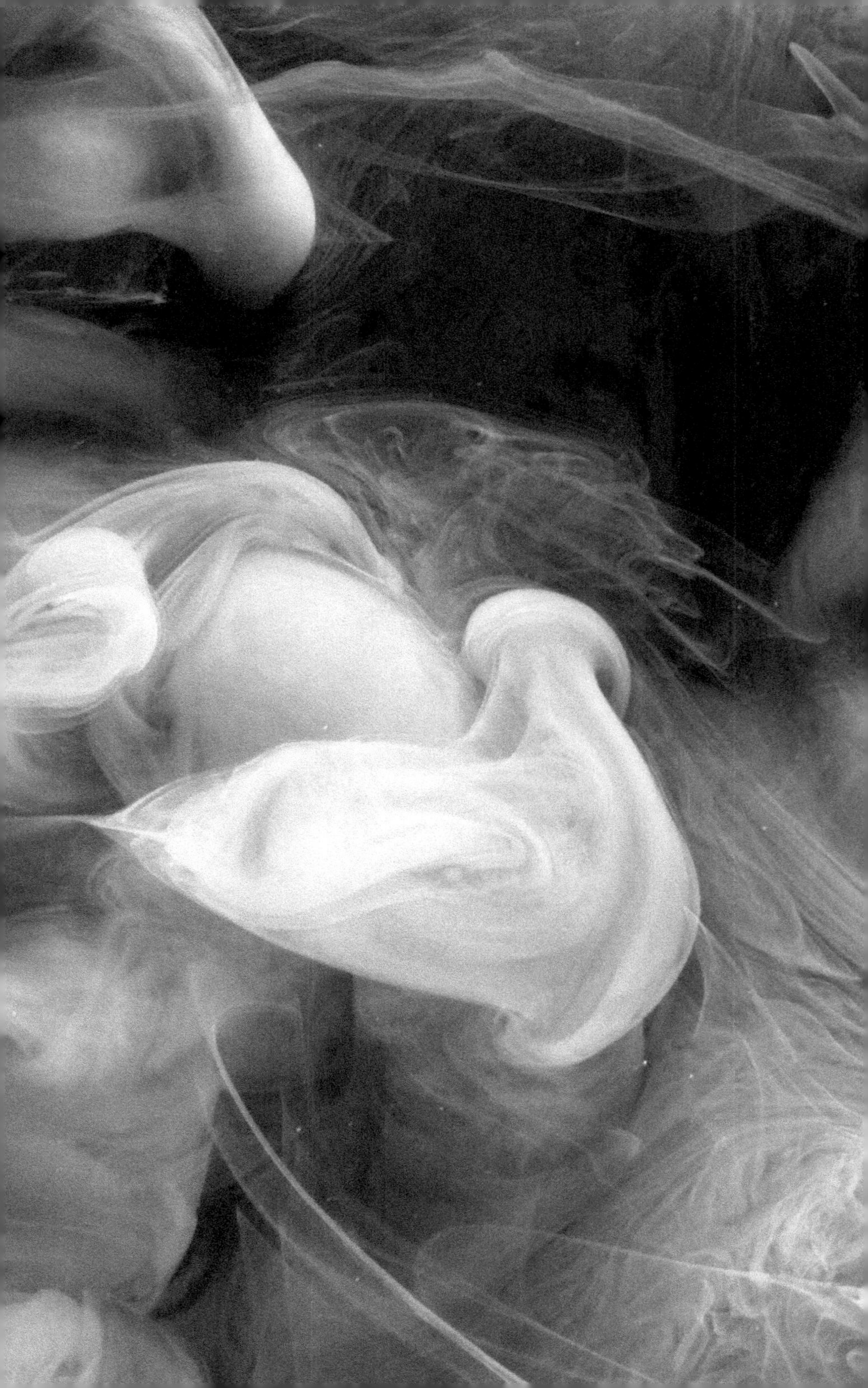

CHAPTER SIX

REMY

An angry sob escapes her, and Rhea shakes her head. "I knew he trusted too much... he did business with far too many shady people."

I laugh coldly before I can stop myself. She doesn't even know the half of it.

"Tell me what happened," Rhea demands, straightening and collecting herself. Her grief turned quickly to anger, and now she wants answers.

Claire straightens, too, grabbing the beer that she'd set before her. She tips it to her lips and takes a long swig that I find myself unable to look away from.

I knew she'd ask this, too. Rhea isn't the type to back down, to accept things the way they're first presented, or to believe everything she's told. Of course, she also expects me not to lie to her in the first place. "He had come to Costa Rica." I begin. "He wouldn't tell me what the business was, but he said it was huge. I think his exact words were 'life-changing'."

"He... was in Costa Rica?" Rhea repeats.

I knew she wouldn't be happy when she found out, but I didn't expect the hurt in her eyes when they flicker to mine. "With you?"

"Well, he stayed with me, yes. It didn't make sense for him to stay anywhere else. But it's not like we were having family dinner every night. I barely saw him."

"You could have told me." She accuses, the hurt as obvious in her voice as it is on her face. "*He* could have told me. I would have flown there so we could all be together for once."

"There wasn't time for all of that." I wave a hand at the ridiculous idea of our family being together again. Whatever reunion my dear sister is imagining we could have had, it's nothing more than a fantasy. "He wasn't planning to stay long. He was there to close a deal, and then he was supposed to fly right back to Zurich. But something went wrong."

"Well, clearly!" She snaps. "Seeing as he is *dead* and all!"

Claire swallows, clearly uncomfortable with the turn our conversation has taken. But I can tell she doesn't want to abandon Rhea at a time like this, and I don't care if she hears it all from me. If they're as close as Rhea says, she'll tell Claire everything anyway.

Claire focuses intently on peeling the label off the beer bottle, and I try not to focus on her.

I'm calm in the face of my sister's rage. I have to be. "Jovich and Dimitri are working on putting everything in order. Obviously, I'm not going to stand for any of this. Whoever was stupid enough to cross our father will pay for it."

"I can't believe this." She lets her face fall into her hands like the weight of these thoughts is too much to keep her head straight. "I thought... I thought he was untouchable."

I stay quiet in spite of the many things I could say. I don't want to hurt her any more than necessary. I've spent my entire life trying to keep her safe and the last few years trying to keep her innocent. I have no intention of seeing that hard work undone.

"Our flight leaves at eight. You'll want to get some sleep. It's not a short trip."

"You're having his funeral in Costa Rica?" Claire ventures, looking to Rhea for confirmation.

"That's where our whole family is buried." Rhea sighs with a roll of her eyes. "We never spent time together while we were alive. I guess they think that there may be some redemption in death."

"There is no redemption for the Boudreaux's." I finish my beer and look at them levelly. I see my sister scowl and wonder if I should be a little less cynical, but I'm not going to candy-coat poison in order to convince my sister to eat it.

"Now is not the time to lament all of your grievances with our family," Rhea warns with one hand up. "We should be... celebrating his life."

"Rhea," I laugh. "That's nothing to celebrate."

Claire considers my words a moment before speaking. "Life is always cause for celebration." She says, nodding shortly like she's trying to convince herself of that. "And death means that there was life, so I'm with Rhea. I say we celebrate."

Of course, she's with Rhea. She clearly doesn't realize the implications of being involved with my family. But then that's just proof that I've done a great job sheltering my sister from all the sordid details of what it means to be a Boudreaux. Claire is apparently like the human version of a Labrador retriever— blindly loyal.

But is it genuine?

I turn and grab another round of beers. "All right." I concede, deciding that if I go full tilt on telling my sister how evil our father truly was, I may just send her running from me. That's the last thing I want. "What are we celebrating?"

"How about you put some clothes on and meet us in the theater room?" Rhea suggests.

I smirk when Claire's eyes fall on me, still dressed in only my boxers. She turns a soft shade of pink and abruptly looks away. Her tongue darts out over her lips before she chases it away with a sip of her beer. She's flustered, and it's really fucking cute. Women don't often get flustered in my presence. They're either so terrified of me that they run away or come straight for me without hesitation.

"Do I make you uncomfortable?" I venture, letting the teasing edge coat my words.

"No." She says quickly, forcing her gaze to meet mine. "I'm fine."

Another long pull on her beer tells me otherwise.

The smirk finds its way back to my face. As I walk past her, I can practically feel the heat radiating off her. I like that.

We just met and already I have such power over her.

I like having power over people, as long as it's the right kind of power. I want power, I want respect, and I want people to fear me. I *don't* want that mix to all come from one person. People who respect you shouldn't fear you, but people who fear you should respect you.

Claire doesn't need to fear me unless she's hiding something.

As I walk into my room, it strikes me that something is amiss. I glance around but find nothing out of place.

I'm alone in my room, but the curtains billow inward with the night breeze. I left the balcony door open in my haste to interrogate Claire. Her shoes and dress still lay on the floor, and I can't help the stab of disappointment that I missed seeing her all done up before she started to undress. Not that I'd trade it for seeing her in that lingerie.

Does she always wear such sexy underwear, or was she planning to bring someone back to my room?

The thought makes my blood run hot, but I'm not sure if it's just my bed that I'm suddenly feeling territorial over.

I shake my head as if that will drive the sinful thoughts of her out of my mind and cross to the balcony, looking down at the woods that separate my childhood home from the rest of town. Everything is calm and quiet. The other side of the house— where Rhea's room is— faces the ocean, which is never still. Perhaps that accounts a little for our personalities. I, too, am still on the surface, a picture of quiet strength and solidarity. But deep within, there are many little surprises... most of which are less than pleasant. Rhea, on the other hand, is wild on the surface. She crashes and dances and screams like the waves breaking on the shore, but she's gentle and serene under it all.

I was pulled under the ocean's surface once. It was actually quite a peaceful place to be. Not a single part of me had any desire to fight to get back above the water. It was Rhea who had pulled me out, though, dragging me back to the shore. She saved me once, and even though I hadn't wanted to be saved, I decided that day that I would spend the rest of my life doing the same for her. Saving her over and over again, protecting her. Nobody else is going to do it. Nobody else can.

The shrill ringing of my phone cuts through the distant sound of crashing waves, pulling me back to reality. I glance at the caller ID.

Unlisted.

Clicking the green button, I wait until a warbled voice comes from the other end of the phone.

"Hello, Remington." It sounds ridiculous—the kind of throaty, high-pitched tone used by overly dramatic killers in nineties slasher films. It's the kind of voice simulator that would send a spike of fear through most women when they answer it unassumingly, but I have to fend off a laugh. I don't have time for theatrics... not now, not ever.

"Who is this?" I demand.

"Let's say I'm... a *friend*."

"I don't have friends," I say seriously. Friends would be a weakness in a profession like mine. "Is there a reason you're calling?"

"I saw your sister tonight." The voice is slow, like the person on the other end is deliberately dragging their clauses apart in a desperate attempt to build tension. "She looks nothing like you. Tight dress, tight body... I bet that pussy is pretty tight too. I'll let you know when I find out for sure."

I go rigid, rage turning my muscles to lead. Just the mention of my sister has me tense. My mystery friend just crossed a line they will severely regret overstepping. "Who the fuck is this?" I growl.

"You'll find out... when I drive a knife through the back of your skull." The man on the other end chuckles.

"You must be either very brave or very stupid to threaten me," I say coolly. "Although, it's pretty cowardly to disguise your voice, so I'm guessing you're the latter."

"I guess we'll see."

"When I find out who you are," I work to keep my voice even and calm. The girls can't hear me from downstairs, but I don't need to let this fucker hear how much his threat concerns me. "I will personally rip you apart limb by limb for even *talking* about my sister. And then we'll see."

The warbled voice on the other end laughs again, the sound like static in my ear. "Sleep tight, Boudreaux."

The line goes dead before I can say anything more.

I clench the phone in my hand, torn between hurling it off the balcony or slamming it against the ground. I decide to do neither, pressing a number on speed dial. Jovich answers on the first ring. "Boss?"

"Tell me you've learned something new today," I command, shutting the balcony doors and letting the curtains fall into place. One last look into the dark of the woods assures me that no one is out there. Not yet, anyway.

"Sure." He agrees, though the flippant way he says it tells me I won't like what comes next. "It seems your father may have crossed both the Russians *and* the Saudis."

"Fantastic," I say drily, pinching the bridge of my nose where a headache is starting to take root. "Add them to the ever-growing list of my father's enemies."

"I have," he confirms, "along with the guy at Boulder Tech."

I sit on the bed and notice Claire's purse abandoned there. A quick glance at the door assures me no one is near, so I grab the strap and drag it closer to me. It's a small black thing with a silver clasp... basic, unassuming, so very tempting.

"Boulder Tech?" I puzzle. "What makes you think they're involved?"

"Call it a hunch."

"Work faster, Jovich. Somebody just called and threatened Rhea. I'm with her tonight and bringing her home with me, but I'm trying to keep her out of all this. Can you figure out who called?"

He makes a sound like a growl. Jovich is probably the second-most person who loves my sister— or third, depending on the extent of Claire's loyalty. "Which cell did they call?"

"The private one."

"I'll reach out to my guy." Jovich says, assuring me it will be looked into swiftly. "In the meantime, don't let Rhea out of your sight."

"Wasn't planning on it."

I end the call and toss the phone on the bed, breathing out my frustration.

I'm tired... not just physically, but down to the marrow. Down to my black soul, I'm tired. My mother had loved to say that there was no rest for the wicked, and the older I get, the more the words resonate. My mom was right about a lot of things over the years, but I can't find it in myself to forgive her for everything. I'm not sure I ever will.

My eyes fall back to the bag beside me. I don't usually make it a habit to look through a woman's stuff. In fact, I could usually care less about what things a lady deems important enough to carry with her. But I want to know if Claire has secrets that could pose a threat to my family. Our first encounter may have seemed like an overreaction to her, but my suspicions aren't without merit. I know the lengths people will go to for vengeance, money, power... all things that can be had by moving the right pieces into the right places on the chessboard.

The clasp is already undone, so I open the purse enough to see that there isn't much in there. Judging by how she's kept my room clean enough that I hadn't even realized she was living there, I guess she is either a minimalist or obsessive about order.

Turning the bag upside down, I let the contents fall onto the bed. A wallet, a pack of peppermint gum, a few crumpled bills, lip gloss, and a single house key. No pistol, no knife, not even mace. She is either brave or stupid enough to think she doesn't need to be prepared to protect herself. I hope my sister isn't as stupid, but

I guess I'm going to have to get them some pepper spray or at least a damn Taser.

I put everything back except for her wallet, which I open. The photo that smiles at me from the ID card is undoubtedly Claire. Those clear, bright eyes are already seared into my memory. Her smile is a bit too chipper for a driver's license photo, but she looks good.

Monroe, Claire E.

D.O.B. 03/24/2002

The address is the one I have Elaine use to send Christmas cards to Rhea, and nothing about the ID stands out. She has a Chase credit card and a Mastercard with the name of an obscure bank stamped on it. A library card, a school ID, a coffee shop loyalty card that is just one stamp short of a free latte.

I thumb through everything, looking for anything that stands out and am just coming to the conclusion that Claire Monroe may actually be a simple girl who just stumbled into Rhea's life by chance, when a second ID catches my attention.

I flip it over to see the same picture as the first one, but the details on this card are different.

Boudreaux, Claire E.

D.O.B. 03/24/1999

The address is the same, and nothing else sticks out to me. But why would she have an Oregon ID with my last name on it? I hold them up, side-by-side, looking for obvious signs that one may be a fake, but they look identical... right down to the anti-fraud emblem that shines in the passing light.

I'm not sure what to make of it. It's suspicious, sure, but it's not exactly a smoking gun either. Either way, it isn't enough to confirm or deny my suspicions of her.

I put everything away and position her purse exactly how she left it.

Apparently, Claire *is* lying about something.

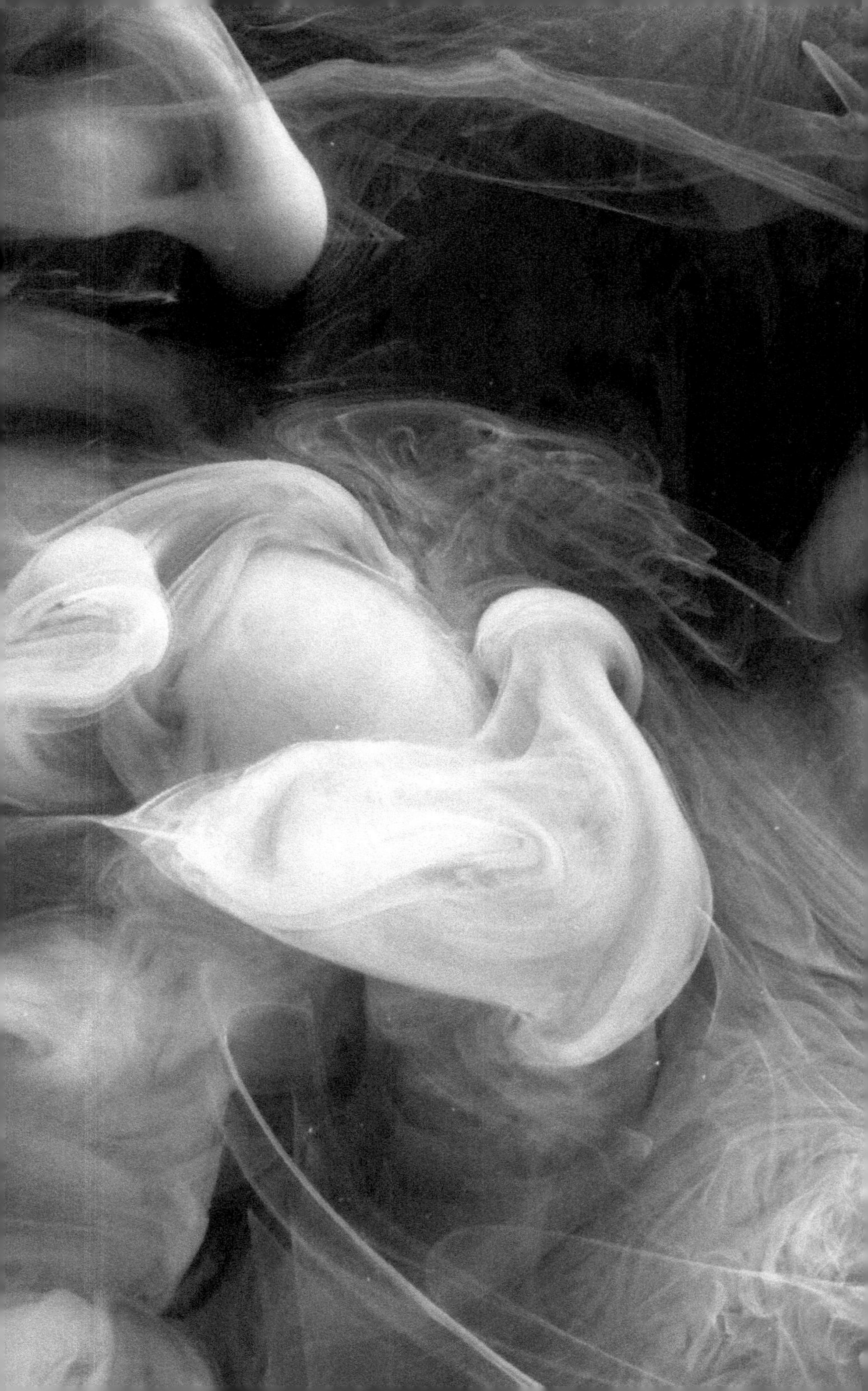

CHAPTER SEVEN

CLAIRE

"That's you?" My laugh fills the theater room and I cringe a little the way I always do when I laugh too loud. Maybe I should slow down on the drinking... my cheeks are hot, and I know it must be from the alcohol pumping through me.

In the photo, a young Rhea with her dark hair in pigtail braids stares dispassionately at me, arms crossed over a pretentious school uniform which still allows me a view of a crest sewn onto the chest of her sweater vest. It's a look I've seen plenty of times—a look that makes men and women alike uneasy. I've never been on the receiving end of her anger, thankfully.

"I seriously wanted to murder my mother over those bangs." Rhea cringes, and I can't tell if it's the mention of her dead mother or the painful memory of her haircut. "I looked like Wednesday Adams, but not as cute." She shakes her head, disgusted. "She always had the maid get us ready for school while she got ready for the day and the one woman—Jolie—she insisted on treating me like a doll. She was horrible. I swear, she tried to put blush on me for my first day of *kindergarten*." Rhea busts out laughing. It's so contagious that I quickly join in.

We've already flipped halfway through a photo album Rhea dragged from a bookshelf and drank a full bottle of wine each. After the day's tumultuous events, it just feels right to sit together laughing. Because if Rhea doesn't laugh, she'll cry, and I'm an empath. If Rhea cries, I cry. I don't need her trying to take care of me tonight of all nights, which is exactly what will happen if we don't keep her spirits up.

"What's so funny?" Remy's voice cuts through our laughter, and I nearly jump out of my skin. He came into the room so quietly that neither of us realized he was there. I think of him upstairs earlier, where I wouldn't have even noticed his presence if he hadn't spoken. Apparently, he's sneaky.

It feels like someone turned up the thermostat, but I don't know if the heat now is coming from embarrassment at the memory of our earlier encounter or his proximity or the fact that his eyes are on me... his beautiful eyes, full of questions and secrets and things he won't show to either of us.

I feel the weight of a knot in my stomach... no, *not* my stomach. It's lower.

Are you serious? Are you really thinking about his hands on you when he just came here to tell his sister their dad died?

But his hands are only the beginning of what I'm thinking about. I'm imagining his lips on me, his weight pressing down on me, being absolutely encompassed by him. Being caught in his touch earlier had felt like the strangest mix of danger and safety; I imagine that sex would be the same.

"You remember Jolie?" Rhea asks, her words pulling me out of my dirty thoughts. I shift my eyes away from him and squeeze my thighs together like that will alleviate the ache there.

"The Russian?"

I can't help it. His voice is too alluring, smoky, and deep. I turn back to see Remy arch an eyebrow, his already-cocky expression deepening when he notices me watching him. I look away, my mouth suddenly dry.

What the fuck is wrong with me?

"She was Ukrainian." Rhea rolls her eyes and shoves the photo album into her brother's chest. "Do you remember when she left me at the park?"

A lazy grin lifts the corner of his impeccably full lips at the memory. "I still don't understand how she could have forgotten you. You never shut up for more than two minutes."

"She still doesn't." I laugh, unable to help myself.

Rhea elbows me in the ribs playfully and then sighs. "I think that's *why* she left me, honestly. But it worked out just fine because mom fired her, and then we had Lenore, and she was perfection."

"She smelled like a French whorehouse." Remy deadpans. I realize he needs to join us, so I start scooting further away from Rhea, leaving space for him in the middle of us. But he walks right by it and sits on the other side of me. He manages to keep a respectful distance between us but still sits close enough that his scent permeates the air. It's the most delicious thing I've ever smelled—sweet and smoky like when you blow out a fragrant candle. It does nothing to help dismiss the arousal that I'm drowning in. In fact, I can feel the electricity rippling over my skin at his proximity.

"Yes, I'm sure you've got a lot of experience with that." Rhea quips. "I mean, she may not have been able to smell for a damn, but her cooking was unparalleled. And she was so sweet... it was like having a real grandmother for once."

"Delores would slap your mouth for that."

"Good thing she's dead." Rhea, who had been thumbing through the album again, finds a picture and points to the woman in the corner of it. "I can't believe we still have a picture of the hag."

I look at the woman in the photo with her enormous black hat obscuring most of her pinched, pale face. "Our mother's mother, obviously," Remy explains. "She was a bit of a—"

"Bitch." Rhea interjects flatly. "Sociopath? Narcissist? I could go on."

"Well, fortunately, there's no need because karma finally caught up to her. How are you enjoying your inheritance, by the way?"

Rhea reaches across me and swats Remy in the arm, laughing. "She had the world's meanest chihuahua, and *that* is what she left me," Rhea explains. "Remington here was always her favorite, so he got the Rolls Royce."

Remy shrugs far too casually. "I sold it off and left the cash with some woman walking her dog. I don't need her cursed car."

"Exactly why I gave Tinker to her housekeeper." Rhea agrees solemnly.

"You guys had a weird childhood."

Weird doesn't necessarily mean bad. It was clearly better than what I had, but I had expected something much *different*. Rhea is so happy, so confident, so capable that I was sure when we'd first met that she had come from a loving, well-adjusted family. I'd gathered enough context over the last few years to realize that isn't necessarily true, and now with Remy's arrival, I'm witnessing it firsthand.

"You are not wrong." Rhea laughs, tipping her wine glass toward me in a sort of toast. "Here's to the dysfunction of the Claremont Boudreaux family."

"Yes, so why don't you tell us what it's like to grow up normal." Remy watches my face like he's looking for any signs of fear. His words do spark it; A tingling spreads beneath my skin, the total opposite of the things he made me feel before. It's a cold tickle that turns to an itch, like all the things I have tried to shove down for so long are trying to claw their way out of me from the inside. I don't like talking about my past, but I've learned the stronger my reaction, the more people become intrigued. Vultures and voyeurs, everyone wants to know the gory details, the dark secrets.

I've learned to disguise my fear well, so I only laugh, keeping my cards close to my chest. "If you're asking me, I'm not sure I fit the mold of what you would call normal. I grew up kind of..." I look around the room with its screen, the length of the wall, and the velvet red couch we sit on. There's a plush rug on the floor before us, a full bar to the right, and a small kitchen to the left. "Well, exactly the opposite of this. My parents died when I was pretty young, so I grew up in foster care. I've lived with a lot of different people, but I wouldn't call that normal." I shrug, hoping my voice didn't tremble and give me away.

"So... you don't have a family?" Remy ventures, his eyes on me with something like interest or maybe suspicion.

"*I'm* her family," Rhea says fiercely, sparing me from having to answer him. She doesn't know the details about all the people I lived with before finally getting my government-granted freedom. She *does* know that my childhood isn't a favorite source of discussion. I don't want to talk about it at length, but I kind of like his curiosity.

"I spent time with some good people, but nothing ever stuck. Some of them had almost nothing, some of them were middle-class. I never had my own room, though... I mean, until I took over yours." I feel my cheeks warm a little more and wonder why I even said that.

"You must have been good in school, then. You're at Darrington on scholarships, right?"

"What the fuck, Remy?" Rhea demands, swiveling toward him. "Is this twenty questions?"

"I'm just trying to get a sense for who Claire is." He shrugs.

I almost laugh but stifle it instead. *Join the club.*

"You did say she is like family to you, after all." Remy turns his eyes back on me, and something in them suggests that he's challenging that assessment. And suddenly, it all makes sense. Why he claimed he thought I was some kind of assassin, why he'd treated me like a threat even when he'd clearly been in control, why he was asking so many questions.

I've never had money or power or anything that people might covet. It has never occurred to me that people may think our friendship is based upon Rhea's financial freedom and that I could be using her for her family's wealth. But apparently, it *has* occurred to him.

Now that the thought has crossed my mind, I can't push it off. Not until I make myself clear. The fact that he may even think that our friendship is financially motivated makes me feel gross. "You don't think my friendship has anything to do with..." I trail off, exchanging a glance with Rhea. "I'm not friends with Rhea for her money. Or her taste in music, for that matter." I laugh, but it doesn't quite sound genuine to my own ears. There's too much hurt underlying it. "And to answer your question, I *was* pretty good in school. I was top of my class, so scholarships cover most of my tuition, and state grants pay my rent and other expenses. What else do you want to know, Remy?" I face him straight on, my chin tipped up in defiance. Other than the past that I keep under lock and key, I have nothing to hide... especially after our earlier encounter.

"Many things, I assure you." His eyes slip from my face momentarily as he fixes me with a simmering glance. "But we have plenty of time for all that."

"Oh?" That catches me by surprise. My indignance at having my motives questioned starts to waver. "Are you staying in the States after the funeral?"

"Rhea and I have a few matters to discuss, but it's not entirely off the table."

"Liar." Rhea dismisses him with an airy wave of her hand. "You'll never leave Costa Rica. You have the perfect life for a bachelor."

"And who says I want to be a perpetual bachelor?" He smirks.

"You did!" Rhea squeals. "Mr. *'I'll never fall in love,' 'I'll never get married,' 'children are God's punishment for our existence.'*"

"Ouch." I laugh. "Someone's got some serious daddy issues."

Remy looks me dead on, and I feel like he's melting a little bit of my soul with the intensity of his gaze. "You have no idea."

His phone chimes at that exact moment—a blessing from the stars because I'm pretty sure I'm staring at him with my mouth open. The phone steals his attention for a moment. When he looks up, his eyes narrow on the theater screen and the movie we haven't been watching. "Why are you watching a Christmas movie?"

Rhea laughs loudly.

"It's July," I explain as if that will make him understand. But it doesn't seem to clear anything up because Remy still stares at me like I've spoken a foreign language. "You know, Christmas in July?"

The blank expression on his face doesn't change until Rhea pipes up to offer me backup. "I'd never heard of it, either, 'til I met Claire. Apparently, it's some sort of marketing campaign, but Claire takes it literally. Just be glad she's not wearing her Christmas pajamas."

"Wait." I turn to her, not bothering to hide the offense. "What's wrong with my Christmas pajamas?"

"Nothing." Rhea smiles sweetly. "Remy, would you put your phone away?" She yells, sending a pillow sailing across the couch. Remy swats it away effortlessly, and it falls to the ground with a soft thud.

"Business never stops."

"Sure." Rhea rolls her eyes.

"What exactly *is* the family business?" I venture, relaxing on the couch. I can feel the exhaustion begin to creep in from our long day. It's a question I've asked Rhea a few times; You don't acquire a wealth like this unless you have part in something big... investments or technology or something. But Rhea says she has no interest in whatever her family does. As an art student, she wants no part in the finances or politics that her brother and father are slaves to.

"Venture capitalism." Remy doesn't miss a beat, but he eyes me, watching my face for any sign that I understand what he means.

"So, you guys just come from old money," I conclude, only half teasing. Rhea has told me that her father and brother are always working and that they earn their money by never ceasing. But there's no denying that they have money because they *came from money.*

"You could say that." He shrugs. "Old money that my ancestors just kept investing over and over again. Our great-great-grandfather turned a hundred dollars into three, and then three into a thousand, and then a thousand into three thousand. Our mother came from a wealthy family."

"How my dad ever got her to fall for him, I still don't understand." Rhea shakes her head.

"It's called a marriage of convenience." Remy's voice is flat. "Mom needed someone to protect her, dad needed someone to flaunt to all his competitors."

"You're not much of a romantic." I surmise, pursing my lips as I wonder what exactly possessed me to say that. "Doesn't that make your life boring? Being all business all the time?"

A mischievous gleam sparks in his dark eyes. "My life is far from boring, Claire, and I make plenty of time for pleasure. You'll see." He winks, sending a warm flash over my skin, and then stands. "You'll need to be ready to leave by seven."

"Seven?" Rhea nearly spills what's left of her drink in shock. "I thought you said our flight was at eight?"

"It is." He confirms. "But I know how you are. If I say eight, you'll be dragging your ass out of bed at seven-thirty, and I'm not paying Simon and Elize overtime to wait on you to get there."

"Touché."

"I'll take the master tonight, and Claire can continue to sleep in my room."

"Oh, you don't have to do that," I say quickly. "I can stay with Rhea... or sleep on the couch."

"There's like ten bedrooms in this house." Rhea frowns. "There's no need to sleep on the couch. Remy is just taking my parents' room as a show of dominance."

"If I wanted to sleep in my old room, I would." Remy's words are bold, chasing a strange feeling over my flesh. "Just do me a favor and lock the balcony door this time. Sweet dreams." He winks at me, dousing that heat over me once again. I hope Rhea hasn't noticed.

"I'll see you at seven," Rhea promises as he walks out of the room.

CHAPTER EIGHT

Remy

The door is barely shut before I hit the redial button on my phone. Jovich answers on the first ring. "What have you got?"

I didn't expect to hear from him so shortly after the last call. Hopefully, that means he has answers.

"Nobody has seen Vazquez in a week."

Not the information I was looking for, but I trust Jovich isn't telling me because he thinks I want to hear his voice. "Am I supposed to care for his safety?"

"No. But you may be interested to know the last person he met with."

I let myself into the huge master suite and turn the lock behind me. "Which is?"

"None other than Alexandre Davos."

"Son of a bitch." I exhale. It isn't exactly a shock, but it's a little bit of a disappointment. "I can't say I'm surprised."

Davos is, for all intents and purposes, my boss. He was an old friend of my father's up until recently when he edged my father out of their business. It's been nothing but bad blood between them for the last year. And yet, Davos is still a fucked up extension of my family. I hate him for what he did to me, for what he does to the world, but he's been fair to me even after the fall-out with my father. But if Vazquez has been hanging around with Alexandre Davos, there's a good chance he's no longer loyal to my family.

"There's more. Davos' great nephew is Tristan Ryan. An old acquaintance of yours, I believe."

"I'm familiar with him," I say dispassionately. It's been years since I last saw the Ryan kid, but he's annoying enough that he's not super forgettable.

I recall the scrawny kid who always followed me around when we were young, trying to insert himself into everything I did. I'd tolerated him because my mother had said it was important to be kind to him, and our families were friends, so I didn't have a choice.

I wouldn't say I ever liked him, but the last straw was when he told Katie Benson I'd taped a picture of her to my ceiling and used it to jerk off. That was the day I punched him in the face, got my first referral, and had my first kiss with none other than Katie Benson, who was apparently flattered by the news. Ryan transferred after that, and I'd never thought about him again.

"Yeah, so is Rhiannon. Apparently, she's been seeing him this summer."

"You're kidding me." I laugh. My sister was never fond of Tristan Ryan as a child, either. The thought of her growing up and stooping to date someone like him is ridiculous.

"Nope."

"Which means he's here in Cove Harbor?"

"He is staying with a friend just outside town. A small home in Marsh Harbor."

Marsh Harbor is a quaint place, and it isn't far. I could be there within the hour, but it would require leaving Rhea and Claire alone, and that's out of the question. I've seen firsthand that they aren't exactly equipped to deal with any real threat, and after that anonymous phone call, there's no way I can gamble with their safety.

"How fast can we get eyes on him?"

"Twenty minutes or less."

"Make it happen, Jovich." I hang up the phone and look around my parents' old room with contempt. Unlike when they were alive, at least I don't have to hide it now. I don't want to stay here. In fact, I'd not planned to step foot in this room at all, but it's the closest to the hall and near the girls. If anything happens, I'll be able to react a lot sooner. Time is crucial in those instances.

If I'd had my way, I'd have grabbed Rhea and dragged her right on the plane with me. She could sleep through the flight, and I'd be able to get out of this house that makes my skin crawl. I'm used to getting my way these days, but I can't let Simon fly us back without getting a good night of sleep, so here I am.

I knew my father hadn't been home in over a year. Part of me suspects that as cold and distant as he was, it was too painful for him to be here without his wife. We own property all over the globe, but this is the home they raised their family in. Even if Johnathan wasn't a great husband or father, blood meant a lot to him. And though I had known for a while that their marriage hadn't been monogamous, my father was somehow completely beholden to my mother, wrapped around her finger. I often wondered just how much she knew about Johnathan's indiscretions, and just how deeply she was involved in his business affairs.

My mother's side of the bed had been closest to the terrace doors because she loved looking out on the beach. That's where I go and open the nightstand. An old leather Bible is the first thing I see lying on top of a large, padded envelope. The gold foil cross etched into the cover seems to taunt me as I set it on the bed and withdraw the envelope. A few photographs flutter onto the duvet as I tip it over, letting the contents pour out. Along with them is a single, folded piece of paper.

I smooth the creases and glance over it at a handwritten letter.

Mary,

I hate to see you like this. Please know you always have a place in my home, as well as in my heart. All my love, J.

I've seen my father's handwriting on thousands of papers and his signatures on assets and lawsuits. The letter isn't from him. And while I've never known my mother to take another lover, considering how often my father had strayed from their marriage, I can't exactly blame her for doing the same.

The photos on the bed, however, are *of* my father. They look to range over a few years' time, and each of them shows him with a different woman in less-than-platonic situations. Some girls half his age with their arms draped around his neck, a woman with her thighs wrapped around his waist. My father never brought other women to our home, but in public, he'd made no qualms about his inability to remain monogamous.

I stuff the photos in the envelope and go back to the nightstand, not sure what I'm looking for. I find a dime-store paperback with a bookmark halfway through it, just waiting for my mom to come pick it back up as if she hasn't been dead for almost four years, a beaded bracelet that was one of Rhea's first art projects, and a sleep mask to block out light. The next drawer reveals a stack of more books and an unmarked velvet bag.

I have a good guess what's in there by the shape alone.

My instincts prove correct when I slip the pistol out of the bag. The silver glints in the moonlight shining through the window at my back. And judging by the weight of it, I'm guessing...

It's loaded.

As much as I want to believe there is no blood on my mother's hands, I am certain that she knew a good deal about what her husband *actually* did. It's not like he was just living a double life—everything about his dark, sordid business bled over into this life... his family.

The gun is either to protect herself from him or to protect *him* from others. I can't imagine her using it, but having it, particularly having it loaded and ready, is a clear enough indication that she wasn't as innocent as she had wanted people to believe.

I place it on top of the nightstand just in case I need it. The gun I came here with is on the dresser in my old room... the room where Claire sleeps. I chose not to grab it in the chaos of our first meeting because I think my sister would have had a heart attack. Now I guess I'll find out if the innocent little co-ed is really as innocent as she claimed. She won't hurt Rhea—if she wanted to, she'd have done it years ago. And if she tries to use my own weapon against me, I guess I'll be ready.

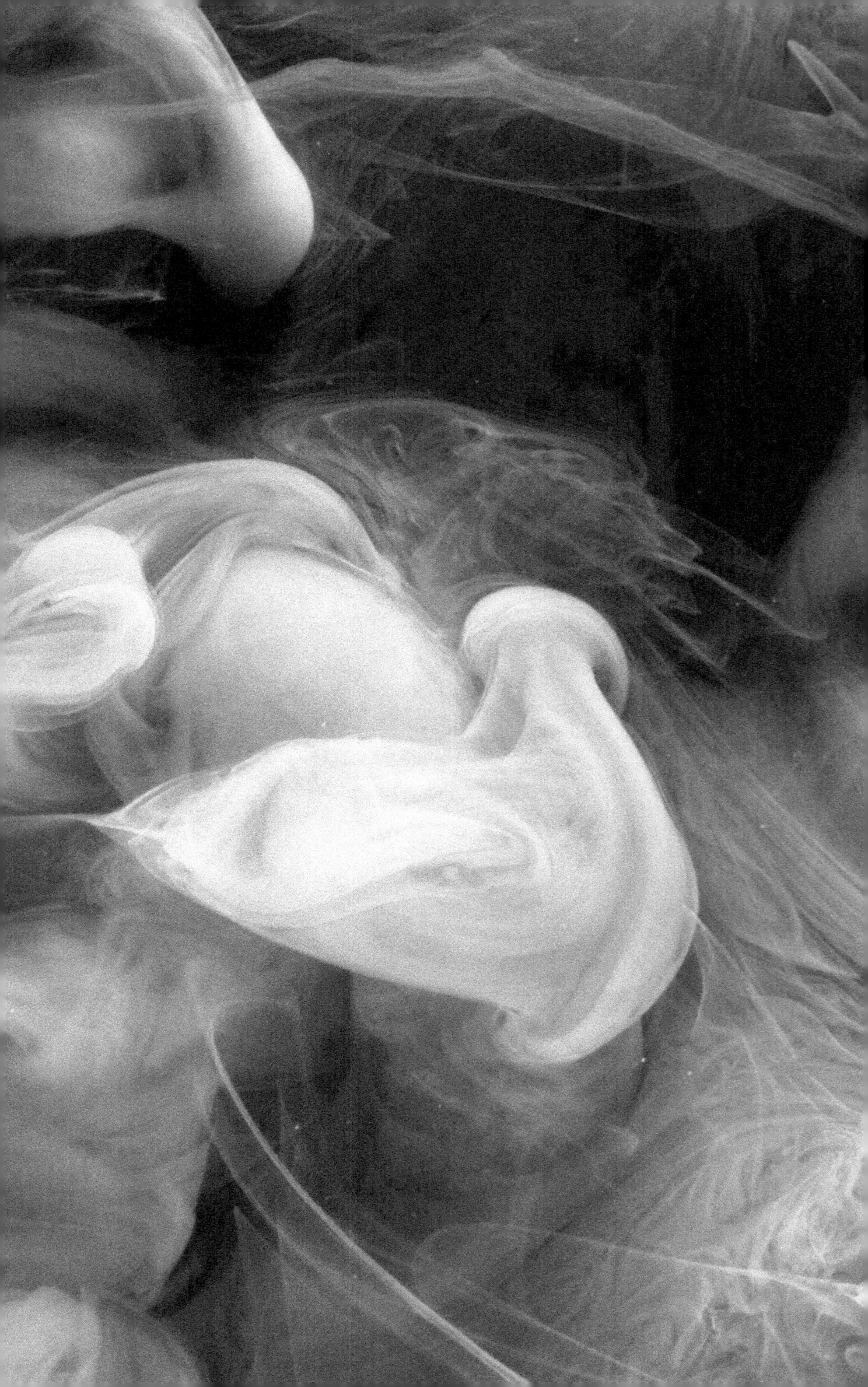

Chapter Nine

Claire

We don't last long after Remy leaves. Rhea starts to drift off to sleep and I debate a long time over whether I should let her stay there or if I should wake her and make sure she makes it to her room. After the chaotic events of the evening, I don't want to deprive her of the peace of sleep. But Rhea has to be up and ready to go in the morning. She needs a good night of rest... something more than a few hours on the couch with a movie playing in the background.

We trudge to our rooms in sleepy silence, and I practically drag Rhea to her bed, where she immediately rolls over and passes out.

I can't say the same for myself.

My mind won't turn off as I lay in the bed I've long considered my own. But now I know better. The man who this bed belongs to is just down the hall, and somehow, my thoughts keep circling back to him. How he'd acted so quickly when he thought I was an intruder was so protective, powerful, and oddly satisfying. Like watching Wes take charge back at The Piazza, only somehow sexier. Having been raised in a multitude of homes with a variety of people, and then at university, surrounded by childish behavior the past three years, it's somehow refreshing to see a man so fierce and possessive. It also doesn't hurt that he is incredibly gorgeous with those thick lashes and stormy eyes that make me feel both safe and oddly vulnerable.

I groan into the pillow, not sure why I can't stop thinking about being so close to him. Clearly, there is something wrong with me for being so hot when thinking about our first encounter. Most women would have been angry or scared, and I was in the moment.

But now I'm obsessing over the feeling of his hand on my hip, his intoxicating scent, the muscles rippling under his gorgeous skin. Perhaps I drank too much. Perhaps it's just been too long since I've had a sexual encounter of my own. Or perhaps I'm just drawn to him because he is my best friend's brother, and that's an obvious no-go.

Most likely of all, it's just a side-effect of my emotional damage. I teased Remy about daddy issues, but what does it say about me that I'm obsessing over the touch of a man who had me at his mercy in such a compromising position? What does it say about me that I am thinking about his hands on me?

Whatever the reason, at least I won't have to deal with it much longer.

In all the years Rhea and I have been friends, Remy has never come around before. A family death is an extenuating circumstance. Tomorrow he'll get on his private plane with Rhea, and I'll never again have to think about how badly I want to be in his arms with his hands on my body. And I... I don't know what I'll do. Rent a room in town and stick out the rest of the summer there? But what I make working for Mama will barely cover a room in a posh town like Cove Harbor. I'd probably be better off going back to school and spending the rest of summer... working out? Cleaning? I don't know, because I don't know what I do when I'm alone anymore.

I hate to admit it, but it strikes me again just how dependent on Rhea I've become. And it's terrifying.

After a lifetime of looking out for myself because no one else was, I sort of latched onto her freshman year. When we met, she came on strong, assuming we'd be best friends just because we lived together. I'd been hesitant, at first, to let her in. After all, we had nothing in common. But it quickly became clear that Rhea must have known something I hadn't because we were inseparable by the end of our first semester. It hadn't seemed like a bad thing then, but now it makes my head spin with things I never needed to consider. Am I holding her back? Am I holding myself back? We're closer than any other friends I've ever known. Is it normal to be so inseparable that the thought of returning to school without my best friend is depressing?

I roll over, burying my face in a cool pillow. I know I've got to stop analyzing myself; It's only making me crazy—or craz*ier*. But my thoughts continue to spiral beyond my control until I can't take it anymore. Finally, I stand and strip down before digging a swimsuit out of the back of one of my drawers. The gun that sits on the dresser is a stark reminder of what sort of man I'm obsessing over. I've never even seen one until today, and yet Remington Boudreaux is apparently the type to keep one on hand. We are not the same.

I slip out of my room and cast a glance down the hall where I know he is.

Is he awake in there, texting someone about the business that demands so much of his time? Is he sleeping? I can't imagine that—he has too much presence for me to be able to imagine him turning it off. I can't picture him vulnerable, but everything remains quiet. Rhea's room is dark, too. I creep down the stairs, avoiding the one that creaks a little under my weight, pad through the halls, and slip out the back door.

The pool is nearly Olympic-sized, with a small waterfall at the deep end. The whole patio is cased in by giant glass panels so that the sun shines through in the day and the stars blink serenely over the water at night. It's my favorite thing about this house, which otherwise makes me feel like the portraits on the walls are judging me.

I don't understand why just seeing water always calms me, but it does. It's part of why I'm so happy to spend my summers here. Apart from being with my best friend, being so close to the ocean just seems to soothe my soul, no matter how chaotic everything around me gets to be. From the minute we step out of the car and stretch our muscles, I feel lighter here.

The water is perfectly still, a mirror image of the sky above it. Tranquil. I sigh as my concerns slip away and then pull my hair back before stepping into the pool.

Rhea once mentioned that the housekeeping staff keeps the water at the perfect temperature throughout the year, so they'd never be too cold or warm. That seems to hold true as I slip easily into the deep end, the water rising to cover me up to my neck. I take a breath and just allow myself to float a minute, dumping all of the anxiety and frustration out of my mind.

I taught myself to swim, just as I taught myself most things in life. Margaret and Dan White had been a decent couple who lived near the community center. I lived with them for two years until Dan got arrested for tax fraud, and then it was on to the next place. During those two years, I spent most of my free time at the community pool. While the other foster kids played sports, read books, or made macaroni art, swimming was my escape. It still is.

The cool water soothes the burn that has raged over my skin ever since I felt Remy's touch. I slip under the surface, letting the water baptize me.

I don't need his touch, his attention. I'm an independent woman, forged in the darkness. Agonizing over the weight of him, his smell, his cocky grin—none of this is me. And yet, here I am, letting him occupy my mind. He's already crawled under my skin, and I don't know how to feel about the fact that I kind of like him there.

After floating a while, I still have too much energy to burn, still feel a longing inside me that I can't ignore, so I swim laps. The pool is huge, but I swim back and forth until I'm breathless and tired enough that my mind is no longer obsessing over the dip of his hips. I paddle over to the waterfall, pulling my hair loose from its tie and let the water flood over me, washing away the anxiety and uncertainty and anything else that dares cling to me at this point.

I fought the better part of an hour to get everything off of my mind, to still the chaos inside of me, and now I'm so at ease that I feel like I could drift off to sleep just like this. I don't think about anything, don't know if I'm awake or in the early stages of sleep. Like this, I just exist without anything else. No pain, no fear, no chaos, or desire, or hunger.

The sound of a car door closing steals my peace in the space of a second, and I go rigid as I stop to consider the sound. It's too close to be from the driveway at the front of the house, and behind it—behind the pool where I've just had my bliss ripped from me— there's only an expanse of sand and sea.

Chills erupt over my arms as I recall the weird events from earlier in the evening. Suddenly, the sound of an approaching car feels more sinister in tandem with the lights turning off on me in the bathroom, my stolen work uniform, and the random assault at the night club.

Maybe it's just my paranoia—a lifetime of looking over my shoulder and trusting no one. Maybe it's the movie Rhea picked last night. Maybe it's just the adrenaline still fluttering around in me, renewed by my shattered peace.

Whatever it is, it's time to go inside and lock the doors.

As I'm wrapping the towel around myself, I hear it: A crack that sounds like thunder in the air.

Glass rains down around me, chunks of it skittering into the pool. I turn, trying to figure out what just happened, and am thrown to the ground in the next moment.

A substantial weight pins me to the concrete and forces the breath from my chest. I cringe into the pavers, everything spinning a little from the fall, and then look into the angry eyes of Remington Boudreaux.

He puts a finger to his lips, warning me to remain quiet, and then stays there a second, looking down at me as my chest heaves up and down. I don't know if he's checking to see if I'm alright or trying to make sure his point sinks in. It doesn't matter because I'm not moving either way. I couldn't if I tried.

He rolls his weight onto his arm as suddenly as he tackled me and stands in a single fluid motion.

I don't even see the gun in his hand until he pulls the trigger.

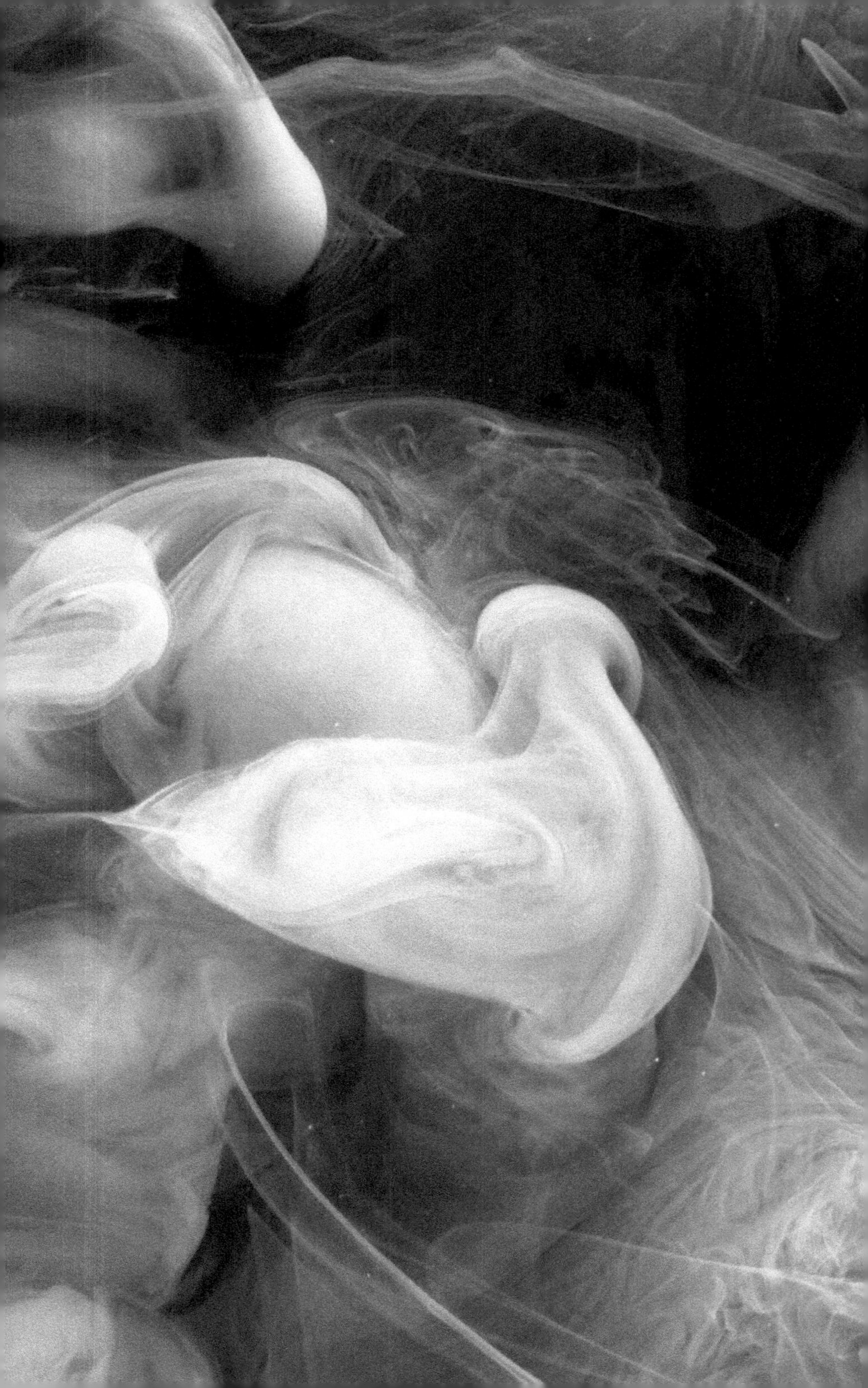

CHAPTER TEN

CLAIRE

My heart squeezes in my chest, and I realize I'm cold. For the last couple of hours, I've been fighting a fire in the wake of this man's touch, trying unsuccessfully to quell the inferno he's awakened in me. And now it's gone without a trace, and I'm colder than I've been in a long time.

Is it the feeling of his weight on me that made my blood run cold, even though I've been thinking about him all night? Is it the way he told me to stay quiet, miming a finger over his lips so that I get the point without him having to break the silence? My heart seizes in my chest, and I don't know if it's because of him or the gun in his hand.

There's an anguished cry, immediately followed by the sound of a car engine roaring to life. And then the sound recedes as it tears off down the beach. Remy watches it for a minute, his sharp eyes taking in whatever he can, and then he extends a hand like he means to pull me to my feet.

When I don't move, he looks at me quizzically, like he's trying to hear the things I'm not saying.

Not used to being shot at Claire? I can imagine him saying. *Rookie.*

He doesn't withdraw his hand, so despite my gut twisting, I reach out and let him pull me to standing. Once I'm situated, his eyes flit over me, assessing the situation. "Are you okay?"

I raise a hand to my aching head and nod, focusing all of my energy on that throbbing pain until everything else recedes. I look at the shattered glass panel; all that remains of it is a twisted metal frame with blades of cracked glass sticking awkwardly out of it. "What happened?"

"Somebody just tried to kill you," Remy says soberly. "Lucky for you, they're a bad shot. Can't say the same for myself. I know I got him."

His words sound like they're coming from the other end of a long tunnel. By the time they make it to me, his mouth has stopped moving. I blink, disoriented.

Someone shot at me?

My chest suddenly doesn't seem to expand enough to let me breathe anymore. "I think... I need to sit." I manage, just before my legs start to go weak.

Remy must recognize my faintness because he manages to scoop me up as soon as my legs start to give. I'm in his arms before I can hit the ground again. "Let's get inside first."

As he carries me to the house, I see where the bullet has lodged itself in the thick metal of the outdoor refrigerator. If I'd been standing a little more to the right, that bullet probably would have made itself at home in my skull. It's a chilling thought— as if I wasn't already cold enough.

Remy locks the door behind him easily and then props me up on the kitchen counter so that his face is level with mine. "You sure you're all right?" He asks, stepping back to take me in. His lips are pulled into a frown. "You look pretty pale."

"I..." I look around the kitchen like anything in there will help me make sense of the last five minutes. Or, for that matter, the last twelve hours. Has this really all been one day? "I don't understand what just happened."

I have an idea, but it's not something I'll give a voice to. Especially not in front of this man.

When I got the call earlier this summer, the number wasn't listed, so I picked it up. I had expected someone looking for Rhea, maybe our airhead roommate Lucy calling from a friend's phone to touch base and ask for the tenth time how much water she should give the plants. I definitely hadn't expected to hear the voice from my nightmares. I didn't expect my muscles to loosen, as if I was about to roll over and play dead, or the phone to fall from my hand.

I said nothing, pressed my hand over my mouth to contain a scream, and blocked the number. Since then, I've ignored every call I've gotten, tensing whenever the phone rings. Fortunately, I've been with Rhea, so the only person who calls me doesn't have any need to. Everyone else just texts nowadays.

It's been years since I escaped, years of healing and nurturing and growth. What are the chances that my past catches up to me, and not even a month later, I'm being taunted in the dark and shot at in the dead of night?

I'm spiraling, my chest not able to expand enough to accommodate my wild heart, but Remy's voice brings me back to earth.

"Being rich and powerful will make you a lot of enemies. My father being dead means they feel bold enough to make moves." He turns to the cupboards and produces a bottle of some dark liquor. The muscles in his back flex and ripple as he moves, and I errantly appreciate that he is shirtless this time. "It's late... or early. Scotch, coffee, or Irish coffee?"

My eyes find the glowing green numbers on the oven. Four twenty-six. No way am I going to be able to sleep now. "Coffee," I say, and Remy sets about making a pot of it, then pouring himself a glass of scotch all before turning back to face me.

"They didn't come for you, but you were in the way. Once you got out of the pool, you made yourself known, and they took their shot. But as I said, whoever it was, they're a miserable marksman. Tells me they're not much of a threat." He swirls the scotch around his glass and then takes a swig. I watch him intently, trying to understand what he's getting at. Remy purses his lips together, savoring the alcohol burn as he considers his next words. "Who goes swimming at four in the morning anyway?"

"People who can't sleep." I snap. "What about you? What were *you* doing awake at four in the morning? Watching me?"

Remy grins and makes no effort to deny what we both know. "I don't sleep much. Tonight, it seems that's a good thing." Turning, he grabs a mug to pour my coffee into. "So, how do you take it?"

I blink, unsure of how to answer that. When his question is only met with silence and the reddening of my cheeks, he glances over his shoulder, his grin more of a smirk. It sends a thrill through me like a bolt of lightning that starts in my chest and goes all the way to my toes, causing them to tingle. "Your coffee, I mean. Dark or with cream and sugar?"

I clear my throat and hope the embarrassment isn't so noticeable on my face. "Creamer, please."

He raises an eyebrow and turns back to the fridge, where there's an assortment of flavored creamers always on hand. We survive summers without six-dollar coffee every day, but only because we keep the kitchen stocked with idiot-proof ingredients to turn our black coffee bougie. I never drank coffee before I met Rhea and now, I can't imagine life without it. "Any requests?"

"Dealer's choice." I wrap the towel tighter around myself as Remy pulls a bottle off the shelf and stirs its contents into my coffee before pressing it into my hands. The warmth is immediate, but deep down, I'm as cold as ever.

Remy seems confident that the shooter wasn't coming for me, but I don't know how else to explain the weird string of events today.

"I guess I'm lucky you were still awake." I say, looking up through my lashes to watch his face.

"Luck has nothing to do with it." He says, softer than I'd have thought him to be capable of.

The chills erupt over me again as I try to understand what exactly he means by that. But he doesn't give me a chance to wonder for long before he plants his hands on either side of me, boxing me in.

"Tell me something, Claire."

His voice is low, and I can't tell if it's because he's trying to be seductive or if he suddenly remembered his sister is asleep upstairs. Meanwhile, I can't keep suspicion from creeping into my voice. "What's that?"

"Is there anything I should know about you? Crazy ex-boyfriends, stalkers, maybe some loser you friend-zoned that would be trying to hurt you?"

The question takes me by surprise. It sounds absurd. I'm not the kind of girl that would attract the attention of a stalker—I've watched enough Dateline to know that the girls who end up with stalkers are all brilliant, bright, kind, and outgoing. *Rhea* is the type who attracts obsessive men.

I am none of those things, and yet...

An icy finger traces up my spine. If Remy wasn't watching me so intently, I'd turn to be sure that no one's behind me, to make sure there's no ghost standing at my back, breathing cold plumes of air on my neck.

"No." I finally answer. "I don't get close enough to anyone to make enemies."

It takes a moment for him to consider that, and I worry that my face or the long pause has given me away. "Smart." Remy nods his approval as if that isn't the most pathetic thing I've ever said out loud. "And Rhea? You two are close?"

"She's all I've got." I nod.

"Does she make many enemies? Long list of ex-lovers, former friends, any of that?"

I scrutinize his face, wondering where this is going. Remy is likely just an overprotective older brother, but I don't want to betray Rhea by answering these questions. I also don't want to lie to Remy if it means danger for Rhea.

"I know she dates around." He says with a dismissive wave of his hand. "You don't have to worry about me judging her or something. Anybody you can think of who would be mad that she's moved on or who may try to take her for ransom?"

It isn't exactly funny, but I laugh. Maybe it's my guilt at the thought that this could somehow be my fault, or maybe it's just the absurdity of trying to reconcile the last three years of my life with the last day. I clawed my way here, and I really thought the past was in the past, but now I'm not so sure.

"We work at a pizzeria, Remy. It's not like we're in an underground society."

"Right." He smiles almost apologetically as if he realizes he's being silly. But this is the same guy who assumed that I was some sort of assassin sent to kill him just a few hours ago, so by contrast, it's not that ridiculous. That dimple in his left cheek reveals itself for a moment before it disappears far too quickly. "No matter. Whoever fired that gun won't be back."

"You don't think?" I clutch the mug between my hands, content to let its warmth leech into me with no desire to actually drink it. My nerves are already jilted enough without adding caffeine into the mix, but the steam still rising up from the surface and the earthy aroma is certainly helping ground me a bit.

"They won't live to see the sunrise." He says.

A shiver passes over me at the finality in his tone and then again as Remy splays his hands out on the counter on either side of me, his strong arms caging me in once more. He's closer this time, the heat rolling off his body tempting me to press myself against him. Those fathomless eyes meet with mine, and I can't help but be impressed with how infinite they are without betraying anything of his soul. I'm certain my lip quivers as I watch his and I have to actively fight the desire to lean into him. "Do me a favor, Claire?"

Anything.

The word springs to my tongue, but I manage to bite it back. When I answer, my voice is thick with desire. I'm torn between praying he doesn't notice and wanting him to recognize it on the off chance he will do something about it. "What?"

"Don't tell Rhea about this. Apparently, she still sleeps like the dead, and I'd rather her not be stressed the entire time we're in Costa Rica. Will you do that for me?"

Lie to my best friend for him? Normally that answer would be a resounding no, but he's right. Rhea doesn't need anything else on her plate while dealing with her father's passing. And if this somehow has something to do with me, I will gladly go to any length to shelter her from it.

I nod.

"Good." He brushes a strand of wet hair off my face as if it's the most natural thing in the world. His touch grazes my cheek, and though I've been wrapped in his arms and trapped beneath his weight, that brush of his finger is the most intimate thing that's transpired between us. It ends far too soon, but the fluttering inside of me lingers even after his hand drops. "I'll have the mess outside taken care of. You should shower and be sure to get the glass out of your hair."

He stares at me like he expects something more, and I stare at him like he's about to do something more. Part of me considers the idea of throwing myself at him for a kiss, but then I remember he's my best friend's brother, he's way out of my league, and he's going back to Costa Rica in the morning.

All the more reason to get him out of your system tonight, says the devil on my shoulder.

All the more reason you can't. Rhea's father just died, says the angel on my other shoulder.

After a moment, I nod, and he steps back. Situated between his legs, he'd not been touching me, and yet his absence leaves me cold.

I slide off the counter and make it halfway out the door before his voice calls me back. I turn upon hearing my name and see him standing there with his phone in hand, not even looking at me as he focuses on the screen before him. "Thank you."

I don't know how to answer that, so I don't. I just drag myself to the shower and stand under the stream for a long time before crawling into bed.

I feel like I've just closed my eyes when Rhea bursts in and throws the curtains open, ripping me instantly away from whatever shred of sleep I'd been clinging to. "Wake up, or we're going to be late!" She demands, flopping onto the bed next to me.

I groan, rolling over and dragging the blanket over my head with me. I don't appreciate the wakeup call or the sudden assault of light in the room. My head hurts and I'm confused for a moment before I vaguely remember knocking it against the ground when Remy pushed me out of the line of fire. "Late for what?"

"Our flight!" I feel her crawl over me so that she can get to my other side and pry the blanket away from me. Once she's on the other side, she bounces a couple times like a child trying to wake their parents on Christmas morning. "Have you even packed?"

Our flight?

I pull the blanket away from my own face to scowl at her. "What are you talking about?"

"Oh my God, did you hit your head or something?"

I did, as a matter of fact. But that has nothing to do with my confusion.

"Do you know what year it is?" Rhea laughs. "Costa Rica. Remember? My dad died, my brother came to get me, the funeral is in Costa Rica? Is any of that ringing a bell?"

I remember it, of course. Remy told her to be ready for the flight at seven. "I don't understand. Why would I go to Costa Rica with you?"

"Why *wouldn't* you?" She laughs. "I mean, I *guess* you could stay here in this big old house all by yourself. Or you could go back to our apartment and read until school starts back up. Or..." She drags the word out, which is impressive, considering it's only a single syllable. "You could come to Costa Rica with me and support me at my father's funeral. Please, Claire?" Her bottom lip juts out in a pout, and she clasps her hands together beneath her chin. Again, she looks like a child begging for ice cream before dinner, and it's part of what I love about her. She's so... innocent and hopeful, even in the wake of tragedy. "I know it's kind of heavy, but I don't know if I can do it alone."

"You won't be alone," I say, sitting up. "You have your brother."

"Remy?" Rhea laughs at his name.

As if on cue, Remy pokes his head in the room. I draw the comforter up to my chin, as if he hadn't seen me in anything less than the tank top I'd put on after my shower. I know for a fact that the bathing suit I wore last night shows more cleavage than this, and that's to say nothing of the bra and panties I'd had under my dress after the club. "Did you need something?"

"Yes." Rhea says firmly. "I need my best friend to come with me to Costa Rica. You don't have an issue with that, do you?"

"I thought that was established?" Remy glances at me, his lips turning into a little frown. "Are you having second thoughts?"

"S-second thoughts?" I sputter. "I haven't had a chance for first thoughts. Nobody told me I was supposed to go."

"I'm sorry," he scoffs. "I thought it was understood."

"So did I." Rhea turns to me again, and now they're both looking at me expectantly.

"I... I don't have a passport."

"So?" Rhea shrugs.

"That won't be an issue," Remy assures me. "Everything's been taken care of."

My mind reels in search of another reason why I can't go to Costa Rica, but I've got nothing.

I look between them, speechless, and finally manage to stammer out a single word, though it comes across as more of a question. "O-okay?"

"Ah! Thank you!" Rhea sweeps me into a hug as Remy turns to go. She squeezes me tight before letting go and standing decisively. "I figure just pack everything, right? We may just spend the rest of the summer in Costa Rica. I mean, why not? I've heard the men are divine!"

"Are you sure you want me to come?" I ask once Remy is out of sight. "This seems like a family matter."

"I'm sure I don't want to go without you." Rhea says firmly, planting her hands on her hips. "And I've told you, Claire. You *are* family."

CHAPTER ELEVEN

REMY

"You've never flown?" I guess, eyeing Claire over the top of the newspaper I'm not actually reading. I can't help myself from stealing glances at her, and even when I look away, my thoughts are full of her. Everything about her is just too distracting.

"What gave it away?" She snaps, turning her eye to the lights on the ceiling and letting go of a shaky breath.

Rhea looks comfortable in an oversized chair with her feet tucked under her and not a care in the world. I'm not sure the last time she flew anywhere, but she acts like she does it all the time. Claire, on the other hand, looks like she has to remind herself to breathe out through her nose so she won't pass out.

"Pale face," I snicker. "Although it's very subtle given your usual pallor."

"Well, we can't all be bronze Gods, now, can we?" Though she snaps that response, too, there's no malice in her words. In fact, they're almost reverent.

My lips quirk the tiniest bit at her referencing me as a god. I have no delusions of divinity, but her word choice is pretty telling of how she sees me. "Someone's feeling extra sassy this morning." I flip a page and shoot another glance at her in time to see her fingertips tighten on the armrests.

"*Someone* got no sleep and then was forced onto a plane to travel across the world without a passport." She speaks fast like she needs to get the words off her tongue, and then her tone changes to pleading. "What if they put me in jail? I won't do well in a regular jail, let alone a Costa Rican one!"

I laugh again, but this time Rhea decides to put her out of her misery. She stands and crosses to the minibar. "You have Ambien up here, right?"

"The cupboard above your head," I tell her.

Rhea rises on the tips of her toes to open the door and, after a moment, finds what she's looking for. She shakes the pills into her hand, puts them back, and then crosses to Claire. "Here. They'll help you relax and catch up on sleep." She passes them to her friend along with one of the mimosas Elize poured before takeoff. Claire only hesitates a moment before accepting it, tossing them on her tongue and following with a long sip from her cocktail.

Clearly, she trusts Rhea with her entire being, which turns out to be a good thing for her because, after just a few minutes, she already looks calmer and less inhibited. She's finally able to chance a glance out the window of the plane to watch as golden light floods through the clouds.

I excuse myself to the bedroom to take a call while Rhea curls up with her sketchbook again. Jovich answers on the first ring like usual. "Morning, boss."

"Did you come up with anything?" I ask.

"Jack went to visit your friend in Marsh Harbor." It's a statement, but it almost sounds like a question. I've grown used to his accent, but on occasion, when I'm waiting for him to get to the point, it grates on me. "The kid let him in and said he hadn't talked to Davos in years."

"Of course, he did." I wouldn't exactly be eager to announce that I was connected to a guy like Alexandre Davos, either. "Any chance he's the one who called about Rhea?"

"Doubt it. Jack tapped his phone with a trojan spyware app. If he contacts Davos, you'll be the first to know."

"And the Russian?"

"He's close. I can smell the grease and piss."

"Do what you have to," I tell him. It goes without saying, but I want him to know we're pulling out all the stops on this one. "We should be there about four. See you at the airstrip?"

"I'll be there." Jovich promises.

I don't doubt him for a minute.

I hang up the phone and go back to the cabin to find Claire asleep, her neck quirked at an uncomfortable angle.

I only debate for a minute about waking her before I reason that the Ambien will pull her under quickly again anyway. I wake her with a gentle hand on her shoulder... apparently, even with a sleeping pill, she's a light sleeper. She startles awake and then turns around, looking into my eyes. Everything I've seen in there to this point is gone, and I don't know if it's her exhaustion that has chased away the embarrassment, the interest, the coyness. The only thing she seems to fix me with is fear. Is it because of me or because of whatever dream I pulled her from?

Tipping my head toward the room I just came from, I tell her, "There's a bed in the back of the plane if you'd prefer to lie down."

Claire straightens up, rubbing the stiffness out of her neck. "No, thanks. I'm fine."

"She doesn't want to sleep in the bed where you seduce unsuspecting stewardesses." Rhea swipes at the paper she's drawing on, using her finger to smudge the pencil lines.

"I don't sleep with women on the jet," I assure her, sinking back into my chair and grabbing my glass. "I did, however, get a very sensual lap dance from an eager journalist in that chair you're sitting in."

Rhea grabs a magazine off the table next to her and chucks it at my head. I dodge it with ease and chuckle. "I'm kidding. She was a news anchor. Channel Six."

Claire takes a deep breath, and then her eyes close again. How many pills did Rhea give this girl? And can she handle them? I eye her warily but decide that if she truly is as important to my sister as I've been led to believe, she wouldn't do anything to hurt her, even unintentionally.

"You're disgusting." Rhea laughs in spite of herself. "I'm glad you got what you wanted though. A life of luxury as a too-legit-to-quit playboy. I'm sure Dad was proud."

"We both know that's not true," I say firmly, attempting to dismiss any further conversation that may stem from there.

But Rhea doesn't give up that easily. "You know, when you left, I thought you were just running. I mean, that's what we do, right?" A small, dry laugh punctuates her observation. She's not wrong. "Mom ran from her obligations, Dad ran from his family, and I ran off to college. I thought you were just trying to get away from it all, but you weren't running from anything, were you?" Smiling a little, she shakes her head before I even get the idea to open my mouth and come up with a response. "You were running toward what you've always wanted, chasing your dreams."

"No, I wasn't." I relax into my chair, aligning my forearms on the armrests to avoid meeting her gaze. "I had nothing better to do. I had no ambitions in life, no goals, no plans. I just did what was expected of me and joined the family business. It's not like I've done anything important."

"I think you did," Rhea says softly. "I resented you for so long for leaving, but I think you did the right thing."

I have a good enough poker face, but under the surface, her words set gnawing guilt in motion. It's like rats busting free from a too-small cage in my stomach and now clawing for an escape, wild with both hope and the realization that there's only one way out.

I know how they feel.

"Save your praise for someone who deserves it." I clear my throat before the weakness can leak into my words, before she can get a sense that there's something I'm not saying. "You, going off to college on your own to a place where no one knows you, that's impressive."

She smiles a little, and the tension in my shoulders eases at the realization I've successfully taken the attention away from myself. "So, what are you planning to do when you graduate? I think you said you're majoring in hospitality."

Rhea makes a noncommittal noise and lifts one shoulder. "Yeah, I am. And minoring in business."

That is news to me. How did that go overlooked? On top of the phone calls I have with my sister on a monthly basis, I've got contacts in place that keep me up to date on her. It's a shame none of them ever told me that her best friend is so damn intriguing. "So, you inherited the entrepreneurial gene?"

"I guess you could say that."

"Well, enlighten me. What sort of business do you want to manage?"

"I'm not telling you." Rhea laughs.

"Oh, come on." I prod with the teasing tone I've used on her our whole lives. "Scared I'll judge you?"

"I know you will. But I'll tell you anyway." She leans forward as if she's secretly excited to tell me what she has up her sleeve. And maybe she is.

All this time, I've pushed her away so that I could keep her safe, but the last couple of hours have had me regretting that decision. She has been safe, of course, and that's my priority. I won't jeopardize my sister for anything, but the way her eyes glimmer excitedly as we finally get to talking about things that matter tells me she's missed me. And God knows I've missed her.

"My first goal is to open a long-term care facility for parentless children so that when they age out of foster care, they have a head start. I'm not talking about a group home or a foster facility. I'm talking about cutting out the middleman. A place where kids go to live with their case workers so there's no bouncing around. A place where they can get their education, where they can mentor other kids, where they're safe, and where they're all family."

I wonder if I should be insulted that Rhea thought I'd tease her over wanting to do something so pure. I have no desire to mock her goals, but I do wonder how she came by them.

When I remain quiet, Rhea takes it as a sign to carry on. "In addition to that, I've spoken to Alonzo about some real estate I'm interested in purchasing to implement that goal... and my other ventures."

"Like what?" I ask, intrigued.

"One life isn't enough for all the things I want to do and be." She sighs, leaning back now that she's reeled me in. "But that won't stop me from trying. I would also like to open my own gallery, and before you say anything, I have met a few great people who can help me along the way."

Art. Now that one doesn't come as a surprise. Not in the way that her humanitarian efforts do, anyway. Our mother had been largely obsessed with art of all kinds, most of which I saw no value in. But that hadn't stopped Father from chasing down priceless paintings in garish frames and odd sculptures that looked as though they'd been carved using Play-Doh and a butter knife. My father had sought to buy all our love. I wasn't certain it had ever worked, but he'd at least bought our time until his own ran out.

"Anything else?"

"Lots of things, but I'll tell you the last of my trifecta." She grins, almost like she's challenging me. "I want to buy a hotel."

That breaks my façade; I raise a brow. "A hotel?"

"I know that sounds... ambitious."

"It's all ambitious." I agree. "I'm sure if anyone could make all her dreams come true, it's you. But why?"

"Why to which part?" She asks. But she doesn't offer me a chance to answer before deciding to explain it all. "Do you remember when we were young and we went to France on vacation?"

"Barely," I say honestly, recalling our view of the Eiffel tower from our hotel room. It hadn't been a glamorous vacation and had mostly faded into the recesses of my memory. Women always talk about Paris like it's some sort of paradise, but I hadn't been fond of the city when we were there. Part of that may have been the crappy weather, but a larger part of it was almost certainly the fact that my dad had dragged us out there under the guise of a vacation, but we didn't do anything fun while we were there. In fact, he'd barely been with us the entire time.

"We went to the Louvre," Rhea says, reminding me of one of the boring things we'd done. "Because, of course, that was the most important thing to mom. I remember being just enchanted by it. The whole place itself is art, but when you consider the treasures inside... I'm not sure there's any other place in the world with that kind of magic. That's where I fell in love with art. Father left early, and then it was just Mom and I, wandering around for hours, staring at paintings and artifacts. You sulked around for the most part. And when it was time to leave, we had no car because Father went off and left us, so we walked back to our hotel."

"I do remember that." My voice is sour thinking about the receding form of my father's back, his shoulders squared, looking completely unbothered by leaving his family alone in a foreign country.

After walking around aimlessly for hours, the walk through slushy snow back to the hotel was imprinted in my mind. I remember how much of it was yellow and melting into the dirty streets and how I decided then and there that Paris was probably the ugliest place I'd ever been. I've still never been back, and I've still not found a city I like less.

"Well, on the way we had just about a hundred grifters on the street trying to sell mom scarves, flowers, silly little trinkets. One man grabbed my arm and tried to get me to convince mom that I needed one of the berets he was selling."

The thought of someone grabbing my little sister's arm spikes anger in me, but that was before I knew just how cruel the world was. Why hadn't I seen that? Why hadn't I done anything?

My anger with myself doesn't burn long before reason breaks through. Though that man's actions had certainly been uncalled for, I doubt that she was in any danger. "Paris has a fairly impoverished population." I concede. "They were incredibly pushy."

Rhea nods. "And mom said no to every single one of them up until we got just outside the hotel. They had guards on the street to chase away the beggars because, of course, they had to protect their image. But there was a man who was sitting against the building before we crossed the street. He was with his family, and when he got up, I noticed they were sitting on a piece of cardboard on the ground with one big blanket across them. I remember him walking straight up to Mom, and I'm not sure why, but I was scared of him. Probably because I'd gotten used to them pushing and pulling at me. But this guy took his scarf off and wrapped it around my neck because I'd lost mine somewhere at the Louvre. Mom thought it was just a good sales tactic at first, but he wouldn't take anything when she tried to hand him money."

I try to recall the memory, but we'd encountered so many beggars during that trip that they all blurred together. I also recall being in a foul mood after being dragged through the museum and trudging back to the hotel in snow that nearly swallowed our shoes, so I hadn't focused on anything more than getting back to the room and warming up.

"Mom asked why he wouldn't take her money, and he explained he wasn't trying to sell her anything, that the scarf was just a gift to keep me warm. He told her in what little English he could manage that he was only between jobs. He wasn't looking for anything, he just wanted to raise his kids to be a part of the good in the world. He didn't know she was fluent in French." She laughs, "Mom marched him right inside and demanded they hire him as their newest bellhop. And you know as well as I do, nobody ever refused, Mom."

I watch Rhea thoughtfully, wondering if she's making this story up on the fly. "I don't remember any of that."

"You ran to the room as soon as we got to the lobby. Maybe it didn't matter to you, but it was kind of a defining moment for me. It was the first time I truly understood how lucky we were to have our family. I mean, Father was as imperfect as they come, but what is it that caused us to be born into all of this money and good fortune when there are people on the other side of the world with only a blanket between them? I still don't understand it." She sighs, her eyes drifting to where Claire is fast asleep, her head on her own shoulder again.

I don't have the heart to tell her that luck has nothing to do with it, unless I count her as lucky enough to be on the right side of the divide. What we have wasn't earned. It was taken off the backs of men and women and children, burdened to us by their pain, their trauma, their lives. I've worked hard to wash the blood off of our family's money, but all it's done is stained my own hands. But I won't tell her any of that... not now, maybe not ever.

"So, you mean to tell me that everything you know about who you want to be was all discovered in one moment by the time you were ten?"

I can't help the envy I feel, but I hope I kept it out of my voice. I'd wanted to do a lot of things with my life at one time. But then I'd been pushed into this lifestyle I never wanted. Now, I'm in so deep that I don't even waste time thinking of who I used to be. Or who I used to *want* to be.

"In a way, yes. Mom asked that guy why they were on the street and whether they had any family to go to, and that's when he admitted he'd raised himself after his uncle died, and he just took whatever paying jobs he could get since he didn't have a proper education. Nobody ever gave him a chance until our mother *forced* the hotel manager to. She also paid his room for a year out, so they had a warm place to go." Rhea laughs, still clearly in awe of our mother's tenacity. "I don't know if Mom had some sort of blackmail over the owner or if they just didn't want to risk losing our business, but I do remember asking her why she did it. She told me that it was because he'd reminded her of an important thing and that he was right. The world would only be a better place because of him raising his children to do good. She wanted to be a part of it."

She pauses long enough to give me a minute for all of that levity to sink in. I don't get to consider my mother's hypocrisy or whether it's just an attempt to counteract her husband's wrong-doing because Rhea sighs. "It was pretty inspirational, but I forgot all about it by the time we were stateside. Then mom died and it didn't seem like there was any good left in the world. I went to college for the escape it was, and I didn't plan to leave with a degree, honestly. I'd assumed I'd take some classes, fall in love, and not worry about choosing a career. Instead of meeting a man, I met Claire."

Rhea looks over again to where her friend is curled up asleep in her chair, strands of golden hair falling into her face. "Honestly, she was just what I needed when I needed it. We got along pretty much right away, and then when she opened up to me about her family situation, it brought up that old memory, and it made me want to do something. We grew up with maids and butlers... hell, we *still* have them. And she grew up without even her own room. She attends school on scholarships and works harder than anybody I know to maintain them, yet everything that she has in the world she has fought for. There's a special kind of pride in that."

I listen thoughtfully and after a few moments of silence, I crack a half smile. "Are you sure you aren't in love with her?"

Rhea rolls her eyes. "Could you blame me if I were?"

Love is so far off my radar that yes, I could blame her. But I decide not to admit as much.

"Just making sure."

"I do love her. I mean, I was trying to hurt you yesterday when I said she was more of a sibling to me than you are, but it also wasn't a lie. Do you believe in soulmates?"

I snort into the glass of whiskey I'd just lifted to my lips a moment before. That's all the answer Rhea needs.

"I figured as much. I think they definitely exist, and I think she is mine. See, they aren't always romantic. I think you can find your soulmate in a friend too. And that's what Claire is. She put me back together when I was falling apart. So no, I am not in love with her. But I do love her like a sibling, like I love you. And I haven't told her yet, but I'm hoping that Claire will stick around to help me manage my future endeavors."

"Fair enough." I concede. It hurts a little to know that someone has replaced my position in my sister's life. But I suppose I'm grateful to Claire for being there when I couldn't. "If she's really as extraordinary as you say, I think the two of you could dominate the hotel/gallery/foster care system."

"Ooh, high praise from the master of business." Rhea laughs. "I can't wait to see what *you've* done with all your success. I'm guessing you have a yacht full of sexy Costa Rican women on standby and no less than three Ferraris."

I laugh, too. "I guess you'll find out."

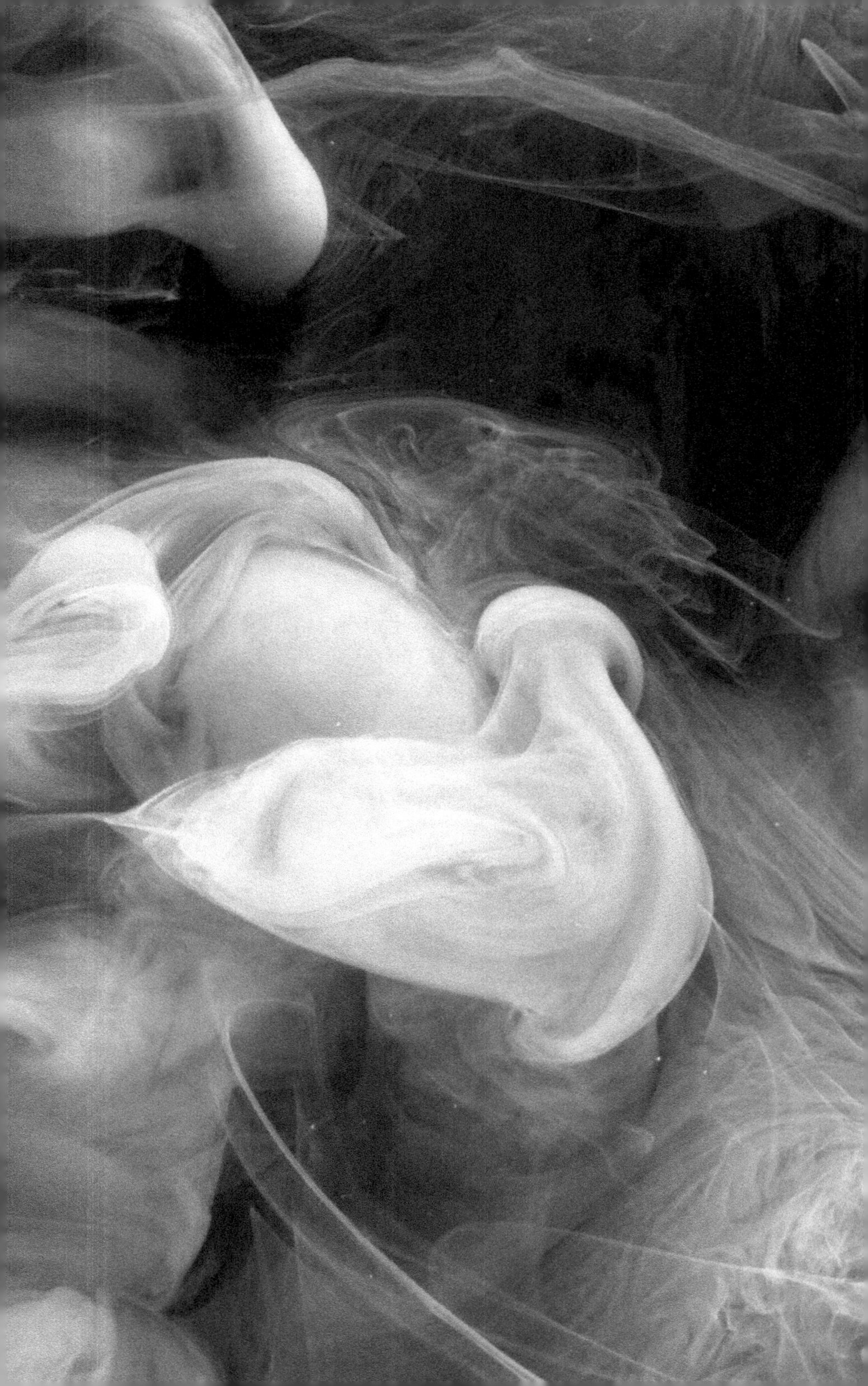

CHAPTER TWELVE

CLAIRE

"Claire?" Rhea's gentle voice cuts through the din of sleep and I can feel the fog lifting as she pulls me from the comfort of unconsciousness. I sigh as it's chased away, the comfortable numbness giving way to a faint headache and achy muscles. If only I'd slept a little longer... last night had been too exhausting.

"Five more minutes?" I try, though the words barely come out around a yawn.

"You slept like the dead." Rhea argues. "You should be good for the next week *at least*. Besides, I've been calling your name for five minutes trying to wake you up. We're here."

Shock prompts my eyes to flutter open. The cabin windows are shut, but it seems brighter than when we took off. I rub the heels of my palms into my eyes, trying to chase away the heavy feeling of grogginess. "We're in Costa Rica?"

"Just landed." Rhea confirms with a nod and a bemused grin.

"That was quick." I stretch my neck, suddenly aware of the stiffness there. I'm going to need a massage after sleeping like that for so long. I wonder vaguely if Remy has a staff of masseuses on standby.

"It wasn't quick." Rhea laughs. "I guess that's my fault. I forgot you're a lightweight and one pill probably would have been the sweet spot. But you needed the sleep, I guess. Now we're burning daylight, so let's go."

I stand up, bracing myself against the table while feeling comes rushing back into my legs. That's not the only feeling that comes back suddenly—I have to pee so bad I could cry. I glance around, but it's just Rhea and I left on the plane, so once my blood is moving, I put one foot in front of the other and follow her to the back of the plane. "There's a bathroom if you need it. The house is still about twenty minutes from here."

She must have read my mind, and I'm grateful.

The bathroom is connected to the little suite, and the bed back there looks like it would have been much more comfortable. I have a foggy memory of Remy waking me to tell me I could move to the bed, but I was too tired to move.

The relief is immediate, and by the time I'm washing my hands, I feel better already. The fog is clearing and my muscles are recovering. And then I catch my reflection—smudged mascara I don't even remember putting on, pale face. No wonder Remy remarked on my pallor. At least it looks a little better when I clean up the mascara and splash some water on my face.

Rhea meets me on the other side of the bathroom door with a grin. "Let's go, slow poke. We've got people to do, places to see."

I blink, trying to make sure I heard her right, and then laugh as she drags me toward the exit.

The sun had been just settling into the sky when we'd gotten on the plane. Now, it's low like it is getting ready to set. I pause at the top of the steps, blinking in awe at the scene before me. I don't like the feeling of having lost a day of my life, but the unhampered view of the sun against an open horizon backed by green trees in the distance is definitely worth it.

Up until today, the most beautiful place I've ever been was definitely Rhea's home in Cove Harbor, with its forest land and water, small-town charm, and opulence all in one place. But this view puts that to shame. It feels like we've just landed in the middle of the jungle. The air all around me vibrates with life, and when I take a deep breath, it's the sweetest, purest breath I've ever taken.

"So, you guys are rich enough that we can just fly into another country, no questions asked?"

"I guess." Rhea laughs. "Someone from customs came in and asked about you, but I believe Remy pays them very well to keep flight logs private. In any case, he had a passport made for you last night so that you'd stop worrying."

I have my questions about the legitimacy of any passport that can be made overnight, but decide not to voice them. I can't, however, help wonder about Remy. "Where is he, anyway?"

"He had to make a call, of course. He should be around here somewhere. And there is our car, right on time." She nods down the steps to where a nondescript black SUV is pulling in.

The driver is a middle-aged man who steps out as we reach the bottom step. He cracks a grin the minute he sees Rhea. "Long time, no see kiddo."

Up close, he doesn't appear as old as I'd initially thought. But it doesn't seem that time has been terribly kind to him.

Rhea only rolls her eyes. "You've gotten gray, old man." She points to her own chin, referencing his grizzled and lightening beard.

"You changed your hair, too. Blonde?" He chuckles and then nods at me. "And you gained a shadow?"

"Jovich, this is my best friend in the whole world, Claire. Claire, this is Uncle Joe."

"Oh?" The surprise is evident in my voice as I look at the man, who bears no resemblance to the Boudreaux's. His accent is decidedly not Costa Rican, though I don't know how that sounds yet. It's also a far cry from the American ones I'm accustomed to. "Hello." I smile at him, but it's met with a blank stare.

"He's not blood, but he may as well be. Jovich has taken care of my family for years. I'm not sure what he could have done to be stuck playing Remy's minion, but it must be bad."

"We have a good thing going," Jovich assures her, opening the door for us to climb in, all without taking his eyes off me.

As I'm buckling myself in, the trunk opens and a man I haven't seen yet lifts our bags into the back. Remy appears shortly after, sliding into the driver's seat while Jovich takes the passenger side. I catch Remy's eye in the mirror. "Glad to see you survived being drugged by my sister. I wasn't sure there was any hope for you."

His voice is thick and smoky, chasing chills over the backs of my arms that I hope Rhea is too busy clicking around on her phone to notice.

"I'm used to her shenanigans." I shrug, trying not to think too much into his words. "It's not the first time she's tried to kill me, and I'm sure it won't be the last."

Rhea elbows me in the ribs, and we both laugh.

Thankfully, it isn't a long ride to Remy's place, and most of it is spent with Jovich and Rhea catching up on everything he's missed since she went away to school. I'm so enamored with the view outside the windows that I tune them out without even thinking about it. Never have I ever seen a place so vibrant and lush, like it's straight out of a fairytale. I sat on the driver's side and am so intent on watching all the shades of green fly by that I don't notice when the coast appears on the other side of the road.

As we approach the drive and Remy begins to slow, I can see the ocean glimmering off to the right and the treetops that dance on the other side. And just like that, I understand why their family would want to be buried halfway across the world.

It almost doesn't seem real.

It shouldn't have come as a surprise that Remy's house is mirrored just like the family home in Oregon. The front of the massive estate looks out to the mountainous forest, but as soon as we pull in front of the home, I can see that the backyard is actually a beautiful white-sand beach, beyond which I can see cerulean waves bobbing along the horizon.

"I haven't been here in years." Rhea sighs, caught in a wave of nostalgia... or maybe just inhaling the scent of coconuts, sea salt, and whiskey. I want to drown in that scent.

"This house has been in your family a while?" I ask, my eyes running along the length of the place. It's even more impressive than their stateside home, though it is smaller and without the refined touch of the Colonial. In fact, Remy's house looks more like a sprawling cabin with tall ceilings and huge glass windows everywhere.

"It was our great grandfather's property. The guest house is actually the original." Rhea gestures to a smaller cabin to the right of the main house. It's a more modest version of the main home, and yet it's certainly bigger than any place I've ever lived in.

"The guest house is, regrettably, under construction." Remy turns the car off and looks over his shoulder at us. "Of course, there is plenty of space in the house."

"Really, Rem?" Rhea rolls her eyes and lets herself out of the car in a huff. "You have no faith in me, do you? You do know that I manage without you, right? I've been doing it the last three years."

"Sorry about the timing." He grumbles. "I didn't exactly plan my remodel around your visit, you know."

Rhea eyes him suspiciously as Jovich goes to retrieve our bags. "Sorry." She mutters, reluctant. "I was just making sure you're not trying to keep me under your thumb. I know you like to think yourself to be in charge."

Remy doesn't argue the matter, but his sly smirk suggests that he doesn't have to *think* he is in charge. "Elaine has already prepared rooms for you, but if you want to choose another room to stay in while you're here, I'm sure she won't mind."

"We'll see." Rhea shrugs, abandoning the fight to grab my wrist and yank me toward the house with all the gusto of a child. "Come on, Claire. You're going to love Elaine!"

Remy leads us up the stone steps to a set of huge oak doors and pushes them open to reveal an impressive, sprawling foyer. In the center of it is a wide staircase that splits into two directions at the top. Sunlight pours in through the open doors near the back of the house, and the sound of the sea can be heard faintly lapping at the shore.

"Wow." It's all I can think of to say. Words won't do justice to a place like this.

"I'll give you a tour later," Rhea promises. "I need a drink."

The sudden ringing of Remy's phone pierces the tranquil vibe and Rhea shoots him a dirty look as he waves us on.

Rhea may not have been here in years, but she certainly remembers where she's going well enough to lead me through a long hall that lets out into an expansive and expensive-looking kitchen. Every surface gleams from the warm sunlight that pours through the open windows, and the air, full of the sound of water simmering on the stovetop and the clap of a knife against a bamboo cutting board, smells delicious.

The petite woman at the marble island in the heart of the kitchen is chopping onions with a massive knife, but as soon as she senses that she isn't alone, she lays it down and eyes Rhea.

"It smells like heaven in here." Rhea sighed.

"I may *be* in heaven because Hell must have frozen over!" A smile splits Elaine's face, and then she's wrapping Rhea in a motherly hug that shoots a pang of jealousy through me. The guilt chases it away as soon as it appears. I shouldn't envy my best friend for anything, as willing as she is to share her life with me.

Rhea laughs, but as she pulls away, I see the guilt in her smile, a mirror of what I feel. "I never should have stayed away so long. I'm sorry, Elaine."

"Oh, hush." Elaine waves a hand as if she can wipe away the past. "I'm proud of you, Sunshine."

"I'm glad you're still here putting up with Remy's bullshit after all these years." Rhea laughs. "Especially because my dear friend Claire and I would kill for a pitcher of your famous sangria."

"Good thing it's already in the fridge, there." Elaine beams as Rhea kisses her on one cheek and then the other before skipping across the kitchen to retrieve the pitcher from the fridge.

Elaine returns back to chopping her onions, but as she glances up at where I stand across from her, the smile slips from her face... and the knife slips from her hand.

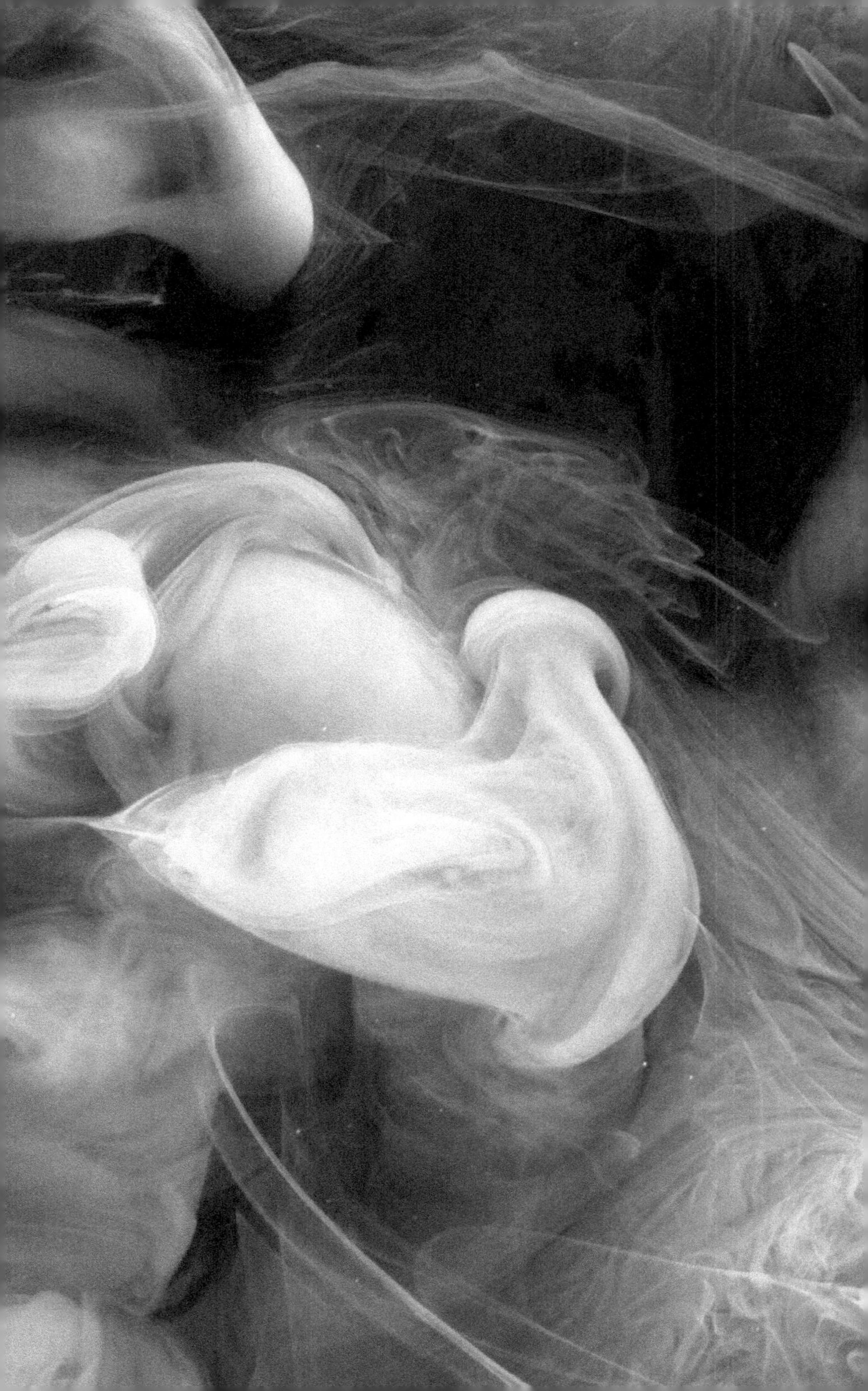

CHAPTER THIRTEEN

Claire

"Oh!" She gasps.

She doesn't even seem to notice that she's cut herself at first, she's so intent on staring at me as though she is looking at a ghost. Despite the blood dripping down her fingers, Elaine is transfixed on me.

It locks me in place for a moment, holding me captive under her strange gaze, and then I see the blood gushing between her fingers. I lunge for the towel on the sink and press it over the woman's hand, uncertain where she cut herself. At the same time, Rhea whips around to survey the damage.

"Are you alright?" I can feel the woman's hands shaking as I press the towel around them.

Elaine meets my eyes, silently at first, and then manages a smile as she withdraws from my touch. "I'm fine, dear. Just a slip and a nick. Happens all the time. Let me clean this up and then I'll be right back."

Elaine rushes off, leaving me to turn to Rhea, bewildered. "That was weird, right?" I don't know anything about Remy's house-keeper. Maybe that interaction is normal for her, for all I know. But the way she looked at me was unsettling—like she wanted nothing to do with me. I wonder if she's a secret psychic and I have some kind of dark cloud for an aura.

"Yeah." Rhea agrees. "Elaine is a master chef. I've never known her to slip."

"She looked... scared of me."

"Scared?" Rhea laughs, turning back to the pitcher. She pours a glass full to the brim with a pungent sangria mix and sets it in front of me. Then Rhea pours another for herself. "I love you, Claire, but you're not very fearsome."

I laugh because it's true. I'm probably still feeling off from the sleeping pills and the long flight and being shot at, not to mention all the weirdness of the last twenty-four hours. I take a sip of the sangria and my tastebuds explode with pleasure.

"Oh my God."

I stare at the glass a moment, wondering if she infused it with magic, before looking up to find Rhea with a slow grin spreading on her face. "I told you it's to-die-for. Elaine has a special touch where everything she does turns out perfect... except for whatever this was supposed to be." She gestures to the cutting board with a few small drops of blood splattered across it.

"What happened?" Remy frowns as he enters the kitchen, looking from his sister to me. "I saw Elaine rush past."

"She nicked herself." Rhea nods at the cutting board and then gingerly picks it up to scrape the contents into the trash.

"Was she alright?" I ask, nervous that she'll need stitches. It really seemed like a lot of blood.

"I'm sure she's fine." Remy says coolly. "She just looked a bit shaken up. She's been handling the details for the funeral and I'm sure it's not been easy."

I nod my understanding as Rhea drops the cutting board into the stainless-steel sink, where it clanks against another dish and then settles. She turns the water on and rinses the blood down the sink.

"We would all be dead without her, and the wicked Boudreaux line would die out." She sighs, wiping her hands on the back of her jeans, and scoops up her drink. "Each funeral, she's there to hold the rest of us together."

"Speaking of which..." Remy straightens to address the business our discussion has reminded him of. "The funeral is Friday, the burial is Saturday, and the reading of the will is Monday."

"Monday?" I look between them, shocked. It's only Saturday. Or is it Sunday now? The time change and jet lag has me all out of sorts. I don't even know how long I slept, but it doesn't feel like nearly enough. "As in *next* Monday?"

"Is that a problem?" Remy raises his brow and something about his severe expression makes my stomach tighten. Well, not just my stomach, actually. My whole body seems to clench under that cocky gaze, every inch of my skin buzzing with the weight of his eyes on me.

"I... I didn't bring enough clothes."

"Again, I repeat, is that a problem?" This time he smirks. If it's possible, the feeling this time is stronger, like butterflies rushing through me and settling down deep. "I quite enjoyed you without clothes."

Oh, God.

I had been certain that he was going to ravage me on the kitchen counter last night—or was it this morning? Either way, the look in his eyes then had been the same then as it is now. Only now Rhea is watching. That fact dampens the need I feel for him, but doesn't take it away.

"Well, I quite enjoy you when you're not here." I snap, blurting out the first words that pop into my whirlwind of a mind. It isn't a good comeback; I'm not even sure what it means. It certainly isn't true, considering that every time he's near, I feel like a live wire, full of energy and possibility. It's a dangerous and delicious combination.

A devilish grin cracked his lips at the implications he's making out of that, and I clench my thighs together, desperately trying to maintain my cool. Why is he so infuriatingly sexy? And even more to the point, why am I falling for it? His little looks and innuendos are prompting my body to react in ways that I don't even fully understand. Yeah, he's gorgeous, but why when he smirks at me, do I react like a trained monkey?

"So, we'll go shopping." Rhea decrees, drawing me out of the tailspin I'm headed in. It takes me a moment to remember what we've even been talking about, but it doesn't matter because Rhea continues. "I've been working on an itinerary for us."

"An itinerary?" I repeat, uncertain I heard her right.

"How often do you go to Costa Rica?" She reasons. "There are a million things to do, and we only have a little over a week to do it. So, *yes*, I put together an itinerary. Is that okay?"

I show her my hands in surrender. I normally do the organizing and planning, but if Rhea wants to take responsibility, maybe it will give me a chance to actually relax during this trip.

Rhea prattles off a list of places she wants to go. I try to listen, but I'm acutely aware of Remy standing across the kitchen just... *watching me*. Every nerve in my body seems alight under his gaze, making it impossible to focus on anything. Fortunately for me, I don't have to pretend to be interested in Rhea's plans for long, because Elaine walks back in and musters a brilliant smile. "Sorry about that. I just got so overwhelmed all of a sudden thinking about everything. Fortunately, I always have extra onions on ha nd... and extra cutting boards."

"Thank you for handling everything, Elaine." Rhea sobers again at the mention of funeral arrangements. She wraps an arm around Elaine's middle and rests her head for a moment on the older woman's shoulder in a half-hug. Elaine pats her hand, unable to do anything else while in Rhea's grip. "And thank God for leading you to us because we never would have made it this far without you."

"Well," Elaine smiles as Rhea pulls away, swiping at a tear under her eye. "Life has a funny way of working out sometimes. I'm making dinner in the slow cooker, so it will be a few hours until it's ready. I'm sure you're tired after such a long trip. Why don't you get rested and changed and maybe we can enjoy dinner by the pool tonight? I'll mix up some more sangria and then maybe margaritas to go with dinner."

"I like the sangria and margaritas part." Rhea muses.

"I like the part where I shower and get some real sleep." Just thinking about a real mattress with pillows and blankets makes me practically salivate. I shouldn't have been too proud to lay down on the bed in the jet. In truth, I was tired enough that I could probably sleep anywhere. But if the guest bed is half as nice as the rest of the house implies, I'm sure I will finally feel alive when I get out of it.

And I'll never take a sleeping pill from Rhea again.

"The whole way here wasn't enough for you?" Remy teases, eyeing me judgmentally .

"Not after you guys drugged me. I need a serious refresh after that."

"Fine." Rhea concedes, pouting a little. "But enjoy it while it lasts, because the rest of the week will be full steam ahead. Good?"

"Whatever you say, master." I laugh when her lips crack into a devious grin, pleased with my response.

"I'll show you to your rooms." Remy offers, setting into the hall before Rhea can finish saying that she knows where she's going.

I follow them back through the hall and up the elaborate set of stairs we passed when we first entered. As we ascend the stairs, I find my eyes drawn to the dome ceiling, which is so clear it almost looks like there's nothing there at all except for the swirling iron pattern surrounding all that glass.

I love that this place is so bright and cheery. The Boudreaux's Oregon residence is beautiful and large, but much darker, as if the house itself has absorbed all of the negative energies that have passed through their halls. And yet, as beautiful as it is here during a bright day, I can't help but imagine how peaceful it must be to sit beneath the dome and watch the rain fall above.

We are nearly at the top when I stumble and come close to falling down the staircase. Fortunately, Remy is paying attention. He steadies me with a strong arm around the waist before I can lose my footing. My skin warms beneath the thin layer of my shirt, acutely aware of how close his fingers are to the spot where I want to feel them.

I thank him without catching his eye, lest he see that the heat in my cheeks isn't just due to that misstep.

Rhea turns right at the top of the stairs, but Remy turns left.

"The rooms Elaine readied are this way." He says, gesturing down the hall.

Rhea's eyes narrow on him in suspicion. "On *your* side of the house?"

Remy laughs. "It's all my house. But yes, my room is down there too. If you prefer the view from over there, I can ask Elaine to fix up two rooms on that side instead."

"No." Rhea waves a dismissive hand. "Elaine's done enough already."

"I'm sure she wouldn't mind changing the sheets."

"It's fine." Rhea sighs, clearly not thrilled with the settlement. "But I'm telling you right now, I don't want to hear your whores moaning in the middle of the night, so set up in another room or something."

"Don't worry." Remy grins, opening the first door to a large room with gauzy curtains covering the length of sliding glass doors. "The walls are fairly soundproof."

"My old room." Rhea looks around with a wistful smile and then dives straight on top of the bed and buries her face in a fluffy white comforter so that when she speaks, her words are muffled. "Oh, the nostalgia."

"Your name is still carved into the floor under the bed." Remy assures her. "I considered replacing it, but Elaine argued that it was a testament of the times."

"It *is* a testament." She agrees. "To teenage angst. I'm glad you didn't replace the floorboards, Rem."

"I'm glad Father didn't kill you when he saw it." Remy chuckles. "Claire, Elaine has set you up just next door. Your room has a private bath, but the shower is across the hall, next to the study."

He accompanies me to the next door, and I open it to a room that is similar to Rhea's with the same sheer curtains covering the balcony doors. The walls are a cheerful yellow that bounces the light around the room. It smells like fresh laundry and the ocean. Though I've never been further from home, it feels just right.

"Don't hesitate to ring Elaine if you need anything." He gestures to the tablet propped up on the dresser. "And I will be just down the hall... if you need anything."

I'm not sure if I imagine the inuendo or if he's simply being his unapologetically flirtatious self. My mouth is dry either way, and I'm sure my cheeks are giving me away. "I think I'll be fine."

Remy nods the slightest bit, but the smile still hasn't left the corner of his pouty lips. "I don't doubt it."

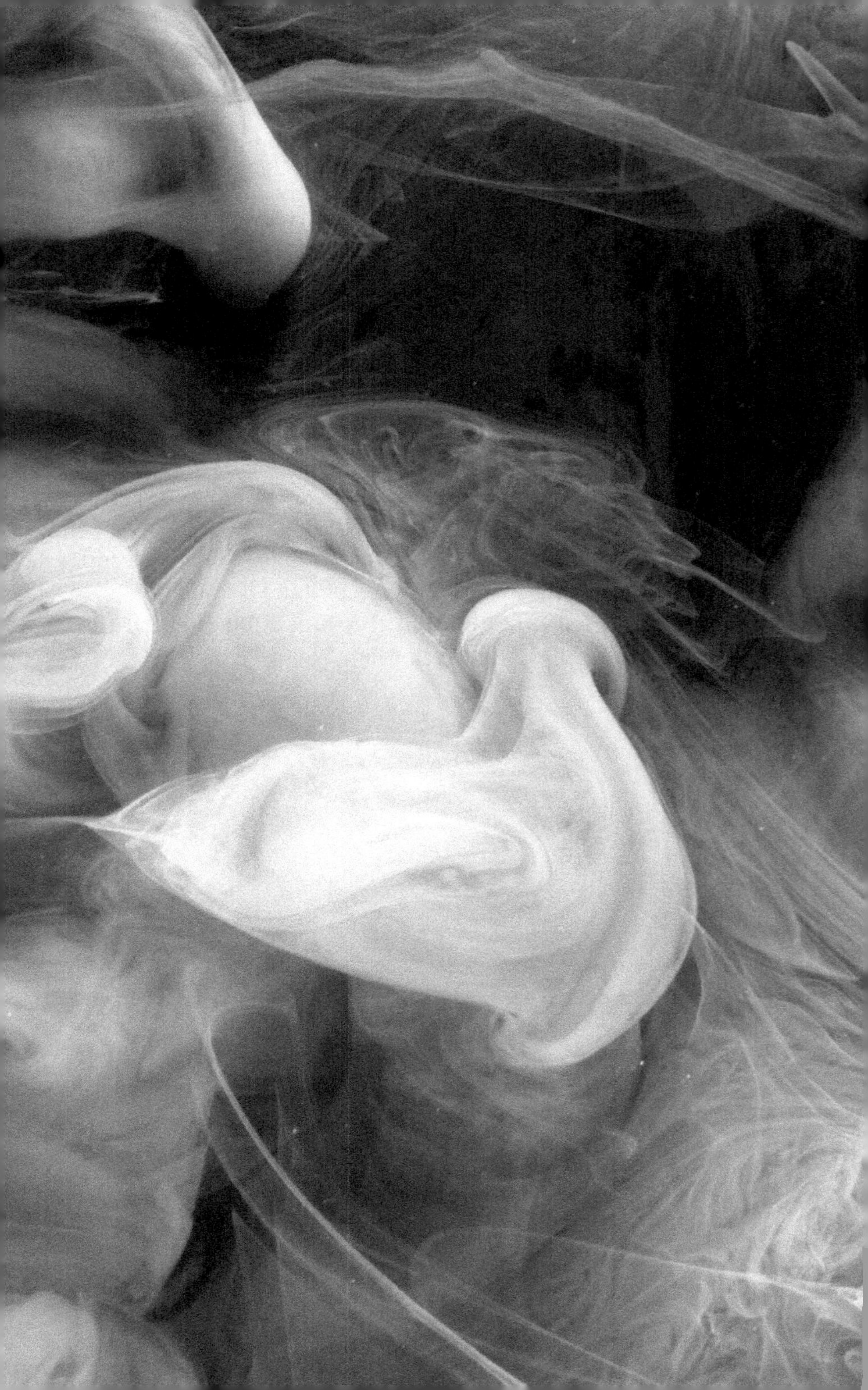

CHAPTER FOURTEEN

REMY

I want to fall down on my bed and let the world fade away. I could truly relax for the first time in my adult life. My father is gone. My sister is safe in the halls of my own home, and so is her dear friend, which means nobody can try to prey upon Rhea's good nature. I can breathe easier knowing they're close, but that doesn't mean that I can rest. There's still too much work to be done to keep my family safe.

"Jack." I say into my phone when the other line clicks as if someone has answered it. There is a brief pause before Jack answers. He probably wonders why I'm calling him myself, given that he's already been in touch with Jovich the last day.

"What can I do for you, Boudreaux?"

"Claire Monroe." Just saying her name sends a fire through my veins that I don't understand. I don't know what it is about her, honestly, but she's managed to consume me in what little time I've known her. Not to mention, I know she is hiding something. I have always loved a good mystery, and the girl staying in the room next to mine is a mystery if ever I've seen one.

"Your sister's friend?" Jack puzzles. "The little blonde?"

I don't grace him with a reply to that question. He knows exactly who I mean. "She's a college student at Darrington. I want to know anything and everything. Where does she come from? Does she have a criminal record? How is she paying her tuition and rent? I want *everything* you can find on her. Do you understand?"

"I'll get it all, right down to her childhood imaginary friends," Jack says confidently. "But you want to tell me what this is all about? She's never caused any trouble in town."

"Just covering my bases." I pull up the tablet Jovich left on my bed and scroll through the photos he loaded. "It's high priority, though."

"Okay," he says. "I'll be in touch."

I set my phone down and sink into the tall-backed chair by the window, continuing to scroll through the photos.

Johnathan Boudreaux had been a busy and well-known man. He was also outspoken and quick to anger, not the kind to make many genuine friendships. He had contacts all over the globe; His clients were among the wealthiest, most influential people in the world, which meant that the list of people who would stab him in the back was much longer than the list of his most devout friends. I knew my father was brazen even when we were younger and he'd had a family that he had to worry about, but as time wore on and our mother died, Johnathan got more and more cutthroat. He had nothing to lose. He'd told me as much, no less than a dozen times.

I tried not to let it bother me. Our relationship had always been strained, as far as I could recall. My father held nothing back and had made it clear on more than one occasion just how much of a disappointment I was. I'd learned to accept it, but what I couldn't ever come to terms with is the fact that he was willing to gamble with Rhea's life.

Unlike me, Rhea has never been a disappointment. She is kind and clever and, the thing my father prized most, obedient. She is a firecracker and feisty, but not obstinate or reckless like me. We don't have the perfect family, but Rhea was always our father's favorite. Which is why, when Johnathan started making promises he had no intention of keeping and gambling with more than he could afford to lose, I was disappointed. I knew my father was willing to take a chance with his own life, and truly, I hadn't cared enough to stop him. I cleaned up what messes I could and did my part to maintain the Boudreaux name, but I hadn't stopped him from walking on the edge.

I also never reached out a hand to pull him back from the ledge.

CHAPTER FIFTEEN

Remy

The water sparkles turquoise under a setting sun and the fresh air still lingers with the decadent scents of Elaine's dinner. Music plays softly in the background, but I'm not listening to what song it is. I don't care. I don't know if it's being home after traveling to the States, or knowing that Rhea is safe, or watching Claire marvel at the ocean in my backyard, but I haven't felt this relaxed in ages.

Claire, too, looks more relaxed than I've seen her yet. Sitting with her legs tucked under her and a gentle breeze teasing her hair loose from the clip on the back of her head, she looks like she would be content to spend the whole week on my patio, eating, drinking, and relaxing. Unfortunately for her, Rhea makes it abundantly clear that relaxation is the one thing that *isn't* on the agenda.

"I made you a copy of the itinerary. Would you like it, so you know how to prepare for the week ahead?"

Claire pulls a face, earning her a sour look from Rhea. "Wouldn't it be nice to just enjoy the moments as they come?"

"Wow." Rhea laughs. "I can't believe that just came from your mouth, Claire Monroe. Miss color coded chore chart is now telling *me* to sit back and wait for life to happen?"

I don't try all that hard to hide my smirk, dipping my head a little in an attempt to look like I'm not judging her. *Chore charts?* I stifle a laugh, but neither of them notice.

"In the real world, at school, I think it's important that we stick to a plan." Claire crosses her arms, trying to hold on to a shred of her argument. "But we're on vacation. Can't we just... see where we end up?"

Rhea wrinkles her nose in displeasure. "Fine. We'll compromise. Take a look at the itinerary and choose two days that you want to 'coast'." She brandishes a sheet of paper, which Claire takes with a roll of her eyes. They flit quickly over it, and then she laughs.

"Clearly, I've rubbed off on you, Rhea. This itinerary looks like it's... color coded."

It's Rhea's turn to roll her eyes. "Yes, as a matter of fact. It is. Coded by importance, with the pink being the most important, naturally, and the teal being the lower priority events."

Claire skims the itinerary. "Shopping, a day at sea, picnic on the beach, day drinking, hiking, shopping again, kayaking... *Rhea*!" She gasps, sounding so aghast that I'm sure Rhea must have included something that was entirely outside of Claire's comfort zone. It didn't take me long to figure out their dynamic... Rhea drags her best friend along to everything with such enthusiasm that Claire never objects. "You put the funeral in teal!"

I laugh out loud and don't bother trying to hide it this time. Rhea shrugs. "I mean, it *barely* won out over sacrificing a virgin to a volcano, so just be grateful it's even on there."

Claire shakes her head, but a small smile on her pink lips betrays her.

"I thought it was funny." I concede. "And you made the right choice. There's no shortage of volcanos here, but good luck finding a virgin."

"Because you've slept with everyone around here?" Rhea quips, clearly pleased with her own wit.

My silence speaks enough that Claire takes it upon herself to quickly change the subject. "Okay, well the funeral isn't exactly negotiable, so that stays. Let's cut out day drinking since we'll likely do that on the boat and at the beach. I'm not sure we need two whole days for shopping, and are you *trying* to kill me by taking me hiking and kayaking? You know I'm not the most..."

"Adventurous? Coordinated?" Rhea laughs. "I'm not going to let you fall off the side of a mountain, Claire. You're my best friend. Besides, I said you could pick *two* days."

Claire sighs heavily, but her lips twitch in amusement all the same. "Fine."

"Perfect." Rhea bounces up out of her chair, grinning like mad. "Did you even look at the whole thing? You fell right into my trap. Now let's go get ready for tonight."

"I—tonight?"

"Yes, tonight. It's right there on your itinerary in purple."

Claire looks down at the paper in her hands. She's showered and done her hair and looks considerably more awake than she'd been after her Ambien haze, but I'm willing to bet she isn't entirely sure what day it even is anymore.

"Dancing?" Claire looks at Rhea, incredulous. "I don't have the energy for that."

"Not the ballroom kind." Rhea winks, slapping her palms on the table. "Which means you're going to need something sexy. And as far as not having enough energy, you can always drink Vodka Redbull."

"Rhea." My voice is firm, not bothering to hide my disapproval. "You can't be serious."

"Of course, I'm serious, Remington. We are in paradise and I'm going to take full advantage."

"I thought we'd stay in tonight." I try. "You know, catch up since we haven't seen each other in years." It sounds hollow even as I say it, but I have to at least attempt something to keep her from going out.

"We talk, Rem. I don't need to stay up all night discussing our feelings, okay? I need to dance, and drink, and maybe find a gorgeous Costa Rican man to keep me warm tonight."

God, no.

Her plans have just gone from bad to worse. My face makes it clear that I'm not thrilled with this listing on her itinerary. But there's no point in fighting her on it. As far as Rhea knows, she isn't here for anything other than our father's funeral. And given her earlier outburst about not needing me to keep an eye on her, I'm on thin ice already. "Alright. We'll go out tonight, but I have a condition."

"We?" Claire asks, at the same time that Rhea says, "Condition?"

"I don't want you bringing strange men into my house." I glance at Claire. "Either of you."

Rhea narrows her eyes on me, as if trying to decide whether I'm being overprotective or territorial. Even if I wasn't worried about their safety, I simply don't want another man in my home. "Define *strange*." She tries, her voice hopeful.

"Okay." I sigh, already worn out by her persistence. I'd forgotten just how exhausting my sister can be. No wonder Claire slept like the dead on the way here. The corners of my mouth betray me when I can't help but laugh. "I don't want you bringing *any* men home. Got it?"

Rhea pouts again, a practiced look that usually gets her whatever she wants. But I know that game, and I'm not playing. "Fine." She huffs. "Come on, Claire."

Claire stands slowly, reluctant to leave the comfort of the patio. She seems like she is usually pretty willing to be dragged along on Rhea's little adventures, but it doesn't escape me that Rhea seems to be pushing her further and further out of her comfort zone. Visiting the Piazza and getting hit on by random teenagers is one thing. Going to a night club in a foreign country where she doesn't speak the native language is a whole different ball game.

Rhea disappears inside as Elaine is heading back to the table. She steps aside but watches Claire's face intently as if she's waiting for something. "Thank you again for everything." Claire smiles at her. "Dinner was incredible."

"You're welcome." Elaine smiles back, but it doesn't quite reach her eyes. It also disappears from her face entirely once Claire is out of view.

"Is something wrong?" I ask, leaning back in my chair to appraise her. "You look... distracted."

"You're right. I *am* distracted. It's not like I was a fan of your father, but I guess I haven't gotten over it." She blinks and shakes her head, like she's just decided that was enough reminiscing for one day.

I appraise her. I've never asked, but I get the impression that Elaine is in her late forties... old enough to be considered a fun aunt. I'd also never asked how exactly she came to know my family, but it doesn't matter. One day she was just there, and then the next day she *was* family. Though she works for me and is often quick to agree with whatever opinion I voice about my family, maybe at one time she'd had her own relationship with my father. Johnathan certainly hadn't discriminated, and as far as older women go, Elaine isn't bad to look at.

"How did you end up tangled in the madness that is the Boudreaux's?" I ask, watching her for any sign that she may have been more than a loyal family friend at one time. I thankfully haven't seen any photos of her with my father, but that doesn't mean she didn't fall prey to him at some point.

"Hmm?" She seems surprised by the question. Her thin lips press together, and for the first time since I've known her, I get the feeling she's trying to hide something. "Oh, it was a long time ago. A friend gave me your mother's number when I was trying to find a job, and we stayed in touch. You know your mother was just that easy to get along with." Elaine shrugs. "So, what's on the agenda? I heard something about Rhea color coding an itinerary?"

I laugh. "I guess Claire's been a good influence on her. Unfortunately, she also doesn't say no to my sister. We're going dancing tonight."

"Oh?" Elaine smiles. "That sounds... nice."

"Not the word I would have chosen." I mutter. But my phone rings in the next moment, so that Elaine never has to know which euphemism I'd have chosen. "Excuse me." I apologize, standing up and accepting the call.

Elaine waves me off, unconcerned, and I walk away to take the call in private. I don't speak until I reach the edge of the patio, where the stone gives way to white sand. "Jack? That was fast."

"Well, I'm not done digging yet, but I thought you may like to know what I've got so far."

"Oh?"

That isn't good. Jack wouldn't call to tell me something arbitrary unless he'd finished his investigation. The fact that he's called back already means that there is, in fact, something wrong with Claire.

"Your girl's a ghost."

"I assure you she's not." I say quietly. I think of our bodies pressed together when I threw her to the ground by the pool, and the way she looked like she wanted me to ravage her on the kitchen counter. She is very much real.

"You're right. She's *half* a ghost. Claire Elizabeth Monroe, born March 24th, 2002 according to her school records. She's had twelve different addresses from kindergarten to the present."

Twelve addresses. I'd have thought she was a military brat if she hadn't already told me she grew up in foster care. Twelve addresses in twenty one years means she doesn't even average two years with each family she was placed with. It's pretty sad, honestly, but I don't get to contemplate it because Jack plunges onward. "Never had anything less than an A, graduated with a 4.0, attends Darrington University on scholarship. She wrote her admissions essay on how she wasn't sure what she wanted to do with life, which is a bit ballsy when you're asking for a scholarship. Her favorite color seems to be green, she's a natural brunette but clearly dyes her hair blonde, she doesn't discriminate in her taste for music, and she looks pretty fucking great in a bikini from what I saw on her Instagram."

I tense at the thought of Jack scrolling through her pictures. I'd asked him to look into her, but that doesn't mean I want him to look *at* her. Are there a lot of photos of her in a bikini online? I make it a point to check. "So, what's the *problem*, Jack?"

"Problem is that the girl has no birth certificate. I did a quick search, but there's no live birth certificate for Claire Elizabeth Monroe on that day anywhere in the U.S."

I'm silent as I consider Jack's words. How is it even possible to not have a birth certificate? Shouldn't the school have one on file? Wouldn't she need it to get a driver's license or a job? "That explains the passport." I say, more to myself than to Jack. "I mean, you said yourself she's had a lot of different addresses. Is it possible that it got lost with one of the families she was with when she was young?"

"A paper copy, sure. You could even go as far as to say she never filed an application to replace it cause she didn't know what state she was born in, or that she hasn't really had to worry about it because she is still in school. But what happened to the state record of her?"

"Maybe her name was spelled different?" I try. The truth is that it doesn't make sense, no matter which way you look at it. And if there is no record of Claire Monroe, then who is in my house right now? Who does my sister live with?

"Like I said, half a ghost. I've got a few things to try and still a bunch of boring stuff in the paper trail, but I figured I'd let you know what I'm working with."

"Well, I know you won't fail me."

"If there's something to find, I'll find it." Jack confirms. "Same goes with Tristan Ryan. His phone hasn't turned up anything suspicious yet, but it's only a matter of time. I'll be in touch soon."

I end the call and stare at my phone, trying to process what I've learned. Claire is either an exceptional actress, or completely oblivious. When I first saw her in my room, I erred on the side of caution, assuming she could be a threat. After a short time with her, I decided she wasn't any danger to Rhea. But now that I have a new reason to question her, I find myself wondering whether she may have created her entire persona to try and get something from us.

I can't believe I'm doing it, but Jack planted a seed and I have to follow through. I navigate to Instagram and type her name in the search bar. The first profile that pops up is the exact Claire Monroe I want to get to know, and when I click on her page, I *do* get to know her. Or at least, who she pretends to be.

Claire is a pretty open book, judging by the photo grid I scroll through. Artfully framed photos of the sky and water, close-ups of flowers, pictures of her and Rhea, selfies, and random snapshots of books. I don't have to scroll far to find the swimsuit photos that Jack had mentioned. Of course, I've seen her in something more intimate than a swimsuit and as much as I had enjoyed the view of her under the hot tub waterfall, her bra and panties are certainly sexier. A sense of primal pride surges through me at having seen a side of her that she doesn't share with the public.

I scroll all the way to the bottom of her page, back to when she only seemed to take occasional photos of the sky. And by the time I look up, the sun is gone from the actual sky in front of me. I slip my phone back in my pocket, deciding that I'm not going to learn who she is or what she wants by stalking her online.

After all, she's in the room right next to me.

I pull up the camera feed on the tablet to see that she hasn't touched it at all. Of course, she hasn't. She's low maintenance, afraid to be a bother. I don't know who made her feel that she was one, but it's clearly ingrained in her. I can see it in the way she holds herself, so unsure that she belongs where she is. Even with my sister, the person she says is the closest to her, she doesn't let her guard down. I'm curious to know if she lets it down when she is alone or if she keeps that guard up all the time, a sort of armor protecting her from whatever she doesn't want the world to see... whatever she doesn't want me to see.

Claire hasn't learned yet that I see everything, but she will.

Her hair curtains her face as she leans forward, lost in some thought. I can't get a good look at her to tell if she's feeling any type of way, but she looks stressed, which is a bit odd given that she is supposed to be on vacation. I mean, I whisked her away to a literal paradise and Elaine plied her with delicious food and drinks, and yet she looks like she's got the weight of the world on her shoulders.

I don't know what I expected to find her doing—opening the window for a partner in crime to sneak through? Calling someone to report her status? I'm so jaded that I can't even trust my sister's best friend. And yet, it's not just my suspicion that keeps me watching her as she moves around the room. It's more of a magnetism, an inability to look away.

I listen half-heartedly when my sister brings her a dress and tries to convince her of why she must wear that exact one, scrolling through my sister's social media profiles to try and pick out any instances with Claire in them. Rhea posts a lot—most of the time with her roommate in the frame as well. But for all the posts she has of baking brownies and selfies and 'date nights', nothing in them stands out as suspicious.

After scrolling for what feels like hours, I reach her first post of the year and a photo of them ringing in the New Year with takeout. That's when I decide I've scrolled enough today. My eyes burn with exhaustion and fatigue from the screen, but I set one aside just to pick up another, focusing back on the tablet as Claire strips down to get ready for tonight.

I should shut the screen off and set the tablet aside. I shouldn't be watching her in the first place. But it's not like I'm just trying to get a glimpse of her in her lingerie. I've already had her wearing that right in front of me. Watching through a screen doesn't do the real thing justice. I'm simply watching her to determine whether she is as innocent as she claims—and with a body like that, I don't know how she could be.

This woman was built for sin, and I'm not sure she knows it.

I guess it's up to me to show her.

CHAPTER SIXTEEN

CLAIRE

"This is... interesting." I laugh, watching the people move around us. *Overwhelming* is the word I want to use, but I don't want Rhea to worry about me any more than she usually does, so I'm doing my best not to look like I feel, which is to say I wanna crawl out of my skin.

We rarely go out like this. Other than summers at the shore, we spend our weekends in more chill ways—playing games at bars and drinking in lounges or staying up all night in the living room. And in the summer, when we go to the Piazza to drink and dance, we know nearly everyone in the place, which means that most people don't really bother us.

Noctambulo is massive and busy, and it's more like a rave than a nightclub. I've never actually been to a rave, but I can imagine it's much like this.

There are three floors of bodies packed in like sardines—surely in violation of some maximum occupancy fire code— with the lights swinging and changing colors so rapidly that the ground seems to be moving along with everyone else. There's a bar in every corner of each floor. Shirtless men and women in tight dresses carry around platters of brightly colored drinks, the likes of which I've never seen. The DJ sits at the back of the building, right on the dancefloor, surrounded by eager fans, and the music varies between Latin songs and some of the hits I recognize from back home. The music pulses through the air and into my bloodstream, echoing in my skull where a dull ache is already building.

"I want to dance!" Rhea announces, slamming her empty shot glass on the counter that's already covered with the four empty shot glasses from our first two rounds. I turned down the third round when my stomach started twisting with the contents... or maybe that was just from the look Remy shot me from across the room. "You coming?"

I look around, trying to find an empty space where we'd even be able to stand, let alone dance. "We just got here." I reason, despite the fact that we've been inside for close to twenty minutes and have just gotten our drinks. "Not yet."

"Boo!" Rhea jeers. "Fine. I'm going out there, but I have my phone. I can't hear it, but if you need me, just text me. When you're ready to go, if I haven't found you by then, just tell the DJ to page me. He'll know what it means." She winks and I can't help the laugh that bubbles up in my chest. Of course, she knows the DJ. Even halfway across the world, Rhea knows everyone. "Are you sure you'll be okay?"

"I'll be fine." I promise, swirling the straw in my drink idly and hoping I don't look as utterly out of place as I feel. Rhea didn't approve of anything that I brought to wear, which doesn't offend me considering I packed for a funeral, not a night of dancing. I'm wearing one of her dresses, which is now adhered to my body like a second skin, but it doesn't feel like one. I feel like an impostor, like I'm trying too hard to fit into the lifestyle my best friend thrives in. "I'm just going to take it slow."

Rhea watches me suspiciously as she backs away into the crowd on the dance floor. No sooner has she stepped away than she's swallowed in a sea of gyrating bodies. I turn my eyes back to the bar, watching the lights flash off the bottles in front of me. A long mirror reflects the kaleidoscope of colors, and I have to look away, dizzy.

"Hola."

I turn to find the person that's trying to get my attention. A tall man with a mess of tight black curls grins at me, revealing a lot of shiny white teeth.

"Umm..." I attempt a smile, trying to remember the two semesters of Spanish I took in high school or anything I overhead when I lived with the Santos family, a period of my life that had been nearly as brief as my interest in learning another language. "Hola."

The man seems to sense my hesitancy to speak... surely the accent is a dead giveaway that I'm not from around here. He nods out to the dance floor. "Quieres bailar?"

Shit.

What is that supposed to mean?

I offer him that same sheepish smile and simply shake my head. That's a pretty universal let-down, right? And it can't be misconstrued as rude when I'm smiling.

"Que tal un trago?" He taps his glass and then leans closer, placing a hand on my shoulder and bringing his mouth to my ear so he can be heard over the music, like *that's* the issue in my lack of understanding. He smells like a cross between a spice cabinet and women's hairspray, and I pull away just enough to get a clear breath of air. "Drink?"

I'm tense under his touch, but still, I force a smile and shake my head.

"Apartate."

The voice that breaks through the noise is strong and steady, and it carries an air of authority that sends a shiver through me. Remy has appeared behind the man, brushing his hand off my shoulder as easily as if he were fending someone off from touching his car. His eyes are unreadable, but his shoulders seem stiff, almost like he's irritated about something. The Spanish rolls off of his tongue and though I have no idea what he's saying, his rich and silky voice sends a thrill through me. "Ella vino conmigo."

The man looks at him for a moment and then me as if considering whether it's worth any more effort. I'm grateful when he walks away, shaking his head. "Let's go upstairs," Remy suggests, tipping his head up at the top floor.

I'm not about to argue the chance to get out of here, so I follow him quietly through the crowd to the staircase in the corner of the room. We climb the first flight of stairs with his touch just lingering over the small of my back like he expects me to fall again. I don't, despite the fact that I feel like a newborn deer in these heels. His thumb grazes my back as he pulls me closer to him while we bypass all the dancers and go up the second flight.

The third floor is considerably less crowded and far quieter, thanks to the DJ being stationed two levels below us. I make for the tables in the corner, but Remy catches my hand and tugs me in the opposite direction, toward another, shorter flight of stairs that ends with a single door painted red. "Where are we going?" I ask, looking around to make sure that no one is going to stop us. My heart pounds a little harder as we approach the door with a big black X painted on it and a laminate sign in Spanish. Even though I can't read it, I'm certain we aren't supposed to go through it. But Remy isn't bothered, and so I walk with him, his hand still holding mine, as he pushes the door open. A gust of sweet, warm air hits me in the face as we step out into the night.

Remy grins as I look around, taking in the little fires that burn every few feet around the roof's perimeter. The sky is onyx, broken by little diamond stars scattered about that shine brighter here than anything I've seen back home. It's beautiful and peaceful and clearly not meant for the general public. "I don't think we're supposed to be out here," I say before I can realize that my voice is a whisper.

"Are you scared to break rules, Claire?" Remy teases. His full lips pull into a smirk, and his eyes speak to mischief. Just like how his sister cajoles me into her devious plans, Remington Boudreaux is taunting me into going along with him.

Damn him.

I bite my own lip as I try to chase away thoughts of his.

"I'm not sure *scared* is the word for it. But I do think rules should be respected." I look around us, trying to decide if it's worth the risk of getting into a little trouble to be out here with him... alone. His fingers reach out and gently snare my chin, tilting it so that we're face to face, our lips inches apart.

"Mmm." It's a noncommittal sound, one that could mean almost anything, but it launches a tidal wave in my stomach that threatens to drown me.

"You disagree?" It doesn't surprise me. Remy comes across as someone who prioritizes his own desire over other people's consequences, and he must be corrupting me because right now, my desire to be close to him is winning out. I mean, really, what's the worst they'll do for us being on the roof? Call us trespassers? Ban me from the club I'll never come back to?

"Some rules are meant to be broken." He shrugs. "So, you claim breaking rules doesn't scare you. I think you're lying, but I'll give you the benefit of the doubt. So... what *does* scare you, Claire Monroe?"

I allow myself to study him a moment before answering. The way he says my name sends a thrill through me that is equal parts excitement and fear.

You.

I nearly say it, but instead, I sip the rest of the drink I ordered when we first got here. "Plenty of things." I assure him. "None of which I'm drunk enough to tell you about."

"Well, that's easily remedied." He grins, recognizing my words as a challenge. "What's your drink?"

That's a loaded question, the answer to which depends upon the objective of the night. If I want to get a decent buzz, it's Tequila. If I want to look sophisticated, it'll be a sweet wine. And if I want to throw caution to the wind and live in the moment... "Jack."

Remy blinks, his sooty lashes fluttering over surprised eyes. That dimple in the middle of his cheek appears. "Jack?"

"Yes." I square my shoulders. "Well, with Coke."

"Ah." Remy nods. "Okay, let's get you another drink, and you can tell me more about yourself."

"I don't think so." I laugh. "There's not much to tell."

It's true. I'm a college student with no clue how to make my life matter. I love pizza and pasta and all the carbs. Netflix and Chill is pretty much my entire personality. What about me could possibly interest a worldly, sexy, wealthy guy like Remington Boudreaux?

"I'm sure that's not true." His hand falls away from my face. I've been so captivated by him that I forgot he was holding me hostage with his gentle touch, but I immediately miss it. "I'm intrigued already."

Something about the way he watches me as if there's nothing else in the world to see implies that he is telling the truth. And something about *that* is exhilarating. "Alright." I agree, seeing how I can use this opportunity to my advantage. "If you want to know more about me, let's play a game. You ask me a question, I'll answer. If you think I'm lying, call me on it. If you're right, I'll drink. If you're wrong, you drink."

He considers it a moment and then leans into me just enough so that his scent surrounds me. A hunger that has nothing to do with food stabs me in the gut. "And how will I know you're telling the truth?"

I don't so much as blink. "I suppose you'll just have to trust me."

"Alright, Claire." He smirks. "Challenge accepted. Let's go fill your drink before we get down to business."

We walk side by side back into the bar, where the girl behind it looks surprised to see him. "Mr. Boudreaux." The wings of her eyeliner are perfect, and the long eyelashes she bats at him can't possibly be real. She's gorgeous.

"Jacqueline." Remy smiles at her. "How are you?"

"Bien. Good." She clears her throat, eyes falling on me. "Just the usual?"

"Actually, no. I'll take a whiskey and cola, and a bottle to go. And if you could keep the soda coming, I have a feeling my friend here will be drinking a lot."

Wild heat spills over me at all the implications in that one sentence. Jacqueline nods and turns to set about fixing my drink.

I'm wondering just how well he knows the busty brunette behind the bar when he catches me studying his face. "What?"

"Nothing." I shake my head. "Do you really think we'll be needing the whole bottle?"

"Well, that depends." Remy grins. "How well can you hold your liquor?"

I laugh nervously, and he doesn't press me for anything further. "We're going to take a seat somewhere a little quieter. Was it too warm outside?"

"No..." I say slowly, glancing at the door behind us. It was perfect, actually. "But I still don't think we're allowed to be out there."

"I'm allowed to do whatever I want." Remy winks. Jacqueline turns back toward us and sets a drink down on the bar with one hand, and a nearly full liquor bottle with the other.

"American whiskey?" She teases. "I thought you disliked everything American." Her eyes sparkle almost as much as the glitter on her eyelids as she looks Remy over. I don't fail to notice how she leans onto the bar in an attempt to offer him a view of her cleavage. But Remy isn't interested, and that fact becomes obvious when he hands me my drink and takes the bottle.

"Thank you, Jacqueline."

He turns away too soon to see her disappointment, but I don't. Hell, I can *feel* her disappointment in the air. I mutter a 'thank you' and follow Remy back to the door we weren't supposed to go through and onto the roof I'm pretty sure we weren't supposed to be on.

The rooftop isn't lavishly decorated, but there is a cozy seating area with some wicker furniture and a fire pit in the center of the terrace. Remy sets the bottle of whiskey on the table as he fiddles with the valve on the propane tank. When the fire blooms to life, he turns around to find me still standing, idly rubbing my arm.

"Cold?"

"No." I sigh, breathing in the night air. "Actually, it feels amazing up here."

A gentle breeze rolls off the ocean in the distance, and though it isn't much, it's perfect.

"Good." Remy sits down, letting me decide whether I'll share the couch with him or take one of the chairs opposite him. To his surprise, I choose to share the couch, though I keep a distance between us that is more than I want it to be. "First question, Claire. It's a bit intense. Are you ready?"

I squirm the slightest bit as I adjust myself on the couch, tugging at my skirt to be sure it isn't riding up my thighs. "Okay." I nod, my head spinning with all the things I think he'll choose to ask. "Hit me."

"Alright, Claire." He lets go of a breath like the question he's about to ask me is a doozy. "Is that actually your name?"

I watch him for a moment, trying to decide whether he's serious. And then I laugh. It's a surprised sound, and even though he asked the question, Remy can't help laughing too. "Of course, it is." I tell him. "I mean, what else would it be?"

He shrugs easily. "Clarice, maybe? Or Clarabelle if you're from the South."

I laugh, grateful that I am not from the south. "Clarabelle sounds like what you name the family cow." I tell him between my laughter. "It's just Claire. Well, Claire Elizabeth."

He watches me for a moment, like he's considering calling me on it, and then asks, "And where were you born?"

I tilt my head slightly, trying to figure out his angle. These aren't exactly the type of questions I was expecting. He's playing softball, but I'm not sure if it's for my benefit. I turn my attention to the drink in my hand. "I'm not sure, honestly. The first fosters I remember lived in Spokane, Washington, so I assume I was born somewhere around there."

"Hmm."

"Are you planning to drink straight from the bottle?" I ask, eyeing him suspiciously. Remy reaches into his jacket pocket and pulls out a flask, setting it down next to the bottle.

"I'm not planning to drink a lot." He admits. "I'm a pretty good judge of character, and I'm great at poker."

"Okay," I say. "You're playing chess, and I'm playing checkers. So, here's what we're going to do... you can ask me ten questions, and then it's my turn. You've already burned your first two, so I'll give you a minute to think of something good."

"Okay." He agrees, grinning appreciatively. "Deal. But I don't need a minute. I know my next question. What do you want to be when you grow up?"

I could take offense to the insinuation that I'm not a grown up, but I don't think he intends it that way. "A nurse." I say it without any kind of hesitation, but he knows the moment the word leaves my mouth that it isn't true.

"You're bluffing." He says confidently. Something about that confidence is wildly attractive, stoking a flame in me that I don't think needs any more kindling. "Drink."

I take a sip and wince a little.

Damn, that's strong. "All right. You caught me."

"I wanted the answer. So, I'll ask again. What do you want to be when you grow up?"

"I don't know." I shrug. "I hate to admit that, but it's the truth."

Remy's hazel eyes narrow on me a little. "You're in your final year of college and close to graduating with a degree, but you don't know what you want to do with it?"

"Is that a question, or are you just judging me?"

He's close... so close. One arm rests casually on the couch behind me, and it gives me an opportunity to lean into him a little more.

"Another Coke, sir." Jacqueline sets a glass down on the table in front of us. I break eye contact, turning my focus on the glass in my hands. Remy isn't the one to look away, and I can still feel the weight of his eyes on me even as he speaks to the bartender.

"Thank you, Jacqueline. Would you bring me a shot glass as well?"

"Of course." Jacqueline smiles before she turns on a dangerous-looking stiletto to saunter away. I watch her go and then turn my attention back to Remy, who still hasn't taken his eyes off me. It's both thrilling and terrifying to be looked at like that... like I have something that he wants.

"I'm changing the game again." He explains. "You're far too good with the banter to waste any more time playing on low difficulty."

I don't know whether to take that as a compliment or not. Remy takes advantage of the moment, placing a gentle hand on my cheek again. Adrenaline courses through my veins, spurred on by his touch, which is both gentle and firm and makes me want to melt into a puddle at his feet. My breath hitches.

What the hell is wrong with you, Claire? Get it together, woman!

"I like you, Claire. Let's stop playing children's games and get to what we really want."

Oh, *God*. That isn't helping matters.

His voice, his words, how he says them... it all twines together, causing my core to clench with need.

I know what I want, but I don't know why. I've never felt so drawn to anyone. He's magnetic, and it's terrifying. The man is like the walking embodiment of sex, and I've never wanted it this badly. Can he tell, or does he just assume this is how every woman feels around him? I finally remember that his words were a proposition. *Let's get to what we really want.* "Which is... what, exactly?"

It's a question I want him to answer, but it's also rhetorical.

Jacqueline reappears with a shot glass. I didn't even hear the clicking of her heels as she approached us. "Can I do anything else for you, Mr. Boudreaux?"

"No, thank you. If I need anything, I'll come to you."

Jacqueline nods and makes herself scarce again. Remy's hand slips from my face, one finger brushing over my lips as a grin spreads over his. "You said Jack was your drink of choice. Can you shoot it?"

I square my shoulders and lift my chin. A small voice in the back of my head warns me that he's trying to get me drunk for a reason, but then another voice in my head screams back that it doesn't matter how drunk I get because I'm hopeless against him. I want this... him. "I can do it. The better question is, do you really want to be cleaning vomit out of the back of your car tonight?"

Remy laughs, a genuine sound of amusement. "It's nothing Jovich hasn't done before."

"Fine." I agree. "So, what's your angle?"

"We take turns asking questions now." He explains, twisting the top off the whiskey and filling the shot glass to the brim. "Same rules apply, only now, if I catch you in a lie, you take a shot."

"So, we're doing the same thing except with shots." I laugh, feeling everything I've drank to this point rushing through my veins. "Well, then you're first. You already asked me three, remember?"

"Fine." He shrugs easily. "What do you want to know?"

I shouldn't ask, but I don't even think of censoring myself until after I've already done it. "Have you slept with Jacqueline?"

The smirk that spreads over his face is a bit condescending. "*That's* your big question?"

"She wants you." I reason. "She was practically begging for you to notice her."

"Do you really think that someone I've slept with would call me Mr. Boudreaux?"

That... is a fair point. "Probably not."

"Were you jealous of Jacqueline..." He ventures. "When you thought I'd slept with her?"

"No." I purse my lips, swirling the melting ice around in my glass.

Remy watches me carefully, then holds the whiskey out for me. "I think you're lying."

I eye the shot and then glance up at him. Those beautiful lips are tugged into a smirk. He has me right where he wants me. I clench my thighs together, trying to ignore the ache in me. He has me right where I want to be.

I reach out and toss the shot back in a fluid motion. He's smug and satisfied as I pull a face, take a sip of my cocktail, and then hand the shot glass back to him. Chasing a shot of whiskey with a mixed drink isn't one of my better ideas, but I'll worry about that later.

"So, you haven't slept with Jacqueline, despite her obvious willingness. Why?"

"Not my type." He says it quickly enough that it seems natural, like he didn't have to lie about that.

"Bullshit. I don't think you have a type."

Remy looks like he's going to say something, but he keeps his mouth shut as he pours another shot and then takes this one himself. "Why are you in college if you don't have any clue what you want to do once you get that degree?"

I laugh and reach for the shot glass again. No sooner has Remy filled it, than I reached out and take it, draining the glass without wincing at the burn this time. When I return it to him, the surprise on his face is evident. I can feel the heat rising in my cheeks, the alcohol warming my veins. I feel lighter, and I don't think it's just the liquor talking. Despite the fact that he's clearly trying to get me drunk, he seems to actually be hearing me. He isn't just asking me questions because he wants to fill the silence—he wants to know me. "I'm not going to lie to you, but I don't know the answer myself, so I figured I'll just get ahead of this one."

"By all means." He gestures for me to continue.

"I mean, what do you do when you have no idea what to do with your life?" I laugh and hope it doesn't sound as bitter as it feels. "You buy more time!" I explain, pointing a finger at him as if he was about to say that exact answer. "My last fosters weren't exactly trying to win parents of the year, and I wasn't going to stay with them a day longer than I had to. And I always liked school, college was always the plan. I just thought... I'd figure it out when I got there."

He looks like he wants to laugh, and I'm suddenly aware of how fast the drinks are hitting me. I take a slow breath through my nose while he waits for me to look at him again. Now, he looks more sober than before.

"What was it like... growing up in foster care?"

I didn't expect that one. It hits different, cuts deeper. I know he's curious, but I don't want to talk about the worst days of my life with him, not on what is shaping up to be one of the best nights. "It's *my* turn to ask a question."

"Sure." Remy relaxes into his seat. "We'll circle back to that one."

Well. I guess the kid gloves are off. He may not realize he's hitting below the belt, but if he is going to insist on knowing about something so personal, I'll give him the same. "What do you *really* do, Remy?"

I didn't expect him to ask me about growing up an orphan, and he certainly didn't expect my question. The shock that flits across his face is brief, but it's telling.

"What?"

"For work." I elaborate, even though he knows exactly what I'm getting at.

"You want to know more about venture capitalism?"

I laugh, taking a sip of my drink and then set it on the glass table so that when I lean into him, there's nothing between us. "No, Remy. See, I'm not buying the venture capital bullshit."

CHAPTER SEVENTEEN

REMY

Claire is so close that I'm not sure whether I'm breathing air or her at this point. She fills my lungs, and I don't mind the thought of drowning in her.

"What?" I ask again, but this time I laugh.

"I'm not stupid, Remy." Claire speaks calmly, but her sly smile tells me she thinks she has me in checkmate. "I know there's something more than what you're telling me."

"Is that so?" I humor her. It's hard not to be amused, honestly.

"You're ridiculously rich, you can fly someone into a foreign country without anybody batting an eye, your father was mysteriously murdered, and let's not forget, I was shot at the other day. Two plus two isn't adding up to venture capitalism." She leans in even more, daring me to try and deny what she is so certain of. "I think you're wrapped up in something bigger."

The fire is reflected in her eyes, and it matches the fire in her. I can tell she isn't going to back down. Funny how a few drinks have silenced her outwardly meek persona, letting me catch a glimpse of someone even more intoxicating than I anticipated.

But is it just an act?

People are nosy; I'm used to their suspicions. I constructed my story so carefully that I don't have to concern myself with overlapping lies or getting caught in my own web. I have plenty of prefabricated answers, but I don't want to get into any of them with her. I don't want to talk anymore at all.

She was so self-satisfied, but as I brush a lock of stray hair from her face, that look melts right into desire. It's almost too easy, the way she abandons the fight. "I'm tired of watching your lips. I want to taste them."

She blinks as if she's trying to decide how to take that, but I don't give her the chance to figure it out. I pull her in and brush my lips against hers, slowly at first, waiting to see if she'll react. It takes a second, but she does. She breathes a tiny little sound like surrender, and I inhale it as I crush my mouth against hers.

I've felt a need for her that I don't even understand from the first time I saw her walking around my room in nothing but a bra and those thin panties, a craving I couldn't satisfy, a temptation I couldn't give in to. Wanting her these last few days has driven me nearly as mad as wanting to unravel the mystery that she is, and if she isn't going to stop me, nothing will. I lean into her, and she caves under me, lying back on the couch as though she's been longing for this moment as much as I. I need to taste her lips, the whiskey, and the remnants of whatever lip gloss she put on, her tongue...

A small gasp of excitement escapes her, and it fuels my hunger. I need more... more of her touch, her kiss, her taste. I need to bury myself in her. But I can't tear my lips from hers. As timid as she acts, I hadn't expected much in the kiss. I thought I would lead, and she'd follow, but damn. She's a good kisser, and she isn't quiet about how much she's enjoying herself. Every sigh, every gasp, I take as a sign that she needs exactly what I'm giving her and more. My cock strains against my pants, desperate to be freed, but I'm enjoying the moment too much to speed things up.

"Boss." A deep, throat-clearing sound tears through our bliss, and I lift my eyes to see Jovich standing by the table.

"What the fuck?" I demand, shifting my weight so that she's no longer pinned under me. Claire's face burns so red I can feel the heat coming off her as she sits up, collecting her breath and adjusting the dress that had hiked up beneath me.

"Apologies." He says, looking from me to Claire and back again. "We have a business emergency that requires your attention."

I scrutinize his face. What kind of emergency can't wait until I'm not in the middle of *this*?

"Is everything okay?" Claire asks, worry coloring her voice as she sits up, smoothing her hair and dress. Her skin is that delicious shade of pink, and I'm not sure whether it's from the heat between us or the embarrassment of being caught. "Rhea?"

"Rhea's fine. It's just a... private matter." Jovich shrugs one shoulder like it's no big deal, but it has to be if he's standing here. He may not be my most intelligent ally, but even he knows better than to bother me for no good reason, particularly in such circumstances.

I have half a mind to tell him to go downstairs so that Claire and I can finish what we started. But looking at her, I can tell the mood has been ruined. Besides, I don't want to fuck her on a couch and run right away. It's not that I want to spoon or anything but fucking her on the rooftop lounge and then disappearing probably wouldn't be the best look. She's here another week still. I don't want to get her emotions tangled up in all this or potentially complicate things any more than they already are. I don't want her getting attached.

"I'm sorry," I tell her sincerely. "Would you like me to walk you back downstairs? I can help you find Rhea."

She shakes her head as immediately as I offer the help. "I'll be fine. I'm just going to take a minute, here." Claire musters a smile.

As we slip into the club, frustration surges through me, dampening my desire. "It had better be important, Jovich," I say, not bothering to hide the bitter edge in my voice. I turn to Rook, the thick-muscled bouncer who watches over the third floor. "There's a woman out there. VIP. See to it that she's well taken care of."

Rook nods his understanding. I turn my eyes on Jovich, ready to know what is so damn pressing that he had to interrupt me in the middle of that.

Jovich is grinning just the slightest bit, but he suppresses it as he speaks. "We've got the Russian."

"Here?" I glance around as if Jovich is stupid enough to march him through my club. To be fair, Jovich is pretty stupid, but even he knows better than that.

He laughs and licks his lips. "Dimitri will take you to him. He should fold pretty easily... I warmed him up for you."

"Watch the girls," I command. "I don't want them out of your sight. And don't let them bring anyone home."

"Of course."

I clap him on the shoulder and make for the corner, buttoning my suit jacket and taking the steps two at a time as I descend the stairs. I take the door that leads out into the back alley. Dimitri is waiting at the curb in a nondescript black car, and before I get in, I turn back and look up at the roof.

Claire can't see me, but I can see her. The moon hangs full and low behind her, illuminating her just enough that I can see her silhouette as she paces back and forth. I can't make out any kind of facial expressions, but as she leans over the railing, she seems to be trying to let go of her frustration.

That makes two of us.

CHAPTER EIGHTEEN

CLAIRE

Remy disappears entirely after that. No matter how many covert glances I toss around, I don't spot him again. I do, however, notice Jovich watching me rather intently. Loyal though he is, something about Jovich doesn't sit right with me. It's an intuitive feeling of unease that I can't shake. Perhaps it has to do with the fact that I'm sure he's killed people as effortlessly as I dress in the mornings. Or perhaps it is just that he doesn't trust me, so I don't trust him. Whatever it is, it leaves me on edge.

To be fair, even Remy seemed to doubt my intentions when we'd first met. It's sad that nobody can trust that I might actually be a real friend to Rhea without an ulterior motive. But then again, we are halfway across the world to attend their father's funeral. In the three years that we've been friends, I never met Rhea's father. That tells me all that I need to know about the Boudreaux family.

Rhea can't shake Jovich's prying eyes the rest of the night, either, until we make it back to the house and he strides away to answer a phone call. I turn to Rhea and sigh my relief. "Is it just me or was he *extra* overbearing tonight?"

Rhea laughs, tilting her hair back so that her multi-colored curls tumble down her back. The caramel pieces catch the light. "It isn't just you. I think Remy told him to make sure we didn't bring anyone home."

I roll my eyes. "He doesn't have to worry about that."

"No." Rhea agrees, studying my face. She purses her lips thoughtfully. "But should I?"

"Should you what?"

"Be worried about you."

I bite my lip with the sneaking suspicion that I know where this is going. But I can't admit as much, even if Rhea will call me on it. "I don't know what you mean."

She appraises me coolly, and then turns away, leaving me to watch her a moment before I catch up. Rhea turns into the kitchen and opens the refrigerator while I climb, none-too-gracefully, onto one of the barstools. When she turns back and sets two bottles out on the counter, the look on her face says it all. "I noticed you disappeared for a while tonight... with Remy."

Even having this conversation with my best friend doesn't stop me from turning red as I realize what she's getting at. I try to play it off, shrugging. "And?"

"And that's got 'bad idea' written all over it." She twists her bottle open and tips it back for a long moment before facing me again. "I love my brother, but he is not good for you."

"I'm not looking for 'good for me'. I'm not looking for anything." I shrug again, hoping to sell her on my indifference. But that's a lie. That kiss left me looking for a whole lot more.

"Remy is not your type." Rhea warns. "And for that matter, you aren't his type either."

"I have a type?" I muse. "Do tell."

Rhea shrugs like she's giving me a hard truth. "Your type is the smart and driven humanitarian. The good to the core, wholesome, 'just wants to love and be loved' type. Like Wes."

I laugh. I'd nearly forgotten about Wes. With his charm, good looks, and manners, Wes probably *is* my type. We only met once, and who's to say what may have come from it? I'd planned to see him again until Remy had sneaked up on me and erased all thoughts of other men from my mind. "Wes." I repeat, trying to keep a straight face. "Is this about Ryan? You want to date best friends, don't you?"

"Ugh." Rhea shudders in disgust. "I do not want anything to do with Tristan Ryan, and now that we're here and I'll likely never see him again, I don't have to coddle his feelings. Which is great, because I met someone tonight, actually."

"Why am I not surprised?" I laugh, wondering how she could have fallen for someone in less than three hours. And yet, I'm not sure I've been able to put thoughts of Remy out of my head since we met the other night, so who am I to judge?

"Because you know me better than I do." She smiles. "And I know you better than you think I do. Please, Claire, just... be careful with my brother."

"I won't hurt him." I tease. "Besides, you said it yourself: I'm not his type."

"You're too pure." Rhea agrees, nodding. "And that's a compliment, my friend."

"If you say so." I focus on peeling at the label on my drink, trying to force all thoughts of Remington Boudreaux out of my mind. "I'm going to try to walk off this buzz. You coming?"

"Hell no. I'm not buzzed enough." As if to illustrate her point, Rhea tips the bottle back again and drains it in a fluid motion. "You have fun, though."

I finish my drink too, and then stand. Jovich rounds the corner as I'm just about to slip out the back door. "Going somewhere?" He asks, eyeing me shrewdly. His large shoulders shroud out the light from the hall behind him, and his face is cast in shadows. If I was wary of him before, I'm even more nervous now.

"A walk." I swallow, gesturing to the door. "Along the beach, if that's okay."

He watches me silently at first, and then finally he nods as if I needed his permission. Honestly, I'm not entirely certain that I don't. I thought I was a guest, but the way Jovich seems so suspicious of me and the way Elaine had regarded me so coldly, I have to wonder if I really am.

I can feel Jovich watching me, his eyes following me into the night, and try not to be bothered by it. I'm in paradise with my best friend and a devastatingly handsome man who has shown a modicum of interest in me. But am I simply falling into the trap that is Remington Boudreaux? I know next to nothing about him except that he kisses me like it's both my first and last kiss... equal parts tentative, respectful, and so deeply passionate that it lights me on fire with need.

Rhea seems to think I'm not capable of standing on my own. I don't fault her for it. We are always truthful with one another, even if that means being blatantly honest at times, and with how heavily we rely upon one another, she's probably just being overprotective. Rhea clearly doesn't hold an esteemed view of her brother's character when it comes to his love life.

But at the same time, I'm an adult capable of making my own decisions. Hell, I'm old enough to drink and smoke if I want to and travel across the world on a moment's notice because, apparently, those are the kind of people I know. Surely that means I am capable of choosing for myself where I want things to go with Remy.

I sigh, realizing that I've gotten ahead of myself. One kiss doesn't mean anything, even if I did feel that kiss all the way down to my toes. Rhea kisses plenty of people, even our old roommates. To some people, a kiss is just that. It doesn't mean that Remy necessarily even wants anything more from me. He effectively disappeared after that kiss, and given that Jovich is intent on tailing me instead of attending to his boss, there's a good possibility he is with someone else right now.

I turn my eyes to the horizon, so dark it's indistinguishable from the sea lying still below it. The moon is nowhere to be seen, and suddenly the darkness seems stifling. When I turn back toward the house, I realize I walked further than I thought. The house lights are just faint pinpricks against the darkness of the jungle behind it.

A breeze ripples through the air, shaking the treetops. I shiver too, but not because of the cold. The distinct feeling of being watched has crept up my spine and chased goosebumps down the backs of my arms. A quick glance around reveals what I expected...

I'm entirely alone out here. Which means Jovich is probably still watching me from the house.

I wait a minute, frozen in time, to see if the feeling dissipates. But it only grows stronger and stronger, until I find myself running back to the safety of the house.

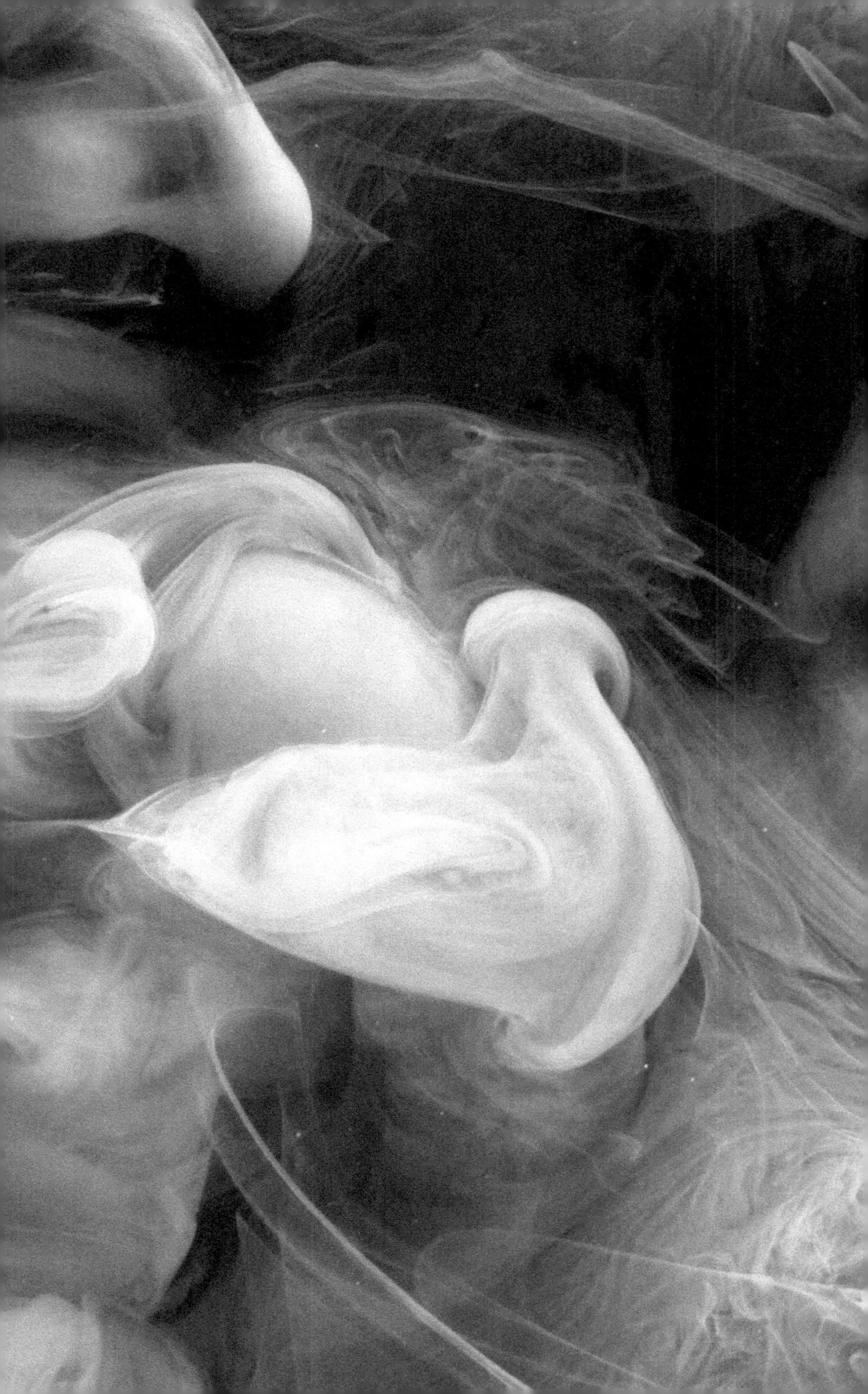

Chapter Nineteen

Remy

"You look a bit pale, Anton." I tilt my head to get a better view of the man bound to the chair before me. His skin is always stark white in contrast to his greasy black hair, but especially with the blood loss, he doesn't look good.

Anton is just one in a long line of people who had bad blood with my father. I've seen that chubby, ghostly face in countless photos, always attached to whatever his newest demands are. Anton thought he was untouchable because his uncle was my father's closest ally. Something tells me he just figured out what I learned years ago:

Nobody is untouchable in this business.

"How are you feeling?" It actually sounds like I care. The thought chills me more than the hatred in his eyes. I'm not supposed to have feelings. Those will only make everything so much more complicated. I've done a good job staving them off for years, and I definitely don't care about Anton.

"*Mu-dak*!" Anton spits, but he's so exhausted it doesn't go far. It just mixes in with the blood slowly dribbling down his chin.

Pathetic.

"I'm glad you're well." I tell him calmly. "Because I have all night. I'm not sure I can say the same for you."

That is true on both accounts. I don't want to be here—the alternative was far more appealing. But the moment has passed, and I won't get it back tonight, so I may as well take my time sourcing the information I want.

"Bastard." His waxy face crumbles in disgust and rage. He knows that, unlike me, he doesn't have all night. Jovich toyed with him before me, and though I can't know the extent of what he did to him, I know that without medical intervention, he has at most a few hours left before there will be more blood on the floor than in his body.

"The apple doesn't fall far from the tree, I'm afraid." I shrug. "Speaking of... are you going to tell me who killed my father or are we going to go another round?"

The chair strains against the metal bolts that secure it to the floor, trembling with the force of Anton's fury as he growls. He looks like he's being electrified... or possessed. He shakes and slams his head forward until finally he stills enough to grin up at me through a curtain of dark hair that's limp with grease and sweat. "I don't know who did it, but they deserve a goddamn medal!"

My eyes flicker down to Anton's, dark as a starless night and full of hatred. They're the kind of eyes that I imagine a demon would possess. Jonathan Boudreaux hadn't been a good man. In fact, I quite agree with the Russian's assessment of my dear old dad. But I can't very well let Anton know as much. So, I sigh and shake my head sadly. I really didn't want to be pulled away from Claire to do this, but my need for answers outweighs my own selfish desires.

"Alright. You want to do this the hard way." I turn around, giving him half a moment to reconsider his answer before I back and punch Anton right in the nose.

Even with using half of my energy, Anton's head jerks back with the force. Blood flies through the air, covering my knuckles. When he readies himself again, his thin lips are pulled into a snarl. "You hit like a woman." Despite that sentiment, he spits blood on the floor, and I notice the front tooth that had been there a moment ago is now missing. Guess he swallowed it.

"So, you don't want to tell me who killed my father." That's fine. That is honestly the least of my problems. "Let's talk about the call I got a couple nights ago."

"A call *girl*?" Anton laughs gruffly. "Surely a ball-less pig like you must resort to throwing money at whores for attention."

I blink, wondering if we've somehow caused brain damage. It's not even a good insult, or a good joke. Even if it wasn't a pathetic attempt at riling me up, I've gotten fairly adept at controlling my temper. It takes a good bit of damage to get under my skin, and that kind of damage doesn't come from insulting me. That's one key difference between myself and my father. I can take the hits just as well as I can dish them out.

"Did you call me and threaten my sister?"

"Your sister?" Anton laughs again. "You think I have any interest in that spoiled bitch?"

I turn my back on Anton again, confident that he isn't going anywhere. He poses no threat in my domain. Here, he is whatever I say he is. Here, he is nothing.

I assess the small armory that Jovich has laid out for me, my eyes trailing carefully over the weapons.

Brass knuckles, a pistol, knives and scalpels, a dirty cloth and a five-gallon jug of water I could pour over his face with a cloth over his mouth to make him feel like he's drowning. A car battery sits on the ground between his legs, the cables clamped on top as an electric hum emanates from them. Jovich is my most fierce employee, but he's always a little too eager to jump to torture, which is why I suspect he got along with my father so well. The two of them probably bonded over the deviant joy they got out of seeking revenge.

I don't enjoy it. Like everything else I do, it's simply a means to an end. But it doesn't hurt to keep up appearances.

"You may want to mind your tongue." I turn back to face him, dragging a finger over the edge of a large, curved blade. "If you have nothing useful to say, I might consider cutting it out."

"Fuck off!" Anton growls.

"Hmm." I muse. "Not useful."

I gauge Anton's reaction, but when the man offers me nothing, I lunge at him. The knife bites into his throat in the next second.

Anton strains against the chair, but I press him further into it so that he sits trapped between the stiff wood and the shiny tip of the wicked blade. My experience with the Russians has proven that they are anything but weak; They don't often relent. And as Anton looks back at me, mirroring my abject hatred of him, it's apparent that he doesn't think I'll follow through on my threat.

I've gotten far on my enemies underestimating me. "Who killed my father?"

Anton stares defiance at me, his black eyes seething.

"Alright." I concede. "Tell you what? You tell me who killed my father *or* who threatened my sister. I'll accept an answer for either. And if you give me something useful, I'll call my guy right now and tell him to go home for the night. I'm sure he'd be thrilled not to have to watch another minute of children chasing around a football."

The shift is almost imperceptible. Despite his foul temper, Anton is a master poker player. He made a good chunk of his money, swindling anyone who would sit down long enough to get hustled by him. But I notice how his shoulders stiffen, and his chest swells with a breath he's straining to control. "What are you saying?"

"Katya has football on Fridays, remember? If the team wins, they'll celebrate at that little café with the kettle on the sign. I'd butcher the pronunciation," I laugh. "but loosely translated, I think it means... the Copper Kettle?"

Terror is a funny look on him, but mostly because it means he *does* have a heart. Even the toughest man is only as strong as his weakness, and his is a six-year old with straight black hair and two missing front teeth.

"You're bluffing."

"No." I shake my head. "I've done my research. My team provides me with *very* thorough reports. Katya's favorite ice cream... it's pistachio, right?" I laugh again, shaking my head. "What kid likes pistachio ice cream?"

If it's possible, Anton pales even more. I can practically see the wheels in his mind turning. He's wondering what the chances are that I would know all of that if I *don't* have somebody tailing his niece?

"You don't look convinced." I furrow my brow at him, mimicking the look of disbelief on his face. "I can have Michael snap a picture of them if you want. I mean, if he can take his hands off Irina long enough. He has said she is quite the insatiable lover." I give him a minute to let the thought of another man touching his sister-in-law take root. He's probably already seeing another hand trace her curves, imagining another man doing the things he's done, erasing him from her mind with every stroke. "But you know all about that, don't you?"

"I'll kill you." He growls, rocking the chair so hard that it grates against the floor. I had hoped not to have to go this route, to avoid bringing innocents into his mess, but if this is the only way to make him sing, then the show must go on.

"You'll never have the chance. Your poor Irina. First, she loses her husband, and now she'll either have to watch her kid die or hear that her new lover—her brother-in-law—is dead too. So much loss for someone so young. But don't worry. Michael is taking very good care of her... and your daughter."

A vein throbs in Anton's now-translucent skin. Sweat that was beading on his forehead now rolls down his cheeks. He looks like he'll be sick. "I don't know about the call." He says. "I don't go after women or children, Boudreaux. Only cowards do."

"A hitman with morals?" I laugh. "Sure. Keep talking."

"And I don't know who killed your father, but I can tell you this. He was in massive debt. Like, all of your houses and cars and private jets combined kind of debt."

"And?"

"Alexei Nyanik. He holds your father's debt. If anyone had motive to kill the bastard, it's Nyanik."

That isn't news to me. Alexei Nyanik made his fortune by loaning money to low-life criminals he knows will never be able to pay it back. When it comes time to collect the bill, men and women both will do whatever they have to in order for him to spare them their miserable lives. He collects the women he favors as playthings and uses the worthy men as assassins. At one point, he was my father's biggest adversary. I could see him loaning money to my father just so that he could own him, but there's no world in which I can see my father swallowing his pride to ask Nyanik for help in the first place.

Nyanik is on my list, but I have to rule out all of the pathetic bottom feeders under him first.

"That tongue of yours has proven useful after all." I roll my shoulders, flexing the blade in my hand as I consider it a long moment before returning it to the table that I collected it from. I slip my phone out of my pocket and hit my first speed dial.

Jovich answers immediately.

"No!" Anton yells, thrashing as best he can. He strains against the rope that binds him to no avail, but that doesn't stop him from trying to break free. He whips around like an animal in a cage fighting for its life. "I told you what I know! Let them go!"

I face him with a coolly practiced apathy. "Our friend will take the first flight back to Serbia. If he's lucky, maybe he'll make it back in time."

I leave it at that, letting Anton use his imagination to figure out what sort of atrocities I'm capable of when crossed. He's despicable, so naturally, his mind goes to a dark place. I can see the panic light in his eyes, his entire body tense.

"Consider it done." Jovich says just before I hang up on him.

With no further use for him, I leave Anton tied up and waiting on Jovich to come free him.

"Bastard!" His screams follow me through the warehouse. I don't bother gagging him again—Jovich will be here before he can scream himself hoarse. And no one is around to hear him anyway. "You said you'd not harm them if I told you what I know!"

"I said *I* wouldn't harm them." I agree. "I never made any promises of my men."

I'm at the door by the time I turn back to take him in. He looks so small and weak against the vastly empty warehouse. Some men have nothing to lose, and they'd die simply to spite me. Most of them are just overblown bullies. Once I find their weakness, I just have to apply the perfect amount of pressure. Then they'll crumble and break. Whether or not I'm successful in breaking a man depends entirely on how much time I'm willing to commit to them. Learning their vulnerabilities, getting in their head, chipping away at their façade to find the chink in their armor. Everyone has a weakness, whether it be love or money or power. Researching my victims isn't usually something I rush, but I'm grateful that Anton was so easy. I have far better things to do.

"Go to them." I tell him without finding his eyes. "If they're still alive when you make it home, take it as your one and only warning shot. If they aren't..." I shrug. "Come find me and settle your debt."

A string of profanity that slips back and forth between Russian and English follows me out the door as Anton screams and growls and barks baseless threats. I let the door close, cordoning off his rage as I step into the cool cover of night. The faint sound of waves crashing in the distance soothes my soul. The tide is coming in. I allow myself a minute to breathe it in and then swipe the screen of my phone open again.

On the other end, Michael sounds bored when he answers. I hear papers rustling as if he's flipping through a newspaper. I can practically picture him, sitting in his car thumbing through the Serbian Scribe, bored out of his mind. "What's up?"

"Jovich will have Anton on the red eye within the hour. How are the girls?"

"Sleeping. Safe."

I sigh quietly enough so that he can't hear me on the other end of the line. "Good. Keep them that way."

"Will do." Michael promises.

I disconnect the call and stuff the phone into my pocket. Anton wasn't hard to crack, but I've been gone for longer than I wanted. The thought of Rhea and Claire in the house without me isn't appealing. Jovich won't leave until I return home, and I know he wouldn't let anything happen under his watch, but it doesn't mean that I'm comfortable with the situation. At the end of the day, there's no one I trust as much as myself. For years, I've had to make the hard decisions. I've had to be the one to do things that I wanted no part in. And in spite of the loyalty they offer, the men who work for me are only bound to me by the cash that I pay them.

I'm not keen on violence, but that doesn't mean I'm opposed to it. All is fair in war, particularly when you've been attacked first. But Anton is prideful; he would likely have died before revealing anything if it was only himself that he had to worry about. That's why, when my father died, I sent Michael to keep an eye on Anton's family.

I'd never greenlight violence against a child, much less murder. But Anton doesn't know that I have come as far as I have because I've worked tirelessly to create an illusion that I don't care about anything. It's an illusion that I was starting to believe; It's why I kept Rhea at a distance for so long.

Shit.

Rhea.

Sunrise is tugging at the darkness on the horizon, which means I have to hurry back to the house and change before my sister or her enchanting friend can catch me sneaking in wearing last night's blood-spattered clothes. I slide into the passenger seat, and Dimitri passes me a towel that I use to wipe the excess blood off my knuckles. It doesn't all belong to Anton. Some of the blood came from my own skin splitting as I pummeled him mercilessly.

"Do you need me to come back and clean up?" Dimitri asks without looking at me. I know what he really means.

Do you need me to dispose of a body?

"No." I stare out the window at the receding form of the warehouse as he puts the car in reverse. "Jovich will handle it."

The warehouse has been in my family as long as the house has, though most people would never know it. My family owns nearly half of the land that the country was built on, including that old building. It was once a textile company—or so the sign used to say. The company declared bankruptcy after a fire that insurance wouldn't cover, and it's been abandoned since. Only the workers ever even knew it was there, and by now, they must all be dead... of old age or curiosity.

Plenty of sordid things have happened in those dirty walls, and the things I've done have been the least of it. Sometimes people die. Dimitri has taken it as his job to clean up the aftermath. He's a problem solver, whether it's dismantling their car so that it's never traced to any of my properties or scrubbing the evidence. He has a knack for making an entire person disappear... not just physically, but their entire cyber footprint.

In the wrong hands, Dimitri is a man to be feared. I know people capable of the same thing, though they use it for far more despicable means.

His place in my company is to be respected. I trust him just as much as Jovich, who has been with my family for decades now. "There is someone that we need to get our hands on, and when we do, the fallout will be cataclysmic."

"Oh?" Dimitri perks up, intrigued.

"Alexei Nyanik," I say, and a low whistle escapes Dimitri's teeth.

"Do you go looking for trouble, Boudreaux?" He laughs. "Or does it just come find you?"

I've been asking myself the same question for most of my life.

I have eventually come to accept that the Boudreaux name is just synonymous with trouble.

CHAPTER TWENTY

CLAIRE

I practically have to drag myself to the shower in the morning. I slept like the dead, which is absolutely not a common occurrence for me. Maybe it's still the jet lag catching up to me or the remnants of an Ambien haze, or the drinks I had. Or maybe it's the fact that the bed is just so damn comfortable I want to sink into it and never leave. Whatever the reason, I don't appreciate the feeling of being so hungover until steam fills the bathroom.

I shower, exfoliate, and shave with all the fancy unopened bottles in the shower, and when I'm done, I feel not just alive—I feel *good*. I smell good, too.

It's still reasonably early, so I take the time to wrap a luxurious towel around me like a dress while I dry my hair and check my phone. When I've wasted as much time as I reasonably can, I get dressed and go downstairs. My reflection in the hallway mirror assures me that I look pretty good too.

When I get to the kitchen, Elaine stands at the sink, fixing a vase of flowers. She straightens upon realizing she isn't alone.

"Good morning!" She smiles brightly at me and then turns to the cupboard, where she produces a coffee mug. "Sit down! I'll make breakfast."

"Oh," I shake my head automatically. "You don't have to do that."

"Please." She laughs. "I'm dying for something to do."

I appraise her for any sign that she really doesn't want to do anything for me, but she looks genuine. "Okay," I agree hesitantly.

sliding onto the barstool as Elaine sets the coffee neatly in front of me.

"French vanilla or hazelnut for your coffee, dear?"

Dear?

Yesterday, I'd have bet money that this woman doesn't like me. The sudden shift in her demeanor is more than a little jarring. Then again, I guess a bit of social anxiety means I'm always worried that people don't like me. Maybe Elaine just hadn't been in the mood yesterday to get to know someone new. Either way, something about her smile as she watches me from over her shoulder while she waits for a response is endearing... almost motherly. "Hazelnut, please."

She hands me the bottle immediately, as if she knew that would be the one that I chose. Her eyes shine with some sort of amusement, like *hazelnut* is a funny answer. "You look beautiful and rested."

I don't miss the compliment; It takes me by such surprise that I don't even address it. "I slept really well, actually."

"Good." Elaine sets about pulling ingredients together as if she's done this a million times, unbothered by my lack of gratitude at her compliment. Her hair is pulled back into a ponytail, which makes her look a bit younger than she did yesterday. She can't be more than forty, and she barely looks a day above thirty. Weird that she has worked for the Boudreaux's so long.

"So, did you have fun last night? I know Rhea was looking forward to it."

I lift the mug to my lips, hoping that will keep my face from giving me away. Rhea always says she can read me like an open book, but is it just because she knows me so well? Or is that because I am notoriously bad about wearing my heart on my sleeve?

Elaine glances up from the tomato she's dicing, and I realize I haven't answered her.

Did I have fun?

Sure. Kissing Remy was certainly not boring. But agonizing over what it means certainly *isn't* fun.

"It was nice." I smile awkwardly, hoping she won't press me for any more details. "Are you sure I can't help you with breakfast?"

"Oh, please. You're a sweet girl, Claire, but no. I usually only get to prepare meals for Mr. Boudreaux. Eggs, coffee, toast, sometimes bacon." She rolls her eyes and then laughs. "He's so boring."

"Who's boring?" Remy's deep voice is a new addition to the conversation, causing me to jump. I didn't hear him come in, let alone sidle up right next to me. He leans his elbows on the counter and Elaine bats him away from her workspace.

"Shoo!" She demands, pointing the knife at him as if she means a threat. But the teasing expression on her face betrays her.

"Fine. I'll pour my own coffee." Remy turns and grabs a mug from the cupboard. His shirt is fitted enough that I can see the hard ridges of his muscles hidden beneath the fabric. His hair is swept back into a perfectly tousled mess that I want to run my fingers through. When he turns back toward us, he's grinning. "What do I even pay you for?"

If Elaine hadn't laughed, I may have missed the joke.

"You pay me to be your friend." She fires back. "I just cook, clean, and deal with all of your affairs because I pity you."

Remy arches an eyebrow, and I'm not entirely sure that one *is* a joke. "Touché."

"You look tired." Elaine says innocently, glancing up at him from below her eyelashes.

"I am." He shrugs. "I didn't get much sleep."

I take a sip of my coffee, trying to avoid catching his eye, and nearly choke on it when a woman saunters into the kitchen, wrapped in one of Remy's crisp white sheets. She doesn't appear the least bit concerned to see us all standing there. Her eyes even light up as they fall on Remy.

"Ah! Coffee!" She sighs and reaches for the cup Remy has been holding. Without even waiting for it to cool, she presses it to her lips and takes a long sip, her shoulders slumping in relief as the taste soothes something for her.

The feeling of disappointment that nestles in my stomach is entirely unfounded, but that doesn't stop it from being there. It also doesn't stop the heat of embarrassment that washes over me or keep my heart from racing like it's about to break free from my chest and run all the way back home.

It was only a kiss.

But after sharing that with him, I didn't expect Remy to bring another girl home.

I try not to look at her, but I can't focus my eyes anywhere else. She is beautiful... tall and tanned with wild chestnut curls that are perfectly rumpled up from an apparently adventurous night. Some women ooze sex appeal, while others try to hide their insecurities by having exactly *zero* sex appeal. This woman is the former, I am the latter.

As if realizing everyone is watching her, the woman looks between us all and then back to Remy. "You don't mind, do you?" Her voice is thick with an accent, sultry and seductive. I can't blame Remy when even I am spellbound by her.

Remy opens his mouth as though he's about to say something, but he doesn't get a chance because Rhea turns the corner and cuts off whatever words had been on his lips. "I thought I told you to stay in bed."

Having no memory of any such conversation, I frown and open my mouth to tell her as much. But it quickly becomes apparent that she isn't talking to me anyway. "I smelled coffee." The stranger pouts as if she's being chastised, but when Rhea snakes an arm around her waist and pulls her in, the pouty lips turn to a kiss. "I'll go back to bed now." She smiles around the room in parting and then ducks out of the kitchen, taking Remy's coffee cup with her.

In her wake, Rhea is the center of attention, which is where she loves to be most. "What?"

"I thought I told you not to bring anyone home?" Remy says, glancing down the hall to make sure the guest is out of earshot.

"Hmm." Rhea helps herself to the coffee and then turns around to shrug at him. "Actually, you said not to bring a *man* home. I didn't."

Unable to help myself, I laugh. I'm torn between amusement at Rhea's loophole and relief that it wasn't that curvy brunette keeping Remy up all night.

"Will you be okay on your own for a bit?" Rhea asks, managing to grin while also looking apologetic about abandoning me. "Teresa has to work in a few hours and I wanna make the most of it."

"I'll be fine." I assure her. "Don't worry about me."

Rhea's liner-smudged eyes flick to Remy and then back to me. "Are you sure?"

"Go." I wave a hand. "Knock yourself out."

"Thank you! Love you!" Rhea blows a kiss over her shoulder and skips down the hall.

Before any of us even have a chance to react, the doorbell rings, drawing us all out of our stunned silence. Elaine shakes her head, wiping her hands on her apron. But I see the wry smile on her face as she walks away to answer the door. That leaves Remy and I to catch each other's eye.

"I thought she just walked in off the street." Remy laughs, clearly too stunned to say much else.

I can't keep myself from laughing, too. I want to tell him I'd assumed she was his lover for the night, but I don't want to show my hand. He doesn't need to know that I've been obsessing over what he was doing from the moment his warm body had moved away from mine last night. Better to let him think I haven't thought about him at all.

"I want to say that I'm surprised, but I guess if I'm being honest, I'm not." I shake my head. "I mean, Rhea's got a lot of love to give."

"I thought she may have been in love with you." Remy's eyes hold mine, gauging my reaction.

He isn't prepared for the fit of giggles that I dissolve into. A smirk creeps into the corner of his lips.

I can't help it. Rhea and I definitely love one another, but nowhere near a sexual way. We're too much like family.

When I regain my composure, it's just enough to ask, "Why would you think that?"

"I just had to be sure." He shrugs, casual, but his eyes are shining playfully when Elaine sets the package on the counter. "So, what did Rhea have on the itinerary for today?"

"Let me see..." I flip to the photos in my phone, where I'd taken a snapshot of Rhea's master plan. "Uh," I try to sort the days out in my head. "It looks like we were supposed to go shopping."

Remy makes a face that matches how I feel. I *do* still need clothes if I'm going to be here for the next week, but I'm not going alone, and the thought of Remy following me through racks of dresses and tops is unappealing. The idea of Jovich stalking through the store in my wake is even more unsavory.

"I'll probably just lay by the pool, maybe go down to the beach, if that's okay?"

He glances up at me from where he has slit the tape on the package. Elaine yells something about him leaving her knives alone and that they have letter openers in the office, but Remy ignores her. "Sounds great. Actually, the best beach bar in the entire Western Hemisphere isn't far from here. They have live music and cheap margaritas. I'd be happy to escort you."

I bite my lip, considering it. I finally feel alive for the first time since we left the States. Do I really want to squander it laying by the pool? I want to do *something*, and I want to be near Remy, so why not? "Okay." I say it quickly, before I can change my mind, and then drop my head to hide the smile creeping across my lips.

Elaine sets a plate in front of me, laden with all sorts of colorful foods I don't recognize. I thank her and watch Remy survey the contents of the box he's just opened. But his face gives nothing away, and he closes the box again, resting his arms on it as he looks across the counter at me. "How do you like it?" He gestures to the untouched plate before me.

I cut off a small bite, wait a second for the steam to subside, and then lift it to my mouth. His eyes are so intent on my mouth that it makes me uncomfortable, but not in a bad way. How am I supposed to eat with him watching me, sending a thrill through me that I still don't understand?

"It's amazing." I answer honestly. He watches me without moving, without blinking. I see the flicker of a smile play on Elaine's face as she sets about making Remy's breakfast.

The silence feels heavy. "So," I clear my throat. "What time were you thinking?"

Remy straightens and tucks the package under one arm. "Maybe about an hour or so. That'll give us both time to get ready."

Without anything else, he sweeps out of the room, leaving me to stare at the plate of food Elaine prepared, and leaving Elaine to stare at me while I pretend not to notice.

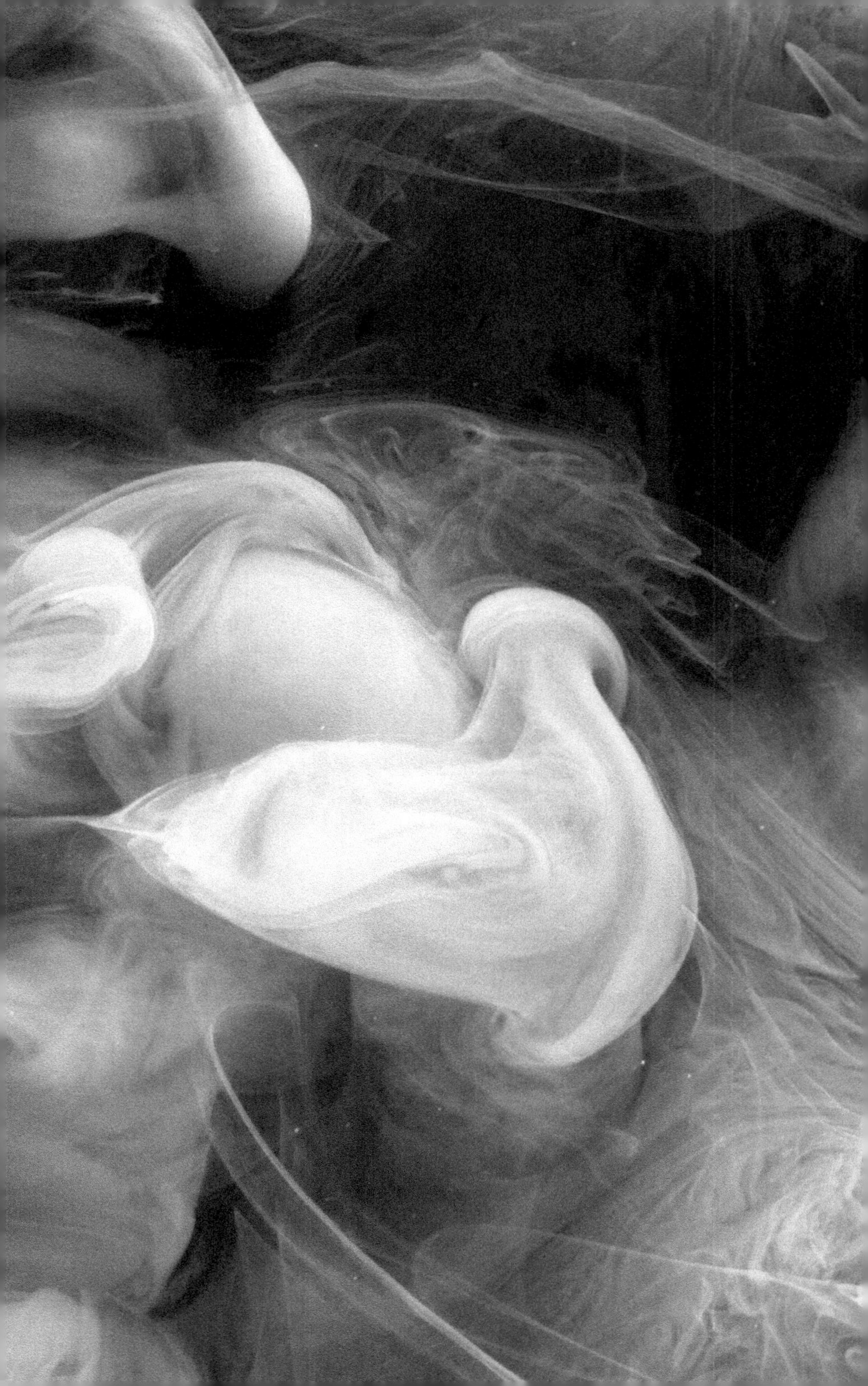

CHAPTER TWENTY-ONE

REMY

"There's no return address?" Jovich muses, rubbing the straggly hair on his chin.

"No shipping address either. Whoever this package is from, they hand delivered it." I had successfully hidden my anger in front of Claire and Elaine, but I'm not holding anything back from Jovich. His eyes flicker from my face to the box, and when he opens it, his expression darkens.

"Sort of a big box for one measly bullet." He reaches in and grabs the little piece of metal, holding it up to the light and squinting. "9-millimeter luger."

"The same bullet I used against whoever shot at Claire back in the States." Jovich narrows his eyes on me in an unspoken question.

He doesn't have to say what he's thinking. In all the time he's known me, I've never been wild about guns. There are other methods of doing a job that are cleaner, easier, more personal. "It was in my mother's nightstand."

That, at least, makes sense. Jovich makes a noise of understanding. "So, whoever sent you this package knows where you live. Not exactly a surprise."

"No." I agree. I don't have my address listed in public records, but it's not like it would be hard to figure it out. "I want to see the security footage from the front door. Whoever brought that box up to the door is either an idiot, or they didn't know what was in there."

"Sure." Jovich says. "I'll have Dimitri pull up the feed and send it to you."

As my tech guy, Dimitri controls access to the security feed. I can access my cameras myself from my phone to see where anyone is at a given time, but archives can only be accessed from the computer, a process I've never bothered to familiarize myself with.

"I'll go ask him myself."

Jovich's voice stops me before my hand falls on the doorknob. "Dimitri isn't here right now. He's chasing some lead."

I bristle, my irritation surging. I don't expect my men to check with me before every step they take, but the fact that Dimitri is gone is news to me. Of course, he isn't here when I need him.

"What lead?" I demand, turning back to glare at Jovich for not telling me sooner.

"Some guy who claims that he knows where we can find Nyanik." Jovich shrugs. "You'll be the first to know once we've got something solid."

I study his face for a moment, wondering why he had stated the obvious. Of course, I'll be the first he tells. "Good." I say slowly. "Have we heard anything from Jack?"

"Jack?" He doesn't bother trying to hide his confusion.

"I asked him to look into Claire for me." I wave a dismissive hand. "If you find anything out, text me. I'll be out for a while. Rhea has a guest, so keep an ear out and don't let my sister leave the house."

Jovich nods, assuring me it will be handled. I open the door just in time to see Claire walking out of her room, wearing a thin white dress that flows around her and yet still offers me a perfect view of the parts of her body that aren't covered by the swimsuit beneath it. "Is this okay?" She asks, pulling at the fabric.

"It's perfect," I tell her honestly. I couldn't care less about the dress. In fact, I'd prefer her without it. And without the bikini, while we're at it. My cock hardens at the thought of tugging at the string behind her neck so that her soft breasts tumble free. I could push her into my room right now and finish what we started last night. A large part of me wants to do just that, but I ignore it. I have other plans for her first.

That delicious pink heat rises up on her cheeks, and I realize I've been staring a little too long. I clear my throat. "I had Elaine prepare a bag for us, so no need to worry about anything."

"Elaine is pretty amazing." She smiles.

"I agree."

I reluctantly tear my gaze from her body and lead her down the stairs. She hesitates at the bottom, preparing to go to the front door, while I turn toward the back porch. "Is it walking distance?"

"No." I laugh but don't stop. I'm testing her again, seeing if she'll follow me into the unknown. After a moment, she catches up to me.

Without turning back to look at her, I can tell there are many things she wants to ask me. I feel the same about her. But we walk in silence as she follows me to the corner of the property, away from the beach.

She follows me obediently between the trees and onto the boardwalk tucked away in my yard. From the house, you'd never know it was there.

The sun darkens as we walk further away from the house and the trees become thicker as we venture deeper into them. Stray limbs start to bow over the path overhead. I make a mental note to get someone to trim them up.

The boardwalk is one of my favorite places to go. It's a treasure trove of unparalleled peace, which is hard to come by in my line of work. It also happens to lead out to my other favorite place to be.

We walk in silence, until I turn back and laugh. Claire's lips are pushed together like she's working hard to keep them shut, and her eyes are wide. She looks ready to run the other way.

"Are you scared?"

"No." She scoffs. "I know you aren't going to murder me, because if you do, you'll have to deal with Rhea."

"You're not wrong." I tell her, turning back to the path ahead.

Murder isn't on the agenda today... not for Claire, at least. I don't want her blood or her life. I just want answers. "Watch your step." I warn as the dock starts to dip.

The trees fall away, and the dock opens up so that we can see the catamaran sitting at the end of it. "You have a *boat*?" Claire asks. The way she says it sounds like she's surprised, as if it's something exotic like a pet tiger.

I stifle my amusement and turn to see the apprehensive look on her face. "Never been on a boat before?" I guess.

"No." She laughs. "Apparently, I haven't done *anything* before."

I could change that if she'll let me. We're from two different worlds, but here we are all the same. I like having her as part of mine, even if I haven't figured out how she fits into it. But I still have to get to the bottom of who she really is and whether it's all an act before I let her infiltrate any deeper. She's already taken over most of my waking thoughts, and I constantly find my eyes drawn to her like she's a magnet for them. If it turns out she's got an ulterior motive to her friendship with my sister or her presence here, she'll live just long enough to regret it. Part of me hopes that she does so I won't feel guilty for not pushing her away as I should.

"Well, let's hope you don't get seasick." I quip, bracing myself against the dock and hopping over the seat. I turn back and offer her a hand, which she takes and uses to pull herself into the boat with me. She tumbles onto the deck, and I catch her against my chest. I feel her entire body freeze for a moment as she gathers her balance and then glances up at me tentatively.

Her eyes are like an ocean on a cloudless day... deep, clear, and enchanting.

Claire Monroe is beautiful, sure. I've known plenty of beautiful women. Women with thick lashes, full lips that can work their way around my cock like it's a treat for them. Women with sumptuous asses and accents that make my name sound like a prayer when they scream it. I don't discriminate, and I've indulged in women of every ethnicity, some of which were simple in their beauty, and others whose looks seems to captivate every man she lays eyes upon. And yet, none of them have ever gotten under my skin the way that Claire has. I've never craved any of them with the intensity that I crave her, an admission that's both thrilling and terrifying. Even before all this, in what feels like a past life, when I loved Monica so deeply that I'd wanted to marry her and live happily ever after, I hadn't felt this inexplicable need to consume her.

Claire bites her lip, and I have to force down the desire to take it between my teeth and do the same. I don't want to scare her off just yet.

"Have a seat." I offer, gesturing to the sundeck as I turn away from her so fast that she nearly loses her footing again.

I set about getting everything ready while she walks the length of the boat, running a hand along the bow as she goes. A breeze picks up, blowing the sun dress out around her and teasing her hair free from the clip at the nape of her neck.

Claire sits gingerly on the upholstered bench and as the engine roars to life, she draws her knees into her chest. I want to laugh, but her fear subsides quickly as the breeze picks up and I cruise into the early noon sun.

She is one sexy distraction, and I have a hard time taking my eyes off of her. Thankfully I know this path well enough to boat it in my sleep.

After a few moments, as I'm motoring into the outlet to the larger sea, her initial anxiety seems to melt away, and she strips off the sun dress, tucking it under her legs so the wind won't carry it away. She leans back on her arms and lets the wind whip through her blonde hair and the sun soak into her body. I don't know if she's trying to look so fuckable, or if that's a happy accident, but either way my dick hardens at the sight of her. She looks like a damn swimsuit model. When I pick up speed, racing us over waves into the clear blue sea, she laughs, enjoying the rush.

We're miles from the house, in the middle of nowhere, when I cut the engine and turn to face her. She seems to sense that I'm watching her, because her eyes pop open, and she smiles a little. "Are we here?" She looks around and realizes there's nothing as far as the eye can see, save for the reedy strip of trees on one side of us and a vast expanse of ocean on the other. Confusion passes over her first, and as I walk closer, a little bit of fear sparks in her eyes.

"What's going on?" She puzzles, crossing her arms over her chest. I wonder if she's punishing me on purpose, taking away my view because she knows I'm not playing anymore.

"I think it's time we finish our conversation."

Her chest swells as she glances around the boat, the first signs of panic starting to set in. She's just realized she may have trusted me too much. Now, she's alone with a practical stranger in open water, completely at my mercy. It's a terrible position to be in, if you pose a threat to my family. Whether she does, still remains to be seen. "Here?"

"Is that a problem?"

"No." She bites her lip again. Irritation surges hot through me; I want to be the one to do that. I want to pull that lip between my teeth and bite it so hard that I taste blood, and I don't even know why she makes me feel so animal. I don't think I'm a cruel person, but I want to take out all of my frustrations with the world on this girl, to take her love and give her pain. I crave her in a way that's unlike anything I've ever known... in a way that doesn't even make sense to me.

"Good." I pull the gun out of my waistband, wrapping my fingers around the barrel.

Claire gasps as she realizes what it is and pulls herself up to stand. I close the distance between us with the handle out, watching her intently as she goes on the defensive, eyes wide and lips parted on a scream that's caught in her throat.

She has her hands up, either to show me she's innocent or because she's prepared to fight me if she has to.

As if she stands a chance.

CHAPTER TWENTY-TWO

REMY

"Take it." I tell her, tipping the gun toward her. "It's loaded."

"I... I don't understand." She looks from the gun to my face, and when I press it into her hands, she accepts it. Or, rather, she doesn't push it out of her grip. She looks like she's going to drop it the moment I let go, but I hope she's got a little more fight than that. I flip the safety off before pulling my hands off of hers, and she flinches at the click likes it's a cannon blast.

I take a step back without taking my eyes off her, but we're still close. I can smell her shampoo in the wind, and the coconut of her sunscreen. The barrel is aimed in my direction but pointed at the ground, exactly the way it was when I passed it to her. If she just reached out her arms and held the muzzle a bit higher, it'd press right into my chest.

"You're not stupid, Claire. Unfortunately for you, neither am I. We're miles away from any sort of civilization. Nobody would hear a thing. So, if you want to try to hurt me, here's your chance." I raise my hands to show her that they're empty. If she's planning anything, now is the time to act upon it. I won't give her another chance.

"Remy." Her voice quivers over my name as she shakes her head. "What the hell?"

"I turned the safety off. If you want to shoot me, you just pull that trigger. But make sure you aim well, because if you miss, you won't make it off this boat alive."

I'm sure I can hear her heartbeat hammering under that delicate skin, see her pulse twitching. "I don't want to hurt you." She says, shaking her head. Her words are thick with desperation or tears, maybe both. Those beautiful eyes are certainly shining with the latter.

"I don't want to hurt you either." I tell her honestly. "But I will if I have to."

She chokes on a sob but does a good job burying it to try and look composed. "Okay." She says slowly. "Tell me what this is about. Tell me what you want to know."

"Who are you? I mean, really. One hundred percent truth?"

"I..." She shakes her head again, confused. "I'm Claire Monroe. Rhea was my roommate freshman year, and we became best friends." Those bright eyes are glassy now, and I can't tell if she's holding back tears or trying to summon them. "I didn't seek her out with the hope of getting close to her millionaire brother, if that's what you're suggesting."

"Let's say I believe you. Why do you have an ID with the name Boudreaux on it?"

Her eyes narrow on me as she realizes what I just confessed to... snooping through her possessions, violating her privacy. She doesn't even know the half of it. "Obviously, that's a fake." She looks like she can't believe we're even having this conversation. "Rhea turned twenty-one before I do, so to get into bars, we had a friend make that up for me. He put the same last name down as a joke because people always ask if we're sisters."

Obviously, I know it's a fake, but I couldn't have guessed why. "Alright." I nod. "And you still carry it because..."

"Because if you look at my other ID, you'll see that I don't turn twenty-one until March."

I had noticed the IDs had different birth years, but I hadn't bothered to do the math. Underage drinking is hardly a drop in the bucket compared to the atrocious things I've done, but if that's true, how is she in the same classes as Rhea? "Rhea turned twenty-one months ago."

"Good for you for knowing that. Do you know how we celebrated?" Anger is cutting into her tone, a bitter venom now that I'm challenging her. "We had a party at our place. We invited half of the junior class, and we both got so wasted that we missed the rest of the week's classes." Claire laughs. "But I know you brought it up because you want to know how I ended up rooming with Rhea at the same age when I should have been graduating high school. Right?" She crosses her arms and doesn't wait for me to answer. "The last family I ended up with... they were shitty. I hated it so much, I couldn't even see the light at the end of the tunnel. And I was sick of being kicked around like the trash no one wants to clean up, moving homes and schools and entire towns every time someone got sick of me. So, I stole pills from the bitch and took a knife from the block on the counter, and I tried to kill myself." She says it flatly, as if that's just a decision one makes as easily as what they have for breakfast. "But I couldn't even do that right, Remy. I was such a fuckup that I couldn't even kill myself. Didn't cut deep enough, I guess."

Her words are raw, and her eyes have taken on a troubling chaos. They reflect the storm clouds gathering on the horizon, and I realize all at once that she is a sponge. Not only do her eyes show the world around her, but she too is a product of the circumstances she finds herself in. Rhea gave her friendship and love, so Claire reciprocated it. But I'm not Rhea. I don't have anything good to give her.

I've known for years that being tied to me is like having a lead anvil tied around your neck. It's why I broke Monica's heart with every measure of certainty. Claire isn't Monica; She's worse. I thought that this girl was light, but she's just a mirror reflecting the light my sister gave her. I can't drag Claire into my darkness if I don't want her to become darkness itself.

But she isn't done talking, and I'm not going to make her stop.

"My social worker, Addie, she's the one who was there when I woke up in the hospital," Claire says. "She's the only person who's been constant in my life until Rhea. She managed to get me out of the psych watch they were trying to force on me, and she suggested I emancipate myself to get out of there. So, I did. I got with my school principal, and took all the state exams to graduate early, and Darrington had already offered me the scholarships, so Addie called and asked if I could be moved up the admissions list. I went to Darrington a year earlier than I was supposed to because if I went back to just trying to survive, I wouldn't have lived." Her hands have been trembling around the gun, but now when I look, she's holding it steady between us. "I can give you a play-by-play of my entire life if you want that, Remy."

"No," I say. Guilt claws at the back of my neck, but I can't let her see it. I can't let myself feel it. Whatever I had expected from her, it wasn't that. "That's not necessary."

"Are you sure? Because I'm not." She laughs bitterly. "It's like you *want* me to be hiding something, like you want me to have an ulterior motive so that you can punish me for it."

She's right. I *am* looking for a reason to push her away. I simultaneously want her to keep her distance and want her. It's a maddening tango. "Tell me what happened to your birth certificate."

Her silence reinforces the look of confusion on her face. Her lips open and then close. "What do you mean?"

"There seems to be no birth certificate on file for Claire Monroe. Not just in your school records but anywhere. Surely you needed one when you applied to Darrington, especially if you're using financial aid."

She lets go of a frustrated sigh. "My social worker did that for me. She sent all of the paperwork since I was locked in the hospital." Claire shakes her head, her lips pressed tightly together like she's being careful about what else to say. "I'm sure it just got misplaced."

I narrow my eyes on her. "Have you ever seen it?"

That gets a laugh from her, though it's more confused than amused. "What?"

"Have you ever actually seen your birth certificate? Or have you just taken the word of all these people who passed you along to the next person? Do you know your name is Claire Monroe because that's what your mother named you or because that's what you've been told?"

I'm pushing her. I've been doing it since I met her, scantily-clad in my bedroom. I wanted to put the pressure on, to watch the house of cards crumble and reveal whatever she's hiding underneath. I've been so convinced that there is something she's hiding that I've never stopped to consider what would happen if I pushed her so hard, only to find out that there are no secrets buried under that sweet exterior. But I've watched her bare her soul to me, forced her to tell me more than she's comfortable with, and now she isn't just hurt.

I see the shift in her, the crack in her spirit that exposes all of the insecurities she's been hiding from everyone... including herself. It's achingly obvious for a moment before she covers it with a scoff.

"You know what, Remy?" She blinks through the tears that are starting to carve a path down her cheeks. Her eyes turn to the gun in her hand, and a lightning bolt of panic tears through me. Not because I fear her turning it on me, but because she just told me she'd tried to kill herself once. And I've pressed her even harder, grinding her between my demands and a wound that will never fully heal.

"Claire." I shake my head, trying to find words to make her understand I wasn't trying to hurt her. But she doesn't see it as she turns the gun in her hands, letting the sunlight glint off of it. Her eyes flicker up to mine, defeated, and the look of hopelessness there knocks the breath out of my chest.

CHAPTER TWENTY-THREE

CLAIRE

"If you're really that scared of me, maybe you should do something about it." I press the gun into his hands the way he did to me. His fingers are nowhere near the trigger, but if he wants to, he could reach it and drive a bullet straight into my stomach. It would likely be over pretty quick and probably wouldn't even make much of a mess. I tilt my chin up so that he can see that I'm not bluffing.

Maybe Remington Boudreaux likes head games, but I don't. I may not be an open book, but I'm not going to great lengths to hide anything from him. I'm not a spy sent to infiltrate his home, not an assassin working to gain his favor. I'm not looking for anything from him that he doesn't want to give me. But maybe he likes to play with his food.

His lips are so close. The air around us smells like salt; It's so thick that I can taste it.

The storm clouds are falling fast around us, the sky darkening with every passing second. I can feel the boat rocking as the waves start to intensify, but I plant myself firmly on the deck, squarely in front of him, and wait. I've just put him in check—time to see whether he attacks like a wild dog or quietly backs down.

If he pulls the trigger and it's immediate, the last thing I'll see is his eyes. They're so much like Rhea's... a kaleidoscope of warm colors that remind me of leaves before they fall in autumn. My favorite season, autumn is proof that there is beauty in decay. It's why I've never been afraid of death—life is so much more painful than it could ever be.

Remy moves so quickly that I don't know what's happening until the gun clatters on the table. I don't have an opportunity to do anything, to register relief or disappointment, because in the next minute, he sweeps me up in his arms.

I respond without even thinking of it. I wrap my legs around his waist as he crashes into me, one hand on my ass to hold me against him and the other threading through my hair, pulling me into him so that I can't escape. As if I would want to.

Our mouths find each other right where they left off last night, tongues tangling in desperation. I need to taste him, to have him taste me. I need to punish him for his stunt and reward him for seeing reason. I need him to erase the ghosts of every kiss before this, to let the fire of our connection consume me until I'm born in ash like a phoenix.

His kiss is desperate, and it's clear that we aren't just courting one another. Love has no place here. This is lust—dangerous and dark and so hungry that nothing will ever satisfy it fully. He gives me passion and hate that aren't even for me, his teeth biting my lip with every bit of intention and making my need grow so that I arch into him more.

The rain begins to fall, slowly at first. My head falls back, and the first couple of drops splash upon my face as he presses me into the bench, wedging himself between my legs like his body is magnetized to mine. I reach out and catch his silky hair in my fingers, needing to grip something as he ravages my mouth, his tongue seeking mine again and again.

His mouth leaves mine cold as it trails to my neck, his hot tongue laving at my skin while his fingers work at the bikini strings knotted behind my neck. I can feel the outline of his cock pressing into me through the thin material of his board shorts, and I want it.

Thankfully, we seem to have a common goal because when the knot comes undone, he tugs at my bikini top so that my breasts spill out, exposing them to the warm air. He tosses the fabric aside, unable to be bothered with it and wastes no time filling his palms with them as his tongue makes its way down to greet them. I gasp as his teeth graze one nipple while his thumb rolls over the other, causing them to stiffen further under his touch.

But while my nipples are hard, the rest of me isn't. I'm melting under him, driven into a puddle of lust as his movements send shudders of pleasure through me. A hunger unlike anything I've ever known nearly rips me in two so that when he moves off of me, I open my eyes, breathless, confused, and feeling cheated. Every inch of me feels raw with desire, and disappointment blooms in my chest.

Why did he stop?

"Fuck." He mutters, and it's not the throaty sound of pleasure I want. He sounds irritated.

I run a tongue over my swollen lips, trying to orient myself to his absence, and follow his gaze up at the sky above me. The sun has disappeared from the sky completely. My head is dizzy with the sudden dam of our need bursting. Have we been out here that long? But no, I realize the sun's just been edged out by the storm that's rolling in.

The rain falls a little faster and Remy hurries back to the wheel, leaving me aching and cold again.

I turn around to get a sense of how close it is. Lightning forks through the sky followed, a moment later, by a clap of thunder so loud I feel it echo in my body. The waves in the distance are angry, and they're riling up the ones closer to us. One crashes against the side of the boat, accompanied by an angry clapping sound. I jump in time for it to just splash against my feet.

I grab my now-wet swimsuit top off the ground and face away from Remy while I knot it in place, attempting to reclaim some of the dignity I threw to the wind moments before. I pull the dress that I'd abandoned over my head and go to stand next to him. "Welcome to Costa Rica." He says, loudly enough that I can hear him over the howling wind. "The weather can change on a dime. We've got to get back to the house."

I nod wordlessly, crossing my arms over my chest. I stay that way as we zip over the waves that roll under the boat, barreling back the way we came. Even under a deck, the rain that follows us pelts me from every which way, soaking me thoroughly.

A glance behind me shows the clouds closing in and the darkness getting deeper. The crashing rain and whistling wind make any further attempt at conversation impossible, which is just as well because I don't know what to say anyway. Clearly, we let passion take the wheel back there, but was it just because we were both so amped up about the fight? What would have happened on the roof if we hadn't been interrupted? What would have happened just now if we weren't in the middle of a storm?

I barely notice when we pass his house because all around us seems like nothing but an endless squall. But Remy seems to know the waters well. He docks and climbs effortlessly over the side, then turns to offer his assistance. The boat lurches against the dock as I'm stepping out, and he picks me up before I can fall. Once my feet hit the ground, he grabs my hand and pulls me into the canopy of trees with him.

I don't even remember to grab my shoes, and as we run, the wood slips under my feet.

The cover of trees offers us a temporary shelter, though I can still hear the angry wind howling overhead and the rain falling in the distance. Remy looks me up and down with concern. "You alright?"

"Yeah," I laugh, breathless. I don't know if it's the adrenaline coursing through me in the wake of our encounter or just the insanity of the circumstances, but I feel delirious with it.

"Things have been so insane around here that I forgot all about Kate."

The strangest jealousy rolls through me as a peal of thunder rolls over us. "Kate?"

"The hurricane." He laughs, tipping his head back toward the storm wracking the ocean. "Costa Rica is nearly untouchable from a hurricane, but we're getting a taste. Come on, let's get inside."

I let him lead me through the darkness of the trees, clutching his hand still so that I don't fall as my feet slip against the wet wood. The storm is quiet in the denseness of the forest as the animals chatter excitedly, surrounding us in a symphony of their croaking, chirping, and humming. When we break out into his yard, the storm's call overpowers that. His hand on my wrist catches when I head toward the patio we came from, and I turn to see him nod at the front door. It's a shorter distance to the entrance, so I let him pull me as we dash across the distance to the front door.

We step into the house and slam the door shut behind us as a gust of wind tries to fight its way in. We stand for a moment, breathless, dripping water on the marble floor. My white dress is plastered to my body, and I have no doubt he can see everything, including my still-hard nipples. He'd seen a lot more than that on the boat, but it still makes me blush a little as I feel him watching me. I want to ask him what to do next, but my voice sticks in my throat, so I turn my eyes up to the ceiling. I'd wondered what it would be like to stand below it during a rain shower, and now I know. It's an incredible sight, but I can't focus on anything other than the rise and fall of Remy's chest as he stands next to me.

"Rhea may still be busy." He says, casting his eyes toward the steps.

My heart thunders in my chest nearly as loudly as the rain does outside. I don't think I'll be able to get the words to unstick themselves from my throat, but then they're out in the chilly air between us, full of innuendo and need.

"What should we do in the meantime?"

Heat flashes in his eyes as he picks up on the words I don't say. We walk quickly up the steps and turn the corner, both of us deathly silent as we creep past Rhea's closed door. Her room is quiet as the crypt, and the hall is dark. I feel like a thief in the night, like I'm doing something irredeemable, something wrong. But this is something that I want to do more desperately than anything I've ever known.

Remy's hand drifts down to my waist before I can turn into my room, catching me before I can lead him in there. I see him tip his head toward his own door... a room that doesn't share walls with Rhea's. His eyes ask a question that needs no answer. I desperately want to finish what we started.

I've just stepped inside his room and haven't even had a chance to look around when the voice comes down the hall. "Remy?"

I close my eyes as Jovich comes to the door, and then press myself into the wall, hoping we haven't been caught. He creeps me out enough under normal circumstances; I don't want him to see me so raw and exposed.

"What is it, Jovich?" Remy growls. He makes no apology and no attempt to hide his irritation. Honestly, Jovich is so good at cock-blocking us that I have to wonder if he's jealous about having to share Remy's attention. Maybe he has a thing for Remy, too. I can't really blame him if that's the case.

His voice is muffled, but I can still make out the words, "I just thought you'd want to know that Jack called."

"You can give me the details later."

"Alright." Jovich agrees. "But I thought you may want to know that your friend Miss Monroe must have some friends in high places. We didn't find the birth certificate yet, but I did find a criminal record."

Criminal record?

It feels as if all of the air is sucked out, first from my lungs and then the room. Fear shudders through me, seizing my heart in its steely grip. Remy is so close that I can feel him tense beside me. What air is left in his room shifts from warm and gentle to cold and static. There's only one thing he could possibly be talking about. I swallow, praying that Jovich wasn't able to see the details of that report. Just the highlights would be bad enough, but if he saw the whole thing...

Nausea rises up in my stomach, creeping all the way into the back of my throat. I suddenly can't feel my fingers or toes, as though the cold's made them lose feeling. My breath is so ragged I am sure he can hear it, and that he knows Remy is hiding me like a fugitive behind the door.

"Oh?" Remy asks without turning to me. If he'd look at me, maybe I could make my mouth work enough to tell him not to listen. Maybe he'd see that I can explain. Maybe he'd let me tell him myself, in my own way, before it's out there.

"Assault with a deadly weapon." Jovich says, and I feel my hope crumble. Of course, they found it. That file was supposed to be sealed, hidden from the world because of my age and because the charges ultimately didn't hold water. "There's another charge too, but it seems that one was dropped." He pauses as if he knows I'm standing there, just around the corner, holding onto a desperate hope that he hasn't seen anything more. And an even more desperate hope that if he did, he won't admit as much. But he barely pauses to let any of it sink in before he says, "Attempted murder."

Remy is silent as he processes the information, and Jovich takes the opportunity to speak again. "It seems the little minx isn't quite as innocent as she's been pretending to be."

"You don't say." Remy muses. I watch his lips form the words, and then he thanks Jovich. I'm not sure if Jovich is even gone before Remy shuts the door or if he just closes it in the older man's face, but when he turns to me, rage sparks in his eyes.

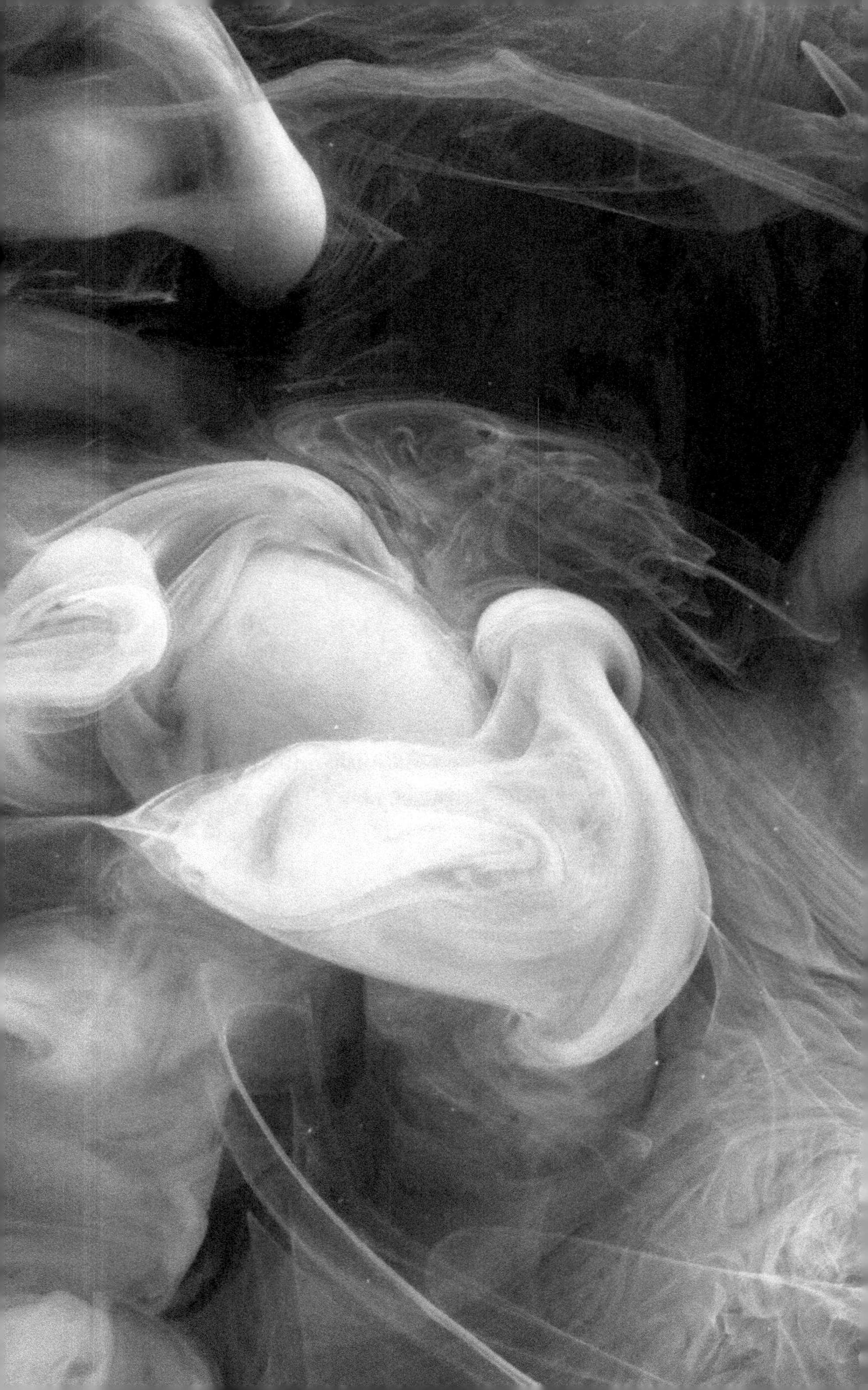

CHAPTER TWENTY-FOUR

Remy

"Attempted murder?" I demand.

Claire's eyes are wide as I close the distance between us. But she doesn't say anything, doesn't try to defend herself. And her silence makes me angrier than her lies. "Start talking, Claire."

Her lip quivers as she looks like she's about to say something, but then she presses it together against her bottom one and shakes her head. She covers her mouth with a hand, so that when she speaks it's muffled. "I can't."

The rage burns like molten fury in my veins as my hands curl into fists at my sides. I've never hit a woman, and I don't ever plan to. But Claire is messing with my head. Her lies are poisoning my mind, and I need her to talk. I could turn her over to Jovich or Dimitri, but that would be a fate darker than my anger. She's already backed herself into the wall, and now she's caught between a rock and a hard place as I shift my weight in front of her and grip her chin between my fingers. She has nowhere to go. I can feel her heart slamming against her ribs. She's like an animal in a cage, which means she's dangerous.

"Who *the fuck* are you?" I growl.

She winces, knocking her head against the wall as she tries to lurch away from my anger. I've given her too many chances. I've tried to be too nice because she matters to the one person who matters to me. I let her tight little body tempt and distract me from the fact that she is just as much a threat to my family as any other stranger on the street... probably more, given that my sister trusts her so completely.

Anger rips through me as I watch her close her eyes. It doesn't stop the tears spilling out from under her lashes. So many goddamn tears. Does she think they'll stop me from getting the answers I need from her? Does she think that I'm so weak that her pathetic whimpering will make me take a step back or let it go?

"Who *are* you?" I grind the words out between clenched teeth and sink my fist into the wall just to the right of her head.

The drywall crumbles around my fist, and bits of it scatter to the ground, a white powdery dust floating in the air. "I've already told you." She sobs. "I don't know what else to say. Please."

"Then tell me who the fuck you tried to kill." I want to shake her, but I can't close my hands on her. If I do, I'm not sure I'll stop until I know she isn't a threat to my family anymore. If I put my hands on her, I'm not sure I'll be able to stop until she's dead.

A deer caught in the headlights, at first, she only stares at me. And then through her crying, she chokes out a name. A name I don't recognize, and one that I can't make out. I grip her chin tighter, force her to look at me, and demand that she repeats the name.

"Eric." Her voice is small. She looks like she's about to collapse, so I shift my weight on my feet, pressing against her. I plant one hand on the wall so my fingers won't drift down to her pretty little neck and start to close around it of their own accord.

"Eric *who*?"

She closes her eyes, letting the last of the tears escape. And when she opens them again, those tears are gone. Her resistance is gone. Her fight is gone.

Because now she's empty.

The shift is noticeable—not like she's dropped a façade, but like she's let go of something she's given all of her energy trying to hold onto. Now she's deflated and hollow, her voice cold and her eyes eerily void of emotion.

"Eric Giante." She says, her voice a whisper like she's afraid saying the name any louder will summon him. "My former foster father."

Her shift in energy drains my anger all at once, the tide waning as I watch her shrink in front of me. I can tell I've made a mistake as soon as she says those words. *Former foster father.* Suddenly, the story she told me on the boat comes back to me, the pieces of the puzzle that she is finally falling into place. The shitty foster family, the pain of not wanting to live anymore. I know immediately that this man did something to her. I can see it in the way her entire body just shut down, the way her brain just turned everything off... to protect her.

I exist in a murky world. It's the kind of dark most people never have to concern themselves with. I *know* how relentlessly cruel it can be, and yet I didn't see the signs.

I shake my head, trying to stop her before she can say the rest of the words I've been demanding. But I'm the one who pressed her into the wall and threatened her for the truth, and I've broken her enough that she's going to give it to me now whether I want it or not. I don't want her to say the words I can feel are coming—I don't want them to be true, and I don't want her to give them to me because I've bullied it out of her. But they slip off her tongue without emotion, detached and automatic.

"The man who raped me."

Once they're said, they can't be taken back. It's a truth that I now know, something private that I forced her to reveal. Something I wish I could undo. But it's too late.

I let go of her like she's burned me and step away from her as I try to find the words to... I don't know what I think my words can accomplish. They can't take back my relentless, obsessive pushing. They can't undo her past or take away her pain. They mean nothing to her.

Claire closes her eyes and raises her hand to her lips like she can take the words back. Or maybe she's going to be ill. Or maybe she's wiping away the feel of my lips on her, another man forcing her to do something she never wanted to.

Whatever it is, it's fleeting, because she turns and runs from my room so fast that I don't have a chance to get anything past my throat. I try to grab her before she breaks past my door, but she's fast and I'm rooted to the spot. Her door slams shut before I even manage to move.

I pinch the bridge of my nose like that will counteract the pressure in my head, which is suddenly pounding with the weight of all the thoughts in my head.

Only one thing right now is clear— I've fucked up. Big time.

I reach for the phone in my pocket and dial Jack's speed dial. "Remington." He sounds surprised when he answers. "You talked to Jovich?"

"Yes." I snap. "I want the records."

Jack lets out a whistling breath. "It was hard to get. I could get in some deep shit if I share the file out. I have my family to consider..."

"You'll be in some deep shit if you don't." I snap, unwilling to bow to his attempt to strong-arm me. We both know it's not his menial police salary that keeps his family living comfortably.

Though he can't see me, Jack seems to sense just how serious I am. He hesitates a moment and then laughs drily. "What the fuck is with this girl, Rem? She got a golden pussy or something?"

The hairs on the back of my neck stand on end as my anger turns necrotic, eating away at what's left of my patience. Jack is lucky to be a thousand miles away because if he was standing in front of me, I'd probably punch him right in the throat. "Send me the fucking files!" I yell. "Now."

"Alright." He sighs, and I hear papers shuffling in the background. "I'll fax them."

"It's the twenty-first century." I growl. "Nobody uses a fucking fax machine. Take a picture on your phone and send it to me."

"Alright," Jack grumbles. "Anything else, Your Highness?"

I ignore the smart-ass remark, grinding my jaw together. "Yeah. Look into this Eric Giante guy and let me know what you find."

I can hear the keyboard clicking as he types the name into his search bar. "Looks like a low-level piece of shit. Domestic abuse, battery, petit theft, grand larceny..." he whistles under his breath. "And the list goes on... domestic abuse, sexual assault, lewd and lascivious acts against a child under eighteen..."

"Just send me the pictures." I snap, hanging up on him before he can go any further.

I feel oddly ill, unsettled. I work for the worst sort of people that humanity has to offer. I've seen what they do to women, to children, to anyone they deem less than them. I've seen men take what they want, and I've seen the women who have had everything taken from them. I had everything taken from me, too.

I relate to Claire more than she will ever know. Just the thought of anyone else putting their hands on her makes me want to explode, but the thought of anyone else *hurting* her? It makes me want to go nuclear.

I try to control my rage, knowing it is fueled by my guilt. My father had made it his mission to destroy people in the pursuit of money and power. I made it my mission to try and lessen his impact, to bring some light into the darkness he created. I try to heal the wounds that he caused, and yet I've just blown a hole through the safety net of someone I care about... someone who crawled her way through the darkness into the light on her own, only for me to come along and kick her back toward it.

My fingers curl around the phone, and I'm just about to chuck it at the wall when it buzzes with Jack's message. I braced myself as I zoom in to read the picture and scroll through the first few paragraphs of irrelevant information.

At 22:13, Officer Timothy Ketty was dispatched to a domestic disturbance at 8420 Prince Park. The caller claimed assault with a deadly weapon and attempted murder.

I, Officer Ketty, arrived at 22:38. There was a woman standing on the porch (Jane Giante, WF, D.O.B. 08/23/69). She was frantic and claimed their foster child had tried to kill her husband. Mrs. Giante took me inside to an upstairs room, where I observed a large man with a superficial cut across his left cheek (Eric Giante, WM, D.O.B. 01/29/1968), and a young woman (Claire Monroe, WF, D.O.B. 03/24/2002) backed into the corner.

I sent Mr. Giante downstairs and asked Ms. Monroe what had happened. She claimed that Mr. Giante came at her with the knife in a rage. He slapped her across the face. Ms. Monroe claims fear for her life. She wrestled the knife away from him and tried to "stop him from hurting anyone again." I observed a handprint on the right cheek consistent with Ms. Monroe's claims, as well as older, unrelated marks and bruises. Her face was wet from crying and upper lip was bloodied.

I questioned Mr. Giante separately. He claims that he entered his foster daughter's room to tell her goodnight when she became agitated and pulled the knife from her nightstand. Mr. Giante claims that he slapped her when she threatened him, and she lunged at him, causing the laceration on his cheek. He says she told him she was going to "kill you". At that point, he wrestled the knife out of her grip and sent Jane to call 911. He commanded her to sit in the corner until the police arrived.

Jane Giante claims she was in the shower when the struggle began, but she heard a "scuffle" and went to check it out. That is when she claims to have witnessed Ms. Monroe with the knife in her hand and that she stood there yelling, "Claire, stop" until her husband instructed her to call 911.

Ms. Monroe and Mr. Giante both denied being the aggressor. Both sustained superficial injuries. I explained that Ms. Monroe would be removed from the home, and The Giante's said they didn't wish to press charges. Current procedure dictates the removal and separation of the aggressor from the victim. Mrs. Giante attempted to solicit a bribe from me in exchange for deleting the report. I was uncomfortable leaving the three of them in the home together, but I didn't have enough evidence to facilitate any arrests. I handcuffed Ms. Monroe and took her to Walsh County Police Department, where Officer Annalise Rickers and I again asked what happened. Ms. Monroe's story was consistent with her first account.

The other children in the care of the Giante's corroborated the family's claims that no abuse has occurred in the home.

Officer Rickers kept watch of Ms. Monroe throughout the night and returned her to her home the next morning at 09:23. No charges have been formally filed against either party, but the state representative for Miss Monroe was notified of the disturbance.

I blink, trying to process the information, and then read the whole thing again.

Attempted murder?

There is no mention of anything that looks like murder. Even the officer who took the report clearly hadn't thought it was an attempt on this man's life. I scroll down a bit and see another report. I skim this one, looking for any sign that Claire had done anything other than defend herself against someone who was supposed to protect her. But there's nothing incriminating... just a hauntingly similar report. Beneath it are the photos that the officer's report had referenced. The girl in the photo is unmistakably Claire, and yet if I didn't know that, I may think it's someone else entirely.

Those eyes that have been haunting me the last week stare out at me, just as empty as they were when I broke her down into a confession. Her face is sharper in the photo than it is now, like she didn't eat enough. Dark circles under her eyes make the bruises on her neck seem all the more vivid, and the handprint emblazoned across her cheek and lip looks as if they'd just happened before the shutter clicked. She looks like a different person... someone who Claire would want to bury once she'd escaped the darkness.

I close the case files and open my browser, searching up the Walsh County Public Records. I type the name Eric Giante into the text box, and before I've even blinked, a long list of offenses appears. I skim through them, finding every indiscretion Jack mentioned and then some. The last one was exactly what Claire had claimed.

I open the link, but there's no report attached. Just the charge and the date.

I click out of the browser and stare blankly at my phone for a moment before deciding to call Dimitri.

"Hello?"

"I have a new task for you," I tell him without offering any kind of formalities. "It's your number one priority."

"Tell me what you need," Dimitri says without any hint of hesitation.

"There's a man I want dead." I swallow the bile at the back of my throat. "No, I *need* him dead. His name's Eric Giante of Walsh County."

Dimitri shuffles some stuff around, clicks a few keys on a keyboard, and after a minute, he says, "Looks like he's out on parole. I can have it done in twenty-four hours. Any requests?"

"No. Take the jet and bring him here. I want to watch him suffer."

"Done." Dimitri sounds like he's about to hang up, but something is weighing on me, so I blurt it out before he can drop the call.

"Dimitri? Don't tell Jovich about this."

He doesn't have to tell me he won't, but he does. "Of course."

When he hangs up, I hang my heavy head, trying to figure out how to fix this before my sister finds out. I may have just broken her best friend, and I got absolutely no pleasure out of it.

I reach for the tablet that I used to watch her flit around her room this morning, but she's not in view of the camera. At first, I think she may have left, gone to tell Rhea that her brother is an ass. But then I hear it—her soft sobs threaten to cave my chest in.

Fuck.

CHAPTER TWENTY-FIVE

CLAIRE

I don't know much about hurricanes, having lived my entire life in the Northwest. I thought you could see them coming before they hit. I thought there were varying degrees of destruction.

If that's true, Remy isn't a hurricane. He's a tornado. His rage appeared from nowhere without warning, and he stopped at nothing until he destroyed everything that was still standing. Until he destroyed me.

Once I got away from him, I locked the door behind me and slid to the ground against it, watching the rain fog up the sliding glass window and cut occasional paths down to the balcony.

Only a few people know the truth about my 'record'. Whether he'll admit it or not, Eric Giante is one of them. And now I can add Remy to that list.

But I saw how quickly he dropped me when I told him who Eric was. I saw the look in his eyes—pity, disgust, rage. I knew from the very first time that Eric came to my room in the night that I was damaged. I've known my whole life that I am. It's why not even one of the families I spent time with ever pulled through for me. And if I wasn't damaged before that night, I knew I was the minute his fat fingers pushed inside of me, digging into me like a pumpkin he was going to carve, scooping out all that was left of my hope for the world. But he didn't give me a face like a jack-o-lantern—he covered my mouth and told me how stupid I was for trying to tempt him with my dresses and braids.

He may not have given me a face, but he taught me how to put on a face. It was under the Giante's care that I learned to grin and bear it, because as long as I was there, he was hurting me and not the other girl I shared my room with. He taught me how to look like I was okay when I was dying inside and how to keep a secret whether I wanted to or not.

Remy's been insistent that I'm hiding something, insistent that I'm keeping something from him. Maybe he sensed it in me from the beginning. Maybe he knew it from the first look at me, from the moment his touch landed on my bare skin. Maybe he could feel who'd been there before, or he could smell the rot that took hold all those years ago. It never went away, after all. You can't cut out something like that, but you can cover it up, bury it deep and try to forget it's there.

Whether Remy knew from the first moment he met me or not doesn't matter. He knows now, and there's no undoing it. he'll forever look at me and see a ruined woman, the layers of rot and abuse hidden under the surface. He'll never want to touch me again. Who would? Eric told me as much every time he came to me, and I believed him. I never told anyone because I knew he was right. I could at least pretend I wasn't damaged with other people as long as they didn't know. But now Remy does, and he proved Eric right immediately. He dropped me instantly, like he couldn't stand to touch something so dirty. He couldn't even look at me, because he found out that I really have been hiding something from him.

I don't know how long I sit there with my knees pulled into my chest, staring out the window and ignoring the hurt I've been hiding for so long... the hurt I thought I'd gotten rid of. I'd done such a good job of burying it that I don't even know how to contend with the reminder of it... with the pain. It sits on my chest, threatening to squeeze the air out of my lungs.

The rain stops just as suddenly as it started. One minute, it's still pouring, and the next, it's gone entirely. That breaks me out of the trance and smashes the cage I've locked myself in since I came in here.

Trying to find any signs of noise coming from either Rhea's room or Remy's, I press my ear against the door. But it's quiet in the hall.

I glance around the room, wondering if I should bother taking anything with me. But I didn't bring much and anything besides my phone and purse will slow me down, making it easier for them to catch me. I came to Costa Rica prepared for a taste of paradise, and my clothing choices are pretty reflective of that. I push my clothes aside, digging through my suitcase before landing on a pair of shorts, a simple top, and sandals. I'm still shaking from the cold and the unexpected trip down memory lane, but at least I won't be stuck where I'm no longer wanted. At least I won't have to know that just down the hall is a man I threw caution to the wind for. Now he's just another in what is shaping up to be a list of men who have only made me hate myself.

I finally strip off the rain-drenched coverup and the bikini underneath it, throwing it on top of my other clothes and shimmy into the dry set, slipping on the only sneakers I brought before I step out into the hall.

I don't have the stomach to look over my shoulder at Remy's room, and I can't glance up at Rhea's door, so I keep my head down. I walk quickly, sure to keep my footfalls as silent as possible as I move to the stairs and tiptoe down them. The entire house is silent, and darker than it should be for the time of day. I glance up and see that the sky is still murky overhead. Though the rain has stopped, dark clouds still press against the glass, swirling ominously.

That's how I walk right into the man standing at the bottom of the steps, who appeared there so quickly and quietly that I didn't even notice his presence with my eyes trained on the roof.

I stifle a scream and then curse under my breath. Jovich grabs my arms like he's trying to steady me, but I tear myself away from him, taking a step back up so we're on the same level. "Going somewhere?" His gray eyes are flat, emotionless.

I swallow. "I'm leaving."

That makes him laugh. "Are you?"

"I get the sense you've wanted me gone from the moment I stepped off that plane. I don't care why you don't like me. I'm not very fond of you either. So, just step aside and pretend you never saw me."

His laugh is too loud as it ripples through the foyer. I cringe and glance over my shoulder, but the upstairs is thankfully still. "Or what? You gonna come after me with a kitchen knife?"

My heart drops in my chest at the words, and my stomach threatens to turn over. It's thankfully too empty to do that, but it doesn't stop the nausea from curling inside of me. Jovich is *mocking* me. Remy asked him to dig up dirt on me, and Jovich pulled through. He isn't going to pretend he didn't, either. I swallow my indignant rage, blink back the furious tears in my eyes, and make to move around him, but his fingers close around my upper arm and squeeze. "I can't let you go."

"Am I Remy's prisoner, now?"

"Nah," He shakes his head, stroking his beard with his free hand. He releases his grip on me, and I look down to see the impressions his fingers made against my skin are already fading. "But I think Rhea would probably fire me if something happened to you 'cause I let you walk off into the middle of a foreign country. It's a cruel world, Claire Monroe." He almost sounds like he's going to laugh, but he doesn't. "I'll give you a ride to the airport."

I narrow my eyes on him. As far as I can tell, he works for Remy, not Rhea. I'm not sure Remy gives a damn what happens to me, especially now, considering he's seemed ready to kill me more than a few times since we met. But Jovich is right in that Rhea will likely be disappointed to discover me gone. If she finds out I walked away from them without any kind of plan to get back home safely, she'll lash out.

"Fine." I sigh.

He turns and fumbles around in his pocket as he searches for his keys. I follow him out the door to the black SUV in the driveway. The paved drive is wet, and the air is heavy and sticky hot. I can feel it in my lungs on the short walk to the backseat of the car. I don't want to be in the same space with Jovich, and I certainly don't want to sit next to him in the passenger seat, but I'm reluctantly grateful when he turns the key in the ignition and cranks the knob for the air to maximum.

That relief doesn't last long before I'm freezing, wrapping my arms around myself to try and warm up a little. I catch Jovich's eye in the rearview mirror and promptly turn away to look out the window. Droplets of water still bead on the glass, blurring the world outside the car even further. Jovich drives faster than Remy did, and as we turn off of the paved road, he presses the pedal further into the floorboard so that every bump we hit jars the vehicle. I don't even remember a dirt road on the way here, but surely, he's taking me to the public airport this time. I probably should have swallowed my pride to ask Remy for that passport he'd had made.

I don't have the faintest idea how I'll be able to get home without one, but it's not something I'm going to bring up in front of Jovich. Maybe I can say that I lost it or bribe a gate agent with tears. It wouldn't be a show, and it wouldn't be hard to summon them—I'm barely capable of keeping them at bay as it is.

The SUV dips into a pothole as I squeeze my eyes shut and focus on breathing through my nose so that I don't throw up.

I can't guess how much time passes before the car slows and I feel steady enough to open my eyes again. The night presses in all around us. I straighten in my seat, trying to take in wherever we are.

But it's too dark to see past the high beams that cut through the hazy night in front of us. Jovich stops and shifts into park, but he doesn't turn the car off. Instead, he turns around to look at me.

There should be lights to direct us, signs, planes.

"This isn't the airport?" I guess. My nerves are still a tangle of raw emotions and anxiety. As I take in the middle of nowhere place that we stopped, they only worsen.

"No." He laughs. "But it is a one-way ticket."

I'm trying to understand what that is even supposed to mean when my door opens. I barely have a chance to look out at the man who opened my door before I feel the sting of a needle in my neck. I try to scream, but as the plunger empties some sort of drug into my veins, the effect is immediate.

A heavy warmth falls around me all at once, and suddenly the darkness outside is the least of my worries.

The last thing I see as I'm dragged out of the car is Jovich's shadowy grin. "Sorry kiddo." He says. "I can't have them find out who you are."

I blink and feel myself falling to the ground, but the same person who ripped me out of the car threads their arms under mine and drags me into the night.

The headlights disappear as Jovich tears out of there as fast as he came.

My eyes are too heavy to keep open, and as they close one final time, his words tease the back of my mind.

Can't have them find out who you are.

The cold and pain disappear, a headrush making me feel light as the world around me falls away. I'm confused, unable to hold onto a single thought, let alone the millions that seem to be flitting away from me just out of reach. But as my eyes close, one thought stays with me.

Who am I?

CHAPTER TWENTY-SIX

REMY

The rapid knocking on the door jars me from the fringe of sleep and I glance around my room, confused.

I don't remember my eyes closing.

"Remy!" Rhea yells my name from the other side of my door, punctuating it with the beating of her fists.

She's pissed, and I'm in for it now. I glance at the tablet, where the screen is still open to Claire's empty room. I guess she told her.

I drag myself to the door and throw it open to stare at her with my jaw set. I don't even have a chance to ask what the hell her problem is, because as soon as the barrier between us is gone, she braces her hands on my chest and shoves me so hard that I stumble backwards. Not because she's strong, but because I certainly hadn't expected *that*.

"What the hell?" I growl.

"What the hell is *exactly* what I wanna know." She snaps. "What the hell did you do to my best friend?"

I sigh as the thought of Claire sends guilt and anger pulsing through me in tandem. I'd known Claire would tell her all about just how much snooping I'd done into her past, and I'd been prepared to stand my ground in the face of her anger. But now, I can't even defend myself against her fury, because she has every right to it.

"I crossed the line." I scrub my hands over my face. "I know she won't want to see me, so I was trying to give her some time before I apologize, but trust me. I know I'm an ass."

"Where is she?" Rhea demands. "Elaine said you guys went out on the boat and that was the last time she saw either one of you. Did you do something to her?"

I blink as I try to orient the pieces of what she's saying into something that makes sense. "She didn't tell you?"

"Tell me what?"

I glance over her shoulder at the door to Claire's room. It's firmly shut, no light leaking out from beneath it. "Tell me *what*, Remy?" When I meet her eyes, Rhea curses. "Damn it, Remy. Did you fuck her?"

"No." I answer honestly. But I can tell she isn't going to believe anything that comes out of my mouth, and truly, I can't blame her.

"I told her to stay away from you. And you knew how much she meant to me." She shakes her head, her eyes sparkling with tears. "You just treated her like some plaything and now she's gone." Her lip quivers as she considers her next words. "Fuck you, Remy."

She turns to go, but I can't let her leave. "Wait! What do you mean, 'she's gone'?"

"I mean, unless you're bluffing and you tossed her over the boat, I'm guessing that you've scared her off and drove her away."

"You checked her room?"

"Of course, I did." She snaps. "Her stuff is still here, but I know Claire. She left like she's not planning on coming back. So, thank you for that."

I glance out the window, at the oppressive blackness pressing in around the glass panes. "What time is it?"

Rhea throws her hands up like she doesn't give a damn what time it is, but she glances at her phone. "11:30."

"11:30?"

Shit.

I don't know what time we got back to the house, or when Claire ran from me. I'd been rereading the police reports Jack had sent when my eyes got heavy. The next thing I know, Rhea was beating my door down. "You said Elaine hasn't seen her since this morning?"

Rhea's eyes narrow on me. "She said *you're* the last person who saw her."

"Dammit." I grab my phone off the bed where it must have fallen from my hands and look at my last call to Jack.

3:30.

My heart hammers against my ribcage as I realize the gravity of the situation. Nobody has seen Claire in eight hours.

"Did you try calling her?"

"Of course, I tried calling her." Rhea snaps. "But whatever you did to her, she isn't answering. So, I'm going to ask you, one last time, and if you give me anything less than the truth, I will never talk to you again." Her chest heaves up and down as she gathers her thoughts. "Did you kill her?"

The question shocks me into gaping at her with my mouth open. "You really think I would do that?"

My fingers had itched to close around Claire's neck when I thought she'd been lying to me. I can't blame Rhea for wondering if I had it in me to take her friend's life. Or, at least, I shouldn't blame her for thinking it. It certainly isn't outside the realm of possibility. "That's not an answer, Remy."

"I didn't kill her." I sigh. "And I didn't fuck her. But I did fuck up."

"How?" She demands.

I pinch the bridge of my nose in a futile attempt to drive away the headache wedged between my brows. It feels like someone is driving an ice pick into my brain.

I'm not sure how much Rhea knows, so I'm not sure if I should tiptoe around the truth or hit her over the head with it. "I've had Jovich digging into her, and I had some questions about things that didn't make sense. I pushed her too hard."

"Well, she's not made of glass," Rhea snaps, her eyes narrowed on me, "so what did you do?"

"I forced her to tell me things she didn't want to... things that I shouldn't have, about her past and that last foster family."

Her suspicion is tangible. "I'm not buying it. She doesn't like talking about her childhood, but it wouldn't make her run away without telling me. So, what am I missing, Remington?"

It hits me then that Rhea *doesn't* know what I do. She doesn't understand the depth of pain, the torture I've made Claire relive as I demanded she explain the violence from her past while threatening her with further violence. I've known I'm a piece of shit, but I didn't realize just how badly until this moment. As close as they are, Claire hasn't ever revealed that private piece of her past to my sister. And within three days of storming into her life, I bullied her into confessing it to me.

The pounding in my skull only grows worse. "Call Jovich and ask if he's seen her. Ask him for the security footage of the front door from 3:30 on." I push past her hard enough that it knocks her slightly off balance.

Rhea plants her hands on her hips and stares daggers after me. I can feel her anger radiating off my back, but I can't be worried about that right now.

I'm already down the stairs by the time her voice calls after me. "Where are you going?"

It's a question I don't know how to answer, so I don't even try.

Elaine is waiting at the bottom of the steps, pacing back and forth. When she sees me, she straightens and positions herself firmly in my way. "Elaine." I tip my head in acknowledgement, expecting her to step aside. Instead, she lifts a hand and presses it firmly against my chest, stopping me in my tracks. I meet her eyes and am surprised at the anger in them.

"Where is she?" Elaine demands.

"That's what I'm trying to figure out." I say impatiently, trying to sidestep her.

"Remington," her voice carries a warning that I've never heard from her, hysteria bordering on a threat. "I swear if you did anything to that girl..."

"Elaine," My jaw is straining as I hold back the impulse to scream at her. "Do you really think I killed my sister's best friend?"

"I want to say no. But I've seen the way that she looks at you, and I've seen the way you look at her. The two of you left together, and now you're here but she's not. You understand how that looks?"

"I'll be the first to admit I'm an asshole. And it's my fault that she's gone, so let me handle it." The tone of my poorly concealed rage tells her there's no use in arguing it any further. She steps aside but her cold eyes follow me out the door.

I glance around the driveway, holding onto a ridiculous hope that she simply stepped out for some fresh air. But there's no one outside.

I call Dimitri first, but it goes straight to voicemail. I curse his name and rake my fingers through my hair as I try to figure out my next move. I don't turn to face Rhea when she walks up behind me. "Jovich hasn't seen her." Her voice wavers and nearly breaks. "He's headed back now and then he'll get us the security footage."

"From where?" I ask, turning around to face her.

"The front door." She shakes her head, confusion mixing with the irritation and worry on her face. "You're the one who told me to ask him for it."

"No, I mean where is Jovich coming from?"

"I don't know." There's a pause as she considers my question, and then understanding seems to take root. "You don't think he's lying?"

Actually, that's exactly what I think.

Jovich has been shifty the last week, and I've chocked it up to the circumstances surrounding my father's death. But it's gotten stronger since I brought Rhea and Claire back with me. There's no denying that Jovich knows something. He was cagey about the security footage this morning. He came to tell me in person about the charges listed against Claire without revealing any of the backstory, because he knew it would look bad, but I know well enough that he would dig into it before passing the information along. Now, Claire's gone without a trace and Jovich has chosen this exact time to step out?

The lights slicing through the night alert me to the car speeding down the road. I turn to my sister and watch the confusion slip from her face as she considers what I'm suggesting.

"Get in the house and lock your door. Don't open it until I come get you. Not Elaine, not Jovich, me."

"Are you serious?" She shakes her head. "I have to help find Claire. I have to—"

"Go!" I yell.

I don't often take that tone with her. Rhea and I don't need to argue. We balance one another like dark and light, and usually our sibling squabbles amount to just the teasing variety. Occasionally we lose our temper with one another, just as she'd done when she accused me of chasing her best friend off. But to really yell at her? It's something I've never done.

She doesn't fight me, turning on a dime and disappearing inside the house just as the car turns into the drive. I cross my arms as he slows, and when Jovich steps out of the car, he looks around questioningly. "What's going on? Rhea said Claire's missing?"

"Is she?" My voice is deceptively calm considering I'm raging inside.

Jovich pulls a face. "You know where she is?"

"Nah. But I think you do."

Jovich laughs, but it's short-lived. When I don't join in, he realizes I'm serious. "What's going on, Remy?"

"You tell me." I step toward him. I have the advantage of height and bulk on a good day, but now my anger eclipses him. "Where is she?"

Jovich opens his mouth like he's going to deny it, but then his lips turn to a grin. "What is so special about this whore? I mean, between you and your sister fawning over her, I'm starting to wonder what the big deal is. And I'm kind of bummed I didn't get a taste of that sweet cunt while I still could."

His words, his casual tone, are a trigger. I feel like I'm spring-loaded, barely holding it together. And once he speaks, that spring snaps. My hands find his throat and squeeze as I press him against the hood of the SUV. The headlights cast us in a haze that makes it hard to see anything beyond the insufferable quirk of his lips. I slam his head into the car, but the grizzled smirk doesn't slip from his face. "Where is she?" I growl, knocking his head again.

I let go just enough for him to catch his breath and answer me. A wheezing laugh claws its way through his throat and his lip curls deeper in amusement. "You should be grateful, Remington. Claire is settling your old man's debt."

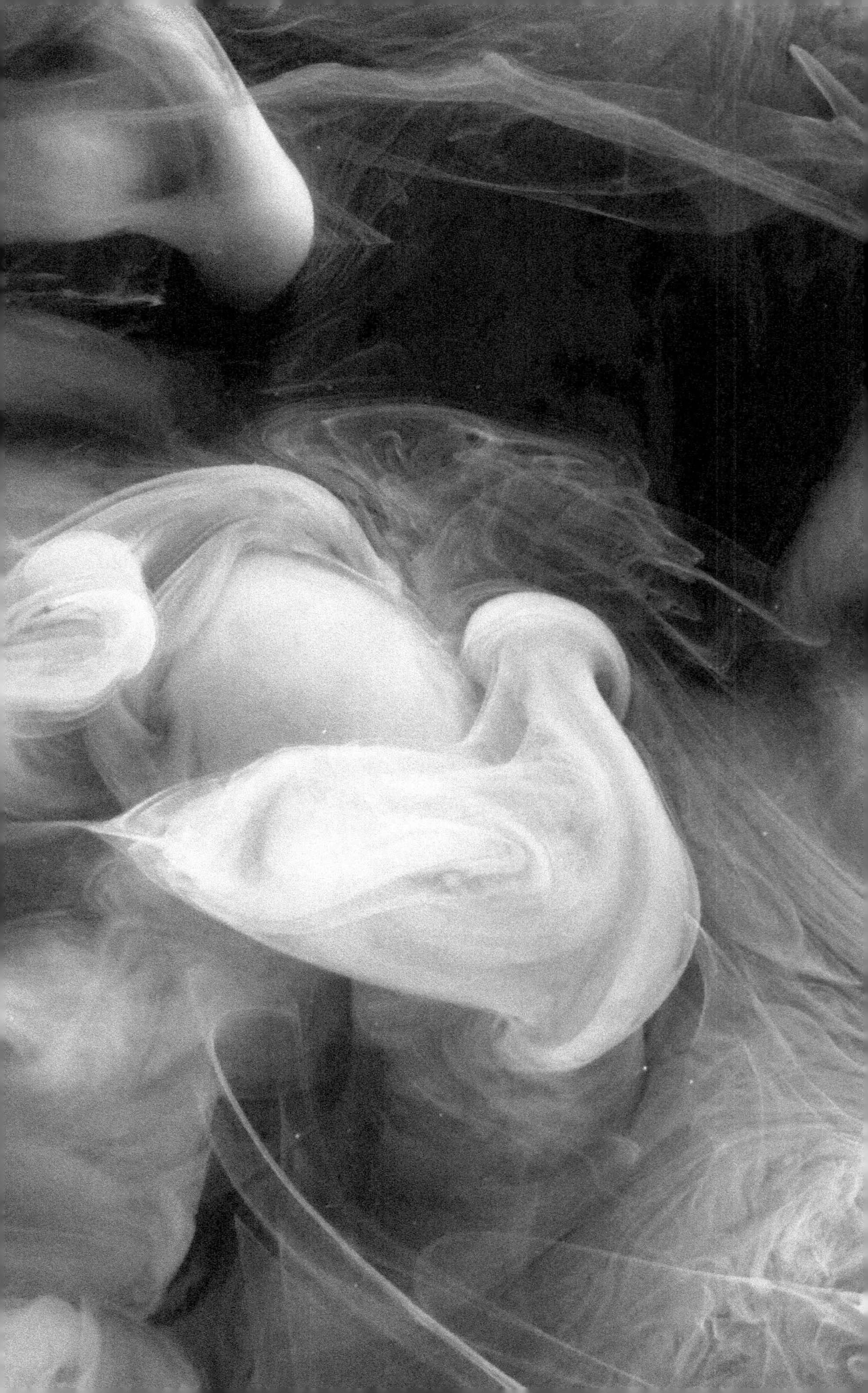

Chapter Twenty-Seven

Claire

A hand whipping across my face wakes me up with a start, a cry on my lips and confusion making my head and eyes heavy. All of me is heavy, actually.

I struggle in vain to sit up, but I'm tied down. Literally.

I can feel the rope rubbing against my arms, digging into my skin, and manage to crane my neck enough to see that it's wound around my stomach, my ankles, my thighs, my chest. Panic tries to bloom there, but it's drowned out by the pounding in my head, like someone is using my skull as a drum set.

It takes a moment for the face hovering over me to come into view, and when it does, I can't figure out where I know it from. His dark hair is pulled back into a ponytail and his similarly dark eyes betray no warmth. In fact, the longer I look into them, the colder I feel. I try to turn away, to look at anything other than those soulless eyes, but he grabs my chin and angles my face toward him.

"Morning, sunshine." He says, grinning around a wad of tobacco in his mouth.

I try to ask him what he wants, who he is, why I'm tied up. But there's something stuffed in my mouth... something dirty and foul that tastes faintly of kerosene. I gag as it slips against my tongue, the edge of it precariously close to slipping down my throat.

"So, you're what all the fuss is about, huh?" His eyes traipse over me. "I preferred you in that little black dress that made my dick tight." He slaps a tattooed hand over his crotch and adjusts himself as if the memory is causing a physical reaction.

I can't keep my head up, so it drops back against the table as I try to blink away the sleep still pulling at me like a fog. My heart squeezes into a fist as I remember where I've seen this face before. Back at the Piazza. Before Costa Rica. Before Remy. This is the man who sent me a drink—the Blue Russian. Did he follow me to another country just to kidnap me?

But he didn't kidnap me. Jovich did that.

I don't remember why—did he give me a reason? I just remember the prick of a needle, being dragged out of the car, his taillights fading into the night.

"I see you remember me." He chuckles, running a finger down my cheek through a trail of tears I didn't realize I was crying, and down to my tape-covered lips. He rips it back all at once and pulls the gag out of my mouth, but I don't have a chance to scream, because he shoves his fingers in its place, pressing hard against my tongue.

If the rag tasted filthy, he tastes like decay. Nausea rips through me, and I turn away as hard as I can so that if anything comes up, it won't get caught in my throat. But there's nothing to throw up anyway, though I still gag from the pressure and taste of his disgusting fingers.

I feel like I've been hollowed out, like someone came along and scraped my insides out. I've felt this way before. The thought sparks terror and I crane my neck to make sure I haven't been opened up and sewn back together, to make sure my clothes are still in place. Beyond the coarse rope, there's nothing amiss. It's a small comfort.

The man steps away and wipes his hands on the crotch of his jeans again. I'm trying to find my voice to scream when I realize there's someone else in the room. I can't see him, but I can hear his words. "Leave her alone, Mack."

"Help me!" I cry, trying desperately to find the source of the other voice. I can't move enough to find another person in the darkness, so I try to entreat them again. "Please, help me!"

"Shut up, bitch." Mack squeezes my lips between his fingers so hard I'm sure they'll bruise, but that is the least of my problems.

My first sound comes out muffled, and Mack laughs, pressing harder. "Do it again!"

This time, I'm able to rip out from under his touch and scream. The air moving through my throat feels like swallowing jagged pieces of broken glass. "Help!"

My voice echoes around me, followed by laughter. "Again!" Mack cries, digging his nails into the thin flesh of my collarbone. I oblige, preparing to call for help again, but the sound doesn't make it out of my throat.

Finally, I can see the second man as he stuffs the rag into my mouth forcefully enough to make me gag again before he steps back. "Cut it out." He warns his companion.

"Aw, come on, Slick. I'm just having a little fun. It's not like anyone can hear her out her." His tone is condescending, and when his gaze slides toward mine it's much the same. "There's no cavalry coming, Princess."

"Yeah, well it's fucking annoying." The second man moves out of sight again.

"She didn't bite." Mack says gleefully, his tone changing completely when he faces his friend. "Submissive little whore. Davos will be pleased."

"He'd better be." Slick says bitterly. "I'm not trying to make an enemy of Boudreaux over some bitch who's been rode hard and put away wet."

Boudreaux?

My heartbeat falters. What do Remy and Rhea have to do with this?

"You used to be so full of adventure." Mack grumbles. "I remember a time when you would have already choked her on your dick. I miss that guy."

"Not this one." Slick grunts. "You'd be a damn fool to fuck with the sister of a guy like Boudreaux."

Sister?

I strain against the rope, trying to see past the tears to get a sense of where we are. But there's nothing around... just unending, vast darkness. Only the space I lay below is illuminated by a large, round fixture on the ceiling. I can see nothing beyond it.

"I'm not scared of a bitch like Remington Boudreaux. What does he know about getting physical? Soy boy probably has his maid do his dirty work." He laughs. "Besides, she's ours. Jonathan offered her to us fair and square."

Slick laughs. "She's no more ours, than she was his to give. She belongs to Davos now."

Confusion clouds my head as I try to keep up with their conversation. I don't understand what they're getting at, but I know enough that it isn't good. The mention of *belonging* to anyone sends a lightning bolt of fear through me.

"You see the prick around here anywhere?" Mack grins, lifting his palms toward the corners I can't see, to indicate that they're the only ones here.

"The prick sent me to make sure you don't fuck it up again."

I tense at the new voice that comes from out of my line of sight. Somewhere in the recesses of my mind, I recognize it. But that recognition is buried under my terror and the slamming of my heart against my chest.

"Oh great, you're here. Can we pump her veins and get this party started?"

"No. The kind of clients that are gonna pay for her aren't the sort of men who want her too doped up to move or feel anything." The voice is slow and deliberate, letting his words sink through me. "Nah, not a high-class whore like Rhea Boudreaux. Trust me, if she's half the lay her mother was, this little honeypot's a goldmine."

Realization slaps me across the face harder than Mack did when he pulled me from unconsciousness. It dawns on Wes' face at the same time, and we stare at each other in silence a moment before he turns away from me. His voice shakes when he says, "What the hell is this?"

Slick edges into view, glancing at me like he's trying to see what's wrong. When he can't figure it out, he turns to look uncertainly at Mack.

"The handprint?" Mack guesses. "She took the mids a little too well. I wanted to make sure I didn't overdose her."

"I'm not talking about the handprint." Wes' voice is tense, like he's trying hard to hold onto a shred of his patience. "I'm talking about the woman tied to this table."

They exchange a glance, and that's when the pieces begin to shift into a picture that makes sense. At least, it makes a little sense. They think I'm Rhea, but Jovich obviously knew better. He probably hadn't been counting on anyone to realize as much. Mack frowns and stabs a finger in my direction. "That's Rhea Boudreaux."

"No." Wes growls. "It's not."

"I saw you with her days ago." Mack reasons. "At that little shithole in the States."

"You don't have Rhiannon Boudreaux on the table." Wes assures them, looking ready to explode. "That's her friend, Claire."

There's a silence as they all let that information settle around them, and then Slick pipes up. "Jovich is the one who brought her to us."

"Then he lied to you." Wes sighs and turns to face me. "Dammit, Claire. How'd you get yourself wrapped up in this?"

I try to talk, but I still can't. Wes understands that, and he peels back the tape, plucking the rag from my mouth. He rubs my cheek idly, rubbing his fingers through my tears like he can soothe away the sting still burning in my cheek.

"Wes!" I pant, the moment I'm able to make my tongue work. "Help me!"

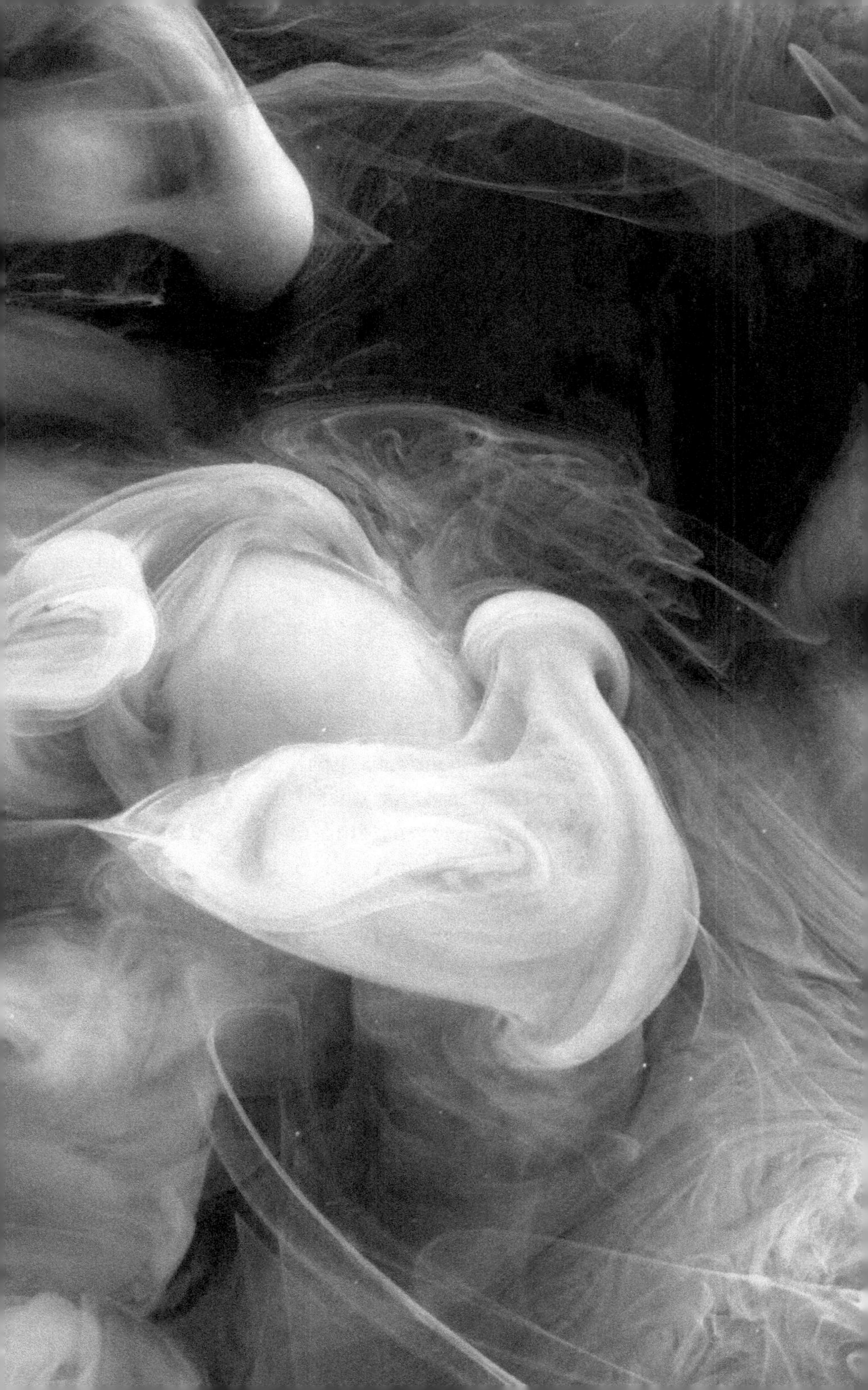

CHAPTER TWENTY-EIGHT

CLAIRE

"Please." I beg, my voice curdling with desperation. "Please, help me! I don't know what's going on."

Wes' eyes appraise my face for a moment as he listens to me plead for my freedom. "It's probably better that way." He pats my shoulder, and his eyes darken as he finds something that interests him. He reaches out and runs a finger over the skin on my neck. "A hickey?" He laughs. "What are you, a fucking teenager?"

A hickey? I didn't realize there was anything there, but things between Remy and I have been intense. He kissed me all over before we'd been driven apart, so it isn't entirely impossible.

"Oh." Wes' lips form the shape of surprise before they turn to a grin. "You're fucking Remington Boudreaux?" He laughs, amused with the realization he's come to.

"No." I shake my head so hard it knocks against the table I'm bound to. "Wes, *please*. Help me!"

He narrows his eyes on me and then looks up at his companions. "All right. This..." He nods like he's working through something in his head. "This can work."

Mack and Slick exchange a look while they await further instruction. "Untie her." Wes commands.

Relief bursts through me so violently that I feel fresh tears burning my eyes. "Thank you." I sniff, trying to hold back the flood. "Thank you."

Mack's face is sour as he undoes the knots on my legs first, and then my arms. As the rope falls away, I rub at my raw skin and sit up, the last of the fog finally fading away. When I swing my legs over the side of the table, the world shifts like the floor is falling out from under me. Mack catches me under the arm and holds me up. Wes appraises me a minute, casting his eyes up and down as we wait for him to tell us how to make everything okay.

"Get her undressed."

An excited laugh leaves Mack's lips as he turns to leer at me.

"What?" My tears of relief turn instantly to panic. "No! Wes, *no!*"

But Mack grabs my other arm and Slick moves in, ripping my shorts away from my body in a swift motion. I twist away from him, fighting to keep them on my hips, but he lifts my legs while Mack supports my weight and tugs them loose. I kick at him and nearly catch his jaw, but he moves out of my path with an appreciative chuckle.

"Grab her waist." Wes tells Mack, who obeys without taking his hands off me.

Slick grabs the hem of my shirt and rips it over my head. I fight against him, trying to curl my chest into my knees. But all I accomplish is giving Mack better leverage. His hand paws at my bra, ready to tear it away without unhooking the latch. Slick steps back, laughing. "She's a real lively one. Whoever breaks her in is gonna go home with his wallet a lot lighter. Push her on the table."

Mack is happy to do as he's told, spinning me around and slamming my chest into the table hard enough that it knocks the air out of my lungs and steals the scream from my throat. Slick kicks my legs apart and tugs at my panties, but his fingers have just grazed my skin, slipping under the elastic when Wes speaks. "Leave her like that."

He's standing on the other side of the table that I'm being ground into and I can feel both men behind me still at his command. "The kind of man that buys a woman like Claire does it because he wants a good girl to ruin. Leave some things to the imagination."

He turns and paces a few feet away before spinning back around and sliding his cell phone from his pocket. Mack weaves his fingers through my hair and yanks my head up. A gasp of pain rips from my throat and more tears spill down my cheeks as I try to get a look at Wes through them. "Mmm." Wes murmurs. "Perfect. Go ahead and cry, Claire. The buyers love that." He snaps a photo—one taken on an old fashioned camera, with a dizzying flash and a loud shutter. White dots from the sudden flash explode in front of my eyes, and I try to blink them away, but everything is spinning and then there's a cell phone in my face.

"You're sick!" I yell as Mack twists his hips, grinding an erection against my ass. "You're animals!"

"Animals." Slick laughs. "What an insult."

I've been holding out hope that Wes will soften and realize how messed up this is, but they seem to be feeding off of my desperation. I dig my teeth into my bottom lip and squeeze my eyes shut, forcing my mind to think of someplace else, trying to escape to that place I used to go where I don't have to be in my body, don't have to feel what they're doing.

But Eric was easy to drown out because he came with routine—always the same excuses, the same string of words, the same motions. It was easy to shut my brain down after the first couple of times, and I thought I'd learned to dissociate to survive. Apparently, it's a skill that you either use or lose, because I can't detach myself now.

Wes rubs a finger over my lips and leans in. I see the steady flash of his cellphone through my closed eyelids. "That's perfect, Claire. You're a natural at this. So fucking sexy."

A whimper breaks through my chest and is halfway out of my lungs when I swallow it back. I can feel him move behind me and hear the camera on his phone shutter. Mack yanks me backward so that I straighten, and the bright light cuts through my darkness again. "Open your eyes." Wes says softly.

I don't move a muscle until I feel the blade press against my stomach. "Do it."

My eyes flutter open to see him holding the tip of a blade against me. But he isn't trying to cut me... he leaves that to Slick, offering the knife in his open palm. "Don't go too deep." Wes warns. "But make sure she feels it. The men want to hear her scream. They want a preview of what they're getting."

"Just the tip." Mack laughs, wrapping his free hand around my neck and pulling me firmly against him.

His breath is hot on my skin. The camera in my face spurs my rage; The light is solid, and I know he's recording.

"You're pathetic. Can't get women to sleep with you so you have to force them? Fucking animals! You're sick!"

Their laughter enrages me further. I strain against Mack until the knife presses into my flesh again, the edge digging into me without cutting. "There seems to be some confusion, Claire." Wes says. "We're not going to hurt you... I mean, not *much*. That pleasure is going to go to the highest bidder."

I don't need to think about the horrors of that threat, but I do. The highest bidder. There are no words for how despicable that is, but I have to try. "You can't just sell people!" I yell. "I'm not cattle."

"As good as." Mack snorts.

Wes leans into me so that there's no mistaking; he isn't bluffing. "Baby, I make women disappear for a living. All it takes is a few friends in all the right places and I can have all traces of you wiped off the face of the earth."

"You're a monster!" I accuse, fighting them the only way I can. But the insult doesn't bother Wes, who just smirks at me.

"I'm just the same as your dear best friend's brother... you know, the one you've been fucking since our date the other night? You move fast, Claire. Get used to it, cause most of the buyers we have love to share with their friends. Give them a taste, show them what they've got, and make them want more. You're a whore, Claire. Just fucking embrace it!"

As if he were acting on cue, Slick presses the knife into my flesh. I try not to make a sound, but the metal bites into my abdomen, and he drags it across my skin a second, making me gasp in pain. I feel the warmth of blood welling up there, running together, but refuse to look down. Slick glances at Wes, who shakes his head. "You can do better."

Slick licks his lips and adjusts his fingers on the knife before driving it a little above the last spot. This time he digs the blade in deeper and pulls it through me harder, though he seems to do it with all the ease of fileting a fish.

There's no fighting it. The pain feels like being ripped in half... which is essentially what he's doing. I've never heard the sound that comes from me. I wouldn't have even known it was human, let alone mine, except it dies when Slick pulls the blade away, turning instead to a strange sound that's something between gasping and sobbing.

Wes' lips twitch in approval. "Pure fucking magic." He says. His voice is deeper, husky. I shiver at the sound of it and his obvious arousal. "Tell them who you are."

I look at the camera wordlessly as Mack's fingers drum against my throat while the other pushes a lock of my hair behind my ear. "Don't be shy, baby. Let them know who they've got a chance at owning."

I grit my teeth around another scream as Mack slips a hand under my bra, his hot palm cupping my entire breast under the fabric. "If you don't want to tell them, we'll just have to show 'em." Slick drags the bloody tip of the knife between my cleavage, creating a thin line of blood that wells up on my chest. He presses against the bit of fabric that holds the cups together, keeping me covered. If he presses hard enough, the fabric will shred and I'll be exposed not just to them, but to whoever views the video. I swallow my tears enough to squeeze out my name as Mack pinches my nipple hard between his fingers. I cry out in pain and rage, trying to squirm out of his grip. He likes me squirming— I feel his erection growing against my ass and will myself not to vomit.

"They already know your name's Claire." Wes tuts, unenthused. "Tell them who you've been fucking."

"I haven't—"

I'm trying to argue that we haven't even done anything but Mack's hot breath rasps against my neck, distracting me. I have never wanted to crawl out of my own skin so badly. I can't even breathe, my heart is hammering too fast in my throat.

I don't know how far they're willing to take this, or how true their claims of selling me off like an old car are, but I don't intend to help them out.

"Claire Monroe." Wes interjects. "This sexy little bitch is 20 years old, a senior in college, and has been spending her summer riding none other than Remington Boudreaux." He laughs. "Bidding starts at three hundred sixty firm and closes at three a.m. Greenwich Mean Time. You don't wanna miss this."

Mack chuckles, his tongue darting out to lick the swell of my cleavage, one hand wrapped around my throat while the other kneads against my other breast. Wes makes no attempt to stop him until his hand drifts over my stomach, running through the blood welling from the cuts Slick made and dipping into the waistband of my thong. "No!" I gasp, crying freely as I try to evade his touch.

"That's enough." Wes commands, slipping the phone in his pocket. Mack pauses, but doesn't let go of me, his hand cupping me like he's considering ignoring Wes altogether. When Wes sees my face, he laughs. "You can dry your eyes now. You should just be grateful you're worth more alive than dead... for now anyway."

Mack moves his hand away from my neck, brushing his fingers down my chest. "And you should be glad that I have a family to feed, or else I wouldn't hold back on showing you just what you're in for." He pulls his hand out from my underwear, grabbing me by the neck and flinging me to the ground, where I stay with my face pressed against the dirty floor until Slick tugs me into a sitting position. He drops his weight on the balls of his feet so that his face is level with mine.

"I wanna say it isn't personal and it's just business." He says, grabbing the rope off the table. "But now that he knows Boudreaux's been with you, it *is* personal."

He pushes my wrists behind me and winds the rope around them, knotting it tightly before repeating it over again. He does the same at my ankles and then connects them behind my back so that I can't move... not even a little. I told them I wasn't cattle, but I'm not sure anybody even treats cattle this cruelly. He pushes me backward and guides me to the ground where he rests me on my side. Now at least, my face isn't on the ground, so I won't drown in my own tears or suffocate in the dirt they left me in.

"You should try and get some beauty sleep." He suggests, as if he didn't stab me five minutes ago. "It'll be a few hours before we know where we're sending you."

I'm fairly certain I'll never sleep again, but as he walks out of sight and flicks the light off, the darkness he casts me into is indistinguishable from sleep.

And my nightmares? Those are indistinguishable from what has become my life.

CHAPTER TWENTY-NINE

REMY

Jovich underestimates me. He foolishly assumes that I'm no good at getting my hands dirty, simply because I *let* him handle otherwise unsavory business that he takes pleasure in. It's a win/win situation and delegating allows me to prioritize, so that I can focus my energy on the true goal. Unfortunately for him, I'm not as meek as he seems to think I am. I handled my own problems before he was sent to keep an eye on me, and I can handle him, too.

"What do you mean, she's settling my father's debt? His debt was paid in his death."

Jovich laughs. "You know as well as I do that the type of debt your father racked up can't be paid in his own blood. He made them an offer and they accepted. Your father being dead doesn't change anything."

"He made an impossible deal!" I yell. "He bargained with a life that wasn't his."

"That's how you see it." He shrugs, far too casual about the circumstances. Jovich has been involved in my father's debauchery for far longer than I have, and he's either desensitized to it, or he enjoys it. "But you know your father always considered women to be his property... his to do whatever he wants to. Your mother, your sister, your housekeepers..."

I curl my fingers around the collar of his shirt and draw him closer. "Tell me where she is!"

"That can never happen." Jovich shakes his head. "And you know that."

"No." I shake my head, my jaw tense as I clench it. When I let go of him and turn, Jovich follows.

"Come on, Remington. It's not natural for you to be in such a twist over one little bitch."

He says it like she's just another victim of the billion-dollar industry I've been forced into. He says it like she's just some random girl who has been pulled off the street, as if that makes it any easier to look the other way.

But Claire is so much more than that, and not just to Rhea. "Where is she?" I growl. "Who did you hand her over to?"

"Remy," He tsks. "Let's go inside, have a drink. Get her out of your head." He claps a hand on my shoulder and squeezes like he thinks he's going to offer me some kind of comfort. I lift my eyes to his. They're flat, unaffected.

I knew he was sick... I knew something in him wasn't quite normal. He enjoys causing the pain and destruction that his job demands of him, but usually it's directed toward men who are so despicable they're barely even human. It's easy to overlook his depravity when it's aimed at men whose wickedness knows no bounds. "Come on," he nods to the front door, "we'll tell Rhea I drove her friend to the airport. She won't even know that I've told you."

Something in me snaps.

I grab his arm and twist it behind his back so fast, so violently, that I feel it pop out of place. He growls and hisses, gnashing his tobacco-stained teeth like a wild animal. "Tell me where you took her, and I won't tell Rhea what you've done."

"Davos' men have her." He hisses. "In a matter of hours, she'll be gone, and I guarantee you'll never see her alive again."

My brain doesn't even register that he gave me a timeline. I'm reeling, trying to deny the truth he just told me. He's lied to me a few times today, but I know that this isn't one of them. There's no merit in a lie like this.

Davos' men?

Rage ripples in me so hard that I start shaking. Davos is an emotionless prick who made his fortune off the backs of women his cronies plucked off the street. He is the most ruthless man in the trade, and also the most powerful. He turned a brothel into an empire with the help of my father. He's also my employer, my jailor, my debtor. I've seen firsthand what his men do to the women he auctions. If Claire is under his control, she'll be dead soon... or, at least, wishing she was.

Jovich is at my mercy, but it doesn't mean he's at my command. I push him so hard that he drops to his knees on the pavement. He faces away from me, hiding the agony on his gnarled features as he works on getting his shoulder back into place. That gives me the distraction I need to slip the gun out of the back of my jeans. When he feels the barrel press into the back of his skull, he freezes.

"Don't point that thing at me if you aren't gonna use it." He warns, still with that teasing lilt in his voice, challenging me.

"Don't make me use it." I counter. "Tell me where you took her."

"I told the idiots she was Rhea." He laughs so hard it shakes his whole body and then growls in pain as it pulls on his shoulder. "They'll figure it out, but by the time they do Rhea can have a totally new identity and you won't have to worry about someone busting her door down in the dead of night... or all the things they'd do to her."

I grab his same arm again, twisting it as I tell him, "Hand me your phone."

"You can't stop this Remy." He bites out, "This is bigger than you."

I raise my arm and strike him with the butt of the gun. "If she dies, I'll kill you. But if you help me find her, I'll let you live." That offer should be incentive enough, but I'm desperate. "And I'll double whatever Davos offered you to make you flip on me."

Jovich laughs. "I didn't take his money. I just needed the bitch gone, and your father's debt needed paid in flesh. Two birds, one stone, as they say."

I bash him with the gun again, and his free arm covers his face, trying to protect his vulnerabilities. Time is running out, and I can't have Claire's blood on my hands, on my soul. She's already been haunting my every thought since I first laid eyes on her. In death, I'm sure she'll torment me. And that's to say nothing of Rhea, who will likely kill me herself if everything unravels and she realizes I put her best friend in danger.

I lower the gun, aim where I know I'll get results, and shoot him right in the back of the knee.

The *bang!* is closely followed by an earth-splitting scream as his kneecap shatters into a thousand tiny splinters and Jovich's blood surges out around him.

Jovich has always seemed to get off on the sound of other people's screams. It's like a drug that makes him giddy. But the sound of his agony does nothing for me. That isn't what I want.

He falls immediately to the ground and writhes in pain, white-faced and sweating. "I'll take that phone now." I cock the gun at his other leg, just in case he tries to deny me.

It takes a minute, but he reaches in his pocket and retrieves his cell, holding it out to me with a trembling hand. "Dial Davos and have him call it off." I command.

"I *can't*!" Jovich roars. For a guy who likes pain so much, he sure can't take it the way he can dish it out. My finger strokes the trigger almost of its own accord, and he groans. "You know it won't do anything."

I blink. He's right. I know that Davos is the worst sort of man to walk the Earth, closely followed by his customers. But I don't have any other option. "Call him."

As he scrolls through the phone, Jovich's whole body quakes with unconcealed agony. When he lifts the phone to his ear, I shake my head. He switches it to speakerphone and drops it on the ground before me as it rings.

Alexandre Davos answers on the third ring. I'm familiar with his guttural Russian solicitation, but it means nothing to me. "English," I demand.

"Call it off, Davos." Jovich yells, his voice hinting at some of the fear he's trying to keep at bay. "I made a mistake."

"I know you did, Jovich. You thought you could fool me?" Davos' deep laugh booms through the speaker. "The deal we had was for Rhiannon Boudreaux. I don't know who you took to my boys, but she's a hit."

"Let her go." Jovich tries again. "Your boys know where to find me. Just bring her back, and we can forget this whole thing ever happened."

"Are you kidding?" Davos laughs again. "You may have pulled one over on my men, but that doesn't mean the girl isn't serving her purpose. The bidding's already begun."

Desperation tangles with rage in my stomach.

The bidding has begun.

I've witnessed their depravity firsthand, and it's hard enough to watch a complete stranger have their life ripped from them. I never thought I'd have a personal connection to someone being auctioned off, but I do. I can't even begin to untangle the web of ways that I feel connected to Claire.

"I'll beat whatever your highest offer is." I say loudly enough to be sure he'll hear me from a distance.

There's a pause as my words hang in the air, and Davos considers the offer. "Is that Remington Boudreaux? To what do I owe the pleasure?"

"You have something I want. Cancel the sale. I'll top whatever she's going for."

"Come on, Remy." He sighs as if he regrets the conversation we haven't even had yet. "I'm trying to run a business here. I can't have my customers doubting my commitment to them."

"You can." I say firmly. "Just this once."

"Remington..." He clicks his tongue in disappointment. "You know better than to get attached."

"Davos." I growl his name through clenched teeth, desperately trying to maintain a sense of calm. "Shut it *down*."

"I wish I could help you, son." Davos sighs for dramatic effect as if he expects me to fall for his lies. "But it's out of my hands now. This girl has got my buyers in a frenzy. I'm already up thirty percent from the opening bid. I suspect you've made an impression on many of my buyers, and they're eager to make their own impression on her."

My throat threatens to close, it's so dry. Claire is slipping through my fingers, and I know what fate awaits her if I let go. "Send me a passkey."

If I can't get Davos to circumvent the auction, I'll have to gain entry to the listing and win her myself. I'll gladly bankrupt myself if that's what it takes to keep her from being turned over to some anonymous predator who probably has a vendetta against my family that they intend to take out on an innocent third party.

"I'm afraid they're all gone. I only sell a limited number of tickets to every auction, you know that. And your little girlfriend has everyone scrambling to come up with funds."

I slam my fist into the hood of the car. It's a poor substitute for the true cause of my anger, but thousands of miles and a whole army of security separates Davos from me. "If you don't shut it down right now, I will hunt you down, and I will guarantee you the slowest, most excruciating death you could ever imagine. Mark my fucking words, Davos, if you take her, I will bring down your whole fucking empire from the inside out."

"Sorry, kid." Davos says, but he doesn't sound very sorry at all. "You can't always get what you want... unless you're me." He chuckles. "In fact, after she sells, I'm gonna offer the buyer a little kickback for first dibs. I am dying for a taste, myself."

Fury rips through my veins, an acrid drug that takes me over.

In my head, I picture him straddling Monica, threatening to have his way with her. That was the only reason he got me to bend to his will all those years ago. Now, he's going to do the same thing to another person I care for. Only, this time it's not a threat. This time, he has every intention of following through.

I shift the gun to Jovich's head as the poison turns everything on the edges of my vision black. "WHERE IS SHE?"

"I feel for you, kid. Your old man just dragged you into this life." He says it as if he didn't threaten, bribe, and blackmail me into being a soldier for him. "But you're here now, so you're gonna have to learn. Check your texts."

I keep the gun trained on Jovich's pale face as I reach down with my free hand and sweep his phone into my hand. There's one new text, and when I open it, the video starts playing immediately. The lips that I've been thinking about for the last few days are cracked and bleeding, and when someone runs a finger over them, it smears red on Claire's tear-soaked face.

I watch in horror as the woman I'm supposed to be protecting is pushed around like an object. She's strong, fighting, trying to keep control and hide just how badly they're hurting her. But her fear is greater than her resolve, and her cries tear through me, stabbing the pit of my stomach.

When the knife slices into her, I yell too. I try not to vomit when the thicker man holding her captive paws at her breast, helping himself to a handful as his tongue darts out to lick her. I can't decide what I'll cut off first when I find this man— his hand or his tongue.

The lanky man presses the blade between Claire's chest and threatens to reveal her to the camera, and I feel the shift in me as easily as if I flipped a switch.

"Like I said," Davos' voice is cold, all business. "That scream has a lot of men scrambling to pull some funds together. It's too late for this one."

The line goes dead just as suddenly as the video ends. Jovich stares up at me, finally looking like he's starting to regret his choices.

But it's too late for that, too.

I squeeze the trigger, emptying the last bullet into his head.

CHAPTER THIRTY

CLAIRE

"There she is."

I hadn't heard a door open anywhere in the room. I hadn't even noticed they'd turned the lights on. But now that I do, I find myself blinking past the fluorescent glare at the feet of the three men. Their shapes are blurred, distorted, and I'm not sure if it's from the sudden light or my swollen eyes.

"Our golden goose." Wes' voice comes closer and then he drops his weight on the back of his legs as he hunches down for me to see him. "You are a legend, baby."

His hand reaches out and strokes my cheek gently. They hadn't ever replaced the tape, and at first, I thought it had been a mistake. I screamed myself hoarse once they left. But that had accomplished nothing other than wearing me out even faster. Now, I barely have a voice to plead with them anymore. "Wes," I whisper, not because I don't want to be heard by the others, but because it's all the sound that I can make. "Please."

"I really was looking forward to going out with you. But you had to go and get yourself involved with all the Boudreaux family drama. There's a price to pay Claire, and that price? It's you. All of you, until someone decides to put you out of your misery."

He stands up and looks at Mack. "Go get the car ready. We need to have her in Zurich by sunset tomorrow."

"Zurich?" Mack asks. "I thought she sold already?"

"She did." Wes nods. "But the boss is going to deliver this one by hand."

"Sure." Mack's laugh echoes around the walls as he walks away. "If she makes it that long."

Slick chuckles too as he saws at the rope connecting my wrists and ankles. When the tension disappears, I'm too sore to move. My spine has been twisted for hours, my shoulders pulled back, my legs bent at the knee. Being released is a relief, but it's not an immediate fix for the last few hours. He tries to make me stand, but without adequate blood flow, my feet can't find steady ground below me.

Wes slips my arms over his shoulder. Though I don't want to be anywhere near him, I can't push away from him either. "The pilot's meeting us on the airstrip in twenty minutes." He tells Slick. "Clean this up and meet us there."

Wes drags me alongside him so that the tops of my feet scrape against the concrete floor, my ankles still tethered to one another too tightly to get them under me. "This worked out well." He says lightly. "I'll have to thank Jovich sometime. The commission from you is going to pay off the rest of my student loans."

"You're a *doctor*." I pant. I'd forgotten about that detail, given the circumstances. Now that I've remembered, it feels like a slap in the face. "You're supposed to do no harm."

His laughter is deep and rumbling. "You really are so *innocent*, aren't you? That's cute, Claire. You don't honestly believe that I'm a doctor because I want to save people, do you?"

I didn't think there was any other option. But I suppose that I'm discounting the one thing that turns otherwise decent people into criminals: money. After all, that's why I'm here, in this position. It's why I'm being sold off to whoever will pay the highest price. "Making people disappear is what pays the bills. But cutting people open and calling it surgery? It's not just a hobby, it's also a damn good cover. I mean, who doesn't trust a doctor? You did." Wes laughs, tossing his dark, wavy hair back as he languishes in his own wit.

He's right; I did trust him. Not because he's a doctor or because he has gorgeous eyes, but because I trust too freely these days. I've known pretty much all of my life that it isn't fair, that it's dark and sometimes twisted. I learned, growing up, that it isn't always pretty. And I had once believed that there was too much dark for any stars to shine again, that the darkness was too infinite for a pinprick of light to make a difference.

Somewhere along the way, Rhea got me to see the good again. I became so used to seeing that light, I'd become disillusioned by it. I forgot that monsters walk among us in the guise of a helping hand, a protector, a caregiver.

Wes stops abruptly as if something is amiss, clutching me against him and pressing a cold hand over my mouth. For a moment, there's nothing but the empty hallway in front of us and a steady *drip, drip!* noise coming from somewhere. But then a gunshot rings out through the building as if the walls are made of aluminum. Wes swears out loud. "Slick!" He hisses. "Go see what that was all about."

Slick brushes past us, gripping the knife in front of him. He moves quietly and quickly, disappearing into the darkness ahead. We wait for what feels like forever for any signs of either Slick or Mack. But when a few long moments pass, and nothing comes, Wes swears again. "Keep your mouth shut, Claire."

My ankles and wrists are still bound, making walking impossible, so he continues to drag me through the darkness. He stops when we're close enough to see a door propped open at the end of the hallway. What I presume to be the high beams of a car illuminate the empty space outside the door. Dust motes flit in the air, and I can hear the low rumbling of an engine. The scene is eerie, filling me with a sense of foreboding that I don't understand. Whatever is out there can't be worse than what awaits me at the end of the line.

Wes lifts a finger to his lips, a warning to be quiet, and then rushes for the door.

We're nearly at the exit when Mack steps in our path. With the light behind him, his face is cast in shadows, but his size leaves no doubt as to who it is. He opens his mouth, but the sounds that come from him are strange—weak little noises like something between a whimper and a groan fill the air between us.

Wes eyes him a moment and is opening his mouth to say something when Mack takes a step forward, allowing the light to bounce off his shoulders and reveal his empty mouth pouring blood. It oozes down his lips and chin and covers his shirt. In fact, his shirt is actually soaked with it... far too much of it to have come from just his mouth.

One arm is pressed against his chest, and the other is gesticulating wildly as he attempts to convey some kind of final message to us. Whatever it is, he can't say, because when he opens his mouth to try again, I realize his tongue is missing.

Mack falls to the ground before us, right at my feet. The knife sticking out of the back of his skull sends a shock through me.

I scream.

Wes grips me tighter and dodges the fallen body without a care, the way someone might sidestep a puddle. When we cross out into the night, there seems to be no one around. But Mack certainly didn't stab himself.

The driver's side door is open, and I can see a rabbit's foot keychain dangling from the ignition. I catch my reflection in the car window, feral and desperate. I don't recognize myself there, but I know who she'll be in a matter of days. Hopeless, broken, a shell of what she strived so hard to become.

This may be my last chance to fight back.

I go completely limp, dropping all of my weight onto Wes' arm so that it bogs him down. As he tries to shift me, it gives me an opening to wriggle loose and break free.

I hadn't just been lying in the dark waiting for them to come back and herd me off to whoever purchased me. Even as I screamed myself hoarse, I'd been tugging at the rope, back and forth, shifting the coils so that the ties loosened and tightened and loosened some more. I know it stripped away some of the flesh… I could feel the searing pain every time I shifted the braided nylon over my already-raw skin, but I clenched my teeth and almost wished they'd put the rag back in my mouth so that I had something to bite down on.

All that pain gave me just a little slack, and I wasn't sure it would be worth it, until I drop out of his grip and fall on the hard ground. The tension between my wrists eases enough for me to shift myself one last time, wriggling my hand free. All the while, Wes watches me with an amused smirk. His form blocks my exit. "You can't escape me, Claire. There's no other way out."

He steps slowly closer to me, the way someone might approach a dog they're about to trap. He doesn't seem concerned about getting bitten so much as having to chase me. I keep my eyes trained on him as he comes near, and when he takes the opportunity to lunge at me, sweeping me off my feet and throwing me over his shoulder, I let him.

"I liked you, so I'm going to give you some advice." He speaks casually, as if he were giving me tips on how to pass a test or budget my money. "This whole hard-to-get thing is cute to me. You're just a delicate little mouse, and I like watching you try to outrun the wheel. But not everyone is going to find it so endearing. If you want to last a while, learn to read your new master. I happen to know he—"

But whatever he knows about my 'master', I don't care. I'll die before letting him ship me off to some rich sadist. I slip my arms around Wes' neck so that the rope still dangling off one of my wrists is wound around his throat. I pull the other end tight with my free hand and force all of my weight into the movement, the rope digging into his skin.

In this moment, all that matters is survival. Mine, certainly not his.

Wes' hands release me to claw at the rope, desperately trying to slip under it and leverage it away from his air supply. But I can't let go. I practically climb on his back, forcing him to his knees as he tries to fight me away, and I double down on the rope against his windpipe.

I'm vaguely aware of his spluttering noises and also a distant yelling somewhere that I don't have a chance to consider the source of.

I cling to him even as it burns my hands, scraping away flesh as he tries to tug the rope out of my grip. Wes seems to realize the only way I'm letting go is when he's dead. He sinks further to his knees and lurches forward, throwing me flat against the ground. In my moment of surprise, he presses into me enough to rip the rope from my fingers and then his neck. It takes him a moment to catch his breath, so I scramble to my feet and try to run past him. I took him by surprise once, but that won't happen again. As much as I've pissed him off, I don't stand a chance against him in a fight.

But if I can just make it to the car...

Wes reaches out and grabs me around the waist, knocking me to the ground again so that the air in my lungs rushes out in a gasp of pain. I try to keep my face from grinding into the concrete as I feel his weight on my back, and then his fist is in my hair, yanking me toward him. "Play time's over, bitch."

I'd assumed Wes wasn't carrying a weapon because he hadn't used one to threaten me yet. I realize I was wrong as I feel a blade press against the soft skin of my neck so hard that I'm scared to even breathe, which is just as well cause I can't when a new voice speaks.

"Funny. That's what I was going to say."

I strain my neck and eyes to look up, straight into the barrel of a gun.

CHAPTER THIRTY-ONE

REMY

The man holding the knife to Claire's throat doesn't look entirely afraid of me. In fact, he almost looks amused.

"Well, if it isn't the man himself. Remington Boudreaux."

My fingers stroke the trigger, torn between blowing his brains across the walls or letting him explain himself. "And you are?"

"You don't know who I am?" He frowns, tangling Claire's hair in his fist tighter so that she gasps in pain and arches her back more to ease the burden on her scalp. But I can't look at her, can't take my eyes off of him for even a second lest he make a move to kill her. "That hurts, Rem."

The man is probably Rhea's age, give or take a year. He's too young to be calling the shots, and yet I know that voice. It's the very same one from the video... the one that had announced the bidding of a live person. Of *Claire*.

He looks innocent enough, a far cry from the tattooed and scarred men who usually do this sort of work. The kid looks like he doesn't usually get his hands dirty, so how did he get wrapped up with the most deplorable men I've ever met?

"Should I?"

The man shrugs. "I'd think you would know your own brother when you see him."

"You?" I laugh. "You're delusional."

"Am I?" His eyes hold the smirk his lips don't quite fulfill. "You don't see the striking family resemblance? I mean, we're practically twins. Your father was a little darker in flesh than mine, but that's nothing to be ashamed of."

"Drop the knife and get off of her." Given the amount of blood present when I'd slit the throat of the lanky one, I know there isn't a chance he's alive. The fat, greasy one lays on the ground at my feet with the knife protruding from his skull, his tongue is in the dirt just beyond the exit, and I'm pretty sure he isn't getting up. But I don't know how many others may be lying in wait. It would have been useful information to get out of Jovich, but I don't regret pulling the trigger.

"As much as I'd love to humor you, we both know it won't do any good. She's already been sold. Even if you can find it in yourself to kill your own flesh and blood, even if you get away with her, they're not going to let it go. They'll come for her."

"Then I'll kill every one of them." I say, pressing the gun into his forehead hard enough that his smooth skin ripples around it. "Get off of her."

His eyes lock on mine as he weighs his options, which aren't much of anything other than die *now* or die *later*. It's as he stares at me that I realize I'm looking straight into my mother's eyes.

"I'm not scared of death." He says. "But they'll kill me if I kill her, anyway." He drops the knife and unwinds his fist from Claire's hair before showing me his hands, admitting surrender.

"Untie her." I demand.

"Fine." He moves off of Claire completely and reaches for her ankles, unknotting the rope.

When the last of it falls free, I tell him, "Help her up."

Claire is already getting to her feet. The kid laughs, but with the gun still trained on him, he does as I tell him to, pulling her up off the ground as she tries to put as much distance between him and her as her exhausted body can manage.

The first time I saw her, she'd been in lingerie similar to what she wears now. But that time she hadn't been bruised, bloody, or relieved to see me. That time, the sight of her had set me on alert, aware of the possibility she could be a threat. This time the sight of her fills me with a sick rage.

I was only eighteen when I was sucked into the seedy world that Davos and his men belong to. It was harder to stomach then, and with time, with my own methods of coping, it's gotten easier. But I never imagined letting myself care about someone, so I never imagined the acute fury and disgust of watching it happen to someone that means something to me. I still don't understand the depth of it.

I stretch my free arm out and fold her against my body. Claire buries her face in my shirt and her arms cling to me like she doesn't have the strength to hold herself up. Her entire body seems to be trembling, so I squeeze her harder against me.

"I want to kill you." I tell him honestly. "People like you don't deserve to live."

"But...?" His tongue flicks out over his lips, anticipating what more I have to say.

"But you might be useful to me. So, I'm not going to kill you yet."

"Oh?" He mocks. "Do you want me to thank you for your mercy, sir?"

"No." I laugh. "I want you to call Davos."

He narrows his gaze on me, suspicion taking over the sharp features of his face. "You want to tell him you win? Really gonna pour some fuel on the fire?"

"No." I shake my head and wave the gun, a reminder of why he's taking my commands. "You are."

The kid laughs and reaches into his pocket to withdraw a phone. He must have Alexandre Davos on speed dial because it's only a few seconds before he has it on speakerphone with the dial tone echoing around us.

"Wes." Davos' greeting is curt, impatient.

"Hey, dad." Wes smirks at me, confirming what my suspicions had already started to put together.

"Are you on the plane?"

Considering he thinks Wes has just made him an ungodly amount of money, he doesn't sound very pleased with his son.

"About that..." Wes hesitates. "I don't think I'm going to make the flight."

"Why?" He growls.

"Because," I say. "Your boy and I have some catching up to do."

"Remington?" Davos sounds confused, but that's crowded out by the fury. I can picture him with his hands splayed on his desk, spitting at the phone in front of him. "What's going on?"

"I told you I would hunt you down. I promised you a slow death. I don't go back on my promises, but you're going to have to take a rain check."

"Where's the asset?" He demands, his voice rising in a glorious mixture of panic and rage. Just an hour ago, he had been delighting in my desperation, and now he's surely feeling the same. "Where is she?"

"Don't worry about Claire. She's safe. Your son, on the other hand? That depends on you."

"You think I care about the kid?" Davos laughs. "He means about as much to me as any of my other employees. Maybe even less."

Wes laughs, too.

"Well, I hope the two I killed weren't ones that you cared about."

There's a beat of silence, and when Davos speaks again, his words are tense. "What do you want, Remington?"

"Simple. Tell me who killed my father."

The laughter from the other end of the line is deep and rolling. Even when he pulls himself together, the amusement isn't gone from his voice. "We both know the answer to that question."

For now, that's all the answer that I need. "I'll be in touch." I tell him.

The line goes dead.

Wes flashes a grin at me. "If I didn't know any better, I'd say he likes you more than me."

"You don't know any better." I say curtly. "Claire..."

She pulls away enough to look at me, and I see her cheeks shining with fresh tears. "Go wait in the car. And lock the door." Her lip twitches like she's going to say something, but she bites it back and takes the gun I offer her.

I don't turn to watch her go, keeping my eyes trained on Wes, but I hear the car door shut after a moment. "What's the deal, Boudreaux? We gonna dance or something?"

"No." I laugh. "Not quite." His eyes flicker to the knife between us. Grinning, I kick it at him. "Go ahead."

But he doesn't move for it. He recognizes the threat in front of him. He isn't going to take his eyes off of me. "The answer to this next question determines if you live. So, you may want to think it through a minute. Take your time before you answer."

"You gonna ask me who killed your father? You think I'll tell you so you can avenge him?"

"No." I laugh. "I already know the answer to that question. What I want to know is, who killed my mother?"

His eyes—my mother's eyes—change with surprise. "Your mother? Why would I know that?"

"You've already told me you're my brother. That means she was your mother too. And I don't know the story there, yet, but I don't think you do either. So, again... who killed my mother?"

"She was sick." He shrugs. "Cancer. You know that."

"Mmm." I nod. "I do know that. I also know that cancer doesn't slit your throat. Any guesses who did that?"

"What's it matter? She was a whore, and now she's dead."

His words don't provoke me. I can't be any more provoked than I already am.

Except now, I know who the enemy really is.

And I know exactly how to destroy him.

CHAPTER THIRTY-TWO

REMY

I have never stopped to consider why a woman like Elaine, who so clearly loves taking care of people, had never had children of her own. But now, I can't help wondering why she's being so fiercely protective of Claire. She all but accused me of murdering my sister's best friend, and now that she knows I didn't, she's still acting as though she can't trust me with her.

She insisted that a hospital couldn't do anything more for Claire than we could, so I allowed her to get Claire patched up and make sure that nothing was broken. But that's as close as I'm letting her get. That's as close as I'm letting anyone get.

The drugs, the pain, and the exhaustion all took its toll on Claire, and once she collapsed from all of it, I refused to let her out of my sight. I can tell that Rhea isn't happy about it, but I've already failed once by trusting someone who only hurt her. There's no chance I'm going to let it happen again, so until she wakes and pushes me away, I'm going to be her shadow.

If Jovich was ever loyal to anyone, it would have been my father. After my father appointed me to the family business, he appointed Jovich to me. I kept my fair share of secrets from him, and clearly, he kept his fair share of secrets from me. But he had been a family friend for years... I never considered that he would be a threat under my own roof. And maybe he didn't mean to be. He had insisted that what he did would protect Rhea. In his own way, maybe he truly thought he was helping. But he didn't understand that Rhea would never forgive him for what he did. And now he never will understand it because he's gone.

Dimitri called me as soon as he secured his mark, and when I filled him in on all that he'd missed, it only took a matter of phone calls before the mess was cleaned up and Jovich's body was taken care of. Explaining it to Rhea, who only heard the gunshot and didn't see any of it unfold, was the hardest part. She didn't understand why he would have done something so cruel, and she doesn't even know the half of it. I told her that Jovich had taken Claire to Davos' men for money and nothing more. There was no love lost between myself and my father, particularly now that I know about Wes, but I can't ruin Rhea's perception of him. She doesn't need to know that she'd grown up in a house with a monster who was so obsessed with power and money that he sold his own family for just a little more.

Claire wakes with a start, sitting bolt upright in my bed and gasping as she does. She searches the room a moment, not recognizing her surroundings, and then relaxes when she finds me sitting in the chair beside the window. "You're safe." I promise her.

She nods and draws her knees into her chest, resting her head on them as she recovers from the same nightmare that she's already suffered countless times. I've watched her float in and out of sleep for the last day, and we've barely talked in that time. All that matters is that she knows she is safe when she wakes, and I know she is safe while she sleeps.

But this time, she looks more lucid than she's been any of the other times.

I stand and walk slowly to the bed, sitting at the end where her feet had just been. I'm quiet as I allow her a moment, and when she looks up, her lips are pressed together while she contemplates her words. "I don't know where to go from here." She says. "That's the hardest part. Maybe that sounds silly, but am I really supposed to just go back to classes and act like I'm okay?"

"No." I assure her. "You don't have to act like you're okay. You don't have to *be* okay. What you've been through... that's not okay."

She laughs and runs a hand through her hair, letting out a frustrated sigh. "I still don't understand what happened. I know that Jovich wanted to get rid of me, but why did they think that I was Rhea? And why were they going to take her?"

It's a question I've prepared for. But that doesn't mean it's any easier to say out loud. So, I meet her question with one of my own. "Do you remember the other night when you asked me to tell you the truth about the family business?"

"Yes." Her voice is a whisper devoid of surprise or confusion. Somehow, I think she sensed that her kidnapping had more to do with business than opportunity. I don't think she knew it when she asked me on the rooftop what I really do for a living—if she did, she'd have run from me instead of allowing herself to be trapped under me. But somewhere between then and the horrors she lived through the last couple of days, she seems to have pieced it together.

"Well," I say. "Now you know."

The confirmation doesn't disgust or horrify her. She just numbly shakes her head. "This can't be real."

"I thought the same thing the first time I found out. When we were kids, it never even crossed my mind to ask what my father did. All I knew was that he was always away on business, on the phone. I never questioned the constant stream of people that came to our house, or the parties, or any of it. Right after I turned eighteen, my father told me I was gonna have to man up if I was going to keep the business alive.

He took me on a trip to meet a friend in Zurich. We got to this big old castle and met with an old family friend and his business partner, Alexandre Davos. I didn't want to go, dreaded it actually. It was all right at first, and then he got weird... asking super unusual questions. He said he wanted to give me a birthday gift, so he took me downstairs to pick one out. And when we got down to the cellar, I was expecting a bottle of whiskey or a cigar... not *people*."

I rub the space between my brows, trying to ease the ache that seems to live there these days. Remembering my first glimpse into the underworld is like a special sort of torture. It's the kind of thing I reserve for the days I feel sorry for myself or when I lose out on a bid because I can't attract any attention if I want to be able to help. I can't help them all, and it makes me sick. The knowledge haunts me, but I can at least make a big difference in the lives of those I do help. And whenever I start to think otherwise, I force myself to remember the way the air changed, the way the sounds of the house above were swallowed by cries and sobs, bribes and threats. I force myself to think of that picture of Monica that had been taped to my car door for the world to see, and of my mother's skin splotched with red when I found her body, and the file that had been pushed across the table with all of the pictures of Rhea, entirely oblivious to the fact that she was being stalked.

Claire whimpers, bringing me back to the present. I place a gentle hand over hers, curling my fingers around hers as a reminder that she is safe with me. "Not just women, Claire... men and children, too. That's when they explained it all to me, every last detail about how they stole people, their money, their lives, and sometimes even their identities. And then they turned around, and they sold all of it to whoever was willing to pay the highest price. When I told them that I didn't want to pick anybody, they offered to let me choose. And when I refused that, they warned me that I had no say in any of it. They threatened to bring my girlfriend into it, my mother, even Rhea."

I sigh, trying not to let the anger grip me. I don't want Claire to see it. She doesn't need anything else to be concerned about right now. "I thought they were bluffing. And then, one day, Davos showed up, and I found him with Monica. He drugged her just to show me he could, took photos of her. She never even knew she was in danger. But the threat was clear the next day when I found those photos left like little breadcrumbs all around my house, my car. It was clear: I submit to their will, or they'd take everyone I cared about. I broke it off with Monica the next day when she almost found one of them in the kitchen cupboard. It wasn't enough.

"Two days later, my mother was gone, and I knew that they were serious. So, I did what my father asked... I got on the first plane to Costa Rica, and I never looked back. As long as they thought I was working with them, Rhea would be safe. And that's exactly how it should have been. But my father was stealing from Davos, little bits at first and then larger amounts. Davos found out, of course, and my father couldn't afford to pay it back. He came here to see if I had the capital to pay his debts, and that was when he found out I'd been lying the whole time. I wasn't moving their money to offshore accounts; I wasn't draining the assets of the people they took. And when my father figured that out, he told Davos he could have something that didn't belong to him... Rhea."

Claire shakes her head again, looking like she's on the verge of crumbling. But she sits up straighter and meets my eyes. "If you weren't laundering his money, then what were you doing? You're just complicit in all of this?"

"I thought for a long time about what I could do to stop it, how I would bring them down. At first, I fantasized about reaching out somewhere—the law, the government. Except you know my father is friends with our governor," I remind her of a photo she's surely seen hanging in the estate back in Oregon, "and they didn't bond over golf. I tried to think of anyone I could trust with this information, but once they brought me into the company and I got a look at their operations, it was clear that there was nobody who could help me destroy them. They'd been at it too long. My father hadn't simply loved my mother; he *selected* her because her family had everything that he wanted... wealth, power, respect. The roots run deep, and they are twisted. This isn't a small-scale operation, Claire. The men and women who looked the other way—and the clients themselves—are officers in some of the most influential positions you could imagine. Government, military, the

United Nations. Even some of the companies that claim to fight for the cause are just a front."

I can tell she wants to cry, but she's still too exhausted to do so. "You didn't answer my question. If you haven't been laundering his money, what do you do? Where does all of your money come from?"

"I could tell you..." I say slowly. "But if you're up for it, I'd rather show you."

She narrows her eyes, suspicion setting in.

Our time together has been tumultuous, and I still feel guilty for how I treated her, but against all odds, she trusts me enough to slip her hand into mine and follow me through the quiet house, out the front door, and to the guesthouse. As I unlock the door, she glances around like she's looking for something.

I don't turn the lights on as I lead her through the house and down into the cellar.

As soon as my hand touches the doorknob, a muffled cry carries up the steps. I feel rather than hear her draw a breath, and then I unlock the door. Before I flip the light on, I turn to her.

Claire knows what I'm asking without me having to say it. Whatever it is, she's already involved, and now she wants answers. She nods, so I let the light illuminate the steps and offer her my shoulder to lean on as we make our way down them.

She takes the stairs slow and steady, handling the exertion well considering she hasn't been out of bed in a few days.

Claire freezes, her entire body going rigid when she sees Wes tied to a chair in the first room, wide-eyed with a rag tied around his mouth.

CHAPTER THIRTY-THREE

REMY

"It's okay." I promise. "He can't hurt you."

She can clearly see that he's bound to the chair, and that's enough for her to gather the courage to walk past him into the next room, letting me shepherd her without sparing him a glance. I hope she isn't sparing him a thought, either.

The man who sits strapped to the chair has a burlap sack over his head, and when I face her, the confusion is obvious. I place a gentle hand on her shoulder, making her jump a little.

"I need you to understand that I'm going to protect you, no matter what. This man sitting here has no power over you, and he never will again. *You* are in control here, Claire."

She nods, which is exactly the sign I was looking for. I reach down and rip the sack off his head unceremoniously.

The man winces from the onslaught of light, blinking as he tries to figure out where he is.

I hear her suck in a breath, feel her hand tighten on mine, and then she pauses. Her voice is small when she says my name, and it sounds like she's forgotten how to breathe. "Remy?"

"Some people are so vile they don't deserve to live with the rest of us. Some people are more monster than man. My father and Alexandre Davos are some of those people. This is another one."

I see the moment the man's confusion disappears and understanding takes hold. Claire sees it too. The man who hurt her so badly she didn't want to live is now chained up in my basement.

"They say if you can't beat them, join them." I tell her. "What my father did, what Davos does, is ruin lives. So, I do my best to save them. I built an empire of my own so that I can afford to buy some of their victims right out from under them. I find them new identities and resources, and then I wish them luck and move on to the next one. But sometimes, that's not enough. Sometimes, I need a little vengeance."

The man tied to my chair is so focused on Claire, yelling against the tape on his mouth and straining against the chains, that he doesn't see me pick up the knife.

Dimitri brought him here instead of to the warehouse so that he could get to work cleaning up the Jovich mess. He didn't know why I requested this man be brought to me, but he'd set up the tools anyway, just the way his predecessor would have.

I choose the knife, hoping he'll appreciate the symmetry. It's what he wielded against Claire all those years ago.

"Remy." She says again. She looks so small in the large room, and I imagine she feels even smaller compared to the large man we're holding captive. He's easily twice her size, so large that he'd probably break the chair if it weren't metal.

"He's going to die, Claire. There's no way around that."

Those sweet lips quiver, and she shakes her head. "You don't have to do this."

"Maybe not." I shrug. "But I'm going to. And I want to offer you the opportunity."

"The... opportunity?" She chokes, uncertainty lingering in the word.

She knows exactly what I'm offering her as I hold the knife in my upturned palm. Her eyes glance from the blade to me, so full of uncertainty.

"You don't ever have to do anything you don't want to do, Claire. You are your own person, and I'll never force you or guilt you into anything again. But he is going to die, by your hand or mine. You can do it yourself, or you can watch. Or I can walk you back to the house and come back for him later. But now that he is here, I won't let him go. He dies tonight."

Giante's muffled scream draws Claire's attention back to him, and he looks like he's trying hard to appeal to her sense of morality, to convince her to help him. I wonder how many times she tried to appeal to his clearly non-existent sense of morality. I wonder how many times she cried for him to stop. And my anger only grows, testing my patience. I'd have painted the warehouse with his blood and fed him to the sharks by now if I didn't think she deserved this chance to kill her own demons.

I can feel the tension rolling off her. Claire's terrified, but I don't know if it's of me or the man before her, or the possibility of taking a life, or maybe the fact that she *wants* to.

"I don't think murder is the answer."

Despite her words, she doesn't sound convinced.

"Maybe it isn't." It certainly isn't a simple thing to do, though it does get easier with time. "Maybe there's a real solution out there to all of the predators and monsters, but if there's a better option, I haven't found it yet. Until I do, I'm just doing my best to protect the ones who can't protect themselves. It's okay if you don't want to take part in that, but I want you to decide for yourself."

"But where does it end?" She asks, searching my face. "I mean, an eye for an eye makes the whole world blind, right?"

"That's a good question," I tell her honestly. I'm not trying to patronize her; It's a question I've asked myself before without answer. It's the question that's kept me awake through the night The only way I see this ending for me is in a pool of my own blood. "Maybe we're all better off blind. Why don't you ask him where it ends?"

She eyes the man in front of her like she's considering asking him and then turns her gaze back to me. "You aren't the first person he hurt," I tell her as gently as I can manage. "And you weren't the last."

I turn and grab the file Dimitri left next to the instruments, flipping it open to the list of names. I can't stomach looking at anything more than their names again. When I first looked at the file, I had to excuse myself to throw up. Monica was nearly eighteen when Davos showed up in my home and violated her in front of me. He held back because he wanted the threat of what he could do to sink in, but it hadn't even occurred to me at the time how she was a child. Hell, I was eighteen, but even I was still a child before I was dragged into this shit.

But this file? It's got literal children. Apparently Eric Giante just decided teenagers were easy prey... the youngest of the girls we know about was thirteen. Claire was fifteen. My stomach twists. I have to get this over with, but I owe it to her to not rush this, not to bully her into participating.

"Cara Thompson, Cindy Jones, Leah Alvarez, Claire Monroe," At first she looks confused, but when I get to her name, realization takes hold and she presses a hand over her mouth. "Amber Smith, Tiffany Evans, and Misty Carter. That's just what my team was able to dig up. You could ask him if there are more, but I doubt he'd tell you the truth."

She stares at me for a long time with her hand over her mouth, like she can keep the horrors inside. And then seems to remember where she is. She doesn't even look at Eric as she walks by him to pick up the file. I'm silent as she flips through, but she isn't. Her breath hitches at the first page, and by the last, she's gasping for air like the world is closing in around her. Through all of it, the tears in her eyes don't fall.

"There were more." She says quietly as the realization settles around her. She presses a hand to her mouth like she's worried she'll be ill. "Before me and... and after." Claire snaps the file shut and lets her eyes close a moment. When she opens them again to look at me, they're full of vengeance.

She's made up her mind.

"Will you help me?"

"Anything." I nod. "Tell me what you want."

She slips her hand into mine and pulls me tentatively in front of the prisoner, her eyes finding mine as she finds the resolution she needs to commit to this.

"I want him to hurt." Her voice is wobbly but certain as she tries to come to terms with the fact that she's asking for violence. "For each of the girls." She opens the file and shows him the first picture, studying his face for any signs of recognition, remorse, humanity. She won't find any of it.

The monster hasn't stopped fighting, but when the picture of the smiling girl is in his face, he looks away. I've never seen or met any of the other women, but I'm sure that girl was forever different after he wrecked her life. I'm sure Claire is.

"I want him to suffer..." She breathes a little sound that makes me want to pull her against me and keep her safe. But I have work to do. "For Cara Thompson."

I flex my knuckles on the knife handle and then drive it into Giante's stomach so deep that all that remains outside of him is the inch of handle that my fist is wrapped around.

The monster yells a guttural sound which grows higher as I twist the blade in the wound. It takes some effort to dislodge the knife, but when I do, blood begins to pour out from the gash in his abdomen, and his attempts to scream turn to sobs.

I look at Claire to make sure she's okay, not about to faint or vomit. But she's well-acquainted with blood after the last few days, and she's no shrinking violet. Suddenly, she has a strength about her I haven't seen before. Her face is set in a mask that betrays nothing of what she's feeling, and she looks a bit peaked, but I can't say whether that's just her post-trauma pallor or if she's being retraumatized right now. I do see her eyes blazing with hatred, and it lights her up. She's fucking beautiful, on fire with purpose.

She nods at me, an assurance I no longer need, and then says, "Cindy Jones."

I stab him again, driving the blade between his ribs and eliciting another anguished cry. Tears stream down his face, but his cruel eyes aren't sorry, aren't confused... just full of anger. Most of the time, I like to have a conversation with the people on the other end of my blade, but I left him gagged and taped because I couldn't risk Rhea or Elaine hearing his screams from the house. I'm glad I did, too, because I'm sure by the look in his eyes that he'd be spouting the most despicable, vile things he could in an attempt to hurt Claire one last time.

"Leah Alvarez." I stab him again, quicker this time.

"Amber Smith." Again.

His blood is spilling from him rapidly, covering the plastic-lined floor.

"Tiffany Evans." I plunge the knife in him, overlapping one of the previous wounds I made. The blade slides in easily, and his attempt to scream is renewed with more effort. He knows he's at the end of his life, and he doesn't want to give it up yet.

My hand is slick with blood.

"Misty Carter." I wipe it on my shirt and adjust my grip before driving the blade through his already shredded shirt and into flesh once more.

I look up to find Claire watching me, and I'm so focused on her eyes, I don't see her stretch her hand out at first. Once I do, I wipe the blade again and hesitate before giving it to her. "Are you sure?" I ask, giving her one last chance to reconsider getting her hands dirty. I tip her chin up with my fingers so that I can appraise every inch of her beautiful face, looking for any signs of hesitation. "If you do this, there's no going back. Once you let the darkness in, it doesn't let you go."

"It won't let me go anyway." She says softly.

It's a reminder that I failed her. I brought her here, and I couldn't even keep her safe. I've never been able to protect the people I cared about, so I don't know what made me think I could protect her. This is my chance to make it up to her, and I want her to take it. I want her to get her revenge. I just want to be sure that she is aware of the consequences. "Murder leaves a stain on your soul. It's a mark that other people can't see, but you'll know it's there."

I don't know if she doesn't hear my words or if she doesn't care. There's no hesitation in her when she answers. "I'm sure."

Claire takes the blade from me and stares at the blood that hasn't been wiped clean. And then she waves it in front of the monster and watches as he shakes his head weakly. If we walk away right now, he'll bleed out on the floor in less than ten minutes. He's already a dead man, but Claire can hasten his end. It will be a kindness, really, to put him out of his misery. He doesn't deserve that kindness, but she deserves the chance to get her own revenge.

"The first time you hurt me, I thought it was a fluke." Her voice only shakes a little as she stands in front of Eric, looking him directly in the eye. "I thought it was my fault. I thought that I did something wrong, said the wrong thing, wore the wrong thing. You told me I tempted you with my dresses... my braids. I stopped braiding my hair after that, but you didn't stop coming to me. The second time, I begged your wife to help me, but she turned the other cheek. By the third time, I'd grabbed a knife of my own right from your kitchen to defend myself."

The monster attempts to say something, but even if his mouth hadn't been covered, the words wouldn't be intelligible. He's fading fast, his eyes getting distant under fluttering lashes. "I didn't tell the police or my social worker what you did to me because I was stupid enough to think that if you used me as your punching bag, that you wouldn't hurt anyone else. When Kaylee got adopted and it was just me in that room and you kept doing it, I thought that you just hated me for some reason. And I figured if you hated me so badly that you wanted to hurt me over and over again, then there must be something wrong with *me*. That was when I decided to kill myself. Do you know how much it hurts to give up on the world and decide to do something like that? To bury the rest of your hopes and dreams right alongside what you took from me? That's when you really ruined my life."

I notice her voice no longer shakes as she carries on. "And now I know you didn't just do it once... you did it seven times. You ruined *seven* lives. And now, I'm going to end yours." She twists the knife in her hand, like she's trying to decide her best angle, and then drives it deep into his stomach, crying out like a warrior running into battle.

His eyes widen as she manipulates the blade, but he isn't making noise anymore. She's already forced most of the air out of his lungs, and now he holds her gaze as the life slips out of him. When she steps away, she whispers loud enough for me to hear, "That one was for me."

I take a step toward her, but Claire turns just as suddenly as she'd decided to kill him and sprints past Wes, disappearing up the steps.

CHAPTER THIRTY-FOUR

CLAIRE

I don't know where I'm running to, but I couldn't stay in that basement a moment longer. I couldn't look at the man slumped over in the chair, couldn't see the faces of the other girls he hurt, couldn't smell his blood. I ran past Wes without giving him a single look and up the stairs, turning into the first room I see.

A bathroom. Thank God, because the way my stomach is roiling, the way my whole body is burning, I'm surely going to be sick.

I suck in as much air as my lungs can hold and then hear Remy's footsteps come to a stop behind me. When I turn, he's standing in the doorframe, his dark eyes full of concern. I can feel myself vibrating with something... shock, or fear, or need. I don't know exactly what it is, but it doesn't matter, because his gaze is so intense, it sends shockwaves through the pit of my stomach, like he'd reached out and touched me. It's that intimate.

And suddenly, I don't care about anything in the world beyond him.

I launch myself at him, and he reacts quickly, like his body is already in sync with mine. He catches me under my ass as my legs wrap around his waist and our lips seek each other. His kiss has already been proven to liquify me, but now it sets me on fire. A desperate sound brushes past my lips and is muffled by his as he deepens the kiss, pulling my tongue into his mouth.

I have no time to waste—I fumble with the buttons on his shirt, eagerly pulling it away from his skin. I need to feel him against me, to have him cover me with his darkness, his light. Remy responds in kind, matching my energy beat for beat, our need synching. He slips the straps of my tank top and bra down in one easy motion before reaching around to unclasp it. As it falls away from between us, I groan and hurry with the last button before sliding the fabric down his arms and pressing myself into him, trying to eliminate any space between us.

He's warm, chasing away the cold in me, but it's not enough. I know he can give me more, and he's going to. I want everything he can give me—the passion, the anger, the fear. I can't even begin to unpack the implications of what we just went through together with him rescuing me from Jovich's betrayal, and that's saying nothing of the fact that we just killed a man together.

My head is dizzy with all the thoughts trying to fight for importance, but only one thought rises above it all, and it's barely a thought so much as an intrinsic need.

More.

I'm vaguely aware that we're moving, and then the bed is pressing against the backs of my knees, and I tumble onto it. Remy falls above me, his strong arms bridging the gap so his weight doesn't touch me. But I need his warmth. I need him to cover me, to consume me.

I reach around his back and pulled him toward me. My lips fall free of his as he pulls away enough to look at me, breathless. The hand that isn't supporting his weight touches my cheek, swirling something inside of me. "Are you sure?"

"Yes." I breathe the word like a prayer, and Remy obliges, covering me with his body so that we're sandwiched together. His skin against my breasts has my nipples tightening with need, and I can feel a similar need coming from him, straining through his boxers. "Please. Fuck me, Remy."

I don't realize I've said it out loud until he pulls away and I see the curve of his lips as he tears his belt off and tugs his pants and boxers to the ground all at once, letting his erection spring free. I feel my entire body quiver as I take him in, so big and so hard. He doesn't let me look long, because then he's pulling my shorts down, taking my already-wet panties with them. We've gotten so close to this, to skin on skin, and every time we've been interrupted. Tonight, I'm not letting him stop. I won't give him the chance.

Remy growls as I lift my hips, brushing against him, but he doesn't let me drop down again. His hand catches me beneath my thigh, hiking my legs around his waist so that he can leverage me closer to him.

He takes control of my mouth again, kisses my lips, my neck, my breasts, running a hand over every inch of me. I'm ready for him, every nerve inside of me screaming for his touch— even the parts that ache. He avoids the bandages from Slick's knife, snaking his way down my navel, pushing away from me enough that he can continue peppering his kisses along my thigh. His breath ghosts over my center, and his eyes flick to mine. He must find whatever he's seeking with that look, because he smirks and then his fingers land right over my already-swollen clit. There's no fumbling, no adjusting—he just finds the part of me that's aching for his touch.

The breath I draw in is sharp, full of excitement even to my own ears. His name rolls off my lips as he strokes a finger away from that delicate bud and down the length of my slit, like he's seeing how badly I want him before plunging a finger inside of me. My entire body clenches with the need for more, and he gives it to me, adding another finger that strokes every last fold inside of me, and then another until I'm surely coating his hands with the proof of my need. But it isn't enough, and my desperate moaning must make that clear, because I feel his fingers move away, and before I've even had a chance to lament my disappointment, they're replaced by his warm breath between my thighs.

I draw in a breath of my own that comes out like a gasp. As if he's been waiting on some sort of approval, Remy presses his tongue to the same place. He teases it over me while he finds a rhythm he likes, circling me with his tongue until I'm clutching the sheets, screaming his name as he stokes the fire he'd built in me until it explodes into an epic orgasm. It comes on fast and hard, the same way the adrenaline did. But it doesn't drop me, picking me up and throwing me back down the way it does when I bring myself to relief.

He continues through it, and then before I've even stopped pulsing with it, he slides into me.

I accept every inch he offers, the desire starting to ripple all over again as his warmth stretches my insides, stroking a place deep inside of me, soothing an ache I've never realized existed. He kisses me back as feverishly as I kiss him, and though I've just come apart against his tongue, my need for him is urgent. With every movement, my fingers brush against his back, feeling his muscles sliding under my fingertips until his pace reaches a crescendo. The heat is starting to build in my belly again, so I plant my hands on his ass and dig my nails in, holding him tight as he thrusts into me over and over again. We fit so good together, him filling me so completely that I can't even think with him inside me, and I love it.

He pushes in one last time before he finds his own release, a hand on my hip gripping me for dear life. I press my hips up and tilt myself against him, the friction against my sensitive clit sending me over the edge in his wake.

He's still careful not to put any weight on me as he falls onto the bed and lays next to me, his arms circling me, loosely enough that they don't feel like a cage, but tightly enough that I feel safe. I'm still panting when I roll over to face him, my chin on his chest. He watches me for a moment, and then kisses me again... softer, slower, deeper.

When he pulls away, I sigh and lay there a moment with my eyes closed, listening to the steady thrum of his heart. I've never done this... never cuddled with someone after that. It's oddly vulnerable, less warm and more uncomfortable.

A cold chill creeps slowly over me, stealing the afterglow as I open my eyes and notice the red spots that paint his chest where blood seeped through the thin fabric of his shirt. I stifle whatever noise is trying to claw its way out of me and then sit up gingerly, taking him in.

He's still smiling a little, though he watches me with growing concern as I stare at him. Remy is exquisite. His body, unfurled in all its glory, is laid out on the bed without a care in the world. His thick muscles look like they've been carved by the gods for man to have something to aspire to, and the way his chest rises and falls is so gentle... normal.

But the light streaks of red that cover his chest, his tight abs, his neck... that isn't normal.

And they're in places he couldn't have touched on himself.

My heart hammers as I realize *I* left those marks on him, and when I look down at my own palms and see the red on them, everything around me falls away.

I feel myself falling through the sky. My breath seems to have escaped my lungs, and I'm not sure my tongue is still there either because when I try to speak, the word congeals in my mouth.

I try again, and this time, a sound comes out. "Remy?"

I'm vaguely aware of him reaching out to me, but it's too late. I'm consumed by the panic, headed for a void so deep it looks like nothing can escape it, a pitch-black nothing waiting below as I hurtle head-first into darkness.

CHAPTER THIRTY-FIVE

CLAIRE

As the high of the orgasm fades, reality comes thundering back to me. One minute, I'm high on adrenaline and euphoria, and the next, the corners are peeling back to expose the reality of what I just did.

I killed someone. The panic holds the air in my lungs hostage, making it hard to breathe.

And then I fucked my best friend's brother before the blood on our hands even had a chance to dry. My skin burns, like it's stretched too tight.

It's wrong. I think Remy is saying something, but I can't hear anything. The world has taken on a sudden silence, like all sound has just been sucked out of it.

Animal. No, not all sound. I can hear my blood rushing through me, an unsettling reminder that I'm alive when just under this floor, someone isn't.

Criminal. I can feel saliva pooling in my mouth, the nausea in my stomach rising like a tide.

I'm a monster. Darkness presses on the edges of my vision, and I feel faint.

Breathe, Claire, or else you're going to have a panic attack right in front of him.

I roll out of bed just as suddenly as I'd flung myself at him and face away, suddenly embarrassed, as I shimmy into my clothes. I can feel his eyes on me, see him pushing himself up to sitting. As much as I usually relish his attention, right now it feels like just another thing trying to grind my ribcage into dust.

"Claire." His voice is gentle as he calls to me, but I can't bear to try and decipher what he's aiming to do with it. Is he trying to comfort me for the murder we just committed or is he feeling guilty about the fact that we just fucked like animals in the blood of our victim? Nothing about what we did was gentle or sensual or loving—it was raw and needy, desperate, and sick.

We're sick... both of us.

And I need air.

"I'll go back to the house first." I say, freeing my hair out from under the neck of my shirt as I face him, fully clothed. It takes every bit of energy I have to sound normal. "I don't want Rhea to see us together and ask what we've been up to."

He says nothing, but I can feel Remy's dark eyes appraising me, but I can't bear to look at him. Without waiting for anything else, I turn and walk out the door, still leaving him there in the bed with one thin, blood-streaked sheet covering the naked lower half of him.

I stumble out of the room, bracing myself with a hand on the wall as soon as I'm out of sight so that I don't trip over my own feet, which suddenly feel heavy. *Everything* feels heavy, now.

Our physical relationship had been progressing to that point, but now that we've done it, regret fills my stomach, flooding my veins. It isn't regret for sleeping with him, though. Even though it was chaotic and unhinged, it was also glorious... a heady, erotic, wild high that I never could have anticipated.

But the events preceding it? Killing someone is bad enough, but then doing what we did with his blood still on our hands?

There are no words for that level of depravity.

I'd cast a glance at myself in the mirror before I dressed and wiped my hands of the blood that covered them, but Remy had said it would leave a stain on my soul. In the moment, I hadn't really considered exactly what he meant, but I can feel it now settling over me: a darkness so thick, so endless that it's trying to smother me.

As I walk out of the guest house, I think I hear him call out to me again. But whatever it is, his words are lost in the howling wind of another storm brewing. The treetops rustle, and rain begins to fall in fat drops from the night sky overhead. I want to stand in the storm and let it pummel my flesh on the off chance that it can purge me and cleanse my soul. But I have to get cleaned up before anybody finds me and starts asking questions.

Once I'm out of the guest house, I can breathe again, the faintness falling away with each step I take until I'm practically running back to the main house. I cross the distance quickly with my head down and open the front door before thrusting my hands in my pockets, all too aware of the way they itch with the thin layer of blood that has dried over them. I take the steps two at a time and walk as fast as my short legs will allow, holding my breath all the while as I repeat a silent prayer that Rhea is fast asleep. If she finds me, how will I explain this to her? Dimitri or Elaine may know about Remy's dark dealings, but I'm sure that Rhea hasn't got a clue what her family really does. If she did, she...

I don't know what she would have done... what she'd do. I don't know what I'm supposed to do with this knowledge, but I'm pretty sure it isn't kill for revenge.

I have no idea what time it is, but the house is dark and quiet.

Please, please, please be asleep.

I've always had my doubts about whether any sort of God can exist while such cruelty is allowed to take place and demons run the world, unchecked. If there is a God, I doubt that he'll be answering any of my prayers after what I just did.

No, there may not be such a thing as divine justice. Maybe it's up to those of us down here who have been wronged to tip the scales, to stop the string of violence before it can continue. Maybe there *is* a need for vigilante justice, angels of vengeance.

Maybe that's what Remy is.

Whether because my prayers are answered or I have a single stroke of dumb luck, I make it to my room without incident and lock the door behind me before letting out all of the breath that I've been holding hostage in my chest. My heart feels like it's been replaced by a brick of coal, shriveled and dark and not even pounding despite my cascading emotions and the fear of what I've done, of who I've become.

I carefully avoid catching my reflection in the mirror this time as I hurry to the bathroom and flick the light on for disappointment to flood me.

Shit.

I forgot my bathroom only has a deep soaker tub with elegant taps, the epitome of luxury and relaxation. It's a place I'm sure you could think of some of your greatest ideas, not a place you'd want to be stuck when you're questioning your existence because you just stole someone's last breath. The shower is across the hall and there's no way I'm taking a bath. It's apparently a quick jump from prey to predator, but I'm not so far gone to consider bathing in the blood of my enemies.

I need to scrub it out from under my fingernails, to get it all off of me and ensure it disappears down the drain. I set about grabbing some clothes and then pause at the door to see if any noise comes from the hall. Nothing moves outside my door—the only sound I hear is my jagged breath, which still hasn't evened out. I throw the door open and dart across the empty hall with my heart in my throat.

Rhea is probably fast asleep, but what about Elaine? Or Remy?

I lock the door behind me before even flipping the light on and take a moment to lean against it. I've feared the dark for so long, but now I'm afraid of what I'll see in the mirror when I flip the switch. I'm not sure it could be worse than what I'm seeing in my mind's eye, which is my fingers curling around the blade that Remy held out for me, Eric's dark eyes widening in realization and fear, his warm blood gushing over my skin. The older memories of his breath on my neck, his stench permeating the small room that was supposed to be my safe place, his rough hands against my soft skin.

I flip the switch and the bathroom comes into full view, chasing all thoughts of Eric away, no matter how brief. He's gone, and now I have to be alone with myself. It's almost more frightening than being at his whim.

Gripping the edge of the sink between my hands, I steel myself to look up at the murderer in the mirror.

Eric deserved to die for what he did to me, for what he did to who knows how many other people. I believe that without the slightest doubt. There was no justice for girls like me when a broken system let him slip through the cracks. He would have just kept hurting innocent girls... children. The world is better off with him gone, I have no doubt. But did he deserve to die like *that*? Tied up and in pain, staring at the faces of the girls he ruined?

He hurt people, but does that mean he deserved to hurt in his final moments?

Nausea swells in me, so I rest my head against the cool glass of the shower and reach around to turn the spray of water on. I suck in a deep breath as the steam fills the bathroom, wishing it could sink inside me and clear away the rottenness deep inside.

I'm gasping to catch my breath by the time I shed my clothes and step under the spray. The boiling water burns my skin, but I don't move or turn down the heat. I simply let it fall, pelting my skin until it's tender, watching the tinged pink water swirl around the drain as the not-yet-dried blood rinses away.

When my flesh is raw with the assault of my shower, I take the loofa and scrub soap over every inch of me, relishing the pain because it's a beautiful contrast to the numbness I suddenly feel inside. I must have triggered something in my brain that's caused it to shut down because all of my fear and anxiety over what I've just done has evaporated.

My motions become automatic by the time I rake shampoo through my hair, and by the time I turn the water off, I feel oddly detached. I've learned to dissociate when I need to, but this is different—this feels like I'm about to faint.

When I step out, the mirror is fogged up, so I don't have to worry about catching a glimpse of myself in it, but I don't dash back to my room just yet. I drop my towel and look over my body, my still-pink skin shiny under the glare of the bathroom lights. All traces of blood are gone. At least, all that you can see.

No matter how hot I made the water or how hard I scrubbed, I can still feel the warmth of it coating my fingers as they slipped against the hilt, sticky when it dried on my flesh. I hadn't thought of that when Remy's hands were on me, painting my body with the blood of our victim as we acted on animalistic passion.

I squeeze the counter under my palms again, trying to get a grip on myself, and lift my gaze to the mirror. I've got to look at myself eventually—may as well see what it's like being in the body of a killer.

The fog has subsided, and now that I see myself, I wonder how I got here. Not even two weeks ago, I was full of light and hope, and other than my anxiety about figuring out what to do with the rest of my life, carefree.

Not anymore.

When I first met Rhea, I had been running from the darkness of my past. She'd helped me heal little by little to where I almost never even thought about the person that I used to be... broken, hollow, with jagged edges like a glass that was put back together wrong. Those edges had been blunted by Rhea's light, casting me in a vignette.

But now that light I borrowed from her is gone.

Her family's darkness chased it away, leaving me broken once again.

Join the Coven!

For more information about what's next, group therapy, or just for funsies, join us at Carly Claire's Coven on Facebook.

Need more Remy? Join my email list for a free novella to learn all about the darkness that forged Remy in this DARK prequel.

https://dl.bookfunnel.com/h2pul15bna

www.ingramcontent.com/pod-product-compliance
Lightning Source LLC
Chambersburg PA
CBHW071553030726
47593CB00001BA/141